TOLD BY THE DEAD

TOLD BY THE DEAD

RAMSEY CAMPBELL

Introduction By *Poppy Z. Brite*

DIP

Design & Layout by Michael Smith
Printed and bound in England by T.J. International

Drugstore Indian Press | Grosvenor House
1 New Road Hornsea, HU18 1PG | United Kingdom

editor@pspublishing.co.uk | www.pspublishing.co.uk

contents

introduction

Ramsey Campbell is the Best of us All

B<small>UT YOU NEEDN'T TAKE MY WORD FOR IT.</small>

The Internet is full of amusing fads. A recent one is the search engine Googlism (www.googlism.com) where you can plug in the name of a person, place, or thing and get back a list of results in the form of simple declarative sentences: a sort of sampling of the Mass Mind. Most subjects will yield a mixture of responses favorable and unfavorable, some funny, some catty, some just plain mean. Only when I plugged in the name 'Ramsey Campbell' did the engine refuse to spit out a single nasty response.

"Ramsey Campbell is one of the most respected writers in the horror genre"

"Ramsey Campbell is such an acclaimed writer"

"Ramsey Campbell is highly regarded for his sensitive use of the language and his ability to create psychologically"

"Ramsey Campbell is one of the finest exponents of the classic British ghost story"

"Ramsey Campbell is not always a nice place"

"Ramsey Campbell is the best of us all"

That last one really seems to sum it up. I don't mean to suggest that Campbell appeals to everyone—you can always go on Usenet and find some bewildered soul complaining, "I just don't get him" but I don't recall meeting another writer of dark fiction who didn't at least admire him. Way back in 1979, when Campbell had published two novels and a good number of short stories, Stephen King devoted a section of his horror overview *Danse Macabre* to Ramsey Campbell's work. "Good stuff," he wrote. "But strange; so uniquely Campbell that it might as well be trademarked." No other writer has a voice like Ramsey Campbell's; though he seldom repeats himself, and has grown tremendously as a writer since his early publications, he has maintained a coherent, instantly recognizable voice.

The present collection, *Told by the Dead,* spans most of his career. The earliest story here ('The Previous Tenant') was written in 1968, the latest ('Tatters', 'The Retrospective' and 'All For Sale') in 2001. There is a collaboration, 'Little Ones', written with his wife Jenny; though many writers consider their spouses or partners "collaborators" in some sense, it's rare (and interesting) to see a story actually *penned* by husband and wife.

The book opens with a recent story, 'Return Journey', which may seem like a fairly straightforward horror tale unless you know it's being written by an author born a year after the second World War's end and raised in a city (Liverpool) that still bore the terrible scars of wartime bombing. The image of children ducking into a burial vault during an air raid suggests resilience—life in the midst of death—but the protagonist is ultimately not to be saved from the long arm of the war. The story contains what must be one of the loneliest definitions of adulthood ever written:

> Her parents couldn't keep her safe now; they had never appeared when she'd called out to them in the night to prove they were still somewhere.

Much of Campbell's recent work, in particular, has contained a menacing humor that can make the reader nearly as uncomfortable as the characters. It's seen in several stories here: 'No Story In It', about the futility of the writing life and the terror of trying to care for a family on an author's dwindling income; 'Becoming Visible', which employs Campbell's genius for the paranoid protagonist perhaps first seen in *The Face That Must Die* (the narrator's imagined description of a rich man's wife—"bristling with jewels and doused in perfume to cover up her smell, her hair glossy as hot tar, the valley of her flesh bared in front of her"—is particularly toothsome); 'The Word', which combines a cruelly accurate send-up of the convention scene with a Salieri-like older writer's hatred for a young, ridiculously successful one.

(I should mention that I had the pleasure of hearing Campbell read 'No Story In It' at Spookycon in San Francisco six weeks before writing this, and I truly think he is the best reader I've ever heard. Particularly when reading one of the blackly humorous stories, his vocal interpretation adds new depths to the material. If you ever have a chance to attend a Campbell reading, don't miss it.)

Ramsey Campbell has never made a secret of his affection for H.P. Lovecraft, and the New Englander casts his gaunt shadow over several stories here, most notably 'Never To Be Heard'. This recent story about an occult symphony being performed in a church at Easter (also the vernal equinox, the pagan season of rebirth) is Lovecraftian in its focus on terrible mysteries never meant to be revealed, and on the irresistible human impulse to reveal them. Campbell's stroke of genius—something Lovecraft wouldn't have thought of and probably couldn't have pulled off if he had—is in telling the story from the point of view of a prepubescent choirboy, one of those performing the symphony. The boy's awakening sexuality seems to make him particularly vulnerable to the insidious effects of the music. The Lovecraftian influence is also evident in 'Slow', a 1975 horror story with science fiction trappings and a monster that—like Lovecraft's "rugose cones"—neither the protagonist nor the reader is sure whether to laugh at or fear. A more surprising influence is suggested in 'Dead Letters', a 1974 tale that put this reader in mind of those short, sharp shockers Robert Bloch wrote during the 1950s and '60s.

Along with the aforementioned 'No Story In It', 'No End of Fun' explores the horror of redundancy, impotence, and uselessness that crops up often in Campbell's recent work. In 'No End of Fun' the sense of redundancy seems to be a payback for a childhood act of brutality. Lionel, a retiree of indeterminate age, forced his female cousin into a frightening semi-sexual situation when they were adolescents. Now his fantasies seem to have condemned the deceased cousin to a hellish version of that same situation. Lionel discovers this when he comes to live in her home, now a boarding house run by her daughter and her daughter's daughter, neither of whom has much time for Lionel. The cousin's fate is nasty, but the most painful part of the story is the dialogue between Lionel and his younger relatives: his increasingly desperate overtures, their weary rebuffs. One gets the feeling his whole life has been like this—in cosmic retaliation for one act of cruelty, or simply because he's the sort of person who invites such treatment? Campbell leaves it up to us.

Written in 1973, 'Accident Zone' might be viewed as a precursor of the modern (and mostly media-manufactured) phenomenon of "road rage." More interestingly, it's a twist on the idea of "bad spots" that have been reported by paranormal chroniclers from T.C. Lethbridge to Colin Wilson. Lethbridge wrote of a seaside cliff in Devon where he and his wife experienced sudden, inexplicable feelings of depression, and where his wife felt some unseen force urging her to jump. Later they learned that a man had leapt to his death from that very spot. Lethbridge theorized that the extreme dampness of the spot somehow created a magnetic field upon which strong emotions could be "recorded." The water droplets that figure prominently in 'Accident Zone', as well as the fact that the story is set in England's Lake District, suggest that Campbell may have had this theory in mind.

There isn't a weak story in *Told by the Dead*, but 'The Retrospective' is probably one of the finest and most disturbing tales Campbell has ever written. (It's also one of the most recent, written in 2001.) Trent, a Type-A architect with little time for anything beyond his career, has an unplanned travel delay in the town where he grew up. He decides to visit his elderly parents, whom he has neglected badly, and finds them confused and helpless. Rather than staying to make things right, Trent cuts short the uncomfortable visit and goes to investigate a new museum of the town's history. The visit home is a heartbreaking exaggeration of the truism that childhood's important sites always turn out to be smaller and more squalid than one remembers, and the museum is a horrible, horrible inversion of that truism, where everything is stretched out, overstated, made abnormal and grotesque. The final paragraph brings the horror home to Trent in a way that won't soon be forgotten by anyone who has ever tried to rise above his past, only to find that its fingers are longer and stickier than he had imagined.

Because he is able to do things like this—because he can horrify us in a way that touches not just our brains or our viscera, but our souls—Ramsey Campbell truly is the best of us all, and his own best is well represented in this collection. As my husband once said, "Ramsey's great—as a writer, as a friend, as a pervert." These stories may be *Told by the Dead*, but I hope Campbell will be alive and telling more for a long, long time.

Poppy Z. Brite
New Orleans
February 2003

TOLD BY THE DEAD

for
Ina
Janet
Ray
Linda
Alan
Gavin
from another of the family, I hope

Return Journey

A S THE OLD TRAIN PUFFED OUT OF THE STATION, PAST THE sandbags on the platform and the men dressed up as soldiers and a wartime poster with its finger to its lips, the three children who were managing to occupy the whole compartment apart from Hilda's seat began to demonstrate their knowledge of history. "I'm Hitteler," announced the girl with orange turf for hair, and shot up an arm.

"I'm Gobble," said the girl whose bright pink lipstick didn't quite fit her mouth.

Hilda didn't know if she was meant to be offended. When Hitler and Goebbels were alive they'd been just a couple of the many things her parents never discussed in front of her. It was left to the third girl to react, clicking all her ringed fingers at her friends and declaring "You'd get shot for that if we was in the war."

"We're not."

"They don't have wars any more."

"You'd get shot or you'd get hung," the ringed girl insisted. "Hung by your neck 'till you was dead."

They must have learned some history to use phrases such as that. Perhaps they remembered only the unpleasant parts, the opposite of Hilda. She was turning to the window in search of nostalgia when the ringed girl appealed to her. "They would, wouldn't they?"

"Did you know anyone that was?"

"Did you ever see any spies being hung?"

"I don't look that old, do I? I wasn't in the war, just in the wars."

They regarded her as though she'd started speaking in a dead language, and then they crowned themselves with headphones and switched on the black boxes attached to them. If they intended to shut up so much of their awareness, Hilda wondered why they were on the train at all—but she wasn't far from wondering that about herself.

She'd seen the poster on the outside wall of the car park of the telephone exchange where she worked. Since none of her colleagues had seen it, she'd felt it was aimed just at her. OLD TIME LINE, it had said, with a train timetable and the name of a town pretty well as distant as her hot and bothered Mini could reach for one of her Sunday jaunts. If she hadn't been aware of having settled into never driving anywhere that wasn't already part of her past, she mightn't have taken the chance.

The town had proved to be even more Lancashire than hers: steep hills climbed by red concertina terraces, factories flourishing pennants of grey smoke, streets so narrow and entangled they might have been designed to exclude any relative of the shopping mall that had taken over the view from her floor of the small house she shared with two pensioners whose rooms always smelled of strong tea. She would have liked to explore, but by the time she'd found a car park where the Mini could recover from its labours she'd thought it best to head for the next train. When she'd stumbled panting into the two-platformed station she'd had to sprint for the train the moment she'd bought her ticket, scarcely noticing until she'd boarded that the railway preservation company had gone wartime for the weekend, and at a loss to understand why that should make her wish she'd been less eager to catch the train.

She rather hoped she wouldn't need to understand while she was on it. The station and whatever it contained that she hadn't quite liked were gone now, and trees were accompanying the train, first strolling backwards and then trotting as a preamble to breaking into a run as the last houses stayed in town. The land sank beside the track, and a river streamed beneath to the horizon, where a glittering curve of water hooked the sun from behind frowning clouds to rediscover the colours of the grassy slopes. This was more like the journey she'd wanted: it even smelled of the past—sunlight on old upholstery, wafts

of smoke that reminded her of her very first sight of a train, bursting out like a travelling bonfire from under a bridge. The tinny rhythmic whispers of the headphones were subsumed into the busy clicking of the wheels, and she was close to losing herself in reminiscences as large and gentle as the landscape when a guard in a peaked cap slid open the door to the corridor. "All tickets, please."

He frowned the children's feet off the seats and scrutinised their tickets thoroughly before warning "Just behave yourselves in the tunnel."

That took Hilda off guard, as did her unexpectedly high voice. "When is there a tunnel?"

"There has been ever since the line was built, madam."

"No, I mean when do we come to it? How long is it?"

"Just under a mile, madam. We'll be through it in less than a minute, and not much more than that when we come back uphill. We'll be there in a few puffs."

As he withdrew along the corridor the girls dropped their headphones round their necks so as to murmur together, and Hilda urged herself not to be nervous. She'd never been frightened of tunnels, and if the children misbehaved, she could deal with them. She heard the guard slide back a door at the far end of the carriage, and then darkness closed around the windows with a roar.

Not only the noise made her flinch. The girls had jumped up as though the darkness had released them. She was about to remonstrate with them when they dodged into the next compartment, presumably in order to get up to mischief unobserved. Excerpts of their voices strayed from their window into hers, making her feel more alone than she found she wanted to be. The tunnel itself wasn't the problem: the glow that spread itself dimmer than candlelight was, and the sense of going downwards into a place that threatened to grow darker, and something else—something possibly related to the shadow that loomed in the corridor as the girls fell abruptly silent. When the guard followed his shadow to Hilda's door she gasped, mostly for breath. "Nearly out," he said.

As he spoke they were. Black clouds had sagged over the sun, and the hills were steeped in gloom. In the fields cows had sunk beneath its weight, and sheep that should be white were lumps of dust. It wouldn't be night for hours yet; nobody was going to be able to stage a blackout, and so she was able to wonder if that was the root of her fear. "Thank you," she called, but the guard had gone.

She remembered little of the blackout. The war had been over before she started school. The few memories she could recall just now seemed close to flickering out—her parents leading her past the extinguished houses and deadened lamps of streets that had no longer been at all familiar, the bones of her father's fingers silhouetted by the flashlight he was muffling, the insect humming of a distant swarm of bombers, the steps leading down to the bomb shelter, to the neighbours' voices as muted as their lights. She'd been safe there—she had always been safe with her parents—so why did the idea of seeking refuge make her yearn to be in the open? It was no excuse for her to pull the communication cord, and so she did her best to sit still for ten minutes, only to be brought back to the war.

The temporarily nameless station was even smaller than the one she'd started from. The closer of the pair of platforms was crowded with people in army uniform smoking cigarettes as though to celebrate an era when nobody had minded. The three girls were beating the few other passengers to a refreshment room that had labelled itself a NAAFI for the weekend, and Hilda might have considered staying on the train if the guard hadn't reappeared, shouting "End of the line. All change for nowhere. Next train back in half an hour."

The carriage shook as the engine was uncoupled, and Hilda grabbed the doorway as she stepped down onto the platform, which displayed all it had to offer at a glance. Most of the female passengers were queuing for the grey stone hut behind the ticket office. The waiting room smelled of cigarette smoke harsh enough for Woodbines. The refreshment room had to be preferable, and she was bearing for it when a pig's face turned to watch her through the window. For as long as it took her to confront it she had the grotesque notion that the building had become not a NAAFI but a pigsty, and then she saw the snout was on a human head.

Of course it was a gas mask, modelled by one of the girls from the train. Three empty masks were rooting at the inside of the window. By the time Hilda grasped all this she was fleeing up the steps onto the bridge over the tracks, and the realisation by no means slowed her down. She walked very fast until she was out of sight of anything reminiscent of the war—out of sight of the station. She saw the smoke of the engine duck under the bridge and rear up on the other side, where the rails used to lead to the next county presumably the engine would turn so as to manoeuvre to the far end of the train—and then she was around a bend of the narrow road bordered by sprawling grass, and the flank of the hill intervened between her and the railway. She didn't stop until she came to a hollow in the side of the hill, where she not so much sat as huddled while she tried to breathe calmly enough to believe she might grow calm.

Breezes and sunlight through a succession of shutters of cloud took turns to caress her face. The grass on the hills that crouched to the horizon hiding the town where she'd joined the train blazed green and dulled, shivered and subsided. She didn't know whether she closed her eyes to shut out the spectacle of the agitated landscape or in an attempt to share the stillness it briefly achieved. While she gave herself up to the sensations on her face she was able not to think—was aware only of them, and then not of them either.

She wouldn't have expected to be capable of sleeping, but some kind of exhaustion had left her capable of nothing else. She didn't dream, and she was grateful for it. Instead, as her mind began to struggle out of a black swamp of unconsciousness, she found herself remembering. Perhaps her stupor was helping her to do so, or perhaps, she thought as she strove to waken, it was leaving her unable not to remember.

Her parents had kept her safe from everything about the war, but there had been just one occasion when she'd had to shelter without them. She'd spent a Saturday at her aunt's and uncle's across town, which meant her teenage cousin Ellen had been required to play with her. Long before it was time for Ellen to see her home the older girl had tired of her. Perhaps she'd intended to be more quickly rid of her, or perhaps she'd planned to scare Hilda as a sly revenge for all the trouble she'd been, by using the short cut through a grave-yard.

They hadn't progressed halfway across it when it had begun to seem to Hilda as vast as the world. Crosses had tottered towards her, handless arms as white as maggots had reached for her, trees like tall thin cowled heads without faces had whispered about her as she'd scampered after Ellen into the massing darkness, and she'd been unable to see the end of any path. Ellen had to look after her, she'd reassured herself; Ellen was too old to be frightened—except that as the sirens had started to howl, a sound so all-encompassing Hilda had imagined a chorus of ghosts surrounding the graveyard, it had become apparent that Ellen was terrified. She'd run so fast she'd almost lost Hilda at the crossing of two paths dark as trenches, and when she'd halted, her voice had betrayed she'd done so largely out of panic. "Down here," she'd cried. "Quick, and don't fall."

At first Hilda hadn't understood that the refuge itself was one source of her cousin's distress. She'd thought it was a shelter for whoever worked in the graveyard, and she'd groped her way down the steps after her into the stone room. Then Ellen had unwrapped her flashlight, and as its muffled glow brightened with each layer of the scarf she removed from it, her breaths had begun to sound more like whimpers. The walls had been full of boxes collapsing out of their long holes and losing their hold on any of their lids that hadn't caved in. For a moment Hilda had thought someone was looking at her out of the box with the loosest lid, and then she'd seen it was a gas mask resting on the gap between box and lid. Gas masks were supposed to protect you, and so she'd run to pick it up in the hope that would make her braver. "Don't touch it," Ellen had not much less than screamed, but Hilda had pulled the mask off—

She didn't know if she had screamed then; certainly she did now. The cry rose to the surface of her sleep and carried her with it, and her eyes jerked open. The view that met them could have been more reassuring. The sun was considerably lower than last time she'd looked, and its rays streamed up like searchlights from behind black clouds above the town past the horizon. One beam spotlighted a solitary oval cloud, so regular she had to convince herself it wasn't a barrage balloon. She hadn't quite succeeded when she became aware not just of the lateness but of the silence. Had the last train departed? Long before she could walk back to town it would be dark, if she managed to find the right road.

As she shoved herself to her feet her fingers dug into the soil, and she remembered thinking in the graveyard vault that when you went down so far you were beneath the earth. She did her best to gnaw her nails clean as she dashed to the bridge.

The platforms were deserted. The ticket office and all the doors were shut. A train stood alongside the platform, the engine pointing towards the distant town. The train looked abandoned for the night, and she was about to despair when the stack gave vent to a smoky gasp. "Wait," she cried, and clattered down the steps. She hadn't reached the platform when the train moved off.

"Please wait," she tried to call at the top of her voice. Her dash had left her scarcely enough breath for one word. Nevertheless the rearmost door of the last of the three carriages swung ajar. She flung herself after it, overtook it, seized the inner handle and with a final effort launched herself into the corridor. Three gas masks pressed their snouts against the window of the refreshment room, their blank eyepieces watching her as though the darkness was. She shut them out with a violent slam and retreated into the nearest compartment, sliding the door closed with both hands and falling across a seat to fetch up by the window.

The station sailed backwards, and the humped countryside set about following. She was glad the masks were gone, but she wished the view would demonstrate the past had gone too. There wasn't a vehicle to be seen, and the animals strewn about the darkened fields were so still they might have been stuffed. She was trying to content herself with the rewinding of the panorama when she remembered that it would return her to the tunnel.

She didn't want to enter it by herself, especially since the lights of the carriage appeared to be dimmer than ever. She would put up with children so long as they didn't try to make anything of the dark. If there were any in her carriage she would have heard them by now, but perhaps there were quieter passengers. She stood up, though the movement of the train was against it, and hauled herself around the door into the corridor.

She was alone in the carriage. The empty compartments looked even less inviting than hers: the long narrow outlines of the seats reminded her too much of objects she was anxious to forget, the choked brown light seemed determined to resemble the wary glow of her memories. Surely there must be a guard on the train. She hurried to the end of the corridor and peered across the gap into the next one, down which she heard a door slide open. "Hello?" she called. "Who's here besides me?"

The carriage tossed, sending her off balance. She floundered towards the gap above the speeding tracks, and had to step across it into the middle carriage. It was swaying so vigorously that the lamps looked close to being shaken out, and she had to reassure herself that the sound like a nail scraping glass was the repeated impact of a blind against the window of the first compartment. If someone had drawn the blinds down for privacy, Hilda was loath to disturb them. Instead she ventured past in search of the door she'd heard opening.

Was the carriage out of service? The insides of the window of the next compartment were so grimy they might have been coated with soil. Through a patch that a hand must have cleared she saw movement—a stump jerking up and down—the movable arm of a seat, keeping time with the rhythm of the wheels. It must be a shadow, not a large black insect, that kept creeping out from beneath the arm and recoiling, though there were certainly insects in the adjacent compartment: fat blue flies, altogether too many of them crawling over those few sections of the windows that weren't opaque, more of them blundering against the rest of the glass, thumping it like soft limp fingers. She was trying to nerve herself to dodge past all that, because next to it was the door she'd heard, when she saw what was wedging the door open. She wanted to believe it had slid open with the lurching of the carriage, which had also thrown an item of lost property off one of the seats to be trapped by the bottom corner of the door—a glove with its fingers twisted into claws and as brown as shrivelled skin. Even if it was only a glove, it didn't look quite empty enough.

Perhaps she didn't see it stir, or perhaps the careening of the train made the fingers twitch. She only knew she was backing down the corridor, leaning against the outer wall for fear of being hurled against or into a compartment, her hands sliding almost as fast over the grimy windows as the twilit hills and fields were regressing outside them. She had to force herself to look behind her rather than retreat blindly over the gap. As she executed a faltering stride into the rear carriage, her lips formed words before she knew where she remembered them from, and then while she attempted not to remember. "It wasn't me," she mouthed as she fled along the carriage, and as she slid the door shut on the corridor that had turned too dim for her to see the end of it and clung to the handle "I didn't do anything."

She hadn't broken into the vault or vandalised the contents, true enough. Days later she'd overheard her father telling her mother that some children had, and she'd realised they must have left the gas mask. "Pity they weren't old enough to be called up," her father had said for her mother to agree with, "and learn a bit of respect," and Hilda had felt his comments could have been aimed at her, particularly since Ellen had persuaded her never to mention they'd been in the grave-yard. After that, every time she'd had to go to the shelter with her parents—down into the earth and the dimness full of shapes her vision took far too long to distinguish—she'd repeated her denial under her breath like a prayer.

"I didn't do anything"—but she had. She'd lifted the mask from the open end of the box—from the head poking through the gap. Whoever had pulled out the box must have used the mask to cover up the head. It seemed to Hilda that some of the face might have come away with the mask, because the vacant eyes had been so large and deep that shadows had crawled in them, and the clenched grin had exposed too much besides teeth. Then the light had fled with Ellen up the steps, and as Hilda scrambled after her, shying away the mask and its contents, a steady siren had sounded the All Clear like a cruel joke. As though summoned by the memory of her having had the light snatched away, darkness erased the countryside outside the train with a stony shout of triumph.

She doubled her grip on the handle until the hot thick stale exhala-tions of the engine began to invade the compartment through the open window. Now that the journey was uphill the smoke was being channelled backwards, and she felt in danger of suffocating. She

lunged across the seat to grab the handles of the transom and slide the
halves together. They stuck in the grooves while her hands grew as hot
and grubby as the smoke, then the halves stuttered together and met
with a clunk. She fell on the seat and masked her face with her cupped
hands, but when she saw her blurred reflection against the rushing
darkness on both sides of her she uncovered her face. At least she'd
shut out much of the uproar as well as the smoke, and the relative
silence allowed her to hear something approaching down the tunnel.

No, not the tunnel: the corridor. She heard an object being
dragged, followed by a silence, then a closer version of the sound. She
was well-nigh deaf from straining her ears when another repetition of
the noise let her grasp what it was. Somebody was sliding open the
compartment doors.

It could be the guard—perhaps he was responding to her call from
before they had entered the tunnel—except that the staggery advance
sounded rather as though somebody was hauling himself from door to
door. She strove to focus her awareness on the knowledge that the
train wasn't supposed to stay in the tunnel much more than a minute.
Not much more, her mind was pleading, not much more—and then
she heard the door of the neighbouring compartment falter open. Her
gaze flew to the communication cord above the entrance to her
compartment just as two bunches of fingers that seemed able only to
be claws hooked the edge of the window onto the corridor. The
carriage jerked, and a figure pranced puppet-like to her door.

It might have been wearing a camouflage outfit, unless the dark
irregularities on the greenish suit were stains. It was too gaunt for its
clothes or for the little of its discoloured skin she could see. Above the
knobbed brownish stick of a neck its face was hidden by a gas mask
looked in danger of slipping off.

For the duration of a breath she was incapable of taking, Hilda
couldn't move. She had to squeeze her eyes shut in order to dive across
the compartment and throw all her weight against the handle of the
door while she jammed her heels under the seat opposite her. As long
as the door and the glass were between her and the presence in the
corridor it surely couldn't harm her. But her sense of its nearness
forced her eyes open, and the figure that was dancing on the spot in

time with the clacking of the wheels must have been waiting for her to watch, because it lifted both distorted hands to fumble with the mask.

Hilda heaved herself up to seize the communication cord, and only just refrained from pulling it. If she used it too soon, the train would halt in the tunnel. Her mouth was yearning to cry out, but to whom? Her parents couldn't keep her safe now; they had never appeared when she'd called out to them in the night to prove they were still somewhere. Her fist shook on the rusty chain above the door and almost yanked it down as the fingers stiff as twigs dislodged the mask.

Whatever face she'd been terrified to see wasn't there. Lolling on the scrawny neck around which the mask had fallen was nothing but a lumpy blackened sack not unlike a depleted sandbag from which, far too irregularly, stuffing sprouted, or hair. All the same, the lumps began to shift as if the contents of the sack were eager to be recognised. Then light flared through the carriage, and Hilda tugged the cord with all her strength.

The brakes screeched, but the train had yet to halt when the lights, having flared, died. The train shuddered to a stop, leaving her carriage deep in the tunnel. She had to hold the door shut until help arrived, she told herself, whatever she heard beyond it, whatever she imagined her fellow traveller might be growing to resemble. But when the handle commenced jerking, feebly and then less so, she rushed across the invisible compartment and wrenched the halves of the transom apart and started to scream into the darkness thick as earth.

Twice by Fire

IT'S LIKE BEING UNABLE TO SLEEP BECAUSE OF A FEVER, BUT it's infinitely worse. It feels as though I may never again be still. I can't tell if I'm cold as naked bones or hot as the heart of a furnace. My skin is crawling like a heap of ash on my body, which is twisted around itself as if to squeeze to death the last of my consciousness. A flickering of flames won't let my awareness take refuge in the dark. Now I'm conscious of the ache of lying on a surface as hard as my bones. The ache feels like the merest hint of worse, but it's clear I can't retreat from it. I open the charred lumps my eyes feel like and admit the light that's snatching at them.

It comes not from flames but from neon, through a gap between two black plastic bags almost as tall as a man. Several bags of garbage loll around me like a drunkard's friends, shaking their heads in a night wind. That must have been the flapping which is the first thing I remember hearing. The bags block the alley in which I'm lying and conceal me. I've hidden here once before. The idea brings me to my feet. My body is readier than I imagined it might be, and I move to the mouth of the alley in the hope of knowing where I ought to go.

The street extends almost straight for miles. Far down it I hear microscopic shouts and screams and a tinkle of glass. A long black car crosses it, so distantly I can't tell whether its lights are on, and vanishes fast as a snake. Above the street the city jabs the sky with towers, some of them clawed or tipped with giant needles, some perforated with light. Beyond the city, on a horizon bandaged with a strip of cloud, is the silhouette of a hill. Some aspect of it fills me with loneliness, so that I feel emptier than the night. I can't make for the hill yet—I have to know why I was here. I cross the street to the bar whose neon sign brought me back to myself.

The signature of a brand of beer glows in the window. The rear edge of the glow sketches booths and tables in the unlit room. Last time I was here I hid in the alley until it was time to go into the bar. The memory feels as if my consciousness is gliding ahead of me on black wings. I close a hand around the chilly doorknob, and the door swings inwards.

As I venture across the bare floorboards a silhouette jerks forward to greet me from behind the bar. It's my reflection in the long mirror against which vampire bottles rest, heads down. My face borrows light from the mirror, and gradually there I am: dark deep eyes, pale cheeks pinched hollow, thin lips weighed down at the corners. I turn away from it and see an object protruding from the shadow in the booth farthest from the door. It could be the thumb of someone lurking in the booth, except that not only the shadow has cut it off. It's a fat half-smoked cigar—one so ostentatious it ought to have a band around it. As I pick it up, its acrid stench is overwhelmed by a memory of smells so vivid that I sway as if I've just inhaled them: carbonised wood, seared brick. Some grief I shrink from confronting is shrivelling my mind into a useless lump of blackness. I stare at the cigar stub, and it tells me nothing at all. I raise my eyes and catch sight of my reflection. "What does it mean?" I hear myself pleading and see myself mouth.

Except that as I repeat the question I see my lips aren't saying it. I think they're struggling to do so until I realise they are forming other words. As they drown in the dimness under the glass they're dredging up the answer. "Look on"—I peer so hard my lips appear to blacken and wither—"the desk."

"Which desk?" Now my face mocks me by mouthing the question every time I ask it, and I'm reaching for a heavy ashtray on the bar to smash the mirror when I understand that some part of me already knows the answer. It feels like blackness and sorrow as sharp and hard as a beak, and I only have to follow where it leads. I drop the stub into a pocket of my coat, a garment so nondescript it tells me nothing about myself. I slip out of the bar and turn towards the hill.

I can't go there yet, I'm certain of that much. It sinks out of view as I leave the bar behind. Half the streetlamps as tall as the fourstorey blocks are shot out, and most of the properties are boarded up. Beyond more than one nailed-over window I hear sobbing or remains of voices. Some of the boards have been ripped away, and in a shop littered with smashed dusty television sets I make out several figures huddled under newspapers and sacks. A woman mumbles in her sleep, trying to fit her mouth around somebody's name. An empty bottle trundles across the floor, and a shape much smaller than the woman—a baby or a rat—retreats into the darkest corner. I'm not sorry when I reach the end of the prolonged abandoned block and cross an intersection where the prosperous stores begin.

A department store occupies most of the next block. Legs wearing shoes stand in a window, torsos without limbs expose their underwear beside an arrangement of half a dozen heads whose lidless eyes are turned inwards, fixed on their nightmares. Light as pale as a mortuary, and rendered meaningless by the desertion of the street, freezes all these objects as though preserving evidence. Beside them are windows that display furniture, and I've passed several when an item snags my attention. Why am I faltering? It's just a double bed with black sheets and pillows and panelled black headboard. Then a fragment of material rises from the foot of the bed and drifts towards me.

It settles on the inside of the plate glass and sticks there, trembling. It might be a black feather, but it looks more like a flake of oily ash—a flake of the substance to which the entire bed has been reduced. I stretch out my hands as if they can take me through the glass to ascertain the truth of what I'm seeing, and stub my fingers on the window. I'm unable to move for the notion that the bed may be about to collapse before my eyes when down the street a car starts out of a side road, howling and flashing its crown of lights.

Its cry fades along the cross street and is lost in the stone maze of the city. It has reminded me where I have to go. I move so fast I remember nothing of the blocks I leave behind except the glitter of used needles in the alleys. In no time that I'm aware of I arrive at the intersection where the car appeared. There's the police station to the left. It's where my desk is.

The long white building set back from the street glares under spot-lights. Several police vehicles are parked outside the glass front doors, beyond which the duty sergeant is reading a self-help book and scratching his head. Preferring for some reason not to attract his attention, I make for the side entrance.

It can only be unlocked by typing the correct digits on a keypad. The combination must bypass my thoughts, because it seems I've hardly touched the first key when I hear the lock yield with a muffled click. I twist the icy handle and step into the bare white concrete corridor that leads past the cells. I recall sliding back the cover of each spyhole as I passed them. One isn't quite shut, and a glance into the cell shows me that a suspect has shed all his clothes and is urinating at the door with a penis as bald and ruddy as his head. I pass by unnoticed and merge with the shadows in the office at the end of the corridor.

The large square room contains twelve desks, most of them strewn with papers. A single fluorescent tube on the far side of the room is lit, isolating a desk next to the door. I know it isn't my desk, yet my photograph is on it, propped against an hourglass whose lower half is full of red liquid. The face in the picture isn't nearly as haggard or haunted as my face was in the mirror behind the bar. I barely glimpse the difference, because the picture isn't alone on the desk. Beside it is a photograph of a young woman and her little girl.

Lisabeth and her daughter Jodie. Lisabeth's blond hair frames the depths of her brown eyes, cups her freckled cheeks and small nose, points with the end of its fringe at her delicate pink lips. Jodie has an eight-year-old version of all these features except for her hair, which is curly and black. I want to reach out to them—them, not their images—but I can only fold myself around an ache at the centre of me. I'm crouched in the darkest corner, and might as well be hiding there, when two detectives enter the room.

The swarthy sharp-faced man is Fortuna; his graceful deceptively slight partner is Chau. Neither of them sees me. They lift their coats from pegs on the wall and gaze at the photographs on Fortuna's desk. "You could take his apartment while I see if she's talking yet," he says to Chau.

I feel in danger of being torn apart by my inability to follow both of them. "Go together," I mouth.

Fortuna shrugs his shoulders into the heavy coat that's only just wide enough for them, then lifts his head as if he heard something. "Or maybe we should both check the apartment so nothing gets missed," he says.

Chau lingers over thumbing each of the buttons on his raincoat into the buttonhole and pulls his belt just exactly tight enough before he speaks. "We should go to the hospital first."

"Got you," says Fortuna, and for no reason except that's what he does at his desk, upturns the hourglass as Chau switches off the light, leaving the red fluid to drip in the dark.

As soon as they're out of sight I follow. By the time I reach the duty sergeant's desk he has grunted at them and returned to his book. He doesn't hear me pass. The doors are swinging together after the detectives, who are heading for a car. "Want to drive?" Fortuna says.

"Walk," I mouth, slipping through the gap between the doors.

"Not this time of night," says Chau to his partner. "Only time the streets are clean."

"Don't get any cleaner," Fortuna agrees, if he's agreeing, and paces Chau out of the car park.

I don't move until they're around the corner and I judge they've walked half a block. They don't seem to feel any need to look back. I trail them alongside a mile of mud-coloured tenements pierced by thousands of windows not much larger than the portholes of a battleship. One street-level window hisses with bright static from a dead television channel, and in another apartment I hear a raw voice ranting at an all-night phone-in show—a voice whose owner may be talking to the presenter or only imagining he is—but otherwise there's nothing to observe except entrance after entrance repeating a view of the foot of a bare stone staircase. I'd rather let that occupy my mind than try to define my grief before I'm confronted with its source. Then an ambulance screeches out of a side road and races into the city, and the detectives turn along the road it came from.

The hospital is close to the main street that leads to the hill I can no longer see. Beyond two parked ambulances a pair of automatic doors are deferring to Fortuna and Chau. I dodge between the ambulances in time for the doors not to need to reopen themselves on my behalf. The detectives are at the reception counter across the lobby, and the receptionist doesn't have to be told what they want. "Jodie Nelson" she says. "Better hustle."

It isn't encouragement I hear in her voice. As the detectives head for the corridor leading to Intensive Care I'm close behind them. They shove each pair of fire doors wide enough to let me pass through a few paces after them. They still haven't noticed me when they veer into a short side corridor that leads to a ward. The ward sister behind her desk raises her eyes to them, and I will her not to say what her eyes are already saying—but though I may be able to make people speak, I can't silence them. "She's gone," the sister says.

"Shit," says Fortuna, and lifts an apologetic hand to his mouth.

Chau curves his little finger to wipe his left eye. "Did she ever come round?"

"No." After a pause the sister adds "Thank God."

"Never said anything either?"

"Hardly breathed."

Fortuna breaks the silence. "Poor little bitch."

None of them is looking into the ward, but I am. Beyond a gap in the screen around the bed nearest the doors a male nurse is loading a small figure onto a trolley. His body almost blocks my view as he covers the contents of the trolley from head to foot with a sheet, but I glimpse the girl's hand. Only it isn't much of a hand any more—it looks as though somebody has tried to make the fingers out of melted wax.

The nurse eases the screen open and uses the trolley to nudge the doors gently aside. He ignores me, and I feel as if he's expressing a contempt I deserve. When he wheels the trolley towards a lift I want to follow, but I need to stay with the detectives. I wait until they return to the main corridor, their backs to me. They're silent as far as the hospital entrance, outside which Fortuna says "They must have known Lee was on to them."

"Maybe they meant to scare him off."

"Do we give a shit if that's all they meant?"

"We do not."

"Maybe we'll find something at his place to show he was investigating them."

"That wouldn't surprise me at all."

I'm Lee. They're going to lead me home. I stay well behind them as they tramp deeper into the tenement district—I feel as if the weight of my grief is slowing me down. Their footsteps are the only sounds in this part of the city, so that I wonder if the way their advance rings through the streets has driven into hiding anyone who prefers not to be observed. When they come in sight of my tenement I know it at once, though I can't see how anyone except a detective would be able to distinguish it. Fortuna is first through the doorless entrance. When I hear his and Chau's footsteps leave the stairs I follow.

The graffiti in the lobby, initials and words of one syllable, crowd halfway up the stairs, where someone has smashed the light at the corner. Concrete dust sifts down where the handrail has been wrenched almost out of the wall. Fortuna is at the top of the flight of stairs, unlocking my door. He uses another of my keys to turn off the alarm just inside, then Chau shuts the door behind himself and his partner.

I don't need a key to open it. No sooner has it admitted me than it's shut as though it hasn't moved. Bedroom, toilet, kitchen. My old colleagues have already opened those doors, exposing how little is beyond them, and are in the main room, where the television is hardly big enough for a solitary person to watch. Some chairs that don't look as if they have ever been introduced squat in front of it. Next to the chair that's sagging from use, charred cork filters without a gap between them ring a glass ashtray. Not many yards away across the threadbare carpet, three straight chairs press against a bare dining table, the only company they have apart from the photographs on a brick mantelpiece with an electric fire in its hearth.

One is a close-up of Jodie's grinning face that makes me have to struggle not to imagine how her face must look now. In the other Lisabeth is showing the camera the diamond on her ring finger. I was behind the camera, and I'm close to remembering too much too soon, more than I can bear all at once. It's a relief when the detectives start talking about me. "So this is how he ended up," Chau says.

"All he thought he could afford, maybe."

"More likely all he thought he was going to be able to."

Are they blaming Lisabeth for that? It would be so unjust that I'm about to declare myself when Fortuna says "He was still a better cop than most."

"Too good not to leave us something if he thought he wasn't going to be able to follow it through."

"Just in case he wasn't, even," says Fortuna, staring around the room.

There's nowhere much for them to search. Chau pulls out kitchen drawers while Fortuna tries the bedroom. I watch him from the darkness of the bathroom, and as he opens the wardrobe I know what he'll find. He has only to reach in the breast pocket of the first of my very few suits to produce a photograph he bares his teeth at before calling his partner. "Like we figured," he says, and holds up the photograph as Chau joins him. "Price and Bilder."

"The old firm."

Though they sound like a partnership of architects, that's far from their trade. The photograph shows them about to dodge into the bar next to the alley where I came back to myself. The more than well-fed man in an expensive Italian suit with a cigar making his small fat mouth round is Price, and his thin swift companion thrusting his narrow-eyed face forward like a fist as if to scare off any watchers is Bilder. I see their faces for barely a moment before Fortuna stows them in his coat pocket, but now I can't stop seeing them. "Enough for a warrant, would you say?" Chau muses.

"No point, the way they cover themselves. Maybe enough for a tap."

"Are you thinking there's a judge who might figure he owes us a favour?"

"When the whole department and some people higher up would appreciate it."

"Let's talk to the chief and then we can buy our judge the kind of breakfast he drinks."

That's too slow for me. As the detectives head back along the corridor to switch off the lights I slip out of the door. I don't need to wait for them to lead me. I never had to: I simply followed them to prevent myself from learning too much too unbearably quickly. Now I want to finish.

I leave the street at the first intersection. Behind the tenements the buildings shrink away from one another and crouch low, dreaming of violence. In front of the lawns, which are a mass of weeds and litter, the streetlamps have lowered themselves so as to be easier to smash. Empty cartridge cases glint on a lawn, and in the darkness on the next there's a sprawled body—an animal's, I hope. Once I hear a clash of machetes, but by the time I reach the place the sound came from there is only a trickle of blood leading into a house. All the doors will be reinforced, because the windows are— more than one is cobwebbed with the impact of a missile, and two sides of a corner house have been decorated with the spray of a machinegun. A girl too young and undernourished and scantily clad to be waiting alone in the night shivers under an intermittently lit streetlamp. A limousine with windows as black as its body and hers glides alongside her, and she stoops towards it as though she's flinching away from a whip. Seconds after its back door creeps open, she's inside.

As the car turns uphill I follow. The houses grow larger and farther apart, fending off the road with spiked railings and brick walls crested with barbed wire. I round a wide curve in time to see a pair of electrified gates meeting behind the limousine as it vanishes along a tree-lined drive. I can't pursue it, I'm not here for it. My destination is too close to ignore—the night has gathered itself overhead to point to it, spreading black wings over me. The road curves back on itself, and at the top of the curve is Price's house.

It's a turreted two-storey Mediterranean castle that gleams white as a false smile. A notice on the railings that are more than twice my height says they're lethal, another warns there are dogs in the grounds. One window on the top floor is lit as if somebody has put a light in it for me. The night above me seems to shrink, to flyover the railings and perch above the window, folding its wings. Its black eyes gleam as I press the button on the left-hand granite column of the filigreed wrought-iron gates.

The camera squatting on top of the opposite column lowers its lens to peer at me as the grille above the button spits out static. "Who is it?"

Despite its metallic croaking, I recognise Bilder's voice. I turn to the camera and stretch my arms wide, and in case that isn't enough, I jam the stub of Price's abandoned cigar between my teeth. "Who does it look like?" I say through the taste of stale smoke.

The camera surveys the road before Bilder speaks again, not to me. "It's Lee. Seems like he's by himself."

"How surprising," says Price across the room. "So why the hesitation, Mr Bilder? Let him in."

Bilder starts to utter what sounds like a protest before the intercom cuts him off. A few seconds later the gates swing open with a whisper of oiled hinges. The camera keeps me in view as I move forward, and I've hardly set foot on the drive, which is so wide and devious it is clearly meant only for cars, when the gates shut again with a clang. It's answered at once by a chorus of snarling, and a Doberman runs out from behind an elaborate shrubbery on either side of the drive.

There's nowhere I can flee, nor any need. As the dogs race to the gates I poise a hand above each glossy slavering head. The animals hesitate, their eyes clouding, their wet lips closing over their teeth, and then they move beneath my hands towards the house. Their claws click on the white gravel, their pelt blackens with shadows of orchids and shines like oil as they trot past lights half buried in the borders of the drive. When I reach the marble steps leading up to the front door I fling the cigar butt across the lawn as green and moist as a swamp. The dogs bolt after their prize, and I go to the door.

In less time than a breath would take I'm past it and it's shut. I'm in an extravagantly wide lobby from which a staircase of the kind a movie star would use for her grand entrance curves upwards. At the foot of the banister, doing duty as a post, is a model of the Statue of Liberty, and I'm tempted to wrench off the torch-bearing arm for a weapon. I've no time, and apparently no need. My rage sends me up the stairs to find my quarry, and I haven't reached the top when I see them.

Price is reclining naked on almost half of a king-sized mahogany bed. The enormous hairy balloon of his stomach has his tiny penis for a mouthpiece. He's gazing out of the window, from which Bilder, dressed in boxer shorts twice as wide as his scrawny thighs, is watching the city. Price's penis inches out of its nest of grey hair at the sight of me—it tries to point at me as the small neat automatic in his pudgy fist is doing. "We've company, Mr Bilder," he says in his high soft voice. "He can be thoughtless sometimes, Mr Lee. He can get a little too full of himself."

Bilder turns only his head and touches his temple with a finger, which he then aims at me. "He's not arguing."

"Forgive our not having come down to admit you, Mr Lee, but our door doesn't seem to have taxed your professional skills. Perhaps you'll tell us how you dealt with it after you've indulged me for a few moments. Do make you comfortable," Price says, and waves his free hand above the expanse of empty bed. "You're just in time to watch a spectacle arranged by Mr Bilder."

I don't know if he's mocking me or convinced he has some power over me that is capable of persuading me to join him on the bed. I take hold of a cushioned antique stool in front of the dressing-table laden with cosmetics facing the army of them in the extravagantly framed mirror. The stool is heavy enough to knock the gun out of Price's hand and smash his head and Bilder's, but I need to see what's about to happen so that I'll know everything. I plant the stool at the end of the bed and sit on it with my back to Price.

I can see his reflection in the window against which Bilder is pressing himself, sweat flaring on the glass around his hands. The pane shuts out the sounds of the city, and I realise how it lets Price and Bilder observe the poverty and despair and crime down there as though it's a movie being projected for their benefit, however much of it they're responsible for. Just now it seems there's nothing to watch, until Bilder closes his fingers and thumbs one by one, their sweat fading from the window as he counts off the seconds. At the moment when he makes another fist, a flame blooms in the shadow of the tenements. "Ah," says Price.

Another flame appears, and another. The windows of a house are blowing out. The blaze spreads around each of them and streams towards the roof, which starts to expose its blackened skeleton before it collapses into the box of fire the house now is. Fire engines as small and ineffectual as toys race across the city to add the blinking of their lights to the glow of the fire. "Exquisite as always, Mr Bilder," Price says, his hand straying towards his swollen penis. As that dwindles he levels the gun almost casually at me, laying the barrel along his thigh. "Mr Lee, we've neglected you long enough. We never expected you to honour our little shack."

The fire flickers next to the reflection of his penis, from which a molten jet of liquid appears to be arcing. "Whose house did you burn down?" I say through my teeth.

"Nobody but someone who owed us more than they were worth. I don't need to tell you what thieves are like. Are you still looking out for the underdog?" Price enquires, and gives my back a grin that squeezes out a fat tongue. "I find concern so fascinating."

"Maybe he's here because he's concerned," says Bilder.

"Is that the case, Mr Lee? Is that your tale?"

Rage twists me as though I'm at the heart of a fire. I step back from the stool and face both men. "I've come from the hospital."

"You had the measure of him, Mr Bilder. Concerned till the last."

"No stopping him."

"What tidings of the injured, Mr Lee? What are you here to report?"

"She's dead," I say, so viciously that Bilder swings around from watching the engines struggle to control his fire. "Eight years old and you killed her."

"A regrettable oversight, would you accept, or shall we say a surplus of enthusiasm? Mr Bilder has been known to express the view that a property with nobody in it is only half a fire." Price folds three fingers around his renewed erection as if to determine its length. "A craftsman ought to love his work, don't you agree?"

"Not just do a job because your father did," says Bilder.

He's talking about me. They're both gazing at me with a mixture of contempt and, even worse, of something not too far from sympathy.

"Did you think that meant I'd give up?" I demand. "Did you think you'd scared me off?"

"At least that, didn't we surmise, Mr Bilder?"

"I don't scare," I tell them, taking hold of a leg of the stool. "Let's see if you do."

"Crude, Mr Lee. An abuse of hospitality." Price looks regretful, perhaps because his penis is drooping again, as he trains the gun on my chest. "If there's to be unpleasantness, you might have the grace to tell me first how you managed to penetrate this house."

"Nothing could have kept me out when I'm here for Jodie," I say, raising the stool with both hands. "I don't think you want to use that. You like to keep your killing away from your home."

"I believe we can rely on Mr Bilder's talent for disposing of the unwanted."

"Good job one of us knows how to hide stuff," says Bilder.

Is he comparing himself with Price or with me? I've no time to wonder. I'm poised to throw the stool at the gun. Even if Price fires, the upholstery will either absorb the shot or reduce its impact before it reaches me. I can take that and more: my fury that cares only for revenge has made me feel invulnerable, and so I fling

The stool hasn't left my hands when the first bullet rips through upholstery and wood. My arms begin to shudder as the bullet thuds into my chest. The piece of furniture sags in my weakening grasp and then, somewhere far away, falls on the floor with its helpless legs in the air. It seems considerably less present than the plaintive caw of a bird that greeted the shot. How could I have heard that through the sound-proofed window? Price looks as if he's considering that question, but he must be contemplating how much he has injured me, since with hardly a pause he fires twice.

A punch that thrusts deep into my body slams me against the wall. The third bullet pins me there like a dead insect. Still pointing the gun at me, Price reaches across himself to an ornate bedside table and plants a cigar between his lips. Instead of a band the cigar is wearing the diamond ring I last saw on Lisabeth's finger.

My rage is a physical force that jerks me away from the wall. I hear another caw outside, but now it's a cry of triumph. The power that has entered me focuses on the lumps of metal lodged in my body. I feel them soften and begin to trickle out of the holes they made. The pain feels like the start of purification. "Take your best shot," I say, framing my chest with my spread hands as I advance on Price.

He fires again, and again. I scarcely feel the bullets as they pass through me, melting as they go, and spatter the wall. I move slowly only because I want him to see his death approaching. At last he shies the empty gun at me, and I bat it aside with a forearm. "Bilder," he screams.

Bilder is dashing for the stairs, and I ignore him. I'm at the service of the power within me. I stoop like a blaze in a gale and take hold of Price's feet. He shrieks, much louder as they catch fire. There's so much fuel in him that his legs and two wide swathes of the bed are ablaze in seconds. A stain spreads to meet the flames, but they acknowledge it only with a terse hiss as they merge at his crotch. As his torso squirms wildly back and forth, flailing its arms as if to beckon the eager fire, I leave him. I hear his cries give way to a bubbling as I race downstairs after Bilder.

Though the front door is open, he hasn't got far. He's trying to talk his way past the dogs—his running must have made them think he's an intruder. He doesn't hear me behind him; he's unaware of my presence when I lay a hand on his head. His scalp goes up at once, but I don't withdraw my blessing until more than his hair is on fire. His brain must be for him to perform such a grotesque dance, dodging from side to side of the drive and kicking up the gravel as he clutches at his head while it and then his arms drip flames. Well after there seems to be too little of him to stand up he prances about, and then what's left of him sprawls in the middle of the drive, still kicking. As his heels exert a last convulsive shove I make for the gates.

Bilder must have opened them from the house. Once I'm through them I look back. The dogs stand over Bilder's smouldering remains, guarding them or about to tear at them. Flames pour from the bedroom window, and smoke in a shape that appears to be pecking at the window and spreading its wings over the roof. Its outline flutters, and the sight loses its hold on me. I have to find Lisabeth and tell her I've done everything I can.

Shouldn't I be heading down towards the hospital? Instead my instincts are leading me uphill, where trees close around houses that gleam like tombs. The foliage cuts off the leaping glow of Price's house and later a howling of fire engines. A willow by a dormant fountain imitates the shape the water will take; a mournful statue averts her face from me and draws her marble robe about herself. The slope of the hill flattens towards the summit, the houses grow smaller. I remember thinking they're like servants' quarters for the mansions below them, except Lisabeth was never anybody's servant.

I can't see the city when I reach the house I recognise. Like its neighbours, it's a wooden bungalow. A child has painted big bright flowers on the fence—Jodie painted them, and that's her swing with a toy rabbit slumped on it in the concrete front yard, though her favourite place was a little clearing in the bushes behind the house, where she used to lie at night and watch the stars. The memories sharpen my grief, so that I know I haven't begun to deal with it, but how? I unlatch the waist-high gate and cross the yard to the lit porch.

Lisabeth is sitting in the middle of the bulky leather sofa in the front room. She's gazing at a painting propped against the wall, the only painting she ever kept for herself—the portrait of her with five-year-old Jodie hovering above her hands. I never knew if that meant she'd just thrown Jodie into the air or if she was suggesting that the child was coming down to her from somewhere else. I'm afraid to move, because there's a stillness about everything—the quiet room, Lisabeth's steady gaze and her fingertips touching her lips as if to hold in a thought or a sound, the house itself—that feels intensely vulnerable, protected only by the black wings of the night overhead. Then Lisabeth turns her head and looks at me.

The sorrow in her eyes is beyond words. I'm hopelessly unequal to it, but where can I go except to her? The door swings inwards, though I'm unaware of having touched it. I move towards her and stretch out my hands, but her expression and the utter stillness halt me well short of her. "I'm sorry," I say, and my hands sag.

Precisely because her face doesn't alter I understand at least part of its message for me: my words and my grief aren't enough. I'm opening my mouth to ask what more I can do, though the words seem too stupid to utter, when I see movement in a bedroom off the main room—Jodie's bedroom. In a moment Jodie comes out and sits beside her mother and takes her hand.

There isn't a mark on her, nor on the T-shirt and jeans and sneakers she loved to wear. She gazes at me with the same wordless sorrow as her mother. They're waiting for me to understand. If she looks uninjured when I saw how she was at the hospital—if she can hold Lisabeth's hand like that, it means not just Jodie but also her mother must be—Only there's worse than that to grasp, and in a moment I see what I've misunderstood. Their sorrow isn't for each other. It's for me.

At last I remember why I had to come back. The knowledge wrenches my mouth as wide as it will go, but crying and grimacing won't help. I have to speak—I have to confess everything, to Lisabeth and Jodie and myself. "I hired Price and Bilder," I say in a voice that tries not to be heard. "I told them I'd leave them alone if they did this job. It was me."

Their faces don't change, though the faintest hint of red like a reminiscence of a fire glimmers in their eyes. The approach of dawn is beginning to tint the sky above the city, and some instinct tells me I've very little time. "I thought I'd made sure nobody was here. I called you, Lis. You said you were on your way out with Jodie to meet me. I shouldn't have waited so long at the restaurant. I did come to find you, but I got here too late."

The memory blinds me with itself: my fists punching through the block of fire the front door had become, my glimpse of two bodies on the sofa in the midst of the house, the entire roof collapsing as I ran to them . . . "Bilder came when you were leaving, didn't he? What did he do, tie you both up?"

I'm hardly entitled to rage at the thought of him. In the glow before dawn the bushes behind the house are starting to be visible through the wall, and through Lisabeth and Jodie. Is my slowness in owning up causing them to fade, to withdraw from me? "The insurance would have been for us," I plead. "We'd have gone across the border. I couldn't touch the money I stole. A crack dealer's money we found on a raid, and me and my partner took half. More than one dealer. It got easier after the first time, and I got careless. The department was waiting for me to go for it and they'd have had me. I must have been insane. I just wanted us to be together. I wanted you to have to come with me."

They're grieving for everything I destroyed. I've told them nothing they didn't know, but I had to recognise it. I can see the leaves of the bushes through them now, leaves red as flames. "I finished Price and Bilder," I say, "but I realise that isn't enough. What has to happen to me?"

My voice falters, because Jodie huddles closer to her mother at the thought. Lisabeth strokes her hair with a hand no more substantial than smoke and gazes at me. Her eyes brighten, perhaps only with the dawn, and her lips part. "We still—" she says, and then the dawn streams through the house, which vanishes instantly like mist, taking her and Jodie back where they came from. I'm left standing in the midst of the sketch of a charred foundation on burned earth.

What was Lisabeth about to say? They came back, they waited for me, and mustn't that mean they still care for me, however undeserving I am? The dawn focuses itself on me, and I prepare to vanish—and then I understand what I must go through if I'm ever to have a chance of finding Lisabeth and Jodie again. Their sorrow wasn't only for my past, it was for now. I can feel the fire of which I was the vessel beginning to consume me from within.

I know what it felt like to be buried under the roof, but that was over in seconds. This fire will take all day to spread through the whole of me, as long as there's sunlight to stoke it. I crouch over the blaze at the centre of myself and stumble through the scorched bushes, and fall down in Jodie's clearing. It won't protect me from the fire that's being raised within me, but perhaps it will help me think of her and Lisabeth. I draw my legs up and wrap my arms around myself and close my eyes. I taste dust and ash, singed earth, parched grass. I would try to breathe deeply for calm, but of course I have no breath. I can only wait until at last the day is over and the crow of night bears me away to rest.

Agatha's Ghost

HE'D DONE HIS BEST TO HIDE HER RADIO, BUT HE'D FORGOTTEN to switch it off. That was the voice like someone speaking with a hand over their mouth she heard as she awoke. She was seated at the dining-table, on which he'd turned all four plates over and crossed the knives and forks on top of them to show that crosses were no use against him. She didn't know if it was daytime or the middle of the night, what with the glare of the overhead bulb and the grime on the windows, until she recognised the voice somewhere upstairs. It was Barbara Day, presenter of the lunchtime phone-in show.

Agatha eased her aching joints off the chair and lifted her handbag from between her ankles so that she could stalk into the hall. Was he lurking under the stairs? That had been his favourite hiding-place when he was little, and now, with most of the doors shut, it was darker than ever. She stamped hard on every tread as she made her slow way up to find the radio.

It was in the bathroom, next to a bath full almost to the brim. When she poked the water, a chill cramped her arm. Now she remembered: she'd been about to have her bath when the phone had rung, and she'd laboured downstairs just in time to miss the call, after which she'd had to sit down for a rest and dozed off. He'd got her into that state with his pranks—what might he try next? Then she heard Barbara Day repeat the phone number, and at once Agatha knew why he was so anxious to distract her. He was trying not to let her realise where she could find help.

She clutched her bag and the radio to her with both hands all the way downstairs. She sat on the next to bottom stair and trapped the bag between her thighs and the radio between her ankles before she leaned forward, dragging agony up her spine, to topple the phone off its rickety bow-legged table onto her lap. She pronounced each digit as she lugged the holes around the dial, but she was beginning to wonder if he'd distracted her so much she had dialled the wrong number when the bell in her ear became a woman's voice. "Daytime with Day," it announced.

"Barbara Day?"

"No, madam, just her researcher. Barbara is—"

"I'm quite aware you aren't she. I can hear her at this moment on the radio. May I speak to her, please?"

"Have you a story for us?"

"Not a story, no. The truth."

"I get you, and it's about . . . "

"I prefer to explain that to Miss Day herself."

"It's Ms, or you can call her Barbara if you like, but I need to have an idea what you want to talk about so I know if I can put you through."

Agatha had dealt with many secretaries when she was selling advertising for the newspaper, but never one like this. "I'm being haunted. Haunted by a wicked spirit. Is that sufficient? Is that worthy of your superior's time?"

"We'll always go for the unusual. Anything that makes people special. Can I take your name and number?"

"Agatha Derwent," Agatha began, then shook her fist. The paper disc had been removed from the centre of the dial. "My number," she cried, not having given it to anyone since she could remember, "my number," and grinned so violently the teeth almost came loose from her gums. "It's may I please go to the party."

"I'm sorry, I'm lost. Did you just say—"

"My number is may I please—" Since even talking at half speed seemed unlikely to communicate the message, Agatha made the effort to translate it. "It's three one six—"

"Double two three five. Got you. If you put your phone down now, Agatha, and switch your radio off we'll call you back."

Agatha planted the receiver on its stand and held them together. She wasn't about to switch off the radio when it might refer to her. She was listening to Barbara Day's conversation with a retired policeman who built dinosaur skeletons out of used toothbrushes, and staring at the darkest corner of the hall in case the twitch of spindly legs she'd glimpsed there meant that her persecutor was about to show himself, when the phone rang, almost flinging itself out of her startled grasp. "Agatha Derwent," she called at the top of her voice as she grappled with the receiver and found her cheek with it. "Agatha—"

"Agatha. We're putting you on air now, so can you switch us off and not say anything till Barbara speaks to you."

The minion's voice gave way to the policeman's, requesting listeners to send him all their old toothbrushes, and Agatha's sense of his being in two places simultaneously was so disconcerting that she nearly kicked the radio over in her haste to toe its switch. Then Barbara Day said in her ear "Next we have Agatha, and I believe you want to tell us about a ghost, don't you, Agatha?"

"I want everyone who's listening to know about him."

"I'm holding my breath. I'm sure we all are. Where did you have this experience, Agatha?"

"Here in my house. He's always here. I'm sure he'll be somewhere close to me at this very moment," Agatha said, raising her voice and watching the corner next to the hinges of the front door grow secretively darker, "to make certain he hears everything I say about him."

"You sound a brave lady, Agatha. You aren't afraid of him, are you? Can you tell us what he looks like?"

"I could, but there'd be no point. He never lets me see him."

"He doesn't. Then excuse me for asking, only I know the listeners would expect me to, but how do you know it's a he?"

"Because I know who it is. It's my nephew Kenneth that died last year."

"Did you see a lot of him? That's to say, were you fond of each other?"

"I'd have liked him a great deal more if he'd acted even half his age."

"Will he now, do you think? I've often thought if there's life after death it ought to be our last stage of growing up."

"There's life after death all right, don't you wonder about that, but it's done him no good. It's more like a second childhood. He always liked to joke and play the fool with me, but then he started stealing from me, and now I can't see him he does it all the time."

"That must be awful for you. What sort of—"

"Clothes and jewellery and photographs and old letters that wouldn't mean a sausage to anyone but me. He had my keys more than once till I made certain my bag never left me, and now he's started putting things in it that aren't mine to show me it isn't safe."

"How old is he, Agatha? I mean, how old was—"

"Far too old to behave as he's behaving," Agatha said loud enough to be heard throughout the house. "Forty-seven next month."

"And forgive me for asking, but as one lady to another, how old would that make—"

"I'm retired from a very responsible job, maybe even more responsible than yours if you'll forgive my saying so. What are you trying to imply, that I'm growing forgetful? I'd know if I owned a brass candlestick, wouldn't I? Do you think anybody would be in the habit of keeping one of those in their bag? Or a mousetrap, or a tin of dog food when I've never owned an animal in my life because my father told me how you caught diseases from them, or a plastic harmonica, or a tin of lighter fuel when all I ever use are matches?"

"I was only wondering if you might have picked up any of these items somewhere and—"

"That would be a clever trick for me to play, cleverer than any of his, since I haven't stirred out of this house for weeks. I bought enough tins to last me the rest of the year, and I've been waiting to catch him at his wickedness, but he thinks it's a fine game keeping me on edge every moment of the day and night. Do you know he whispers in my ear when I'm trying to get to sleep? I thought I could deal with him all by myself, but I won't have him wearing me down. One thing I'll tell you he's wishing I wouldn't: he doesn't want me to get help. He hid the phone directory, and he even tried to take away my radio so I wouldn't have your number. He doesn't want anyone to know about him."

"Well, all of us certainly do now, so I hope you feel less alone, Agatha. What kind of help—"

"Whatever has to be done to send him away."

"Do you think you ought to have a priest in?"

"I went to the one up the road, and shall I tell you what he said?"

"Do share it with us, please."

"He told me they don't"—Agatha made her voice high-pitched and supercilious—"believe in such things as ghosts any more."

"Good heavens, Agatha, I'd have thought that was what they were supposed to be all about, wouldn't you? I'm sure some of our listeners must believe, and I hope they'll phone in with ideas. That was Agatha from the city centre, and let me just remind you if you need reminding of our number . . . "

At the start of this sentence Barbara Day's voice had recoiled from Agatha, who felt abandoned until the researcher came between them. "Thanks for calling. You can turn your radio on now," she said.

Agatha found the switch on the radio with one of the toes poking out of her winter tights before she fumbled the receiver into place. She returned the phone to its table as she levered herself to her feet with the arm that wasn't hugging her bag, in which she rummaged for her keys to unlock the front room. None of them fitted the lock, he'd stolen her keys and substituted someone else's and then she saw that she was trying to use them upside down. He'd nearly succeeded in confusing her, but she threw the door triumphantly wide and grabbed the radio to carry it to her armchair.

When she lowered herself into the depression shaped like herself the chair emitted a piteous creak. It was the only one he hadn't damaged so that her friends would have nowhere to sit. He'd made the television cease to work, and she suspected he'd rendered the windows the same colour as the dead screen, to put into her head the notion that the world outside had been switched off. She knew that wasn't the case, because people who were on her side had started talking about her on the radio. Ben, who sounded like a black man, wanted Agatha to keep stirring a table-spoonful of salt in a glass of water while she walked through the entire house—that ought to get rid of any ghosts, he said. Then there was a lady of about her age who sounded the type she would have liked to have had for a friend and who advised her to keep candles burning for a night and a day in every room and corridor. That sounded just the ticket to Agatha, not least because she'd bought dozens of candles the last time she'd felt safe to leave the house. She'd stored them in—She'd bought them in case he started making lights go out again and pulling at the kitchen chair she had to stand on to replace the bulbs. She'd put them—The candlestick he'd planted in her bag would come in useful after all. The candles, they were in, they were in the kitchen cupboard where she'd hidden them, unless he'd moved them, unless he'd heard the lady tell her how to use them and was moving them at that very moment. Agatha grasped the arm of her chair, avoiding holes her nails had gouged in the uphol-stery, and was about to heave herself to her feet when Barbara Day said in a tone she hadn't previously employed "I hope Agatha is still listening. Go ahead. You're—"

"Kenneth Derwent. The nephew of Agatha Derwent who you had on."

The kick Agatha gave the radio sent it sprawling on its back as she did in the chair. Was there nowhere he couldn't go, no trick he was incapable of playing? He'd clearly fooled Barbara Day, who responded "We can take it you aren't dead."

"Not according to my wife. Just my aunt, and that's the kind of thing she's been making out lately. I must say I think—"

"Just to interrupt for a moment, does that mean everything your aunt said was happening to her—"

"She's doing it to herself."

Only Agatha's determination to be aware of whatever lies he told kept her from stamping on the radio. "I did wonder," Barbara Day said, "only she seemed so clear about it, so sure of herself."

"She always has been. That's part of her problem, that she can't bear not to be. And I'm sorry, but you didn't help by talking to her as though it was all real, never mind letting your callers encourage her."

"We don't censor people unless they say something that's against the law. I expect you'll be going to see your aunt, will you, to try and put things right?"

"She hasn't let me in since she started accusing me of stealing all the stuff she hides herself. She won't let anybody in, and now you've had someone telling her to put lighted candles all round the place, for God's sake."

"I can see that mightn't be such a good idea, so Agatha, if you're listening—"

Agatha wasn't about to, not for another second. She threw herself out of the chair, kicking the radio across the room. It smashed against the wall, under the mirror he'd draped at some point with an antimacassar, and fell silent. She stalked at it and trampled on the fragments before snatching the cloth off the mirror in case he was spying on her from beneath it. She was glaring at the wild spectacle he'd driven her to make of herself when the phone rang.

She marched into the hall and seized the receiver, not letting go of her bag. "Who is it now? What do you want?"

"Agatha Derwent? This is the producer of Daytime with Day. I don't know if you heard some of our listeners who phoned in with suggestions for you."

"I heard them all right, and they aren't all I heard."

"Yes, well, I just wanted to say we don't think it would be such a good idea to put candles in your house. It could be very dangerous, and I'd hate to think we were in any way responsible, so if I could ask you—"

"I'm perfectly responsible for myself, thank you, whatever impression somebody has been trying to give. I hope you'll agree as one professional lady to another that's how I sound," Agatha said in a voice that tasted like syrup thick with sugar, and cut her off. She pinched the receiver between finger and thumb and replaced it delicately in order to control her rage at the way she'd been made to appear. No sooner had she let go of it than the phone rang again.

She knew before she lifted the receiver who it had to be. The only trick he hadn't played so far was this. She ground the receiver against her cheekbone and held her breath to discover how long he could stand to pretend not to be there. In almost no time he said "Aunt Agatha?"

"Are you afraid it mightn't be? Afraid I might have got someone in to listen to you?"

"I wish you would have people in. I wish you wouldn't stay all by yourself. Look, I'm going to come round as soon as the bank shuts, so will you let me in?"

"There's nobody but me to hear your lies now, so stop pretending. Haven't you done enough for one day, making everybody think—" Suddenly, as if she had already lit the candles, the house seemed to brighten with the realisation she'd had. "You are clever, aren't you? You've excelled yourself. All the things you've been doing are meant to make me look mad if I tell anyone about them."

"Listen to what you've just said, Aunt Agatha. Can't you see—"

"Don't waste your energy. You've confused me for the last time, Kenneth," she said, and immediately knew what he was attempting to distract her from. "You got out by going on the radio, and now you can't come back in unless I let you, is that it? You won't get in through my phone, I promise you," she cried, pounding the receiver against the wall. She heard him start to panic, and then his voice was in black fragments that she pulverised under her heel.

She knew he hadn't finished trying to return. She drew all the downstairs curtains in case he might peer in, she hauled herself upstairs along the banister to fetch a blanket that she managed to stuff into the tops of the sashes of the kitchen windows. Once the glass was covered she crouched to the cupboard under the sink.

He hadn't got back in yet—the candles were still there. She had to put her bag down and grip it between her wobbly legs each time she lit a candle with a match from the box that wasn't going to rattle her no matter how much it did so to itself. She stuck a candle on a saucer on the kitchen table, and found another saucer on which to bear a lit candle into the dining-room. The candle for the front room had to make do with a cup, because he'd hidden the rest of her dozens of saucers. Her resourcefulness must be angering him, she thought, for as she carried another cup with a flickering candle in it along the hall she began to ring the bell and pound the front door with the rusty knocker.

"Aunt Agatha," he called, "Aunt Agatha," in a voice that didn't stay coaxing for long. He tried sounding apologetic, plaintive, command-ing, worse of all concerned, but she gritted her teeth until he started prowling around the outside of the house and thumping on the windows. "Go away," she cried at the blotch that dragged itself over the curtains, searching for a crack between them. "You won't get in."

He did his best to distress her by shaking the handle of the back door while he made his knuckles sound so hard against the wood that she was afraid he might punch his way through. The illusion must have been his latest trick, because all at once she heard his footsteps growing childishly small on the front path, and the clang of the garden gate.

She held onto the banisters for a few moments, enjoying the peace, though not once she became aware of his having made her smash the phone. If she hadn't, might he have been trapped in it for ever? Suppose he'd angered her so as to trick her into releasing him? She hugged the bag while she stooped painfully to retrieve the cup with the candle in it from the floor.

She was less than halfway up the stairs when the flame began to flutter. She took another laborious step and knew he was in the house. All his play-acting outside had been nothing but an attempt to befuddle her. "Stop your puffing," she cried as the flame dipped and jittered, "don't you puff me." It shook, it bent double and set the wax flaring, and now she was in no doubt that he wasn't just in the house; he'd crept up behind her—he was waiting for her to be unable to bear not to look. She swung around without warning and thrust the candle into his face. "See how you like—"

But he'd snatched his face away as though it had never been there. Nothing was in front of her except the air into which the cup and its candle thrust, too far. The shock loosened her grip on her bag. She tried to catch it and keep hold of the cup as the latter pulled her off her feet. The bag fell, then the candle, and she could only follow them.

She didn't know if the candle went out as she did. She didn't know anything for she didn't know how long. When she grew aware of darkness, she found she was afraid to discover how much pain she might be in. Then she understood that she was fully conscious, and there was no pain, nor anything to feel it. He'd got the best of her in every way he could. He'd stolen her bag, and her house, and her body as well.

She was in the midst of the remains of the house, a few charred fragments of wall protruding from the sodden earth. All around her were houses, but she couldn't go to her neighbours; she wouldn't have them see her like this, if they could see her at all. None of them had believed her when she'd tried to tell them about Kenneth. For a moment she thought he'd left her with nowhere to go, and then she realised who would believe in her: those who already had.

She heard their voices as they'd sounded on the radio. They weren't just memories, they were more like beacons of sound, and her sense of them reached across the night, urging her to venture out and find them. She felt as she had when she was very young and on the edge of sleep—that she could go anywhere and do anything. She was free of Kenneth at last, that was why, and yet now that he was gone she was tempted to play a few of his tricks, in memory of him and to prove she still existed. Maybe this was her second childhood, she thought as she scurried like the shadow of a spider across the city to seek out her new friends.

Little Ones

GILL AWOKE WITH A COLD HALF OF BED NEXT TO HER. As she groped for the alarm clock to shut it up she heard Brian in the kitchen, whistling a bit of opera until he had to stay in tune by singing some words he'd made up. She grabbed the frosty dial and closed the handful of clock into the box that was its base, and changed her sigh into a quick smile as Brian brought through the breakfast tray. "I have to get up for school, you know," she said.

"I thought I was saving you time," he protested, and put on his hurt look. "Thought we'd have some of it for other things."

"Drop that, I don't mean drop it before you make out I did, and come here." She raised her face to meet his with a kiss and draped her arms around his shoulders. When his hand found the hem of her nightdress and began to glide it over her knees, however, she captured his wrist. "We haven't time now, truly."

"We hadn't last night either."

"You saw all the paperwork I had to do, as if teaching my class wasn't tiring enough."

"How about Sunday?"

"How about it?"

"You didn't seem to have much of a wad to get through then."

"We wouldn't have wanted the landlord banging on the door, would we? Nearly being caught by him once is quite enough, thank you, until we can afford to buy somewhere together. You know how he comes around hunting for sinners after he's been to church."

"You're right. You're absolutely right. You're right as always," Brian said, and straightened himself until she had to let go. "I may as well be off. I don't want any breakfast."

"Stay and we'll talk."

"No, they want us at the shop before the crowds arrive. We've the biggest tape and seedy sale ever starting today, until the next one. It'll be wall-to-wall teenagers as soon as whoever's unlucky opens the doors."

"Just you make sure you stay on the far side of the counter, then."

"If I can," he said with a smile that was rather too close to a swift grimace. He was already on his way into the short narrow rectangle that passed for the hall of the apartment. She heard the hallstand from the Oxfam shop wobble and rattle its prongs as he grabbed his coat. He reappeared in the bedroom doorway, shoving his hand through the sheepskin sleeve to grant her a wave. Before she could finish responding to it he was pulling both bolts on the door to the landing with a single clank. The door slammed, and she heard him skipping down the stairs, and whistling as he reached the street.

She could only hope he wasn't as happy to leave as he sounded. She knew there was one sure way to keep him, but she wasn't ready for that—no risk of children until she and Brian were married, not a single one of her pills missed. Brian stayed over at her flat most nights, but very often he'd spend the evening out with his mates while she slogged through the forms that had come as such a shock to her this year. When he got in he had his way, though by then she was almost always half asleep, exhausted by the strain of her first year's teaching. There must be better years to come, she told herself as she saw her toast off with four quick munches and took her mug of coffee to the bathroom.

The shower clanked and stuttered as she persuaded it to stay hot, and then she had to keep wiping the mirror while she brushed her hair and pinned it up to keep it out of the way of the mites at school. By the time she'd put on a white blouse and one of her dark suits it was almost time for her bus, if it came. She had to leave her breakfast things next to the crumbs Brian had scattered by the sink. "Stay in your holes," she told the mice she kept thinking she heard, and ran down the mostly carpeted stairs into a rain that seemed to have been waiting for the cue of her appearance.

She was just in time for the bus at the end of her road. Clutching her guitar with one hand and her bag stuffed with papers in the other, she struggled to the end of the aisle, where the only free seat was. Three twelve-year-olds preparing to light up made just about enough room for her and wished they hadn't when she gave their cigarettes a grimace each to keep them unlit. By now the bus was out of the streets full of weather-beaten houses that were several times as full of flats. As it passed a rank of new red bungalows which always seemed to Gill to be trying to huddle out of sight of the high-rise blocks that hulked over them, she peered through the window grey with recycled breaths for a peek at Mrs Lavelle's bungalow.

There it was, in the middle of the row, and by now she knew where to look for Mr Lavelle. One of the children rubbed a swathe of glass clear as the bus passed the house. Through the thick net curtains of the front room Gill could just distinguish a man's hunched figure, seated as always no more than a yard from the television. She saw the gleam of his balding bent head, and thought she glimpsed a movement of his face, or perhaps that was only the flickering from the screen. Then the bungalow swam away in the rain, leaving Gill dismayed by the thought of someone sitting all day in front of the television while he waited for his wife to come home.

Ten minutes later the bus lumbered to a halt by the school, a long two-storey building behind bars. Like the houses packed around it, it was the colour of rain even when the sun was out. Gill staggered off the platform of the bus, her shoulder bag swinging unprotected in a district where this was tempting fate. Where's a child when you want one? she thought irritably as rain streamed down her hair into her face as fast as the children were pelting into the school. At the sound of footsteps behind her she instinctively made to secure her bag until she heard Lee Smith's voice. "Hi, miss. Can I carry your guitar?"

"Lee, I thought no-one was going to ask. Yes please, that would be super." She kept her smile steady as she looked at him. His torn jacket had no zip, and he was wetter than anyone should be on this cold morning. "Then if you help me with this lot into my room I've got a couple of jobs that need doing, if you wouldn't mind, and you could put your coat and maybe your jumper on the radiator to dry while you're being such a help."

It was her good deed more than his, she thought—continued to think as Mrs Lavelle rewarded him with a frown as he bore the guitar past her in the corridor. "Be careful if you're carrying Miss Dowson's instrument, Lee Smith," she said.

Lee visibly wondered how there could be any doubt that he was. "He's a useful little chap given a bit of encouragement," said Gill.

"I suppose he'll do by today's standards," Mrs Lavelle said, only to start taking it back. "I remember him from kindergarten. I'm afraid he wouldn't be able to compete with any of my little ones."

By now Gill knew that meant the Lavelle children, however long ago they'd been little—knew that none of the children at the school was ever going to measure up to them. She gave Mrs Lavelle a polite smile and squelched after Lee into the Year One classroom. Once as many of his clothes as he could be persuaded to part with had been draped on the radiator Gill fabricated some emergency pencil-sharpening and book sorting while they dried at least partially. "How come you haven't got a car like all the other teachers, miss?" he asked. "Mr Ingles says his is a Rolls Canardly. Rolls downhill and can hardly get back up."

"I've decided that I'd like a house before a car," Gill said, keeping to herself the thought that neither seemed imminent while she was saving so much more than Brian. "Anyway, I'm going to grab a quick cup of coffee. When the bell goes, head straight for Mr Ingles' room. Don't go out to line up and get wet again. And thanks for your help."

The staffroom was even muggier than the bus had been. Beyond an assortment of chairs that would have looked haphazard in a junk shop, a sweating metal urn stewed its water and befogged the cracked sash window. "Morning," said Pete Ingles as she stepped demurely over his legs to make something like coffee of the powder in her mug. "Did I see my little treasure Lee acting as your enthusiastic donkey just now?"

"I was very pleased with him."

Pete looked embarrassed. "It's good you're getting on with kids from further up the school as well as your own mob, but I shouldn't make a habit of leaving Lee in your room unattended. Things tend to sprout legs around him."

"There's not one of them worth the space they take up, the Smiths." This was Mrs Lavelle from the depths of her personal armchair, where nobody else would have even dared to think of sitting. "Sandra's plying her trade with her mother by the docks already, and Lord knows where Lee goes pinching while they're out. You wouldn't find any of my little ones out of the house by themselves, I promise you."

"Hasn't Lee a father?"

"A Norwegian sailor was the likely candidate." Mrs Lavelle shuddered extravagantly, shivering her china teacup in its saucer. "As if just one man wasn't—well, it isn't a fit subject for young ears."

This had to refer to Gill, who said "I'm quite a big girl really."

"You won't hear me arguing," Pete agreed with a wink. "Just don't tell my wife."

Mrs Lavelle included both of them in a lingering look of reproof. "I'm afraid the kind of understanding I came to with my husband is out of fashion these days."

Gill wasn't anxious to clarify that. "How is Mr Lavelle? I see him most days on the bus."

"On the—" Mrs Lavelle steadied her cup as it almost toppled out of the saucer. "From it, you mean, I see. One should always try and be precise in one's language if one wants to teach. Mr Lavelle has been housebound since he retired from the hairdressing business. Instead of dealing with people in chairs he had to learn to deal with one himself. Has to sit still for me now," she said, and dabbed at her pale lips with a lace handkerchief as if to wipe away the cackle she'd emitted.

"So long as you're happy," Pete said.

"Indeed, and I speak for both of us. You're courting, aren't you, Miss Dowson? Please don't be shy if you ever want a private word."

Gill felt Pete giving her an amused look which, if the assembly bell hadn't rung just then, might have put paid to her determined sobriety. "Thank you, Mrs Lavelle," she called after her as the oldest teacher turned the corners of her mouth down at the sight of children in the corridor.

Gill's morning was what she'd learned to expect: haphazard and noisy if she let it be, all too frequently frustrating but with enough minor achievements—major, considering some of the tiny minds she had to work with—to make her glad she'd struggled to work. She heard children read, sometimes a whole paragraph. She helped them paint, wiped noses, called a halt to fights before they could get started, worked a bit of history and what geography would fit into the lesson, and gave the children and herself a reward for it all by leading a song with her guitar. It was all as different as it could be from Mrs Lavelle's classes, where the children had to sit silent in rows and in what Gill could only assume was old-fashioned terror. But she would have been much happier with her morning if it hadn't started with a shamefaced appearance by Lee Smith, bearing a bagful of her classroom erasers, sharpeners and a little plaster gnome that had been presented to her by one of her pupils. Worse still, Mrs Lavelle across the corridor had seen him.

Gill didn't think she would be able to bear having Mrs Lavelle resurrect the incident in the staffroom at lunch. She felt stupid, but the only person she wanted to admit that to just now was Brian, who wouldn't dare agree or patronise her. Besides, their unsatisfactory parting at the flat had begun to nag at her. Walking to the shop and back would take less than half her lunchtime, and since hers coincided with his there would be time for a drink. It had been weeks since he'd suggested they meet in the pub by the shop.

Five minutes' walk from the school took her out of reach of any traffic. Another five, and a city centre shopping mall shut out the town and the rain. A tape was filling the mall with a song about favourite things as she came abreast of the pub. She was making to hurry past the fountain of Venus with its mock-marble feet in a bowl full of drowned coins when she caught sight of Brian. He was talking to a young woman at a table in the pub.

Gill had seen her behind the counter with Brian; why shouldn't he have a drink with a colleague now and then? She was blonder than Gill, and slimmer, and if she wasn't younger she was doing her best to look it. None of these was a reason for Gill to feel out of place, no matter how friendly a chat they appeared to be having. She edged the pub door open and advanced on the booth where Brian and his friend were ensconced.

She heard them over the top of the booth before they were in sight. "It's the same with me exactly," Brian was saying. "After being brought up in a big family I'm never happy without a few people around."

"But being an only child she just wants you to herself, not that I blame her."

"That's part of it, only she always seems uncomfortable when we visit my folks, as if she can't cope with a lot of people at a time."

"She has to when she's teaching, doesn't she?"

"They're kids. Maybe that's her trying to compensate."

"Trying to compensate for what you don't seem in a hurry to give me, you mean."

Both heads poked over the booth at the sound of Gill's voice. The woman looked at least as caught out as Brian did, and shut her mouth with her knuckles while he said "Gill, we were just—"

"Such as a place we could both call home so we could have a family in it. Quite a big family. You might have realised I'd like that if you'd occasionally listened to me."

"Gill, do you think we'd better save it for—"

"Oh, am I still not supposed to talk about myself? It's only you and your friend who are allowed to discuss me in here, is it? I'm surprised you didn't say that dealing with other people's children is easier than having some of my own."

The woman tried to intervene. "Gill, if I can call you Gill, I'm on your side. I was only trying—"

"I've a good idea what you were trying. Now if you'll both excuse me I'd better be off back to the only crowd I seem to be able to cope with."

"Gill," Brian pleaded, but she was on her way to the door. As it shut behind her she glanced fiercely over her shoulder to see that he hadn't left the booth. Through the window she saw him beginning to stand up, having no doubt told the woman that he ought to. Gill showed him her clawed hands to deter him from following and let the rain stream over her eyes as she marched blindly back to the school.

She had to forget him in order to work. She was especially attentive and tolerant all afternoon, not just in class but in the staffroom, where

Mrs Lavelle seemed to think better of mentioning Lee Smith. Or might the glance she aimed at Gill, so secret and preoccupied it was virtually blank, have meant she was thinking of something quite different? Gill had no time to ponder that either no time for anybody except her children until she was on the bus home.

She'd acted the martinet at the bus stop, so impressively that the children lined up and even made way for her before piling on after her, and for once she had a seat upstairs. It had stopped raining, but it was almost dark, and the twilight and the dregs of rain had merged to turn the windows grey. As the bus cruised past Mrs Lavelle's house Gill saw the teacher drawing the curtains of the front room. Over the net curtains, and through the closing gap, Gill had a glimpse of more than one figure seated in the room. Neither of them was Mr Lavelle, she thought; they were too small, even if her viewpoint was foreshortening them—she would have taken them for children if she hadn't been almost certain that their hair was grey. Or was that an effect of the grime on the bus window? Before she had finished deciding how likely it was that Mrs Lavelle would have any children to visit, the house had retreated into the dark, and it was nearly time for Gill to struggle downstairs.

She didn't let herself think much about Brian. Even on a good night, he was never at the flat within an hour of her. She liberated enough cartons of food from the old vibrating refrigerator to feed two people, and then she devoted herself to the evening's heap of paperwork. Two hours later she microwaved enough dinner for herself, and left nearly all of it. Two more hours later she finished watching a comedy film she hadn't laughed at once, and set about getting ready for bed. There was a limit to the amount of time she could spend doing that, after which she lay in bed and told herself to go to sleep. If Brian had decided not to come round or even to phone, she certainly wasn't going to phone him. It was up to him to make the next move.

The empty half of bed seemed colder every time she wakened beside it. Once she had to pull her arm back fiercely from reaching across it and hugged herself instead. She was glad when the alarm announced it was time for her to stalk about the flat. If he wanted to sulk, let him. If their altercation, or its having been overheard by his blonde friend, seemed enough of an excuse for him to ditch Gill, that just showed how shallow he was. Thoughts such as these kept her going all the way to school—kept her so deep in herself that she didn't think to glance at Mrs Lavelle's house. But they deserted her once she learned that Lee Smith had been arrested for shoplifting.

"He'll be back next week," Pete Ingles assured her at their morning break. "Like as not with a social worker in tow, and a probation officer when he gets older."

"It's time people like the Smith woman were sterilised," Mrs Lavelle declared. "I'd go further and say anyone who starts having children they aren't fit to keep."

"People who are nothing like you, you mean."

"If I may say so, Mr Ingles, you know not the least thing about it," Mrs Lavelle said, and took her time about looking away from him. "You're very quiet today, Miss Dowson. Lee Smith wasn't your responsibility, after all."

"I don't feel as if I've anything to offer," Gill said, not sure how sarcastic she meant to be. "It doesn't look as if I'll be having any children of my own to learn from, not when my used to be boyfriend likes to talk about them to everyone but me."

"I'll bet there's another lucky feller along soon," Pete said.

Mrs Lavelle turned her back on him and gave Gill a blankly secretive look. Gill had even less idea than yesterday what it was supposed to communicate. Perhaps it meant that Mrs Lavelle was continuing to speculate about her, because at the end of the afternoon, as Gill was presenting her two most helpful pupils with items to carry for her, Mrs Lavelle stalked into the classroom as though she'd made a difficult decision. "Forgive me if I guard my words in front of big ears, Miss Dowson, but were you implying earlier that you wanted a private word with someone about children?"

For a moment all the pressures Gill had undergone recently seemed certain to explode, and then she remembered last night's glimpse of Mrs Lavelle's front room. Suddenly it struck her as mysterious enough to need investigating. "I wouldn't mind," she made herself say. "Only I don't think here is private enough, do you? I expect your husband will need you to get home, so shall I come with you?"

This time there was no question that Mrs Lavelle's look was speculative. "You're a discreet enough girl. We'll be friends." She might have been speaking purely for her own benefit. "Take Miss Dowson's things out to my car," she said, so sharply and abruptly that not only the children but Gill jumped.

Mrs Lavelle's car was an ancient three-wheeler that had been the butt of quite a few staffroom quips, but it hadn't previously occurred to Gill to wonder how comfortable Mr Lavelle could find the passenger seat now he was disabled. There was just room in the back for her guitar and both the teachers' bags. As soon as the car was loaded the children fled, leaving Gill with a pitying glance they might have given one of themselves.

The car lurched out of the schoolyard with a series of oily hiccups and veered straight into the road without a care for the oncoming traffic. Though it took less than ten minutes to reach Mrs Lavelle's bungalow, Gill had a good deal of time to wish she'd caught the bus. Her colleague jumped out with unexpected sprightliness to unlatch the gates of her drive, and didn't return to the car until she'd unlocked the front door of the house and pushed it wide open. If Mr Lavelle complained of the draught, she ignored him as she ran back to sprint the car through the gates.

Gill was climbing out when Mrs Lavelle grabbed both bags and the guitar and bore them into the house. She was stronger than she looked, thought Gill, and saw something else for the first time: there were two layers of net curtain at the front window. No wonder it was so hard to see in. She stepped into the boxy spotless panelled hall, which led past three closed doors to the kitchen in which Mrs Lavelle was divesting herself of her burdens. "Tea for two?" Mrs Lavelle said.

"Isn't your husband having one?"

"Mr Lavelle hasn't much to do with liquids these days." As Gill ventured into the kitchen, the other woman sidled past her, gripping her shoulders in passing. "Would you make a pot while I see how things are? There's a good girl."

Gill would have felt more patronised if she hadn't been so busy shivering. She had never known a colder house. Perhaps Mrs Lavelle was trying to save her pay, but how did her husband react to the temperature? As she filled and switched on the chipped electric kettle she heard Mrs Lavelle drawing the curtains in the front room, and her murmur: "We'll be in the kitchen."

It didn't sound like an invitation so much as a warning to someone to stay where they were—at least, that was Gill's interpretation while she listened to the closing of the front-room door. Then she heard the teacher open the next door, which must lead to the only bedroom, and mutter exactly the same words. Was she talking to herself? If so, in which case? Gill found herself edging towards her guitar and her bag. Whatever was going on, she was starting to think she might prefer not to be alone with it. She hadn't reached her belongings when Mrs Lavelle reappeared, still wearing her overcoat. "Won't be long," she said with a lop-sided smile she presumably meant to look hospitable. "Good old thing."

Even when Gill realised she was referring to the kettle, that wasn't much of a relief. Mrs Lavelle had sat down on a pine bench that faced its twin across a matching table, all of them between Gill and the door. For a few moments she watched Gill as if waiting for a waitress in a restaurant to serve her, and then she said "It hasn't turned you against having children, then."

Gill was too nervous to refrain from sounding rude. "What?"

"Why, our job that used to be a vocation when I took it up."

"It hasn't yet. I hope it never does. Why do you think it should? It didn't put you off."

"Did it not, Miss Dowson? Where do you obtain your information about me?"

"From you. Things you've said."

"Oh, those. Sometimes I find it advisable to say what's expected of me." Mrs Lavelle let her gaze stray beyond Gill's shoulder, where she appeared to see some presence silently raising itself. "Do make the kind of tea you like. I always think one can judge character from the strength of the brew."

She was watching the steam from the kettle, of course. Gill grasped it by its handle and felt as though she would be found wanting if she used a towel to protect her hand. She did so anyway, and threw a third tea-bag into the pot for luck or her image, and stirred the contents before she turned round with the pot, to find that Mrs Lavelle had set two cups and saucers, not to mention spoons and a sugar-bowl and milk-jug, on the table without making any noise that Gill had noticed. "Pour, there's an angel," Mrs Lavelle said.

Gill was sure she was going to miss the cups and flood the saucers, but her job had taught her not to seem nervous after all. Mrs Lavelle watched expressionlessly, then sipped her tea, and sipped again. "Not too weak," she said.

Gill decided to take that as a compliment, and as encouragement too. She fed herself a gulp of milkless tea, having blown on it, and dared to ask the question that was clamouring to be asked. "Who were the children I saw yesterday?"

"You're being careless of your words again, Miss Dowson. Where would these children have been?"

"In here."

Mrs Lavelle replaced her cup minutely on the saucer without glancing away from Gill's face. A brownish thread began to trickle down a wrinkle at the right corner of her mouth. "And how did you contrive to see in my kitchen?" she said.

"In the front room, I mean. I saw in it from the bus last night."

"Did you indeed." Mrs Lavelle dabbed at the trickle of tea with her handkerchief and continued not to blink. "I shall be dealing with that," she said.

This sounded not like just a declaration of secrecy but a warning, and Gill was tempted to take it as such and finish her tea or not even finish it before fleeing. Except the older woman's stare wasn't leaving her alone, and if she had to say something, what else was there? "So who—" she said, and broke off, telling herself she'd been stupid, promiscuously imaginative as any child. "Of course, you don't need to tell me. They were your grandchildren, weren't they."

"Most unlikely, Miss Dowson, I'm afraid."

The speculative expression had resurfaced. It was the look of a teacher trying to coax a child to see the obvious, Gill thought—or was it the look of someone wondering how much they could get away with? "Why's that?" she blurted.

"I thought I had made myself clear. Before we were married Mr Lavelle and I agreed we would be sufficient companionship for one another. In those days if anyone thought that odd they kept their opinions to themselves."

"You mean you never—" Once again Gill silenced herself, not only from embarrassment. "Then—"

"Not our nieces, no, nor our nephews." Mrs Lavelle buried a cackle in the stained handkerchief. "What else might there be, do you think? You're my first visitor for nearly a year, you know. Would you like to see?"

At once Gill was sure she wouldn't, not at night and by herself. "Actually, Mrs Lavelle, I should be going. Thanks so much for the tea. I've so much work to do when I get home, I'd better make a start."

The older woman seemed not to have heard her. "They're my companions now. They're quiet as can be, they're what children ought to be. They take after Mr Lavelle, one might say. Come along and you shall meet the family."

Gill stood up and bent to retrieve her belongings, but the older woman was off the bench and swiftly round the table and grasping her by the arm. "Leave those for now. You don't want to drop your guitar and break it, do you?" Her voice had all the reasonableness of a teacher elucidating a requirement to a pupil, and her grip was quite as firm. By the time she'd finished speaking she was at the door to the front room, and blocking the hall between it and escape. She didn't let go of Gill's arm until she had twisted the doorknob and pushed the door open. "It used to be polite to say hello," she said.

Apart from the flickering of the silenced television, the room was dark. As Gill took one reluctant step towards the doorway, a smell of pear-drops met her. She had to advance one more step, then another, before she could see in. Three small figures with their backs to her were sitting motionless on a sofa that faced the television. There was something odd about their heads, she knew. "Do go in," said Mrs Lavelle. "There's nothing you can't see."

Gill reached around the doorway and fumbled at the wall. "I can't find the light-switch."

"Go in, dear." Mrs Lavelle might have been addressing a small niece, to reassure her or to prepare her for a treat. "Nobody will trip you up."

Suddenly furious with herself for being made to feel like a child, Gill stalked into the room. "Hello," she said, more fiercely than she wanted to, but there was no response from the trio on the sofa. The fluttering light tugged the walls closer to her. The smell of pear-drops grew sharper in her nostrils, and all at once she knew she wasn't smelling sweets but a kind of glue. She dodged around the sofa, which was lit by the blaze of an explosion in a cartoon, and saw what she'd spoken to. They were three old-fashioned baby dolls, naked and sexless.

Their unblinking fish-eyes seemed to light up as they saw her, their peeling lips shifted. Those were only effects of the glow from the television; they weren't why Gill almost cried out. None of the dolls was bald, as they should have been. Their scalps were spiky with lumps of grey hair.

"Shall I put the light on, dear," Mrs Lavelle said, "or are you happy as you are?"

She was about to shut the door, Gill thought—about to shut her in with the little ones. It must have been her dash for the door that caused two of the dolls to nod their heads together as if they were discussing how to stop her. She shoved Mrs Lavelle aside and ran: not for the front door, since the older woman was cutting off that route, but for the back. Only that door was locked, and the key was nowhere to be seen.

"Finishing your tea?" said Mrs Lavelle. "You'll want to see Mr Lavelle now, I expect. I'll wheel him out to you. Try not to be too surprised by how he is."

Gill made herself sit down on the bench with her back to the hall. Reflected in the window she could see Mrs Lavelle approaching, halting within what looked like arm's length of her, opening the bedroom door. "It's a bit of a miracle, you know," Mrs Lavelle said, "the way his hair keeps growing."

Gill saw her move out of the reflection of the hall. In an instant she was on her feet and grabbing her bag and her unwieldy guitar. The instrument in its case swung in her hand and almost scraped one wall, then the other. She hugged it one-armed to her and tiptoed swiftly past the bedroom, which was lit only from the hall. She nearly didn't look, and then she did. The next moment she was sprinting for the front door, no longer caring how much noise she made. She had to remember to put the guitar down in order to turn the latch. The rain slashed at her face as she seized the guitar by its neck and fled down the drive, through the gate.

She was afraid to hear Mrs Lavelle run after her, but the only sound was of the front door being closed with a discreetness that went with the house. Gill struggled home, nearly blind with rain and with the memories that seemed to have lodged in her eyes. She couldn't be sure how much she had glimpsed in the bedroom—in the wheelchair Mrs Lavelle had been turning towards the hall. Not much had appeared to be sitting in the chair, but its grey locks had been longer than Gill's, at least on one side of its head. The left side had been bald except for a few curls like the first new growth in a vegetable patch. She didn't know if she could tell anyone, nor what she would do tomorrow, but she knew her life could never be the same. She knew that when she came close enough to her flat to be certain her window was lit, it was the most welcome sight she'd ever seen.

The Last Hand

WHEN MARTIN SAW THE BLOTCHES MOVING DOWN the compartment window, against the thick twilit streams of smoke, he thought at first that it was raining. Then he realised the blotches were flies nuzzling the pane, hurling toward him like curdled drops of the smoke. Already one fat fly like a lump of soot was crawling toward the gap at the top of the window, through which a breeze had flapped at Martin's face all the way from Liverpool. He sat for a moment waiting until the fly entered, so that he could kill it; then he threw his book of crosswords into his case and made for the bar.

"If you give up your job, Martin, I shall leave you."

Many of the compartments on the rocking corridor were curtained; Martin thought of a spy film. But there was nothing mysterious about this train: a dog's nose impressing its seal on a window, the open mouths of sleepers, children laughing or looking sick at the sway of the carriage, a suitcase inching its way to the edge of the rack. Through one window, limned against the Stanlow oil flare across the Mersey sand-flats, Martin saw the scuttling skeletal legs of a fly as it fluttered with him.

"We have to talk about it. You can't write your book if you keep your job, and you'll never write it without me. I wish I didn't have to tell you this."

He strode through the restaurant car, past the gathered white curtains and the lamb chops. He was hungry, but if he could restrain himself as far as London it would be less expensive.

"You haven't got the will or the capital, and you need me to tell you that you've got the talent. But I can't and I won't. I've got to make my own way, and I shall in London. I know you'll want to live with me, but that's just second best. It should be me living with you."

Peals of Birmingham laughter came from the bar. He bought a can and poured the metallic beer into a paper cup. Beneath the Runcorn bridge the Mersey drained from sandbanks like moist indolent flesh in a clogged bath; as the train rushed through the bridge the pattern of the lattices flew silently whirring across his eyes. A fly clung trembling to the window, as if thrown out by the hectic pattern.

"I know you'll keep thinking of me and that won't help your writing. I want you to, because I love you. But I don't love insecurity."

The train flew past a hotel which seemed to have been torn in half, leaving a raw jagged wall and a space for the building's twin, and came to rest in Runcorn station. On the road across the line rain hung like a web from silver lights; shadows on the drizzle ran along the platform, slamming doors. Somewhere Martin heard a buzzing.

"If you've got a job—*if* you've got a job—"

When the train moved out Martin ground his cup into a ball and made his way up the corridor. The diluted smoke billowed ahead of him. He reached the compartment and halted. Three men were sitting beneath his case, playing cards.

The dealer was huge, wet with rain or perspiration. His tall thin companions seized their cards and scrutinised them. As if they were messages, Martin thought—as in a spy film: messages coded through cards. There was the seed of a short story. He stood musing, but the idea slipped away. He dragged back the compartment door and entered.

The dealer looked up; his great eyes glittered like rain on mud. "How are you, friend?" he shouted. "Didn't I say someone must be joining us?" he added, protruding his hands from his bulging black sleeves at his friends.

"Why, a fourth," said one, his sleeves fluttering on his rapid arms like wings.

"A gift from God," the other said thickly, his head turning rustily to Martin.

"Are you going far?" the dealer demanded. "If you want to sleep, old boy, we won't disturb you. I'm sure we can find someone else who'll join us in a good profitable game. You see, I'm being honest with you."

"You can deal me in for a round if you like," Martin said, sitting next to him but not too close. "I'm bound for London."

"Have you high hopes, old boy?"

"No," Martin said.

"It'd hardly be sporting to ask you to join us if you're not too well off. No offence, old boy. No need to be ashamed."

"I can manage," Martin said.

"Well then, let's see what poker does for us!" The dealer snatched the cards from the thin men and shuffled them; he engulfed the pack in his hands and pulled them apart, pouring the cards between them. Colours and numbers flashed at Martin, sketched faces peered. For a moment he thought the figures on the court cards were full-length and, which was odder, full-face and grinning; but in the next shuffle he saw only the familiar twinned profiles.

"One thing, though," Martin said as the dealer thrust the first card into his hand. "The deal passes in rotation, and dealer's choice."

"The Shorrock method, eh?" the dealer laughed. "All right, old boy, dealer's choice it is. I don't think that'll upset us, do you?" he shouted, not waiting for his companions' huge eyes to glance at him and their heads to shake hastily and lethargically.

Martin fanned his cards and sorted them: two kings, two tens, an ace. "Your bet," the dealer said.

Martin rummaged in his pocket and threw sixpence on the windowsill. Outside the pane, numerous flies were crawling silently like delirium.

"My dear chap, sixpence? We can't be so timid now, can we?"

"You'll never be one of us that way," said the slow thin man, bending to the sill with half-a-crown.

"That's more like it! Two half-crowns and one for me as well! Is this your game, old boy?"

"It has to be," Martin said.

"No, no, not at all. Just as you like. We mustn't force ourselves upon you."

"Of course it's as I like," Martin said. "You're not taking me for a loser, surely? Half-a-crown and one card, please."

In exchange for the ace he received a seven. Reaching back, he turned on the reading light. The others were not using theirs. His eye caught that of the thin man nearest the window. "You get used to this kind of light," the man blurted.

"Presumably," Martin said. "Half-a-crown."

"That's better, that's more confident. But we don't frighten, do we? See, he's twice as confident."

"And another half-crown."

"Ten shillings, old boy."

Martin examined his cards. "No," he said.

"You disappoint me, old boy. It's only confidence that sees you through this life, you know. All right, I'll see ten shillings. Seeing? Well, it looks as if my pair of queens has it. Control your face, old boy, there's no need to be so open to us."

"My deal," Martin said. "Same again."

The hands of the man by the window seemed not to belong to him; they dragged at the knees of his trousers like the hands of a hysterical child. "I could do with something to eat," he muttered.

"Just be patient," the fat man advised. "It'll be all the better for waiting."

Martin dealt himself two aces and three meaningless cards. He answered half-a-crown and redealt himself two threes and a six. The twitching thin man raised the stakes to five shillings. His companion pushed a slow hand into his pocket, reached across the restless legs and inserted ten shillings beneath the pile. The fat man followed. Martin thought for a moment. "A pound," he said.

"That's right, that's good! You'll be one of us in no time! Are we scared?"

The leaden man folded his cards together, leaned over for the pack and pushed them into place. "I'm trembling," he said.

The man by the window almost dropped his cards; they flapped and crackled like dry wings. He thrust two pounds beneath the silver and caught the pile wildly as it fell.

"You're doing well, old boy! Rid of one of us already! I think you're on your way now. Two quid."

I mustn't raise again, Martin thought. I must save some money for the next hand in case. And for London. As if the little that he had could make a difference. But he might win. "I'll see you," he said.

"You shouldn't have, old boy. Three nines, that's all I can show you. Only two pair? Bad luck, old boy. Brave try."

"I think you can deal me out now," Martin said. "I'll just adjourn for a few minutes."

"All right, old boy." As Martin reached the door the fat man called "But you will be back, won't you? Don't make us come looking to give you your money back."

In the bar Martin leafed through his wallet and counted ten pounds. He felt he should have more, but he'd under-estimated the cost of the train ticket. He could still win, though, perhaps by changing the game on his deal. Assuming the game wasn't rigged, of course. Absurd, he thought. How could the game be rigged—his brief idea of messages in the cards? Hardly; that was what came of allowing his imagination to use him rather than the reverse. The men were simply grotesques and as such fascinating, perhaps even stimulating when you knew them better. He crumpled the paper cup and left the bar. A large wet fly bounced from the window.

About to open the compartment door, he halted. The three men had laid aside their cards and were passing something between them. It must be a sort of gambler's charm—a small pale object in which points gleamed like eyes. He watched fascinated, for as they tossed it from hand to hand, the motion and the dim light made it seem to struggle. The door jammed momentarily, and when he glanced at the men again, they were returning their cards to the pack.

"Another game, old boy?"

"If you like."

"No, no, if you like. We mustn't stay where we're not wanted."

"Well, stay," Martin said. "We've a long way to go yet."

The man opposite stirred his legs like sticks in mud; water was trickling down his painted black hair. "That's true," he said. "And we must give you a chance."

Martin arranged his cards and automatically followed half-a-crown. He had four clubs; he threw away a diamond and took the first joker he'd seen. He gazed at his hand. "Well, don't read them," stuttered the thin man at the window, staring out at the swarming wet flies. "Play them."

"Five shillings," Martin said, thinking wistfully of his crosswords and their anagrams, and read the cards. Ace, Ten, Nine, Eight, the joker would be King of Clubs—ATNEKC—CANT KE—but if the joker represented any letter, CANT BE—

"What's the last bid?"

"A quid. Come on, old boy, you can't leave us now!"

"Two pounds, then."

"No, I tremble again."

"Four!"

"Six!"

"Eight!" Martin cried with all the conviction he could summon.

They were seeing him. He switched on his reading light, which someone had turned off. "Ace King flush," he said.

"Two pair," the trembling man muttered in despair, drawing his knees up close to him.

"Dear, dear, that sets us back, I think. Although I'm sure there's something I could do with this joker. Why yes, old boy, I'm afraid there is. Nines over fives. Full house."

Martin dropped his cards in the thin man's shivering lap. "Sorry about that, old boy," the fat man said.

The thin man shuffled, pulled at his hands as if to wrench his arms from their sockets, and held out a card to Martin. "All right," Martin said. The money was meaningless, anyway, and so was his trip to London. The man opposite was gazing at him and running his fingers down his cheekbones, drawing the flesh back from his glittering eyes.

Martin followed half-a-crown. He peered at his cards; the light behind him was dimming. Ace, Eight, Three, Two of Hearts and a joker. AT THE (K). CANT BEAT THEM.

"Let's see what you've got, old boy," the fat man shouted. "Why, you've won!"

The silver jingled into Martin's lap; cards were thrust at him. He glanced up; all their eyes glittered; the flies crawled against the grey boiling night, and the pattern on the upholstery seemed to squirm grubbily at the corner of his eye. Ten and Eight of Hearts, Ace and Nine of Diamonds, and a joker—he threw half-a-crown blindly—if he read Ace as One, THE DON—THEY DON—

"Bad luck, old boy. Never mind, the cards are yours."

Suddenly he didn't want to read the message, even though he realised vaguely it was the aspect of the game that gave him a sort of chance. "I'll pass the deal," he said, standing. "I'm going to drown my losses." He piled the cards on the seat and slid back the compartment door.

Perhaps all the corridor lights had fused. Perhaps the train had halted in a tunnel. Perhaps smoke had massed somehow in the corridor, for no light from the compartment penetrated the blinding darkness beyond the door. Martin's foot flinched back. He glimpsed himself snatched away and dwindling, like a fly whirled away on the wind. All at once his despair reversed itself, and he wanted desperately to live. He turned. Like a framed illuminated painting, the three men held out the cards to him. Behind him in the impossible darkness a dry horde swarmed rustling. He reached for the handle and, panting, slammed the door.

"I thought we'd come too far for you to leave us just yet. One more game won't hurt, old boy. Will it?"

"Hurt?" said the slow man, sucking the syllable. "That's not the word."

"I have no money," Martin said.

The fat man laughed open-mouthed; his tongue flapped like a stranded fish. "Old boy, surely we know each other well enough by now not to think in terms of money."

Martin crushed the cards between his sticky hands, thrusting them into place like the teeth of a machine. He could feel the eyes on him. How could they glitter when the light was so dim, and how could there be so many? He glanced up, scattering the cards, and saw only the six wide eager eyes. No light filtered through the window now; the pane was alive, like a black honeycomb. THEY DONT what? His mind struggled to complete the message before the cards were dealt. Suddenly he said "Ace counts low. Low hand wins."

"I don't know about that, old boy," the fat man said, gesturing back his companions.

"Dealer's choice, remember. You agreed."

"So we did," the fat man said slowly. "And we can't break our word."

"But we always play ace high," the thin man cried, ploughing his fingernail along the base of the window.

"Be sporting, old boy."

Martin said nothing. He shook his head ambiguously and threw each of his cards into sight as if it were lethal. Eight and Ten of Spades. Seven of Diamonds. Ace of Clubs. Joker. ETSSDAC.

"No use prolonging the agony, old boy. We might as well show."

"Wait a minute," Martin gasped. "What do jokers count?"

"In your game they're not worth anything."

T USE CADS. THEY DONT USE CARDS.

"You two show," the fat man shouted. "Come on, we're nearly there!"

"Flush," stammered the man by the window. The cards sprang from his hands.

"Pair of eights," said the man opposite Martin, showing them with the lethargic movement of a melting plastic skeleton.

"Pair of twos," the fat man said and grinned. "Not doing too well that round, are we, old boy? Don't you wish you were playing straight poker?"

"Not really," Martin said. "Whether it's low or high, I have an ace."

The three heads turned. The great eyes glittered, and the mouths worked moistly. Behind them Martin saw that the gap at the top of the window was black and blocked by a mass which crawled. The fat man gripped Martin's knee hotly and levered himself to his feet. The three of them stood over Martin. At once the lights went out, and shapes bumbled softly against him.

They've cheated, he thought in bitter desperation. So does everyone. Wind whipped rain from the windows; the train rushed on, and a buzzing form buffeted him hugely. Struggling, he was twisted about and came face to face with the dark intensely fearful oval of his head in the compartment mirror. Then he saw more, and began to struggle frantically as his unseen captors enclosed him.

Someone had opened the window wide; black rain sneaked in, and the train curved and gathered speed toward a tunnel. The tunnel's lips worked. Their outlines crawled minutely and changed, and black spittle flew from them only to return and crawl. Somehow, as the train shouted as it plunged into the tunnel, what lay ahead was displayed in the mirror for him. At the end of the tunnel as if far down a telescope he saw a station like a black ship, sinking beneath swarming clouds of blackness.

A shock thrilled through him, and he managed to throw off his captors for a moment. It was as if the train were moving in two directions simultaneously: the forward rush he felt and the impossible opposite direction in the mirror. It challenged all sanity. And yet they must give him a chance, they couldn't break their word; his mind was still alive and determined to live. "I'm not letting you win!" he shouted and threw himself toward the door, through darkness that buzzed furiously. He had grasped the handle when the first lights of Crewe station blazed into the empty compartment.

Or almost empty, for his feet weren't free. He glared down and saw that they were buried in a mound of silver and notes. He kicked. Then he stooped and began to gather the money. From beneath it crawled three weak flies, which he crushed. He pulled down his case and threw the money in, crumpling it, throwing in the silver from the other side of the compartment, laughing. Suddenly he flung in the rest and, closing the case, strode out onto the platform. He ran through the dim brown light, past waiting figures like forgotten waxworks, toward the platform for Liverpool. Somewhere he heard a buzzing.

Facing it

IN THE MORNING JESSICA TOLD HERSELF IT HAD ALL BEEN a dream. After such a night, no wonder she felt as if she wasn't fully awake. Even the first sting of the shower failed to rid her of the impression that her awareness was somehow muffled. Steam clung to the bathroom mirror as she towelled herself, but why should she find that reassuring? "Get it together," she told herself, and rubbed the glass clear. She stared at her face until it began to seem meaningless, then she dressed and sent herself out of her apartment, into New York.

On the subway faces surrounded her. Whenever the train halted, more of them crowded in; whenever it left a station behind, twice as many swarmed out of the dark that enclosed the train. The train was as hot as a bathroom, and she remembered turning from jonathari's bathroom mirror to find someone faceless waiting for her. Only a dream, she told herself. When she emerged from the subway the October air felt like a promise of wakening.

The elevator hummed to itself as it raised her to the fifteenth floor. Most of the desks in the acres of open-plan office were occupied by her colleagues, who said "Hi" or "Happy Halloween" to her. The concealed lighting appeared to have seeped beneath the skin of each face, rendering them mask-like. Jessica felt herself smile and heard herself return their greetings as she headed for her desk.

The senior editor had already left for a long weekend in Connecticut. Jessica sorted through his mail and then set about copy-editing the typescript of a layman's guide to Heisenberg and the uncertainty principle. Beyond the wide tall windows, traffic streamed up Park Avenue towards Grand Central. Usually the sight reminded her how the city never slept, but now it seemed simply mechanical. When the lines of type began to grow restless under her scrutiny she made for the water cooler.

Jake the art director was sipping from a paper cup. "What's happening?" he said.

"I seemed to spend all last night dreaming."

"Yeah? Me too."

The water in the cooler churned and gurgled like a nervous stomach as Jessica filled a cup. "What did you dream?" she said.

"Some weird stuff. We were all of us heading for Central Park, it seemed like just about everyone in New York was."

"Do you remember why?"

"Can't say. All I know is we each had to bring something sharp." He must have seen that disturbed her, because he added quickly "You weren't there."

Somehow that wasn't reassuring. Jessica returned to her desk and worked for an hour, which was as long as she could force herself to concentrate. She kept reaching for the phone to call Jonathan at the *Voice* and not quite managing to pick up the receiver. She must have dreamed she'd met him last night—she couldn't actually have met him, since the rest of it couldn't be real. By the time she made herself phone he had gone out for lunch.

Jessica bought herself a hero sandwich in the deli on the ground floor and sat with some friends from the publicity department. Several times she thought of asking if they'd dreamed last night, but the question kept shrinking back. She went up to the office and tried to work, but it wasn't long before she found herself reaching for the phone. This time she reached Jonathan. "Jessica," he said.

Could she hear a hint of secret eagerness? She swallowed and said "I know this is a crazy question, but I didn't see you last night, did I?"

"Sure did."

His eagerness had danced into the open. Jessica felt her mind turn over. "So if I saw you . . . " she faltered.

"You know I'm with you."

She knew either nothing or far too much. "I've got to talk to you face to face," she said, perhaps to delay realising.

"I'll be ready. Give me till this evening."

"Where?"

"I'll find you there. You're on the way. Just remember you're not alone," he said.

She let the receiver fall into its cradle and gazed along Park Avenue. Everything felt like a mask she was wearing. If she had really met Jonathan last night, was the rest of it true? Not just the newscasts about the discovery of yet another corpse without a face, but the way her old friends had seemed to know more about Jessica than she did herself? Today she'd been behaving as though the newscasts had made her dream her friends had told her that she was somehow responsible for the mutilations, but if she had really fled from her friends to Jonathan . . . If she had, only to find someone faceless handing her a razor in his bathroom, how could she not recall anything beyond that? How had she got home?

She felt as if she were close to accepting concepts vaster in their implications than she could grasp, or to bursting out laughing without knowing why, or both. She had a sense that there was nowhere for her to go, nothing to do except wait. She resumed poring over the typescript, but the theories it discussed seemed simple-minded by comparison with the notions hovering at the edge of her awareness. She stayed bent low over the typescript, as if she was trying to escape being noticed, until the office was almost deserted and Jake stopped by her desk. "Time to go," he said.

Wasn't his tone a shade too urgent? "I'll be okay. I want to finish this," she told him.

He hesitated, then shrugged. "We'll see you soon."

He turned quickly and left the office, but not before she glimpsed the expression on his face: a look of bewilderment mixed with anticipation—a look of almost knowing. She leafed onwards through the typescript, and then she grabbed the phone and dialled the *Voice*. There was no reply at all from the switchboard at the newspaper.

Jessica didn't know how long she held onto the receiver, having redialled twice to make sure of the number, before she realised that something larger was wrong. The murmur of New York had changed.

She ran to the window and leaned out. All the traffic had stopped. The streets were choked with cars. The only sound from down there was the shuffling of countless footsteps. The sidewalks were invisible beneath an apparently endless crowd, which was heading towards Central Park. As the figures passed beneath the street lamps Jessica saw objects glinting in their hands.

The spectacle entranced and appalled her. When she heard the door opening behind her and footsteps approaching, she couldn't turn. There was no need: above her on the tilted window she made out a ghost of the office and her own face hovering in the night sky like an apparition over the city. Before long Jonathan's face appeared beside hers. "It's starting," he said.

"What is?"

"The millennium."

"What are they doing?" she demanded, though she felt she knew.

"Releasing themselves from their faces."

"Why, for God's sake?"

"Exactly."

Now she could sense what was happening. Waves of a sensation too extreme to be called pain were reaching her from somewhere out of sight, a silent explosion that seemed to make the buildings shiver. "We can go and see if you like," Jonathan murmured.

The idea dismayed her almost as much as the sight of the crowds tramping towards their fate. "Where are they going?"

The question seemed meaningless until he answered it. "Towards the new world."

"What kind of world can it be without faces?" she demanded as if just one question, the right question, might halt everything.

Jonathan didn't answer directly. He moved aside so that the only face she could see was her own. "Faces are the lies we tell ourselves every time we look in a mirror," he said. "They're what prevents us from making the great change. They're why the world is dying of its own lack of wisdom. What you're seeing is our last chance."

All she was seeing was her own face in the sky. Both sky and face appeared to tremble. "You're crazy," she whispered.

"Everyone but you, huh?" He made a sound she couldn't interpret.

"Maybe you're right," he said. "Look beyond."

Again she had the impression of already knowing. His voice hardly sounded like his any more; it seemed to be expressing her own most secret thoughts. "Two thousand years ago a man came to earth to show us what we might be without our bodies. A thousand years ago there was only darkness. Now again there's someone who can change the world."

She heard herself ask without moving her lips. "Who?"

"Who else?"

The answer was before her: her face. Now that she wasn't speaking aloud it reminded her even more of a mask, a gigantic image hovering above the destination of the crowds like an evangelist's face projected on a screen at a rally. The lights of the city were beginning to fail, windows blinking on and off in patterns which seemed about to reveal a meaning, but the waves of ecstatic agony reaching for her were a promise of illumination. "I don't want this," she cried into herself.

"You still have a choice."

Was her face displaying choices to her? It had acquired an evangelical look, lips set, eyes wide and unwavering, but then it changed. A strip of black cloud attached itself to her upper lip like a painted moustache, and all it needed to complete the image of Groucho Marx was a cigar. If she began laughing and couldn't stop, would that help?

"God has two faces," the voice said, "and the third is under your own."

Perhaps Jessica was holding a cigar; certainly there was an object in her hand. "The God of the fundamentalists can only bear an ordered universe," the voice was saying, "but Groucho God plays dice with his. You have to choose which universe we'll inhabit for the third millennium. Hello, I must be going. In the Groucho universe even time is sometimes an illusion."

Jessica made herself focus on what she was holding. It wasn't a cigar, it was a cut-throat razor whose blade was folded into the handle. It looked very like the one she had been handed in Jonathan's bathroom, and perhaps she was still there; perhaps everything she had seemed to experience since that moment was a prophetic vision, or perhaps she had already chosen the universe where time could flow in any direction. All she could see was her own face, reflected by a plane of glass that might be a window or a bathroom mirror.

She felt her free hand dig a fingernail into the object she was holding. For the moment it wasn't clear whether she was inserting her nail into a recess in a razor blade or into the skin of a cigar. It wouldn't be clear until she made her choice. Nobody could make that for her, she thought, nobody could help. But as she took a breath that felt like her last on this earth, she sensed the face of the world turning towards her to watch.

Never To Be Heard

A S THE COACH SWUNG INTO THE DRIVE THAT LED TO THE Church of the Blessed Trinity, Fergal jumped up. He would have reached Brother Cox before the coach gasped to a halt except for tripping over lanky Kilfoyle's ankles in the aisle. Boys of all sizes crowded to the doors ahead of him, waving their hands in exaggerated disgust and denying they'd farted and blaming red-faced O'Hagan as usual, so that by the time Fergal struggled down onto the gravel Brother Cox was playing doorman outside the arched stone porch, ushering in each of his favourite choirboys with a pat in the small of the back. "Sir?" Fergal said.

The choirmaster gave him a dignified frown, rather spoiled by an April wind that, having ruffled the trees around the church, disordered the wreath of red hair that encircled his bald freckled scalp. "Shea, is it, now? O'Shea?"

"Shaw, sir. Sir, is it true Harty's mum and dad won't let him sing at the concert?"

"I believe that may turn out to be the truth of it, Shaw, yes."

Fergal found his eyes wanting to roll up, away from the choirmaster's inability to talk to him straight that was bad even by the standards of most adults, even of most teachers. If he looked above him he would see the pointed arch that reminded him uncomfortably of the naked women in the magazines making the rounds of the dormitory. "Sir, so if they're stopping him—"

"I'm not about to discuss the rights or otherwise of their decision with a choirboy, Shaw."

Fergal didn't care about their decision, let alone their objections to the music. "No, sir, what I meant was we'll be a tenor short, won't we? Sir, can I be him? My voice keeps—"

"Don't be so eager to lose your purity." Brother Cox was no longer speaking just to Fergal, who felt as though he'd been made to stand up in front of the whole of the choir. "You'll grow up soon enough," said the choirmaster with a blink of disapproval at the single hair Fergal's chin was boasting. "Sing high and sweet while you can."

"But sir, I keep not being—"

"March yourself along now. You're holding up half my flock."

Fergal bent sideways in case the choirmaster found his back worth patting, and dodged into the church. More than one window was a picture of Christ in his nightie, a notion Fergal wouldn't have dared admit to his mind until recently for fear of dying on the spot. Not only was the building full of pointed arches to inflame Fergal's thoughts, the broad stone aisle was an avenue of fat cylindrical pillars altogether too reminiscent of the part of himself that seemed determined to play tricks on him whenever and wherever it felt inclined. Choirboys were streaming down the aisle as their echoes searched for a way out through the roof. In front of the choirstalls on either side of the altar, a conductor was pointing his wand at members of an orchestra to conjure a note from them. Between him and the orchestra a woman was typing on a computer keyboard, and Fergal's interest nearly roused itself until he remembered why she was there—the stupidest aspect of the entire boring exercise. The computer was going to produce sounds nobody could hear.

When the Reverend Simon Clay had written the music there had been no computers: no way of creating the baser than base line he wanted for the final movement. The score had been lost for almost a century and rediscovered just over a year ago, not by any means to Fergal's delight. Even its title—*The Balance of the Spheres: A Symphony for Chorus and Large Orchestra*—was, like the music, too long to endure. Last year, when the choir had won a choral competition, some of the boys had sneaked away afterwards for a night in Soho, but now that Fergal felt old enough to join them, everyone was confined to quarters overnight and too far out of London to risk disobeying. He'd given up on that—he only wished he were anywhere else, listening to Unlikely Orifices or some other favourite band—but all he could do was take his place among the choirboys with hairless baby chins and wait for the orchestra to be ready. At last, though not to his relief, it was time to rehearse.

Brother Cox insisted on announcing the title of each movement, no matter how high the conductor raised his eyebrows. "The Voice of the Face That Speaks," said the choirmaster, all but miming the capital letters, as the stout radiators along the walls hissed and gurgled to themselves, and the choir had to sing a whole page of the Bible while the orchestra did its best to sound like chaos and very gradually decided that it knew some music after all. "The Voice of the Face That Dreams," Brother Cox declared at last, after he and the conductor had made the choir and orchestra repeat various bits that had only sounded worse to Fergal. Now the choir was required to compete with the orchestra by yelling about seals—not the sort that ate fish but some kind only an angel was supposed to be able to open. The row calmed down as the number of seals increased, and once the seventh had been sung about the brass section had the music to itself. The trumpeting faded away into a silence that didn't feel quite like silence, and Fergal realised the computer had been switched on. "We shall carry on," the conductor said in an Eastern European accent almost as hard to grasp as his name.

"Best take it in stages, Mr . . . " said Brother Cox, and left addressing him at that. "This is the hardest movement for my boys. Quite a challenge, singing in tongues."

Fergal had already had enough. Even if he'd wanted to sing, his voice kept letting him down an octave, and singing in the language the Revolting Clay had apparently made up struck him as yet another of the stupid unjustifiable things adults expected him to do. Brother Cox had acknowledged how unreasonable it was by giving each choirboy a page with the words of the Voice of the Face That Will Awaken to use at the rehearsal. Whenever Fergal's voice had threatened to subside during the first two movements he'd resorted to mouthing, and he was tempted to treat all of the Reverend's babble that way rather than feel even stupider.

It looked as though that was how he was going to feel whatever he did. Keeping a straight face at the sight of Brother Cox as he opened and closed his mouth like a fish gobbling the gibberish was hard enough. The choir commenced singing what appeared to have been every kind of church music the Reverend could think of, the orchestra performed a search of its own, and Fergal was unable to concentrate for straining to hear a sound he couldn't quite hear.

He felt as though it was trying to invade everything around him. Whenever the choir and orchestra commenced another round, more than their echoes seemed to gather above them—perhaps the wind that flapped around the church and fumbled at the trees. Shadows of branches laden with foliage trailed across the windows, dragging at the stained-glass outlines, blurring them with gloom. Once Fergal thought the figure of Christ above the choirstalls opposite had turned its head to gaze at him, but of course it was already facing him. His momentary inattention earned him a scowl from Brother Cox. Then the choir climbed a series of notes so tiny it felt like forever before they arrived at the highest they could reach, while the orchestra contented itself with a single sustained chord and the computer carried on with whatever it was doing. Well before the top note Fergal did nothing but keep his mouth open. The conductor trembled his stick and his free hand at them all, and when at last there came a silence that appeared to quell the trees outside, he let the baton sink and wiped his eyes. "I believe we have done it, Brother," he murmured.

"If you say so."

Either the choirmaster objected to being addressed like a comrade or resented not having had his well-nigh incomparably straightforward name pronounced. His dissatisfaction was plain as he gestured boys out of the stalls row by row. Fergal was among the last to be marched past the amused orchestra, who were within earshot when Brother Cox caught up with him. "O'Shea," the choirmaster demanded, and even louder "Shea."

"It's Shaw, sir."

"Never mind that now. You've little enough reason to want anyone knowing who you are when you can't keep your eyes where you're told. Maybe you were dreaming you'd be singing low tomorrow, so let me tell you a boy from this very church will be taking Harty's place. A prize soloist, so don't you go thinking you're the equal of him."

On the coach he renewed his disapproval. "I want every boy's eye on me tomorrow from the instant he opens his mouth. There'll be no sheets for you to be consulting. After your dinners we'll spend all the time that's needed till every single one of you is letter perfect."

The choir groaned as much as they dared, and some of the boys who'd heard Fergal being told off glared at him as if he'd brought this further burden on them. The coach wound its way through the narrow Surrey lanes to the school where the choir was suffering a second night. The boys who ordinarily put up with it had gone home for Easter, but the monks they'd got away from had remained, prowling the stony corridors with their hands muffled in their black sleeves while they spied out sinful boys or boys about to sin or capable of thinking of it. The choir had hardly taken refuge in the dormitories when they were summoned to dinner, a plateful each of lumps of stringy mutton that several mounds of almost indistinguishable vegetables applied themselves to hiding. The lucky vegetarians were served the same without the lumps but with the gravy. Some of the resident monks waved loaded forks to encourage their guests to eat, and the oldest monk emitted sounds of what must have passed in his case for pleasure. After the meal, even the prospect of rehearsal came as almost a relief.

Brother Cox made the choir sit on benches in the draughty bare school hall and repeat the stream of nonsense Simon Clay deserved to be cursed for, and then he collected the pages with the words on and mimed trying to lift an invisible object with the palms of his hands to urge the choir to chant the whole thing again, and yet again. He mustn't have believed they could have learned it so perfectly, because he tried requiring each boy to speak it by himself. When it came to Fergal's turn the boy felt as though all the echoes of the repetitions were swooping about inside his head, describing the patterns of the absent music, and he only had to let them become audible through his mouth. "Nac rofup taif gnicam tuss snid . . . " He didn't even realise he'd finished until Brother Cox gave him a curt nod.

By the time Brother Cox dismissed the choir they were so exhausted that hardly anyone could be bothered with horseplay in the communal bathroom. As Fergal crawled under the blankets of the hard narrow bed halfway down the dormitory, a long room with dark green glossy walls as naked as its light bulbs, he wondered if anyone else was continuing to hear the echoes of the last rehearsal. There was only one kind of dream he wanted to have in the intimate warmth of the blankets, but the echoes wouldn't let it begin to take shape. They seemed to gather themselves as he sank into sleep seemed to focus into just three voices, one to either side of him and one ahead. That in front of him began to lead him forwards while the others were left behind. Soon he was outside time and deep in a dream.

He was trudging towards a mountain range across a white desert that felt more like salt than sand. He'd been in the wilderness, his instincts told him, for three times thirteen days. He was bound for the highest mountain, a peak so lofty that the river which rushed down its glittering sheer slopes appeared to be streaming out of the bright clouds that crowned it. He thought he might never reach the water that would quench his thirst and lead him to the mystery veiled by the shining clouds, but in a breath the dream brought him to the river. It darkened as he drank from it and bathed in it, because he was following it downwards through a cavern he knew was the mountain turned inside out and upside down. Surely it was only in a dream that a river could run to the centre of the world, which would show him the centre of the universe, the revelation he'd journeyed so far and fasted so long to reach. Now, at the end of a descent too prolonged and frightful to remember, he was there, and the blackness was glowing with an illumination only his eyes could see. Around him the walls of the cavern were fretted like jaws piled on jaws, ridged as if the rock might be the skeleton of the world. Ahead was a pool so deep and dark he knew it was no longer water—knew the river was feeding a hole so black it could swallow the universe. A figure was rising from it, robed in rock that flowed like water. Was the universe creating it just as it had created the universe? Its eyes glinted at him, more than twice too many of them, and he struggled to awaken, to avoid seeing more. But he could hear its voices too, and didn't know whether his mind was translating them or trying to fend them off. In its image, he found himself repeating, in its image—

Brother Cox wakened him. "Get up now. Sluggards, everyone of you. Rising bright and early is a praise to God."

He sounded so enraged that at first, bewildered by apparently having dreamed all night, Fergal thought the choirmaster was berating him for the dream. At breakfast, chunks of porridge drowning in salt-water, it became clearer why he was infuriated, as the head monk flourished a newspaper at him while trying to placate him. "I just wanted to be certain you're aware what you and your charges will be involved with, Brother Cox."

"I'm aware right enough, aware as God can make me. Aware of how the godless media love to stain the reputations of the saints and anybody with a bit of holiness about them." Brother Cox said no more until he'd gulped every chunk of his porridge, and then he sprang off the bench. "If you'll excuse me now, I've a coach driver needs phoning to be sure he presents himself on time."

After a few moments of staring at the abandoned newspaper Kilfoyle ventured to say "Sir, can I read it?"

The head monk pursed his thin pale lips. "Perhaps you should."

Since Kilfoyle was by no means a speedy reader, when he didn't take long over it Fergal knew he'd given up. The newspaper was passed along the table, making increasingly brief stops, until it arrived in front of Fergal. Of course the article was about Simon Clay—all the stuff Harty's parents had objected to. Fergal was making to pass the paper to O'Hagan when the headline stopped him. **CLAY'S FIRST SYMPHONY: WHAT KIND OF PILGRIMAGE?** The question reminded him of his dream, and he read on.

It was mostly information he couldn't have cared less about. Simon Clay had revived the classical church symphony, starting with his Second . . . He'd composed nothing but religious music . . . During his lifetime he'd maintained that his first symphony was lost . . . Before he was ordained a priest he'd been a member of the Order of the Golden Dawn, and the original score had recently been discovered among the papers of a fellow occultist, Peter Grace . . . It hadn't previously been identified as Clay's work because he had signed it with his occult name, Indigator Fontis, Seeker of the Source . . . Grace had scrawled a comment on the first page: "fruit of the secret pilgrimage" . . . One wonders (wrote the critic) whether Clay's subsequent output was a prolonged attempt to repudiate this score and its implications. Yet the issues are less simple than has been stridently suggested by some members of the press. Underlying Clay's determination to outdo his contemporary Scriabin in terms of passion and ecstasy writ large and loud (Fergal no longer knew why he was bothering to read) is a radical attempt, so harmonically daring as almost to engage with atonality, to create a musical structure expressive of the cosmic balance to which the title alludes, a structure to which the sub-audible line of the third movement is crucial. Given that Clay wrote above this line the comment "Never to be heard"—

The newspaper was snatched away from Fergal. "Heavy reading, is it?" roared Brother Cox. "Let's try the weight of it." When he eventually finished slapping Fergal about the head with the paper truncheon he turned on the rest of the choir. "Eat up your breakfasts, all of you, that our hosts were so kind they provided us. And just you keep your minds on what you have to sing today instead of filling them with nonsense."

Fergal might have retorted, if only to himself, that nonsense was the word for what they'd learned, except that he was no longer sure it was. The ache Brother Cox had beaten into his head prevented him from thinking as he trudged away from breakfast and eventually to the coach, which threw his head about as it rewound yesterday's journey. Amid the chatter of his schoolmates he kept thinking somebody was practising the words of the last movement on either side of him. His mind was trying to retrieve the sentences he'd glimpsed as Brother Cox had snatched the newspaper. Had Simon Clay meant that the symphony never would be heard, or that it never should be? A more insistent question was why Fergal should care, especially when attempting to think sharpened his headache.

Cars were parked along the quarter-mile of lane nearest the church. Members of the audience for the world premiere that would be broadcast live at noon that Saturday were strolling up the drive while a small group of protesters flourished placards at them over the heads of several policemen who would clearly have preferred to be elsewhere. **GIVE EASTER BACK TO GOD ... KEEP THE DEVIL'S MUSIC OUT OF GOD'S HOUSE ... RAISE YOUR VOICE TO GOD, DON'T LOWER IT TO SATAN ...** As the coach drew up beside the porch a man stalked out, pulling at his hair to show that he worked for the BBC. He wasn't happy with the cawing of rooks in the trees, nor the noises the doves made that put Fergal in mind of old women around a pram. He was especially distressed by the chorus of "Onward Christian Soldiers" outside the gates, and flounced off to speak to the police.

Fergal was trapped in the choirstalls when he heard the protesters being moved on. As a verse of "Nearer My God to Thee" trailed into the distance, his urge to giggle faltered, and he realised he'd been assuming the protesters would ensure that the premiere didn't take place. There was plenty to be nervous of: the audience and the conductor and Brother Cox, all of whom were expecting too much of him; the BBC producer darting about in search of dissatisfaction; the microphones standing guard in front of the performers; his sense that the church and himself were liable to change, perhaps not in ways to which he'd begun to grow used; the imminence of an occasion he was being made to feel the world was waiting for ... As the conductor and Brother Cox took up their positions, Fergal gave the stained-glass window opposite him a look not far short of pleading. What might his old beliefs have been protecting him from? "It doesn't look like a nightie really," he almost mouthed, and then he heard a bell start to toll.

It was noon, even if the sky beyond the stained glass appeared to be getting ready for the night. The twelfth peal dwindled into silence not even broken by the hissing of the radiators, which had been turned off, and then the echoes of the footsteps of an announcer dressed like a waiter in an old film accompanied him to a microphone. "We are proud to present the world premiere of Simon Clay's *The Balance of the Spheres*. Despite the controversy it has engendered, we believe it is a profoundly religious and ultimately optimistic work ... " All too soon the conductor raised his baton and Brother Cox, as though gesturing in prayer or outrage, his hands, to let the music loose.

Fergal managed to sing about the creation without dropping any notes, and could hear Harty's replacement was equal to the task. If Fergal started to be less than that he could always mouth—except the notion of leaving the choir short of a voice made him unexpectedly nervous, and he sang with such enthusiasm that Brother Cox didn't glare at him once during the first movement. He felt pleased with himself until he wondered if he was using up too much of his voice too soon.

Why should it be crucial to preserve it for the final movement above all, for the last and highest note? He set about appearing to sing with all his vigour while employing only half. The display seemed to fool Brother Cox, but was it the choirmaster he had to deceive, and if not, wasn't his attempt to play a trick worse than ill-advised? As the last seal was opened he sang as hard as he could, and was able to rest his voice while the trumpets blared. They fell silent one by one, and as the seventh prolonged its top note he saw the woman at the computer reach for the keyboard. The incongruity made him want to giggle: how could they broadcast a sound nobody could hear? Then the fragile brass note gave way to that sound, which crept beneath him.

He might have thought he was imagining the sensation—it made him feel he was standing on a thin surface over a void—if all the birds hadn't flown out of the trees with a clatter that was audible throughout the church. The conductor held his baton high and stared hard at the windows as the computer sustained its note. Was he waiting for the branches to stop toying with the stained-glass outlines? Freeing himself from a paralysis that suggested the sound under everything had caught him like quicksand, he waved his wand at the forces he controlled.

The words of the last movement filled Fergal's head and started to burst from his mouth. Even if he didn't understand them, they were part of him, and he felt close to comprehending them or at least to dreaming what they meant. He had to sing them all or he might never be free of them. He had to reach the highest note, and then everything would be over. He had to sing to overcome the sound that was never to be heard.

Or could the choir be singing in some obscure harmony with it? He was beginning to feel as if each note he uttered drew the secret sound a little further into him. He tried not even to blink as he watched Brother Cox, whose scowl of concentration or of less than total contentment was in its predictability the nearest to a reassurance he could see. His breaths kept appearing before him like the unknown words attempting to take shape, and he told himself the church was growing colder only because the heating was off. He tried to ignore the windows, at which the darkening foliage had still not ceased groping minutes after the birds had flown, unless the trees had stilled themselves and the glass was on the move. The thought made the robed figure at the edge of his vision seem to turn a second face to him, and then another. He almost sang too loud in case that could blot out the impression, and felt his voice tremble on the edge of giving way, dropping towards the cold dark hollow sound that underlay everything, that was perhaps not being performed so much as revealed at last, giving voice to a revelation Simon Clay had spent his life trying to deny he'd ever glimpsed. Fergal didn't know where these thoughts were coming from unless they were somehow in the music. The choir and the orchestra had begun to converge, but they had minutes to go before they reached the final note that was surely meant to overcome the other sound. If he was failing to understand, he didn't want to—didn't want to see the stealthy movements in the window opposite. The choir had arrived at the foot of the ladder of microscopic notes, and he had only to sing and watch Brother Cox for encouragement—not even encouragement, just somewhere to look while he sang and drew breaths that felt as if he was sucking them out of a deep stony place, precisely enough breath each time not to interrupt his voice, which wasn't going to falter, wasn't going to let him down, wasn't going to join the sound that was invading every inch of him—

When Brother Cox's face twisted with rage and disbelief Fergal thought the problem was some fault of his until he saw movement beyond the choirmaster. A man had darted out of the audience. With a shout of "Grant us peace" he seized two power cables that lay near the broadcasting console and heaved at them. The next moment he tried to fling them away while, it seemed to Fergal, he set about executing a grotesque ritual dance. Then the computer toppled over and smashed on the stone floor, and every light in the church was extinguished.

The orchestra trailed into silence before the choir did. Fergal was continuing to sing, desperate to gain the final note, when a cello or a double bass fell over with a resonant thud. He was singing not to fend off the darkness that filled the church but the sight it had isolated opposite him. That was no longer an image in stained glass. The window had become a lens exhibiting the figure that was approaching while yet staying utterly still, its three faces grim as the infinity it had lived and had yet to live, its eyes indifferent as outer space, the locks of its multiple scalp twisted like black ice on the brink of a lake so deep no light could touch it. The figure hadn't moved in any sense he could grasp when it entered the church.

In the instant before the last glimmer of light through the windows went out, Fergal saw the three faces turn to one another, sharing an expression he almost understood. It was more than triumph. Then he was alone in the blind dark with the presence, and he struggled to hold every inch of himself immobile so as not to be noticed. But the presence was already far more than aware of him. For a moment that was like dying and being reborn he experienced how he was composed of the stuff of stars and the void that had produced them, and of something else that was the opposite of both—experienced how he might be capable of partaking of their vastness. He hadn't begun to comprehend that when his mind shrank and renewed its attempt to hide, because the presence had unfinished business in the church. Even if it had taken the man's dance of death as a tribute, that wasn't enough. Fergal felt it draw a breath much larger than the building so as to use every mouth within the walls to give itself a voice.

"I want to praise the choir for their self-control and their presence of mind at the concert on Easter Saturday. As the rest of you boys may be aware, a gentleman under the mistaken impression that the music was sacrilegious interrupted the performance but was unfortunately electrocuted. Some of the orchestra and some members of the public were injured in the panic, but our school can be proud that its choir kept their seats and their heads. It is regrettable that the effects of the technology used at the concert apparently damaged the building. I believe that is all that requires to be said on the matter, and I shall deal harshly with anyone who is caught circulating the superstitious rumours that have been invented by some of the gutter press. Let your minds remain unpolluted by such rubbish as we start the summer term."

As the headmaster's complexion began to fade from purple to its customary red, Fergal glanced at the choirboys seated near him. None of them seemed inclined to disagree with the head-master's pronouncements. Perhaps they were cowed, or perhaps they preferred to forget the events at the church; perhaps, like all the members of the audience Fergal had seen interviewed on television, they actually believed that nothing more had taken place than the headmaster had said. For the moment Fergal was content to pretend he agreed. As the row of boys including him filed out of the school hall under the frowns of the staff, his fingertips traced like a secret sign the outline of the folded page hidden in the pocket against his heart.

It was from the newspaper the headmaster had condemned. Fergal didn't care what it said, only what it showed: the lopsided church in the process of twisting itself into a shape that seemed designed to squirm into the earth; the distorted stained-glass figure of Christ, an expression hiding in its eyes, a broken oval gaping above each shoulder. Fergal shuffled after the rest of the procession into the classroom and cramped himself onto the seat behind his desk, and put on his face that looked eager to learn. Of course he was, but not at school. The weeks to the next holiday seemed less than a breath he'd already expelled, because then he would return to the church to discover what was waiting, not just there but within himself. If Simon Clay had been unable to cope with it, he must have been too old—but Fergal had been through the fear, and he vowed to devote the rest of his life to finding out what lay beyond it. As the first teacher of the day stalked into the room, Fergal was on his feet a moment before the rest of the class. Pretending only promised a future reward. "Good

morning, sir," he said, and sensed his other voices holding their
tongues until he was alone with them in the dark.

The Previous Tenant

H E CLOSED THE CUPBOARD DOOR AND CROSSED TO THE window. The pane exhibited ghostly strokes of soap, like the paint sketched on the sheet of paper he'd crumpled up last week. In the next room his wife moved a table, which screamed. He stared out. The roofs were a jagged frieze against the colours spilled to mix on the horizon; below, the red streetlamps tasted of raspberry, tinting the trees like attenuated pinecones separated by the ruler of the pavement. A car passed, hushed as the evening, casting ahead on the road what seemed already a splash of yellow paint. It wasn't enough for him to express on canvas. He turned back to the flat room, the wallpaper's pastel leaves whose meaning had been lost through countless prints, the bed he must never touch without having bathed. He had remembered what he'd seen as the cupboard door had closed.

The imprisoned books rebuked him; already, on the Renoir, a coil of dust curled and fidgeted like a centipede. What he'd seen was crushed beneath Matisse and Toulouse-Lautrec; he hoisted them and slid it out. It was a photograph of the girl who had owned the flat: one leg high on a wall, her skirt taut, her hand arched on her knee, her eyes beneath an arch of lustrous hair smiling at whoever held the camera; how could she have become a scream above the city, a broken figurine beneath the window? His wife coughed. At once he thrust the photograph into his pocket. At the door he turned to check the cupboard. It was closed.

His wife was cross-legged on the carpet, surrounded by the glasses from the cabinet, considering the space available. "I've done the best I can," he said.

She dabbed a bead of lacquer from her forehead. "It's not your books I object to, you know that," she told him. "It's just that there's not enough space, that's all."

"I don't remember you complaining when we looked it over."

"Who'd complain at a flatful of furniture?" Above her stood the antique chairs, the glass-topped tables, the mirrors with which the girl had surrounded herself. "But there's such a thing as being over-generous, you know."

He was silent; he didn't want to say "We should be grateful."

"If we get rid of a few of these things you could have your painting on the wall."

"There's no point." Not in one painting and a hundred crumpled scraps of drawing-paper.

"It might brighten the place up a little."

"That's a profound analysis." He watched her stretch her legs, hemmed in by the glasses; it seemed a perfect symbol—he would have transferred it to canvas if he had been able to paint her.

"I know I don't have your intellect." She picked up a glass; in a club she wouldn't long have held it empty.

"I've never said so, have I? What you don't have is a sensitivity to this flat. It's the girl's life. There's the chair where she must have sat when she composed the note. Or is that what's bothering you?"

"It doesn't bother me at all, you know that. I'm not the one who lies awake." She spread a cloth on the table and filled two glasses. "Just a few things of my own, that's all I ask. I don't like charity."

And the men at the ballroom? What did she call the drinks they bought her at their clubs? "You're not in all that much," he said.

"It's not my fault if you won't come with me."

"Can't afford to come with you, you mean." His words thrust like a tongue toward an aching tooth. His fingers traced his inside pocket, the photograph symmetrical with his heart.

"Don't, don't. You're hurting yourself." She carried a glass to him. As he took it, she laid her hand on his within the concealed rectangle.

"You can't be both a civil servant and a painter. Don't try for so much or you'll lose everything," she said. "Let's leave the flat to look after itself for tonight. Our room is ours."

"Do hurry," she said, "I'm so tired." Deflated, he lay back. In a minute the moonlit sheet over her breasts was rising and falling like surf. He inched to sit up. His side of the bed was a scribble of shadow like paint scrawled in fury. Perhaps this might be meaningful on canvas. *Bedroom Scene, The Marriage Bed*—But he couldn't express their marriage. She had been a civil service typist; as she'd passed him, glanced and smiled, his pen had become erect between his fingers; the next time she passed he had sketched the memory. When she came to look he'd said "I'd like to paint you."

"That would be nice," she'd replied, "but not nude." Baulked, for she had destroyed his dream, he'd postponed the offer through months of clumsy dancing in ballrooms where smoke billowed to meet clouds of false stars, of hands across club tables at one in the morning; seeking to possess her, he'd foregone the rushing skies, the stretched clouds, the combed and recombed grass, which met at his easel and poured into his brush, and he'd suffocated. When they emerged from the cramped registrar's he'd found he couldn't paint. On the wedding night she'd cried out; briefly he'd possessed her. Yet before the honeymoon was over he'd yearned for something more; he'd gazed from the hotel at rumpled trees, humped hillside walls where the girl from the photograph might have stood and smiled. "Don't forget to give in your notice," he reminded his wife. "I'll keep you." Perhaps thus he could possess her. But his walks possessed the breasts of the hills, the splayed thighs of the valleys. Then one night he'd been whipped home by a storm and had found her gone. An hour later she'd slammed the front door, gasping happily, thrilled by the leaping rain, and had halted at the sight of him sunk deep in a dark chair. She'd stroked his hair; rain coursed down their merged faces like tears. They'd gone upstairs to find the house was cracked; rain dripped somewhere. They couldn't afford the repairs, and at last they'd agreed before a landlord's card bulged and distorted by the first drops of a new rain: this flat, close to the country as she'd said, closer to the raw red sign of the ballroom round the corner as he'd thought. He slid down the bed to mould himself to her, but she was still asleep. He turned over. The moonlight fell short of the wardrobe, where his suit hid the photograph. The cupboard of books was held within skins of sleep, which weighed on his eyes; next to it, his easel was a dusty blackboard. As he drowsed into sleep, he thought the cupboard opened.

"Wear your nice suit today," she said. "I like to see you in it."

"All right, for you." The sunlight slid from cars and coated leaves with light; it might become a painting. He collected pens and wallet from the table by the bed and followed her into the living-room. As he entered she drew the table-cloth across a brilliant sheet of pressed sunlight and pinned it down with bowls of cereal; through the sheet he'd seen its carved legs, shaped as by caresses. "If you think we can't afford furniture," she mused, "I could always go back to work."

"I don't think that's called for." Shaped as by caresses. His hand stole beneath the cloth and touched the wood. Slowly, exquisitely, his fingers traced the curves. He saw the leg braced on the wall, the taut skirt. His wife picked up her spoon; it blazed at the edge of his eye. Unlacquered, her hair glowed. Suddenly ashamed, he reached out and stroked her knee.

"Not when you're eating, please," she said. "Your hands are greasy."

At the door he realised that he couldn't go back for the photograph; if he did his wife would know. Instead, he looked up at the window through the leaves piled like her hair. The pane was white as an empty canvas; within, a figure shielded her eyes and waved.

When he came home that night his mind was covered with sketches, erased lines, sheets half-torn and reassembled with conjecture. He'd imagined the tree-lined street washed by headlamps as the girl had seen it, staring down, perhaps for a last glimpse of whoever had abandoned her—the unknown hand on the camera shutter no longer holding hers. In the lunch-hour he'd sketched on the back of a form, but the sketch had lacked a sight of the reality. "Don't lay the table yet," he told his wife as he veered into the kitchen, "I have an idea I want to get down." The people in the flat below were across the city when the girl had screamed and fallen, but they were sure that she had been abandoned; a drained husk, perhaps she'd thought that she might float toward the empty landscape. He set up his easel before the window. The room seemed more cramped than he remembered; he would have to sit on the bed. He projected the girl on the pane, but she refused to pose; her foot poised on the sill, the weighted falling sun shone through her skirt. That wasn't what he wanted. Already the streetlamps were raw wounds on the night; a tree shed a leaf like a flake of skin. If he could see her perhaps he would be able to persuade her to pose. He crossed to the wardrobe and felt in the pocket for the photograph. There was no pocket. The suit was gone.

You did that on purpose, said his nails biting into the wood. The sun sank and touched the black horizon. He tramped into the kitchen. "So you got rid of my suit," he said.

"You don't think I wouldn't ask you first?" Behind her head a curtain swayed like a skirt. "It's only at the cleaner's. You're an artist— I'd have thought you'd care how you looked."

"So that I'll get on, I know. I didn't think you'd go behind my back."

"If there was anything in it you wanted I'm sorry, honestly I am. I couldn't find anything."

"Nothing I haven't already got."

"This table really is too small, you know," she said. The cruet came down hard on the clothed glass. She knows! it exclaimed. Or had she fumbled it rather than thumped it down as a protest? No, he was sure she had the photograph. She withdrew herself from him by sleeping, then she stole his souvenir. The carved leg pressed his. "I like the flat as it stands," he told her. "It welcomes me."

As he stood before the cupboard plates chattered in the kitchen. No doubt the girl had washed up for her lover; perhaps they'd eaten at two in the morning, their hours based on their shared rhythm, not imposed from outside—the sort of life he meant when he yearned to be bohemian. Arms about each other, they'd tire together when at all. He opened the cupboard door; he would find a book that might suggest a detail to extend across his empty canvas. In the shadows the titles were dim. He knew each by its place. He touched the tip of a spine, and a finger flattened beneath his own.

He wasn't menaced; he didn't recoil. Instead he reached up and brought the glove to his face. It glimmered white on his palm. The fingers were stiff, perhaps starched. He held it by the knuckles and let the fingers rest arched on his hand.

In the kitchen a knife scraped. His wife had finished. Carefully he laid the glove over the books, where it posed lightly, coquettishly. He closed the door softly, as if apologetic, and returned to the easel. In a moment the girl in the photograph might move as desired and stare from the window. But the sun's last shards were blunted; at a cross-roads in the centre of the landscape, traffic-lights tripped up and down their scale. Two glasses chimed. He cursed his wife; jealous, she'd driven away his model. He strode out of the bedroom. "Are you going out?" he demanded.

She arranged the first ring of glasses, encircling the table leg. "I want to do as much as I can tonight," she said. "Anyway, I thought you might like me to stay in."

"When I'm painting?" She turned to him: surely he could have left that unsaid. "Watch what you're doing!" he shouted, but too late; kneeling, she overbalanced and her hand, flinching away from the glasses, caught the table leg. The table reared. The glass top came down on the arm of a chair, and a star flew out between them.

"Oh, I am sorry," she cried, on the edge of tears. "I didn't mean to." But he'd rushed to the table and grasped a carved leg. The ruined top ground and splintered. He whirled, brandishing the leg, topped with a head of jagged glass like an axe.

"I didn't do it on purpose. I wouldn't have done that." She tried to catch hold of his hand as it drooped. "We'd better get rid of it before someone gets hurt," she said.

"Throw away the glass but leave the legs. I may be able to use them sometime. In a carving," he added bitterly.

In the night he sat up. His wife's face lay upward on the pillow, helpless. The black sun was hot beneath the horizon, like a coal about to set fire to the air. He plodded through the flat and turned on the kitchen light. The carved legs were piled in a corner; above them an edge of the curtain swayed. He thought he heard his wife call out. He would fight her; he would complete a painting to express the flat. If only he could see the girl, find the photograph. Behind him the door banged and sprang back. Someone moved silently to stand behind him, her hands almost touching his shoulders. She didn't tint the white tiles of the kitchen. He swung about. Only the restless door moved. "I wouldn't have left you," he said almost to himself.

His wife was propped up by the pillows, waiting. "What were you doing?" she asked.

"There was something I wanted from the kitchen. I didn't expect to find you awake."

"There's a rat in your cupboard," she said.

"Nonsense. What would a rat want in there?"

"I heard something scratching at the door. If you're not going to look, I will."

She slid out and was round the bed before he could move. Aghast, he slapped the light switch. Electric light thrust out the moonbeams. She pulled open the door and craning on tiptoe, leaned her head inside. At last she decided "It must be in the wall."

As she returned to bed he extinguished the light. "You haven't closed the cupboard properly," he said. He opened the door as if to shut it with a slam. A moonbeam partitioned him off from the bed. He laid his hand on the rim of the cupboard, waiting, and the glove fell on his fingers like a caress.

Dear Sir, I am in receipt of your letter—On the back he sketched the glove. At once his pencil traced her poised arm and ranged over her curves, the lead point sensitive as his fingertips. It smoothed her hair and formed the framed oval. But her face eluded him. The shutter of his mind had jammed. Was she facing him or smiling secretly in profile? He drove the point into the paper close to her hair, and the pencil snapped.

"We'll have to eat in here tonight," said his wife from the kitchen. "I know it's crowded."

He threw his overcoat on the bed; he should have an overall to welcome him, a vortex of colour like petrol after rain.

She was wearing a grey sweater; she looked young as a rediscovered photograph. Opened, the oven door exhaled the heavy heat of steak. She encircled the meat with potatoes and smiled. "When I was dusting your books—"

His knife froze in the meat. "You were dusting my books?"

"I thought it was the least I could do. I found a glove. I thought at first it was the rat."

And he'd torn up the sketched hand. "What have you done with it?" The knife gouged; the meat tore.

"I threw it away, of course. It would have ruined your books. It was covered with—I don't know, it was all wet."

"With tears, perhaps. No, no, it doesn't matter."

The pillow gasped as his fist drove in. The bedroom was void. He left his easel in the corner. Already the girl's presence had attenuated; she'd begun to fray, to be absorbed into the flat like mist. Or to drift out of the window; his wife was systematically driving her out, destroying the expressions of her personality, his tokens of her. Clouds bulged from the lacklustre sky like wet wallpaper. He stared at the unlined sheets, willing even the curve of her leg to form. One sight of her face and he would possess her. But he felt sure the photograph was ashes. Suddenly he caught up his easel and bore it toward the window. There would be a suspended silent moment before the easel smashed and scattered on the concrete. He thrust the window high. A breeze breathed into his eyes, and for a second a cloud smiled beneath hair. At once he knew. With gestures sure as sketched lines he set up the easel. Then patiently he lay back on the bed to wait.

He leapt up. His wife was sorting plates and cutlery on the kitchen table. "I won't be in your way," she said. "I won't be, will I?"

Without a word he clutched the carved legs and returned to the bedroom. Each leg was wood. Unprepared for the end of a curve, his fingers constantly fell into space. He laid one leg against his; when he moved the edge cut into his flesh. The wood was lifeless. The cupboard was empty. One side of the canvas had slipped low; a corner encroached on the wide dull landscape. The girl was elsewhere. Even the touch of the glove had been too light to suggest so much as the ghost of a hand. Abandoned once, she would never return again if rebuffed. And yet, he thought—and yet his painting might provide her with a hold. She might become the painting.

Light resonated in the glasses like a soundless chime. He stood before the kitchen door; his throat was dry. The kitchen was her last refuge. Surely it contained nothing that his wife might shatter. The girl knew this as surely as he did. Yet he was afraid to enter; it would be their first meeting. And his wife would be alert.

The door swung in his wake. She came to meet him. Yet not quite; her presence was lent a harsh immediacy by the white tiles, compressed by the pendulous sky, but not formed. She was still preparing for him. He must wait. As he whirled, impatient, he glimpsed his wife's face, flat as a painting against the wall.

He paced the bedroom. The sky was close as the walls, encasing his eyes. He found that he could hear himself breathing, almost suffocated. He wrenched open the cupboard door and dragged out a sketch-pad. A title for his painting. Anything. But the edges of the pencil were insufferable as the angles of a rusty threepence. A book to calm him. The art-paper scraped beneath his nails, agonising as tin. He dropped the book and rushed into the kitchen.

"Oh, what is it?" his wife cried. "Don't keep going away from me!"

At the sound of her voice the girl fled. The kitchen rejected her. He stared slowly at his wife, the neat ranks of cutlery, the handkerchief bulging the arm of her sweater like a muscle. "God. God. God," he said.

And then he fell silent.

Behind her head, like an embryo born of the breeze, the curtain swelled. A thrust of air created cheekbones from its folds. Above them hollows might harbour whatever expression he called forth. The line that linked the hollows fell away into an arch. As the curtain swayed a wrinkle smiled, but shyly.

His wife followed the line of his gaze. "Oh, the curtain," she said. "Why didn't you say it was crumpled?"

She shook it straight. For a moment it was sucked against the window-frame, as if clutched in panic and relinquished. The tips of a tree were veiled, then sprang bright.

The table shook at his clutch. "Won't come back," he muttered.

"Sorry?" But his face was frozen as a portrait. "You look so lost tonight," his wife said. "Can I give you something?"

The planes of the kitchen were flat as the untinted tiles. He would never know what colour of dress the girl had worn: nor that only skulls lack a nose. He peered through a wavering mist at the table. His hand closed on a carving knife. "This'll do," he said.

Becoming Visible

"DUNBOBBIN."

"Is that Mr Dunbobbin?"

"Charles Dunbobbin."

"Good evening, Mr Dunbobbin. I'm calling on behalf of Clearview Windows. We're going to be in your area and we're looking for people who'd like to take part in—"

"No thank you."

"Why not?"

"I beg your pardon?"

"You should."

"Sorry, what was, quiet a minute, everyone. What did you say?"

"I said why not?"

"Well, this is rich. Here's a prodigy. I've got a salesman on the phone demanding why I won't let him perform his routine."

"Bet his neighbours hide when they see him coming."

"That's it, drink up. Plenty more champagne. Does anyone think I'm being rude to our uninvited guest? Think I should let him gate-crash the party now he's got a foot in the door, so to speak?"

"You could see what he's offering, dad."

"You want me to give him a chance, do you, Amelia? Very generous of you. Hello there on the phone? Are you still with us?"

"Just try getting rid of me."

"Hush for a moment, you girls. I missed that. Hello? I didn't catch your name."

"You won't, either."

"Contain yourselves briefly, people. That passed me by too. Quell the revels while I attempt to be polite. Hello again? We're windowed, I'm afraid. We can see everything we want to see."

"You can't see me."

"Granted, but so?"

"You'll wish you could."

"I'm sorry?"

"Too late."

"What's wrong, Charles? What is he saying to you?"

"Nothing you'd believe, Jonquil. Quite funny, really, but more than a hint of the odd."

"That's me summed up, is it, Charlie? You think I'm a little queer."

"I've no idea what size you are, and no interest in your sexual preferences either. It's all right, everyone, my marbles are secure. Can't speak for our caller, though. Hello there for the last time. I think we've had enough amusement now."

"Not yet. Not by half."

"Very well then, let me have an estimate."

"I couldn't start."

"An estimate for what you're selling."

"You want someone to come for a look, do you?"

"That has to be the way you do business, hasn't it? What was the name of your firm again?"

"If you're as clever as you reckon, you tell me."

"I'll need to know the name if I'm to have the work done. You won't want to cheat yourself out of your commission."

"At least I won't be out of a job like you'd call up to make sure I was, but then I'd have to be brainless."

"Now why should you think I—"

"I'd have to be like you," I'm already saying as I poke the button to turn him into even more of a drone than his voice was, and straighten up at my desk. My mouth is full of the taste that started when he interrupted me, stale bacon fat and milk sour with acid. It's the flavour of hate, and it tastes good. I lick my lips before I swallow some of it and let my eyes creep from side to side, to be sure nobody heard anything I said.

Of course they didn't, not even the ones whose desks are closest to mine—Madge to my left, her acne growing redder now she's middleaged and on the turn, Gordon to my right, still convinced the way he combs his hair leaves him lessbald instead of only icing the shoulders of his shabby jackets with dandruff. He and Madge are too busy pleading into their own phones, wasting half their energy on not sounding desperate while they put the rest into trying to persuade another faceless voice to give a chance to the effluent we sell. We crouch behind our computer screens in the long broad room with its slick walls white as scum. I see the others bowing down to the customers while I lower myself to their level—the level of imagining you're worth something because you make enough to pay for an expensive house and stuff it with a family and all the junk they won't stop whining till they get. I've never lowered myself further than I did to reach Charles Dunbobbin, and I can't wait to do it again.

Only I've got to earn my feed, and so I make a few calls first. One woman agrees to have the window merchants visit so her neighbours will have a better view of how well off she is, and a man actually sounds grateful to have his house surveyed for an alarm, though he wouldn't need it if he didn't own too much. They bring the taste back to my mouth, and I duck lower once I've dialled Dunbobbin's number.

One ring, two gold rings, three with diamonds in "Dunbobbin."

I can sound even posher than he can, and I do. "Mr Charles Dunbobbin?"

"The very same, and you are . . . "

"Please say if this isn't convenient, sir. I was ringing for a quick chat about wine."

"You sound like a man to know. What kind of wine?"

I'm beginning to see him. He'll have blue eyes and all his teeth, and hair he's spent too much money on, and a big chin he sticks out whenever anybody disagrees with him. The cursor on the screen twitches like a nerve as I crouch lower and say "Have you much time for champagne?"

"We've quaffed a drop too much of that tonight if I'm to be truthful, old boy. Not much call for it at the restaurant, though."

"What was the occasion, sir?"

"Our younger daughter's results. We've had a few of her friends and a popping of corks."

"Who are you speaking to, Charles?"

That's his wife, bristling with jewels and doused in perfume to cover up her smell, her hair glossy as hot tar, the valley of her flesh bared in front of her. "Just a man about a bottle," he tells her.

"Odd hour to phone. Don't be long. The girls are dancing with anticipation of the fireworks."

I'm afraid he may cut me off before he learns how he's been tricked, and so as soon as his cheek presses against mine I say "Did you mention a restaurant, sir?"

"We own one. You may have heard of it. The Groaning Board."

Of course I haven't, since I've never eaten in a restaurant, not when my father showed me all the cuttings he'd collected about diseases people caught there, but I say "I know it has a reputation."

His chin edges forward. "What kind are you saying that would be?"

"Your kind, Mr Dunbobbin."

Maybe he thinks I said he was kind, because when he speaks it's only "You were going to talk to me about wine."

"Your kind."

"You keep saying that, and it signifies . . . "

"The kind you're going to make."

"I wonder if you've confused me. What sort of wine are you under the impression I make?"

"The sort whiners do."

"Who is this?" he demands, low but so fierce I hear his spit rattling the mouthpiece. "By God, you crazy lunatic, you've rung once already, haven't you?"

"That's me," I say, grinning down at him, but I'm about to tell him how his insult has worsened his situation when a fat hand with one finger bulging out of a ring plants itself on top of my computer monitor.

I lift my head slowly to give my grin time to straighten itself. Mr Maudlin is protruding his purple waistcoat at me as his donkey teeth force his sloppy lips apart. "Are you winning?" he inquires with the stupid heartiness I always think is meant to contradict his name.

"I'm not whining." I can't resist that answer, not when the voice I've crushed against my ear is snarling "You call this number once more and I'll have you traced." I kill it and let the corners of my mouth lift my face towards the supervisor.

"That's what I like to hear," he brays, but then "Are you ill?"

I dig my knuckles into my mouth until I've finished swallowing. "Just a taste."

"I should give it some medicine when you get it home. Shift's finished."

Sometimes I feel as if he put me at the end of the room the same way teachers used to sit me at the back of the class because I wouldn't waste my time with the drivel they had to teach to live, but my position means nobody can overhear me or watch me from behind. "See you tomorrow," I say, sounding enough like the rest of them to fool them, not that it takes much.

I let my bicycle off its chain on the cold sweaty pipe in the Gents and carry it down the worn concrete stairs and out of the side door. A puppy or a rat scuttles down the alley, away from the bins outside the Chinese restaurant, where the kitchen is full of jabbering not much more alien than the talk that surrounds me every day. Above the senseless assortment of roofs the clouds are a slab of grease, holding down the heat of all the drudges who tramp the streets at lunchtime. They've gone home now to pretend they've lives worth living, only some have changed into this season's uniform and are swarming to the lights of clubs and pubs. I pedal past couples stuck together by their hands and imitating dummies in shop windows, past people who've given up pretending that a home is worth the effort and are nesting in the doorways of dead shops. Then there are buildings that are being smashed and burned, and a park with a lake that litter is soaking up and trees that move about so much I have to keep my curtains shut. I cycle through, past two children undressing each other in a shelter, and then I'm where I try to live.

The faded stale three-storey house smells of stewed tea and charred vegetables. On the ground floor Mr Dunn and his parrot are screeching at each other to shut up. On the middle floor Mrs Venable is talking to a play on the radio as if she's got friends in. I haul my bicycle to the top, over the threadbare carpet narrower than the stairs under the grudging bulbs. I slip past my door and shove it closed with the back wheel.

The threads I tacked at ankle height between the skirting boards are undisturbed. I switch on the lights in the bathroom and kitchen and the room that's everything else and empty disinfectant into the bath I only hope is hot enough to kill the day's germs. When it finishes stinging and starts lulling me to sleep I dry myself and sit at my table. The first page of the book I'm going to write remains blank, and I find myself putting faces to the voices in the play under the floor. I'd rather do that to people who haven't been made up. I listen for the Dunbobbin phone to stop ringing as I crawl under my mother's old quilt on the couch.

A girl answers, not one I remember having heard. "Hi, it's Theodora."

"Theodora Dunbobbin?"

"That's me."

"Amelia's elder sister."

"Is it me you want?"

"Don't you worry, you'll do."

"No, I meant did you want her? I call her Me."

"You must be close. That's good. That's what I like to hear."

"Are you a friend of hers?"

"As much as I am of your father. She did well, I hear."

"At her exams? She did, but she nearly gave herself a breakdown. I keep telling mum and dad not to push her so hard."

"People survive breakdowns, take my word for it. Maybe it's the only way she can live up to your example."

"You're joking, aren't you? I didn't do half as well."

"Not a jealous inch in you though, is that right? Still looking after your little sister. Feeling a trifle unnoticed all the same, I can see."

"A bit."

"What do you do when you want to be noticed? What's your talent?"

"I don't know. I used to dance."

"You still can then, can't you? You never forget. It's like cycling. Go and fetch your father and we'll show him what you can do."

"I don't get this."

"You will, and so will Charles. I guarantee he'll be impressed."

I'm in control. No sooner have I drawn a breath that makes my chest throb than she's back. "I've brought my dad."

"I don't want to speak to him this time, but give him a message."

"He wants me to give you a message, dad. Don't take the phone. He sounds serious."

"Tell him I can see you and if you don't do as I say he'll know I can."

She tells him, and I hear him gasp "It's him."

"That's who I am. That's who it's going to be whenever any of you picks up the phone. Tell Charles to lie on the floor. Do it now."

"Dad, he wants you to lie on the floor. You better had. I'm frightened."

"Is he down? Tell him to stay down till he's told he can get up. Now then, let's show him a routine he won't forget. Let's see you dance, Theodora. Dance on him."

"Dad, he wants—"

"Never mind telling him, show him. Dance all over him. Start on his face."

"Christ, Teddy, what are you—Oh, oh God, my—"

"Dad, I'm sorry. Don't try and get away, he can see you. I'm so sorry, dad."

The trouble is, I can't see her. That's so frustrating I wish I had a phone, except there's nobody I'd want to hear from. I unclench my hands on the quilt and roll over, away from the overhead light I can't sleep without, and pull the quilt over my face. I watch Dunbobbin being danced on until he has too little of a face to keep me awake.

In the morning I can't see him at all. I want to see him realise what he's brought on himself, but for that I need to hear him. I send some of the stale taste of hate down to the ache in my stomach with a glass of milk and force down the contents of a can of beans. My mother always said that if food wasn't in a can or wrapped in cellophane it would have germs. I move my chair around the table and rest my face on the blank page, which has nothing for me but a smell of paper. I spring to my feet and stalk between the threads and out to the phone box on the far side of the park.

There's no response from the Dunbobbin house. Charles and his girls are either out or sleeping off the party, in which case I hope he's dreaming about me. He will. I'm so eager to renew our acquaintance that I cycle early to work.

"Good to see a smiling face," Mr Maudlin chortles as I tramp to my desk and call Charles. Perhaps the happy family is at the restaurant, but when I find the number an answering machine is waiting, as if I'd ever be trapped like that. Now the drudges are at their desks, and I add my pleas to the mumble of the room. I've succeeded in netting two fools by the time Jonquil Dunbobbin's voice takes over the machine's job. "The Groaning Board."

"Are you the restaurant?"

"Part of it," she thinks she's quipping, with a flash of her teeth and her jewels as idiotically extravagant as her name. "What can we do for you?"

"Can you fit in a mob of twelve people tonight?"

"What time?"

"About eight?"

"That's our busiest, but let me look. We should be able to accommodate you."

"I ought to have said thirteen people. I nearly forgot myself. Can you cope with that number?"

"That many more the merrier, but we do like a deposit when it's a large party."

"I don't think I can get in before eight. You're where my daughter wants to celebrate passing her exams."

"We've had some festivities ourselves."

Shouldn't she be thinking I'm the same kind of creature she is, a victim of parasites called children? My mouth is filling with the taste as my skull begins to tingle with frustration when I hear Gordon on my right, and I'm inspired. "I'd be able to bring a deposit if I didn't need to be here for my daughter," I say into the secret place between my hands. "She's in a wheelchair, you see."

Jonquil Dunbobbin exhibits a caring smile that gleams like her necklace. "In that case there'll be no problem. We'll look forward to seeing you and your party at eight."

"I'm looking forward already," I assure her, and that's true for hours, so that I scarcely hear myself talking to the faceless, even the several we manage to snare. A few minutes before eight I call the restaurant and tell a waitress the party will be there in half an hour. Half an hour later I tell her we've broken down on the way. I let the Dunbobbins have a good stare at the thirteen empty places while I speak to three people as unimportant as Charles, and then I ring back. As soon as the waitress asks when I think we may arrive I hear Charlie shout "I'll speak to him."

I lower my head to meet him and see his chin stick up at me. "May we know what the problem is?" he says.

"It's you."

"You'll forgive me, but I don't follow."

"It's you, Chas. It's you."

"Sorry." He sounds as if he very slightly is. "You've the advantage of me. Should I know you?"

"Don't you wish you did?"

His chin tugs his lips so tight his voice can barely escape. "Have we spoken recently?"

"Chas, you remembered."

"It's you."

There's so little to him that he even has to steal my lines. "Are you always that quick?" I say through my tilted grin. "Maybe just in bed with Jonquil, eh?"

"Good God, what kind of—" He rubs his mouth to loosen it, and a different tone of voice comes out. "Look—"

"I'm doing that, believe me. Me and God."

"Look, if I offended you the first time you called I—I apologise. I know we've all got to make our living as best we can."

"Like you, you mean."

"There are worse ways, I should think."

"Like mine."

"I didn't say that, did I? I'm trying not to offend you. I just hope that if I did you feel you're even."

The taste of hate is bigger than my mouth, so that a pool of saliva appears on the desk. It froths as I say "You think I'd want to be even with you?"

"What do you want, then? What's this supposed to be about?"

"I'll tell you what I want," I say lower than ever, and the pool shivers like a lake under a storm. "I want you to know how worthless you are, and everything you've spent your money on. I want you to see how nothing you've got can protect you from someone like me."

"Well, that's intriguing. That's certainly ambitious. Are you in a mood to give me an idea of a few of the ways you might try to bring it off?"

My senses have almost closed around the sight of him when I hear Gordon repeating "Clearview Windows", and I know what Charlie's up to—he's using all the words he can in the hope of overhearing where I am. "You'll find out," I say between my hands. "Part of it's the waiting."

"If you—" he starts, but I've gone. I rub away the pool on my desk and come back into the room. My grin jerks my head up, and Mr Maudlin matches the expression. Anything he approves of doesn't deserve approval, and I see how petty I've been—how I've done nothing worth doing to Charlie so far.

In the morning my hatred has a new taste. The world tastes of it, a cold flavour of metal and ash. Leaves on the trees in the park wither as I glare at them. Water by the kerbs holds litter in its icy traps. It's my day off. I know I can call from the phone by the park, but I walk to where the houses have bigger ideas of themselves. I shut myself in a booth and dial Charlie's number while the taste spreads out of me and turns the mirror above the phone as grey as the end of the street that leads towards his house. Two glittering rings and a girl's voice says "Hello?"

"It's Theodora, isn't it? Theodora Dunbobbin."

That takes her off guard, and my face is gone before she says "How did you know?"

"Because I can see you." Which I can, skirt too short to have cost half as much as it did, and half a shirt that lets her stomach peer out one-eyed, and too much expensive makeup, and hair that's a costly mess. "Do you understand? I see you, and I'll see if you don't do exactly as you're told."

Her breaths and her voice shrink into themselves. "What do I have to do?"

"Answer this question first and don't do anything but answer it. Is your father there?"

Her lips pinch together, pulling up her big chin that I bet she blames him for. "He's in the next room."

"Don't make any fuss, but call him. I want him to be watching you as well."

"Dad." When that doesn't work her voice goes higher and louder. "Dad."

His chin is first into the room. "Is it . . . "

"I think so."

"You think you know me, do you, Theodora? You don't know a scrap of the worst." Presumably because her father's there, she doesn't sound nearly as apprehensive as she should. "When did Chas last see you with no clothes on?" I say, rubbing my grin clear in the mirror.

"Why are you asking me that?"

"Because it's going to be now, only this time there'll be someone else watching. Take that top off for a start."

"Dad, he wants—"

"Don't tell him, show him. Take it off or you'll find out I haven't even started doing what I can do to you and yours."

"It's coming off. You said you could see."

I can. Her bare breasts flop into the open, pink-nosed as newborn rats. My skull rises, throbbing with my talent. I've taken control of her—I've been able to ever since I dreamed her name. I feel my mind closing around the Dunbobbins, but I'm opening my mouth to have her remove her skirt when the phone screams in my ear. "Who are you, you sick swine? What are you saying to my daughter?"

"Jonquil. Hello."

"Don't you dare talk like that to me. You leave my children alone or I'll find you and deal with you before the police do," she cries, jabbing and scratching at the air with the light on all her jewels, and tries to damage my ear by slamming down the expensive antique phone. It only makes the noise phones make when they're cut off, and I grin as I hang up its frustrated monotonous moan.

I could call them back at once, but they'll be expecting me. I want to see them when they don't know they're being watched. I walk to their house rather than cycle, since that would single me out as too thrifty for their district. The houses pale as they retreat and try to hide from me, but the cold makes me shiver. I detour to a store that sells clothes for people who don't want to be noticed. I buy a padded grey coat, and as I catch sight of myself in a mirror that bows to me I see I've another reason to grin.

By the time I reach Charlie's street I'm as hot as I was cold. I might feel closed into myself if I didn't see through the show the properties are putting on, stagecoach wheels leaning against them, old lamps sticking out of them, curtains tied back as if the front rooms are stages. I'm expecting Charlie's house to be called Dunbobbin, but it hasn't got a name. It's only as big as its neighbours, not nearly as impressive as he made it sound with his champagne party—it has to leave space for a Mercedes and a Toyota in the drive. I've pulled up the hood of my coat, and I don't grin until I've strolled by. But my grin doesn't last, because I couldn't see a single Dunbobbin. All the curtains are drawn.

Charlie and his sluts must be afraid I'm watching, but they're making their house look how I kept my parents' house until the landlord went and opened the curtains. My parents were the only people I ever met who were worth knowing, but however hard I thought, I couldn't stop them and their minds shrivelling and dying. My brain is stronger now, and I ought to feel pleased to have driven the Dunbobbins under cover, but I want to see them so that my thoughts can seize them. I walk to the end of the street and swing around a thin tree sprouting from the pavement and with half its branches snapped. I've just come abreast of Charlie's house when the front-room curtains twitch like an eye standing on end and pretending to be asleep.

I don't run, I only twist my hooded head aside. Once there's a tree between me and the house I walk faster, my clenched teeth aching with rage. I'm close to the end of the street when I hear a front door open, and at the corner when Charlie calls above his stuck-out chin "Excuse me . . . " I sidle around the corner, and then I do run, into an alley that leads behind his house. I try his back gate as I pass in case I can hide in his home—it would be like squatting in his mind. The gate is bolted, and I dash out of the alley and across another road where all the houses are infected with alarms and into an alley that takes me even further from where I live.

Most of an hour later I slam myself into my flat. The pretentious streets I had to detour through haven't driven away the smell of the waste in the alleys at the backsides of the houses; they've only turned it into more of a flavour of hatred. My skull is blazing with all the heat my flight trapped inside my coat—with fury at my having had to act like a coward, a criminal, a Dunbobbin. I fling myself on the couch and grab my eyes, and as soon as the light stops pounding enough to let me see I grope downstairs and find my way to the phone box.

When Charlie answers my lips peel back, because he doesn't sound nearly so sure of himself—he doesn't sound quite like himself. "Hello?"

"Hello?"

"Can I help you?"

Just in time I understand that I'm seeing his chin deflate not because he's beaten but because it isn't Chas at all, and I'm seeing the real face. "Can I help you?" I say in as much of his voice as I can steal.

"Who is this, please?"

I'd repeat that too if it wouldn't make me almost as stupid as him. I can see his helmet now, and his uniform as dark as the clothes of the men who took away my parents. He wants me to talk long enough to be traced. "Nobody you'd like to know," I say and hang up. I'm halfway to my flat when I dash back and grab the receiver to wipe off my fingerprints.

I eat my dinner to keep the fear down, vegetable soup straight out of the can even though my mother said you should cook everything. Maybe I'm trying to make myself sick so that I can stay off work. The thought of the police arresting me in front of everyone—bringing me as low as them—glares in my eyes, harder when I try to sleep. I do my best to change the thought into a rage at it, which urges me off the couch in the morning, the way my mother used to get me out of bed, saying this would be the day when everyone would see how special I was.

I'm so hungry to speak to Charles I do without breakfast. The chill ashen taste of the day is sufficient to fill my mouth. When I speed into the car park and vault off the bicycle, the way I used to make my mother gasp and cheer, a gust of paleness like my breath grown huge seems to sink into the concrete of the building. I'll make Charlie's house blanch like that, and him. I dig my nails into the seat of my bicycle while the lift raises us, then I wheel my companion to the Gents and chain it up. Once I've shaken the padlock hard I stride along the corridor, tasting some of what I'll say to Charles. But Gordon is already in the office.

His coat is, at any rate, the coat he always wears outside as soon as he begins to moan about the cold. Cycling has kept me hot enough, a heat that concentrates itself in my head. I'm wondering if I have time to focus it on Charlie when Gordon appears, heralded by the squeal of the door to the Gents. He must have been the grunting and complaining I could hear in there. He looks more harassed than ever, but if he's waiting for me to care he'll die of waiting. He mutters about the weather and his family and the ends they have to make meet, and I'd tell him to get rid of some of his problems, starting with the family, if they bother him so much except I'm saving my thoughts for Charles. I manage to agree with everything Gordon says until Mr Maudlin and his minions gather and I can stop feeling expected to talk to anyone in the room. "Good luck, everyone," Mr Maudlin chortles once the desks have trapped their drudges, and claps his fat hands to indicate it's time to start work.

How fast can the police trace a call they're waiting for? Maybe I should confine myself to phones away from the office, however furious having to hide among the drudges makes me. I'm ducking lower to hide my grimace at being forced to pretend I resemble them when someone sneaks into the room.

Before he stoops over Mr Maudlin's desk I see he has a small black moustache as straight as his face is lopsided, and temples eating away his hair. One of his shoulders jerks up and wags about, lifting his jacket to display more of his pale blue suit than is worth a look, as he talks rapidly and low. Mr Maudlin tries a smile, but not for long. "You called earlier," I see him whisper.

"Let's step outside," the man whispers back—challenging him to a fight? Mr Maudlin follows him into the corridor, and I'm forgetting the man's face when I hear Charlie's voice outside the door.

The pool of froth that appears on the desk drags my head low so fast I feel as if I'm going to disappear into it. I can't grasp what he's saying until I realise only two men are talking out there. The bearded man is using Charlie's voice to say "Apparently he can't deal with rejection. He turned very nasty when I wouldn't buy his spiel."

If that's meant to make me lose my temper, it almost does. I grind the dead phone against my jaw as Mr Maudlin says "That's not on at all. I tell all my people to always, whatever the response, not that I'm saying for a moment yours was anything but courteous, be polite."

"That wouldn't be anyone's word for him. When I wouldn't buy he accused me of whining, let me tell you, and then he rang up the restaurant my wife and I run and made a false booking. And yesterday he called my daughter and made suggestions I won't repeat."

"I can only offer you my deepest apologies, Mr Dunbobbin. hope you've informed the police."

"Not yet."

He's trying to throw me, I see that now. He's trying to convince me my talent is less than it is. Maybe he's talking while the bearded man keeps mum. "I wanted to remember the name of the firm he was calling for," he says. "I knew I'd heard it, and this morning it came to me."

"The trouble is, Clearview could be more than one of my chaps."

"I'll know him." In order to infuriate me even more than he and Mr Maudlin already have, Charlie dares to laugh. "Would you believe it, he thought my daughter was following his instructions when all she was doing was sticking out her tongue at him. He seemed to think she was someone else. Kept calling her by some stupid name we'd never have dreamed of burdening her with."

The pain of bone and flesh ground down beneath plastic spreads up my face to the white-hot core of my head. My body has grown stiff as metal, and I'm about to stalk to the door when Charlie says "All the same, it's no laughing matter. The man needs seeing to. He didn't only lose us business at the restaurant, he had the gall to claim the party was for his daughter who was in a wheelchair."

I hear a clatter to my right. Gordon has finished a call and dropped his phone. Though nearly all the drudges are talking, I hear a breathless silence underlying the murmur. It feels as if I'm poised to take control. Then Mr Maudlin, more subdued than I've ever heard him, says "If you wait here I'll have a word with someone."

"I'd rather come in, thank you. I told you I'd know him," Charlie says and marches into the office, or the bearded man does. His gaze starts at the front of the room and rises slowly as a gun to level itself at the back row of desks. It fixes them as he paces towards them, and I meet it with a blank stare behind which all my power is hiding. I'll betray nothing if I can just stop my legs from shivering under the desk as my power leaves the rest of my body for my skull. I'm about to lift the phone and place a call when Gordon steps away from his desk, having tangled with his chair, and grabs his fat grey hooded coat from the stand. The man is in the far aisle, and gestures at Mr Maudlin to cut Gordon off. "It's him."

Gordon shoves one arm into the coat and lurches towards the door. The coat snags on a computer monitor and almost tips it over. When Mr Maudlin trots at him, trying to look both sympathetic and reproving, Gordon shouts "Leave me alone." Mr Maudlin tries to catch his less fat arm, but Gordon shoves him away and dodges into the corridor. "Leave me alone, can't you," he yells as Mr Maudlin and the bearded man chase him. More of that fades down the stairs, and I stare at Madge as if I've no more idea of what's happening than she has. Eventually only Mr Maudlin reappears and watches everyone until they, we, go back to work.

Having to drone so as to go unnoticed is close to unbearable. I feel as if my talent is guttering somewhere in the dimness of my skull. I repeat the formulas over and over while I struggle to understand what happened, but I can't think for performing my idiotic toil. If Gordon has drawn the chase away from me, he has also taken the credit. At last I'm allowed to go home, but even when I stare at the blank page I'm unable to think. I hear my mother tell me "Always know you're better," and in my sleep too, what there is of it. In the morning she's gone, but the blank page stays ahead of me as my body cycles to work.

Mr Maudlin is waiting for me. When I try to head for my desk he beckons me over. The power starts to reach for my eyes until I hear what he wants—what he would have told whoever was first into the office. Gordon won't be coming back. It seems he's heading for a breakdown. He was working at two jobs to buy things for his daughter in the wheelchair, but he'd only told the tax people about one. Charlie has taken pity on him and won't be calling the police.

"You think you know people," I say, and stroll to duck behind my screen. I can't have him wondering why I'm grinning as comprehension lights up the inside of my skull. My talent is as strong as I knew it was—it made Gordon take the blame. It wasn't as powerful when I called Charlie, which is why I saw him wrong, but now I know how he looks. I've only his word that his daughter isn't named Theodora or that she didn't do as I said. Soon I'll find out, when they least expect it, and there will be others. The world is my blank page. Before I'm finished its parasites will see me for what I am. I stroke the phone and wait for the drudges to gather, to give my voice somewhere to hide.

No End of Fun

"YOU DON'T MIND, DO YOU, UNCLE LIONEL? I'VE GIVEN YOU mother's old room."

"Why should I mind anything to do with Dorothy?"

"I expect you've got happy memories like us. Is it all right if Helen sees you up? Only we've got paying guests arriving any minute."

"You really ought to let me pay something towards my keep."

"You mustn't think I meant that. Mother never let you and I'm not about to start. Just keep Helen amused like always and that'll be more than enough. Helen, don't let my uncle lug that case."

"Are you helping with the luggage now, Helen? Will that be a bit much for you?"

"I've done bigger ones."

"That sounds a bit cheeky, doesn't it, Carol? The sort of thing the comics used to say at the Imperial. Is that old place still alive? That can be one of your treats then, Helen."

"Say thank you, Helen, and will you please take up that case. Here are the boarders now."

When the thirteen-year-old thrust her fingers through the handle, Lionel let it go. "You're a treasure," he murmured, but she was apparently too intent on stumping upstairs to give him his usual smile. Remarking "She's a credit to you" brought him no more than a straight-lipped nod from her mother. He had to admit to himself that Helen's new image—all her curls cropped into auburn turf, denim overalls so oversized he would have assumed they'd been handed down if she'd had an older sibling—had rather startled him. "So how have you been progressing at school?" he said as he caught up with her, and in an attempt to sound less dusty "You can call me Lionel if you like."

"Mum wouldn't let me."

"Better make it uncle, then, even if it's not quite right. Great-uncle is a mouthful, isn't it, though you liked it one year, didn't you? You said I was the greatest one you had, not that there was any competition."

All this, uttered slowly and with pauses inviting but obtaining no responses, brought them to the third floor, where he held onto the banister and regained his breath while Helen preceded him into the room. Dorothy's sheets had been replaced by a duvet as innocently white, but otherwise the place seemed hardly to have changed since her girlhood, when children weren't expected to personalise their rooms: the same hulking oaken wardrobe and chest of drawers she'd inherited at Helen's age along with Dorothy's grandmother's room, the view of boarding-houses boasting of their fullness, the only mirror her grandmother's on the windowsill. As he stepped into the July sunlight that had gathered like an insubstantial faintly lavenderscented weight in the room, he thought he saw Dorothy in the mirror.

It was Helen, of course. She resembled Dorothy more than Carol ever had—elfin ears, full lower lip, nose as emphatic as an exclamation mark, eyes deep with secrets. As she dumped Lionel's suitcase by the bed, the mirror wobbled with the impact. The oval glass was supported by two pairs of marble hands, each brace joined at the wrists; the lower of the left hands was missing its little finger. He lurched forward to steady the mirror, and his arm brushed the front of Helen's overalls. He expected the material to yield, and the presence of two plump mounds of flesh came as more than a shock.

She twisted away from him, and her face reappeared in the mirror, grimacing. For a moment it exactly fitted the oval. The sight set his heart racing as though a knot of memories had squeezed it. "Sorry," he mumbled, and "I'll see you at dinner" as she slouched out of the room.

Laying his socks and underwear in Dorothy's chest of drawers and dressing her padded hangers in his shirts and suits made him wonder if that was more intimate than she would have liked. By the time he'd finished he was oppressively hot. He donned the bathrobe that was waiting for him every year and hurried to the attic bathroom, to be confronted by a crowd of Carol's and Helen's tights pegged to a clothesline over the bath as though to demonstrate two stages of growth. Not caring to touch them, he retreated to his room and transferred the mirror to the chest of drawers so as to raise the sash as high as it would wobble. Hours of sunlight had left the marble hands not much less warm than flesh.

He might have imagined he heard the screams of people drowning if he hadn't recognised the waves as the swoops of a roller coaster. Soon he was able to hear the drowsing of the sea. Its long slow breaths were soothing him when he saw a passer-by remove her topmost head. She'd lifted her small daughter from her shoulders, but the realisation came too late to prevent Lionel from remembering a figure that had parted into prancing segments. He lay down hastily and made himself breathe in time with the sea until the summons of the dinner gong resounded through the house.

Even in their early teens he and his cousin had squabbled over who sounded the gong, until Dorothy's mother had kept the task for herself. While it was meant to call only the guests, it reminded him that he didn't know when he was expected for dinner. He was changing, having resprayed his armpits, when a rap at the door arrested him with trousers halfway up his greying thighs. "Would you mind taking dinner with the others?" Carol called. "We're not as organised as mother yet."

"I'd be happy to wait till you have yours."

"We eat on the trot at the moment. You'd be helping."

In the dining-room a table in the corner farthest from the window was set for one. All his fellow diners were married couples at least his age. A few bade him a wary good evening, but otherwise none of the muted conversations came anywhere near him. He felt like a teacher attempting to ignore a murmurous classroom, not that he ever would have. As soon as he'd finished dinner—thin soup, cold ham and salad, brown bread and butter, a rotund teapot harbouring a single bag, a pair of cakes on a stand, everything Dorothy used to serve—he followed Helen into the kitchen. "Would you be terribly upset if we didn't go anywhere tonight?" he said.

"Don't suppose."

"Only driving up from London isn't the picnic it was."

"She wouldn't have been joining you anyway. It's dirty sheet night," Carol said, wrinkling her nose.

He did all the washing-up he could grab, and would have helped Helen trudge to the machine in the basement with armfuls of bedclothes if Carol hadn't urged him to tell her his news. Now that he'd retired from teaching there wasn't much besides the occasional encounter with an ex-pupil, and so he encouraged Carol to talk. When her patient responses betrayed that she regarded his advice about the multitude of petty problems she'd inherited with the boarding-house as at best uninformed, he pleaded tiredness and withdrew to his room.

At first exhaustion wouldn't let him sleep. Though he left the window open, the heat insisted on sharing his bed, Dorothy's ever since she was Helen's age. He found himself wishing he hadn't arrived for the funeral last December too late to see her. "We never said goodbye," he whispered into the pillow and wrapped his arms around himself, covering his flaccid hairy dugs.

He wakened in the middle of the night and also of the heat with the notion that Dorothy had grown an unreasonable number of legs. He raised himself on his elbows to peer sleepily about, and realised she was staring at him. Of course it was her oval photograph, except that there was no picture of her in the room. As he jerked upright he saw her face balanced on the marble hands, crammed into the mirror. She looked outraged, unable to believe her fate.

Lionel snatched at the overhead cord to drag light into the room. The mirror was deserted apart from a patch of wallpaper whose barely discernible pattern gave him the impression of gazing straight through the frame at the wall. When the illusion refused to be dispelled he turned the light off, trying not to feel he'd used it to drive Dorothy into the dark. She was gone wherever everyone would end up, that was all; how could dreaming summon her back? Nevertheless he felt as guilty as the only other time he'd seen her in the mirror.

It had been the year when she'd kept being late for dinner. One evening her mother had sent him to fetch her. He'd swaggered into

Dorothy's room without knocking; they'd never knocked at each other's doors. Although it wasn't dark the curtains had been drawn, and at first he'd been unsure what he saw—Dorothy stooping to watch her face in the oval mirror as she'd squeezed her budding breasts. While she hadn't been naked, her white slip had let the muted light glow between her legs. The smile of pride and quiet astonishment she had been sharing with herself had transformed itself into an accusing glare as she'd caught sight of him in the mirror. "Go away," she'd cried, "this is my room," as Lionel fled, his entire body pounding like an exposed heart. He hadn't dared venture downstairs until he'd heard her precede him.

The breakfast gong quieted his memories at last. In the bathroom he was relieved to find the tights had flown. He showered away most of his coating of mugginess, and thought he was ready for the day until he opened the kitchen door to hear Carol tell Helen "You're not to go anywhere near him, is that understood?"

Surely she couldn't mean Lionel, but he would have been tempted to sidle out of reach of the idea if she hadn't given him a wink behind Helen's eloquently sulky back. "A boyfriend she's too young to have," she said. "Do you mind sitting where you did again?"

Lionel had hoped they could have breakfast together, but tried to seem happy to head for the dining-room. "Morning all," he declared, and when that stirred no more than muted echoes "I'm her uncle, should anyone be wondering."

Did explaining his presence only render it more questionable or suggest he thought it was? He restrained himself from explaining that Carol had divorced her husband once she'd resolved to move in with her aging mother. He made rather shorter work of his breakfast than his innards found ideal so that he could escape to the kitchen. "Are we going for a roam?" he asked Helen as he set about washing up.

"Too many rooms to change," Carol said at once. "Maybe we can let her out this evening if you can think how to occupy her."

He strolled up to the elongated Victorian garden that was the promenade and clambered down a set of thick hot stone steps to the beach. The sand was beginning to sprout turrets around families who'd staked out their territories with buckets and spades the colours of lollipops. He paced alongside the subdued withdrawn waves until screams rose from the amusement park ahead, and then he laboured up another block of steps to the Imperial.

The theatre was displaying posters for the kind of summer show it always had: comedians, singers, dancers, a magician. It took the mostly blonde girl in the ticket booth some moments to pause her chewing gum and see off a section of her handful of paperback, which was proportionately almost as stout as its reader. When she said "Can I help you?" she sounded close to refusing in advance.

"Could you tell me whether there are any, you won't take offence if I call them dwarfs?"

She met that with a grimace she supplemented by bulging her cheek with her tongue. "Any. . . "

"Small performers. You know, a troupe of dinky fellows. They used to perform here when I was a child. I don't know if you'd have anything like them these days." When she only tongued her cheek more fiercely he grew desperate. "Tiny Tumblers, one lot were called," he insisted. "Squat little chaps."

"The only little people we've got are Miss Merritt's Moppets."

"That's fine, then," Lionel said with an alacrity she appeared to find suspicious. "Any chance of a pair of your best seats for tomorrow night?"

"Best for what?"

For persuading Carol to give Helen an evening off, he hoped: she was working the child harder than Dorothy had ever worked her. "For watching, I should think," he said.

From the theatre he wandered inland. Behind the large hotels facing the sea a parallel row of bed and breakfast houses kept to themselves. Victorian shopping arcades led between them to the main street, which was clinging to its elegance. Among the tea shops and extravagant department stores, not a pub nor an amusement arcade was to be seen. Crowds of the superannuated were taking all the time they could to progress from one end of the street to the other, while those that were wheeling or being wheeled traversed the wide pavements more slowly still. When Lionel discovered that matching the speed of the walkers made him feel prematurely old, or perhaps not so prematurely, he turned aside into the park that stretched opposite half the shops.

Folding chairs could be hired from a spindly lugubrious youth decorated with a moustache like two transplanted eyebrows. Lionel plumped himself and the swelling that was breakfast onto a chair close to the bandstand. The afternoon concert was preceded by an open-air theatre of toddlers on the lawns and secretaries with lunch-boxes, a spectacle he found soporific. By the time the elderly musicians in their dinner jackets assembled on the bandstand, he was dozing off.

A medley of Viennese waltzes failed to rouse him, as did portions of Mozart and Mendelssohn. He was past being able to raise his head when the orchestra struck up a piece he would have thought too brash to win the applause, much of it gloved, of the pensioned audience. Though he couldn't name the opera responsible, he recognised the music. It was the Dance of the Tumblers. Far from wakening him, it let a memory at him.

A few days after he'd seen Dorothy at the mirror, her mother had taken her and Lionel to the Imperial. She'd made them sit together as if that might crush whatever had come between them, but Dorothy had sat aside from him, knees protruding into the aisle. She had seemed to take half the evening to eat a tub of ice cream, until the scraping of the wooden spoon had started to grate on his nerves. As she'd lifted yet another delicate mouthful to her lips, the master of ceremonies had announced the Tiny Tumblers, and then her spoon had halted in mid-air. Two giant women had waddled onstage from the wings.

He'd never known if Dorothy had cowered against her seat because of their size or from guessing what was imminent. The longhaired square-faced figures had swayed to the footlights before the flowered ankle-length dresses had split open, each of them disgorging a totem-pole composed of three dwarfs in babies' frilly outfits. The dwarfs had sprung from one another's shoulders, leaving the dresses to collapse under the weight of the wigs, and piled down the stairs that flanked the stage. "Who's coming for a tumble?" they'd croaked.

Lionel had felt Dorothy flinch away from the aisle, pressing against him. If she'd asked he would have changed places with her, but he'd thought he sensed how loath she was to touch him after his glimpse in her room. As two dwarfs had scurried towards her, swivelling their blocky heads and widening their eyes, he'd dealt her a covert shove. Her lurch and her squeak had attracted the attention of the foremost dwarf, who'd shambled fast at her. She'd jumped up, spilling ice cream over the lap of her skirt, and fled to the sanctuary of the Ladies'. Her mother had needed to ask Lionel more than once to let her past to follow, he remembered with dismay. Part of him had wanted to find out what would happen if the dwarfs caught his cousin.

He came back to himself before the thought could reach deeper. He'd grown unaware of the music in the park, and now there was only clapping. He was awakened less by the discreet peal than by a sense that his body was about to expel some element it was no longer able to contain. His midriff strained itself up from the chair as the secret escaped him—a protracted vibrant belch that the applause faded just in time to isolate.

He excused himself as quickly and as blindly as he could—he had a childish half-awake notion that if he didn't see he wouldn't be seen either—but not before he glimpsed couples staring as if he'd strayed from the Imperial, which they barely tolerated for its appeal to tourists. Several pensioners on the main street frowned at his excessively boisterous progress, but he was anxious to take refuge in his room. Since Carol and Helen were busy in the kitchen, only shortness of breath delayed him on the stairs. He manhandled the door open and slumped against it, but took just one step towards the bed.

Whoever had tidied up had returned the mirror to the windowsill. It must be himself he could see in the oval glass, even if the face appeared to recede faster than he stumbled forward. Presumably his having rushed back to the hotel made him see the face dwindle beyond sight, carried helplessly into a blackness that had no basis in the room. He rubbed his eyes hard, and once the fog cleared he saw nothing in the mirror except his own confused face.

The marble hands had stored up warmth. They brought back the touch of flesh, which he'd avoided since losing his parents, not that he'd encountered much of it while they were alive. He planted the hands on the chest of drawers and turned the glass to the wall, then lay on top of the duvet, trying harder and more unsuccessfully to relax than he ever had after a day's teaching, until the gong sent its vibrations through his nerves.

He didn't eat much. Besides being wary of conjuring another belch, he felt as though someone who knew more about him than he realised was observing him. When he took the last of his plates into the kitchen, Carol gave him a harassed disappointed blink. "Dinner was excellent," he assured her, though it had been something of a repeat performance of last night's, with cold beef understudying ham. "I'm just not very peckish. I expect I'm too excited at the prospect of a date with my favourite young lady."

"Do you still want to go out with my uncle tonight?"

Helen had kept her back to his comment, but turned with a quick bright smile. "Yes please, Uncle Lionel."

That was more like the girl he remembered. It lasted as far as the street, where he said "Shall we just go for an amble?"

"To the rides."

"Best save those till I've been to the bank."

"I've got some money. If we aren't going to the rides I don't want to go."

He felt as if she knew he'd manufactured his excuse. "It's your treat," he said.

All the way along the promenade he had to remind himself that the screams from the tracks etched high on the glassy sunset expressed pleasure. The sight beyond the entrance to the amusement park of painted horses bobbing like flotsam on an ebb tide provided some relief. He halted by the old roundabout to regain his breath. "Shall we," he said, and "Go on here?"

Helen squashed her lower lip flat with its twin. "That's for babies."

He might have retorted that she hadn't seemed to think so last year, but said "What shall it be, then?"

"The Cannonball."

"I thought you didn't care for roller coasters any more than I do."

"That was when I was little. I like it now, and the Plunge of Peril, and Annihilation."

"Will you be awfully offended if I watch?"

"No." The starkness of the word appeared to rouse her pity for him, since she added "You can win me something, Uncle Lionel."

He felt obliged to see her safely onto the roller coaster. Once she was installed in the middle carriage, next to a boy with an increasingly red face and the barest vestige of hair, Lionel headed for the sideshows. Too many of the prizes were composed of puffed-up rubber for his taste—he remembered a pink horse whose midriff had burst between his adolescent legs, dumping him in the sea—but they were out of reach of his skill. He had yet to ring a single bell or cast a quoit onto a hook when Helen indicated she was bound for the Plunge of Peril.

He was determined to win her a present. Eventually rolling several pounds' worth of balls down a chute towards holes intermittently exposed by a perforated strip of wood gained him an owl of shaggy orange cloth. He would have felt more triumphant if he hadn't realised he'd betrayed that he wouldn't have needed to go to the bank. He was just in time to see Helen leave the Plunge of Peril.

She glanced about but didn't notice him behind a bunch of Teddy bears pegged by their cauliflower ears. As he watched through the tangle of legs she shared a swift kiss with her companion, the red-faced boy crowned with grey skin, and tugged him in the direction of a virtually vertical roller coaster. Lionel didn't intervene, not even when they staggered off the ride, though he was unsure whether he was being discreet or spying on them or at a loss how to approach them. He was pursuing them through the crowds when their way was blocked by two figures with the night gaping where their faces ought to be.

They were life-size cartoons of a man and a woman sufficiently ill-dressed to be homeless, painted on a flat with their faces cut out for the public to insert their own. Lionel saw Helen scamper to poke hers out above the woman's body. Her grimace was meant to be funny— she was protruding at the boy the tongue she'd recently shared with him—but Lionel realised that too late to keep quiet. "Don't," he cried.

For a moment Helen's face looked trapped by the oval. Perhaps her eyes were lolling leftward to send the boy that way, since that was the direction in which he absented himself. She emerged so innocently it angered Lionel. "I think it's time we went back to your mother," he said, and thrust the owl at Helen as she mooched after him. "This was for you."

"Thanks." On the promenade she lowered a mournful gaze to the dwarfish button-eyed rag-beaked soft-clawed orange lump, and then she risked saying "Are you going to tell mum?"

"Can you offer me any reason why I shouldn't?"

"Because she'd never let me see Brandon again."

"I thought that was already supposed to be the arrangement."

"But I love him," Helen protested, and began to weep.

"Good heavens now, no need for that. You can't be in love at your age." The trouble was that he had no idea when it was meant to start; it never had for him. "Do stop it, there's a good girl," he pleaded as couples bound for the amusement park began to frown more at him than at Helen, and applied himself to taking some control. "I really don't like being used when I haven't even been consulted."

"I won't ever again, I promise."

"I'll hold you to it. Now can we make that the end of the tears? I shouldn't think you'd like your mother wondering what the tragedy is."

"I'll stop if you promise not to tell."

"We'll see."

He was ashamed to recognise that he might have undertaken more if she hadn't dabbed her eyes dry with the owl, leaving a wet patch suggesting that the bird had disgraced itself; should Carol learn of Helen's subterfuge she would also know he'd neglected to supervise her. Carol proved to be so intent on her business accounts that she simply transferred her glance of surprise from the clock to him. "I've a job for you as long as you're here," she told Helen, and Lionel took his sudden weariness to his room.

As he fumbled for the light-switch he heard a scream. It sounded muffled, presumably by glass—by the window. He couldn't tell whether it signified delight or dismay or a confusion of both, but he would have preferred not to be greeted by it. A memory was waiting to claim him once he huddled under the quilt in the dark.

Yet had he done anything so dreadful? Days after the incident at the Imperial, her mother had taken him and Dorothy to the amusement park. On the Ghost Train his cousin had sat as far from him as the bench would allow, though when the skull-faced car had blundered into the daylight they'd pretended to be chums for her mother's camera. For her benefit they'd lent their faces to the painted couple, ancestors of the pair behind which Helen had posed. Lionel had been growing impatient with the pretence and with Dorothy's covert hostility when he'd seen all six dwarfs, dapper in suits and disproportionately generous ties, strutting towards them.

He must have been too young to imagine how she might feel, otherwise he would surely have restrained himself. He'd grabbed her shoulders, wedging her head in the oval. "Look, Dorothy," he'd whispered hotly in her ear, "they're coming for you." In what had seemed to him mere seconds he'd released her, though not before her struggles had caused her dress to ride up, exposing more of her thighs than he'd glimpsed in her room. As she'd dashed into the darkness behind the cartoon he'd heard her mother calling "Where's Lionel? Where are you going, Dorothy? What's up now?"

In time nothing much was, Lionel reassured himself: otherwise Dorothy wouldn't have invited him to spend summers at the boarding-house after she'd inherited it. Or was it quite so straightforward? He'd always thought that, having forgotten their contentious summer, she had both taken pity on his solitariness and looked to him for company once Carol had married and Dorothy's husband had succumbed to an early heart attack, but now it occurred to him that she had kept him away from her daughter. He withdrew beneath the covers as if they could hide him from his undefined guilt, and eventually sleep joined him.

He thought walking by the sea might clear his head of whatever was troubling him. There was just one family on the beach. He assumed they were quite distant until he noticed the parents were dwarfs and the children pocket versions of them. They must work in a circus, for all of their faces were painted with grins wider than their mouths, even the face of the baby that was knocking down sandcastles as it crawled about. Lionel had to toil closer, dragging his inflated toy, before he understood that the family was laughing at him. When he followed their gazes he found he was clutching by one breast the life-size naked rubber woman he'd brought to the beach.

He writhed himself awake, feeling that his mind had only started to reveal its depths. As he tried to rediscover sleep he heard a scratching at the window. It must be a bird, though it sounded like fingernails on glass, not even in that part of the room. When it wasn't repeated he managed to find his way back to sleep.

He felt he hadn't by breakfast time. Being glanced at by more people than bade him good morning left him with the impression that he looked guilty of his dream. There wasn't much more of a welcome in the kitchen, where a disagreement had evidently occurred. When Carol met his eyes while Helen didn't, he said "She'll be all right for this evening, won't she?"

"Quite a few things aren't all right, I'm afraid. Torn serviettes, for a start, and tablecloths not clean that should be." She was aiming her voice upwards as if to have it fall more heavily on Helen. "We've standards to keep up," she said.

"I think they're as high as your mother's ever were, so don't drive yourself so hard. You deserve a night or two off. Is the show at the Imperial your kind of diversion?"

"More like my idea of hell."

"Then you won't be jealous if I take Helen tonight? I've got tickets."

"You might have said sooner."

"You were busy."

"Exactly."

"I think you could both benefit from taking it easier. You and your mother managed, didn't you?"

Carol unloaded a tray into the sink with a furious clatter and twisted to face him. "You've no idea what she was like when you weren't here. Used me harder than this one ever is, and my dad as well, poor little man. No wonder he had a heart attack."

Lionel had forgotten how diminutive Dorothy's husband had been, and hadn't time to brood about it now. "Let me hold the fort while you two have an evening out," he said.

"Thanks for the offer, but this place is our responsibility. Make that mine." Carol sighed at this or as a preamble to muttering "Take her as long as you've bought tickets. As you say, I'll just have to manage."

He thought it best to respond to that with no more than a sympathetic grimace and to keep clear of her and Helen for a while. He stayed in his room no longer than was necessary to determine he had nothing to wear that would establish a holiday mood. He bought a defiantly luxuriant shirt from a shop in a narrow back street to which the town seemed reluctant to own up, and wandered with the package to the park, where he found a bench well away from the bandstand in case any of the musicians identified him as yesterday's eructating spectator. The eventual concert repeated its predecessor, which might have allowed him to catch up on his sleep if he hadn't been nervous of dreaming—of learning what his mind required unconsciousness to acknowledge it contained.

It was close to dinnertime when he ventured back to his room. Rather than examine his appearance, he left the mirror with its back to him. His new shirt raised eyebrows and lowered voices in the dining-room. At least Carol said "You're looking bright," which would have heartened him more if she hadn't rebuked Helen: "I hope you'll be dressing for the occasion as well."

Perhaps Helen had changed her black T-shirt and denim overalls and chubby shoes when he found her waiting on the pavement outside; he couldn't judge. He told her she looked a picture, and thought she was responding when she mumbled "Uncle Lionel?"

"At your service."

She peered sideways at him. "Will you be sad if I don't come with you?"

"I would indeed."

"I told Brandon last night I'd meet him. I wouldn't have if you'd said you'd got tickets."

"But you've known all day."

"I couldn't call him. Mum might have heard."

"You mustn't expect me to keep covering up for you." Lionel supposed he sounded unreasonable, having previously complained of not being let into the secret. "Very well, just this once," he said to forestall the moisture that had gathered in her eyes. "You two go and I'll meet you at the end of the performance."

"No, you. You like it."

It was clear she no longer did. "Where will you be?" he said, and immediately "Never mind. I don't want to know. Just make certain you're waiting at the end."

"I will."

She might have kissed him, but instead ran across the promenade to her boyfriend. Lionel watched them clasp hands and hurry down a ramp to the beach. He stayed on the far side of the road so as not to glimpse them as he made for the Imperial.

The stout girl in the booth seemed even more suspicious of his returning a ticket than she had been of the purchase. At last she allowed him to leave it in case it could be resold. In the auditorium he had to sidle past a family with three daughters, loud in inverse proportion to their size. He was flattening a hand beside his cheek to ward off some of the clamour of his neighbour, the youngest, when someone tapped him on the shoulder. Seated behind him were two of Carol's guests: a woman with a small face drawn tight and pale by her sharp nose, her husband whose droopy empurpled features had yet more skin to spare underneath. "Will you be stopping this show too?" the woman said.

Could she have seen Dorothy chased by the dwarfs? "I don't," Lionel said warily, "ah . . . "

"We saw you at the concert yesterday."

"Heard me, you mean." When that fell short of earning him even a hint of a grin, Lionel said "I expect I'll be able to contain myself."

The man jabbed a stubby finger at the empty seat. "On your own?"

"Like yourselves."

"Our granddaughter's one of Miss Merritt's Moppets."

His tone was more accusing than Lionel cared to understand. "Good luck to her," he said, indifferent to whether he sounded sarcastic, and turned his back.

As the curtains parted, the child beside him turned her volume up. He put the empty seat between them, only to hear the sharp-nosed woman cough with displeasure and change seats with her husband. Before long Lionel's head began to ache with trying not to wonder how Helen and her boyfriend were behaving, and he couldn't enjoy the show. He squirmed in his seat as the moppets in their white tutus pranced onstage. At least they weren't dwarfs, he thought and squirmed again, growing red-faced as another cough was aimed at him.

He had no wish to face the couple at the end of the show. He remained seated until he realised they might see Helen outside and mention it to Carol. He struggled up the packed aisle and succeeded in leaving the theatre before they did. Helen was waiting on the chipped marble steps. She half turned, and he saw she was in tears. "Oh dear," he murmured, "what now?"

"We had a fight."

"An argument, I trust you mean." When she nodded or her head slumped, he said "I'm sure it'll turn out to be just a hiccup." She only turned away, leaving him to whisper "Shall we hurry home? We don't want anybody knowing you were meant to be with me."

They were opposite the ramp down which she'd vanished with her boyfriend when she began to sob. Lionel urged her over to the far corner of her street while Carol's guests passed by. Once they'd had ample time to reach their room and Helen's sobs had faltered into silence he said "Will you be up to going in now, do you think?"

"I'll have to be, won't I?"

Her maturity both impressed and disconcerted him. Each of them pulled out a key, and he would have made a joke of it if he'd been sure she would respond. He let her open the front door and followed her in, only to flinch from bumping into her. Carol and the couple from the theatre were talking in the hall.

They fell silent and gazed at the newcomers. As Lionel struggled to decide whether he should hurry upstairs or think of a comment it would be crucial for him to make, the sharp-nosed woman said "I see you found yourself a young companion after all."

Her husband cleared his throat. Presumably he thought it helpful to tell Carol "My wife means he was on his own at the show."

Carol stared at Helen and then shifted her disapproval to Lionel. Her face grew blank before she told them "I think you should both go to bed. I'll have plenty to say in the morning."

"Mummy . . ."

"Don't," Carol said, even more harshly when Lionel tried to intervene.

"I think we'd better do as we're told," he advised Helen, and trudged upstairs ahead of her. Just now his room offered more asylum than anywhere else in the house, and he attempted to hide in his bed and the dark. His guilt was lying in wait for him—his realisation that rather than make up for anything he might have done to Dorothy, he'd let down both Carol and Helen. He heard Helen shut her door with a dull suppressed thud and listened apprehensively for her mother's footfall on the stairs. He'd heard nothing further when exhaustion allowed sleep to overtake him.

A muffled cry roused him. Heat and darkness made him feel afloat in a stagnant bath. As he strained his ears for a repetition of the cry he was afraid that it might have been Helen's—that he'd caused her mother to mistreat her in some way he winced from imagining. When he heard another sound he had to raise his shaky head before he could identify it. Some object was bumping rhythmically against glass.

He kicked off the quilt and stumbled to drag the curtains apart. There was nothing at the window, nothing to be seen through it except guest-houses slumbering beyond a streetlamp. He hauled the sash all the way up and leaned across the sill, but the street was deserted. He was peering along it when the muffled thumping recommenced behind him.

As he stalked towards it he refused to believe where it was coming from. He took hold of the mirror by its bunch of wrists, which not only felt unhealthily warm but also seemed to be vibrating slightly in time with the sound. He gripped them with both hands and turned the glass towards him. It was full of Dorothy's outraged face, glaring straight at him.

She was so intensely present that he could have thought there was no mirror, just her young woman's face balanced on the doubly paralysed hands. More and worse than shock made his arms tremble, but he was unable to drop the mirror. In a moment Dorothy's forehead ceased thudding against the glass and shrank into it as though she was being hauled backwards. The ankle-length white dress she wore—the kind of garment in which he imagined she'd been buried—was bulging vigorously in several places. He knew why before a dwarf's head poked up through the collar, ripping the fabric, to fasten on

Dorothy's mouth. His outline made it clear that he'd shinned up by holding onto her breasts. Her left sleeve tore, revealing the squarish foot of a dwarf who was inverted somewhere under the dress. Then she was borne away into darkness so complete she oughtn't to be visible, even for Lionel's benefit. He saw a confusion of feet scurrying beneath the hem. One pair vanished up the dress, and her body set about jerking in the rhythm of the dwarf who had clambered her back.

The worst thing was that Lionel recognised it all. It had lived in his mind for however many years, too deep for thought and so yet more powerful, and now Dorothy had become the puppet of his fantasy. He supposed that to be at his mercy the dwarfs were dead too. He didn't know if he was desperate to repudiate the spectacle or release the participants as he flung the mirror away from him.

It was toppling over the windowsill when he tried to snatch it back. He saw Dorothy's face plummeting out of reach as though he'd doubled her helplessness. As he craned over the sill, the button at the waist of his pyjamas snapped its thread. The mirror struck the roof of his Mini, which responded like a bass drum. One marble finger split off and skittered across the dent the impact had produced. The mirror tottered on the metal roof, and Lionel dashed out of the room.

He was scrabbling at the front-door latch while he clutched his trousers shut when he heard the mirror slide off the car and shatter. The chill of the concrete seized his bare feet like a premonition of how cold they would end up. The marble hands had been smashed into elegant slivers surrounded by fragments of glass, but the oval that had contained the mirror was intact. He hardly knew why he stooped to collect the glass in it. When his trousers sagged around his ankles he had no means of holding them up. Not until lights blazed between curtains above him did he realise that several of Carol's guests were gazing down at him.

In the morning Carol said very little to him beyond "I'm sorry you're leaving, but I won't have anyone in my house going behind my back."

This reminded him of his last glimpse of Dorothy, and he had to repress a hysterical laugh. He bumped his suitcase all the way downstairs in the hope that would bring Helen out of her room, but to no avail. "Shall I just go up and say goodbye?" he almost pleaded.

"Madam isn't receiving visitors at the moment."

He couldn't tell if that was Helen's decision or her mother's. He lugged the suitcase to the Mini and dumped it in the boot. "You're sure you don't mind if I take the mirror," he said.

"If you want to try and mend it, be my guest. I've never had any use for it," Carol said, doling him a token wave to speed him on his way before she shut herself in the house.

As the Mini backed onto the street he muttered "Here you go, old bones," crouching his lanky frame lower so that the dent in the roof didn't touch his scalp. On the seat beside him shards of glass stirred in the marble frame, but he could see nothing other than the underside of the roof in even the largest piece of mirror. He scarcely knew why he was taking the mirror with him; could it somehow help him gain control of the depths of his mind and let Dorothy go? The boarding-house swung away behind him, and he wondered what the people in it might be thinking about him worse, what they might be storing up about him unexamined in their minds. For the first time in all his years he dreaded living after death.

after the Queen

WHEN ROBERT ARRIVED IN THE SUBURBAN VILLAGE HE
was twenty minutes early for the film. He stumbled down the
hill from the cinema, fitting his heels into the cracks between the
cobbles, and surveyed the main road. Cars sped past, threshing pools
of rain; bedraggled tattered newspapers drooped from branches in the
nearby park behind railings scaly with soaked rust. Across the road,
beneath the thick night sky stained darker with its burden of rain, the
flat blackened Victorian facades were broken by a blue screen, a laun-
derette window displaying bored children; three doors away shone
the moist yellow lights of a pub. He crossed the road and entered.

He had braced himself for the burst of sound from turning heads,
but the bar was almost empty. One man sat hunched on a stool,
staring into the trademarked mirror between the headstanding bottles
of Scotch and gin above the shelves of beer; as Robert entered, the
man's gaze snapped at his reflection like tongues between wet red
trembling lips. A man in his sixties sat at a table, calmly sipping a glass
of beer. "Good evening, how are you?" he called to Robert.

"I'm fine, thanks. Pint of bitter," Robert told the mostly blonde
barmaid. "And you?" he called as an afterthought.

"Oh, well enough, you know, well enough. Yes."

"That's good," Robert said. He'd better stand at the bar, or before
he knew it he would be involved. But the man huddled before the
mirror had produced struggling from his cuffs a pair of hands like
emaciated crabs, scuttling over his coat collar and pulling it down; his
eyes probed deep into the further inch of reflection he had gained.

Chilled by a drop of rain that had threaded itself through his spine, Robert sat down at a table.

"Could you undo these, please? I'm sorry." Robert glanced up; the man at the other table was holding a packet of Woodbines from whose cellophane his fragile flaking nails had slipped. Robert took the packet carefully, but their fingers touched.

"It's extremely good of you. Have one—go on, please." Their fingers touched again; Robert managed not to flinch. "I seem to have mislaid my matches," the man said.

Robert drew his gun; a flame sprang from the barrel. "Is that Austrian? I was in Austria once, a long time ago," the man said, cupping his hand about Robert's, "One day I should like to see Austria again. Do you live round here?"

"I've come to see a film," Robert told him, gulping beer.

"Oh, yes. There are some good films. At the cinema across the way?"

"That's right," Robert said, taking a breath before the last mouthful.

"I was thinking of going over there myself."

"I didn't mean the cinema just across the road," Robert said hurriedly, staring fascinated at the eyes in the mirror, restless and frantic as if caged. "I meant the one a few streets away."

"I can't say I know that one. Which one is that?" But Robert's throat was open, mute and working beneath the upturned tankard. "Have another on me," the man said.

"I'd like to, but I must rush."

The man touched Robert's elbow. "Don't let him trouble you," he whispered, glancing at the man before the mirror. "He's nervous, that's all. Always was."

"I guessed as much," Robert said. "Well, thank you for the cigarette. I'll see you again."

A breeze wrinkled the puddles. Deep in the park, a portable radio wavered with song and a grey sodden newspaper tore free of a branch. Robert crossed the bare polished road and followed a loud fragmented group of teenagers up the hill.

The cinema slanted with the slope; one poster for *The Dummies of Horror* had been pasted at a tangent with the horizon, but in another the silently shrieking girl and the closing circle of gleeful waxworks seemed in danger of toppling in a heap into the corner of the frame. The pay-box had held its own against the slope, but Robert had to pace uphill, ticket in hand, to reach the entrance of the auditorium— no balcony, only a long stretch of stalls. One girl slipped back giggling against Robert as her soles betrayed her; he grasped her shoulders briefly, steadying, and entered the cinema.

He wasn't sure whether he was levering his way uphill along the row of seats; when he sat down the screen was level with the plane of his vision. The lights were dimming; shadows thickened on the faces around him, ageing them like paper. Or perhaps his eyes were merely bewildered by the subdued light. He accumulated details of the cinema: on either side of the screen, pillars winding their way to the ceiling like overfed pale vines; a dark tear in the curtain across the screen; a gaping hole in a row here and there where a seat had been extracted; couples scraping ice-cream from plastic cartons, many more clustering about the bright light of the ice-cream tray: new arrivals bumping vociferously into unfolded seats.

All at once the lights flickered out; the first advertisement danced blurred on the masked screen and struggled clear within the hole in the curtain; the curtains creaked open and a red firefly leapt from the front stalls—no, a cigarette butt thrown to smoulder before the screen. Robert watched the second-hand transient colours. An anonymous middle-aged man was digging a garden, his wife was carrying him a cup of tea, followed by their children wary of the camera—"For the best gardening tools in town, come to Worthington and Brown!" Robert's gaze wandered to the minute heads bobbing along the foot of the screen, to the red electric Gents'. Ah, yes. He stood up, patted his coat and left it to guard his seat. As he walked down the aisle to the edge of the screen, the image closed into itself, flattened into two dimensions; yet, he mused, the figures within moved untroubled.

He washed his hands and tried to coax a clean inch from the roller towel. The cubicle of cracked tiles was hidden directly behind the screen; the walls resounded with the opening music of the feature, surrounding Robert as closely as if he were in the film. He hurried into the auditorium to regain his seat. As he strode through the audience he felt oddly troubled: the cinema was canted slightly, he was sure, and the askew intent faces were like waxworks, immobile, on which the screen sprayed colours for effect. He toiled to his seat and sat down.

The man had wagered that he could spend a night alone in the waxwork museum. At midnight he sat among the aisles of postured figures, reading the newspaper for which he wrote. The figures were too still; nobody could hold such poses without shifting occasionally: such an effort required a daunting singleness of purpose. He turned a page and started at the crackle of sound. Then he dropped the newspaper. He was sure that he'd heard something else—a faint breath of linen from the Victorian aisle.

He tiptoed in that direction, followed relentlessly by the camera. Jack the Ripper's victim lay, one arm flung almost into the aisle, eyes closed. The linen fluttered again. The journalist climbed over the rope around the scene and bent closer to the girl. Behind him, a finger trembled and flexed. He peered at the girl's face. Her eyes sprang open, and she grinned. As he leapt away from her, Jack the Ripper loomed at his back.

Robert had once read a similar story which perhaps had suggested the film. But this was only the pre-credit sequence. After the title the journalist's unmarked body was discovered; his girlfriend wept and mourned for the first five minutes but then was comforted by the journalist's friend, who suspected the proprietor of the museum—some species of foul play to gain publicity, perhaps. The police wouldn't listen, of course, so they would have to resort to other methods. Near the screen something hollow rattled; a skeleton was running back and forth along a row of seats. Eventually Robert realised what it was: the arms of the seats were hollow, and eight teenagers were fending off boredom with their xylophone. Robert swore; they'd intruded on the reality of the film, were trying to render it unreal because they could offer it no reality. At the waxworks the couple insinuated themselves into the crowd. He began to pin the proprietor down with questions, but the pins kept falling out; she leaned over the rope and examined Jack the Ripper as the crowd drifted away. She reached out to touch him, and the knife fell from his hand to quiver in the floor. She fainted.

And a man hurried into a cinema and paid, urged on by the camera at his shoulder. Robert sat up, frowning. The audience was bored but silent; they hadn't noticed the projectionist's blunder. They were empty, Robert thought: less real than the film. The man entered the empty auditorium, and the film was snuffed out; the image persisted for a moment, framed in a sudden rectangle of blackness. The invisible audience stamped and whistled. An ice-cream carton trundled down the sloping row and halted baffled at Robert's feet; he kicked it away. The soundtrack reared up and the film recommenced. The couple had hidden among the waxworks; the museum was locked for the night. They padded down the aisles, seeking evidence that the dummies had been moved, propelled perhaps towards their dead friend to terrify him. Robert stared down on them from above. They were surrounded by a labyrinth of hands arrested as they gestured or stretched out, of eyes which glinted alertly but seemed still.

He knew the couple was trapped, but he was helpless. Then he found himself between them as they talked, decided to separate and explore again; he was yet more frightened, and struggled to be free. But when he looked down on them once more as they parted and paced away like duellists, he almost cried out. From above he could see that the waxworks had closed in unnoticed; every aisle was a cul-de-sac.

He realised at once what had happened. The dead journalist had infected the dummies with his own introverted terror; they were puppets of his death, and moved now as they sensed fear. The girl turned. The end of the aisle at which she had entered was blocked by a guillotined corpse. She gasped and began to run in the other direction; but Crippen stood there, a little abashed. Her friend was yards away; she could scarcely be further from him; but she froze at the thought of running the gauntlet of those treacherous pale wax hands, ready to move as soon as she turned her back. She screamed. And staring down, pulse thumping, Robert saw that the man was also boxed in.

Of course there was a happy ending. The museum's manager had heard sounds and had phoned the police. Shuddering, the couple explained that they'd had themselves locked in to win a bet. One policeman lit a cigarette, whirled around at a noise he might have heard, and the light from the flung match fled up Marie Antoinette's skirt. As the altercation continued outside the blazing museum, the couple slipped away and kissed—but the Queen leapt through their approaching lips to smile between the closing curtains as from a vignette. The audience avoided her eyes and hurried out; Robert strode down the aisle to the tiled cubicle.

When he emerged the cinema was empty, long and regimented as a barrack-hall. Many seats were still down, waiting, as if the audience might at any moment return. The smoking light was yellow and stained as a wash-leather. Robert began to plod up the tilted aisle. Through the dim windows of the projection booth he glimpsed movement. The projectionist was crouching. Robert couldn't see his head, nor indeed anything recognisable as a framed limb. Robert had passed only the first few rows when the lights began to flicker out.

Don't worry, I'm leaving, he was ready to shout. Then his shadow was trailed before him, pulled out of shape by the cant of the screen. He turned to determine the source of the light. The curtains had crept back, and a film was moving blurred about the screen.

Robert groped his way to a seat. The film was the one he'd seen briefly adumbrated half an hour ago. Gradually the blur cleared. This could hardly be the opening of the film; it must be an amputated reel included by mistake, which the projectionist, curious, was running through. The man on the screen had found a seat in the cinema; Robert squinted at his face but was unable to make it out. Then he was gazing at the back of the man's head from far behind him in the cinema, perhaps from the projection box. Oddly, the screen that confronted the man was blank and shadowed.

After a minute or so, still gazing, he wondered what the man's head was meant to communicate. If this were an experimental film, it failed to reach him. Robert rested his hands on the arms of the seat, patted them twice and made to stand up. At that instant he discovered that the camera was stealthily moving towards the seated man.

He strained his eyes again at the man's face, but it remained dark and featureless as the screen within the screen. Suddenly he knew it was not the man's face that should concern him. He glanced about the cinema within the screen. It looked remarkably like the one in which he was sitting, and he wondered briefly whether the film had been shot there—by the projectionist, perhaps.

The ranks of darkness within the screen seemed empty. Before Robert could reassure himself, however, he was once more behind the man and creeping unwillingly closer. The closing empty frame menaced him, like the walls of a murderous room. Empty, yet not quite; at the foot of the stealthy screen clung a hirsute blot of fluff, an intruder on the projector's lens.

Robert had been dragged to within a few feet of the man. In a minute he would leave: as soon as his prickling hands relinquished their grip on the arms of the seat. Again he found himself staring into the oval of darkness that was the man's face. Still the rows at the man's back were empty, though his head and shoulders blocked that part of the cinema directly behind him. The screen's frame was clean; the projectionist had blown the fluff from the lens. No, there it was, creeping with Robert towards the back of the man's head. They were barely a foot away now. At any moment he must turn. The blot of fluff rose up behind him, swaying and quivering.

Robert had grabbed his coat and had run to the front of the cinema, to the exit beneath the screen, before he saw that the double doors were padlocked shut. He whirled. The tiered rows flickered faintly with the film. They were empty. All of them. Though he couldn't see them clearly, he was sure they were empty. He couldn't count them, but there were a great many to run past. His back was to the screen; the film must be reaching its climax unseen. For some reason he felt chilled, and ran back to his seat.

He threw his coat over the back of the next row; but losing its hold, it slipped heavily to the floor. Distracted, Robert stooped to catch it up. As he rose he glanced overhead and froze, crouching. Above him the cinema was dark. No beam of light linked the projector and the screen.

Gasping, Robert turned directly to the screen. The man's head had twisted back over his shoulder. His expression was invisible; there was no sound. A second later the screen blanked out, leaving Robert in total darkness.

He fell into the aisle and trembled between the rows, alert, straining the darkness for sounds. His feet inched forward, towards the unseen exit. Then he remembered his coat. He snatched it from the row, and a seat slammed back. Robert started and almost yelled aloud. The silence held for a moment; then there came a sound of seats closing one by one, a rattle of hollow armrests, rapidly approaching him.

If he hadn't reasoned frantically that the first seat had disturbed the others like ninepins, Robert would have been convinced that something was pursuing him along the arms of the seats. He bundled his coat together and began to walk up the aisle, faster, faster. His thudding feet were vibrating the seats, for the armrests rattled as soon as he had passed.

He panted upward, through the darkness. Each rattle was closer. All at once he knew why: his feet on the tilted floor were being guided blindly towards the seats with each step. He corrected his path as best he could and laboured onward. The next armrest to rattle was closer than ever.

Closing his eyes, he ran. He had not run three steps when the corner of a row struck him, punching the breath from him. He fell.

His fingers crept forward over the rough fabric carpeting the aisle. He knew they must touch something. A spent match, a fragment of crackling cellophane, the cold iron supporting a seat. Above him an armrest creaked and rattled faintly, as if someone perched or leaning on it had shifted restlessly, waiting.

He recoiled, stuttering. He splayed out his fingers to thrust himself to his feet. He was staggering sightlessly when the auditorium doors exploded open and a carpet of light unrolled swiftly towards him. "Come on! I can't find the light switch!" a man shouted. "Not much further! Come on!"

Robert ran wildly, focusing himself on the centre of the track of light, never glancing into the darkness beyond. In the bright foyer he dragged the exit doors shut and turned shaking to the man who had befriended him in the pub. "Thank you," Robert said, gripping his hand. "Thank you."

"You'll be all right," the man said. "It's happened before."

"But does the manager know?" Robert demanded. "Why doesn't someone tell him?"

"Oh, the manager," the man said, pointing to an open pale-green door next to the pay-box. "Don't you see? He was the first. He knows if anyone does."

Robert stumbled forward and peered in. The manager had his back to him; but his frantic eyes met Robert's again for a second in the mirror above his desk before they withdrew and began once more to brood.

Tatters

"PERFECT," GOLDMAN SAID. THE GENTLE DAWN LIGHT lent the bricks of the warehouse apartments a glow as contented as a fire in a hearth. Across the river, which might have been holding itself still to be filmed, the faintly misted city waterfront was a dream of prosperity. Above the skyline that was scribbled with distant lines of trees interrupted by three church spires a reddish sun was edging into view. "Mark," he called.

Simonette brandished the clapperboard but kept its wooden jaws locked as she blinked over her shoulder. "What's that?"

A shadow was advancing faster than the sun along the alley between the warehouse they were about to film and its neighbour. Goldman held up a hand to delay Stephanie Maple beyond the black glass doors of the lobby, and the spectator halted out of sight. "Filming in progress, please," Goldman shouted. "Mark."

Simonette named the shot and clapped the board with a sound that drove only half the anxiety out of her small fragile face. Vane; shrugged the camera an inch higher and squinted through the viewfinder while Lezly planted her dungareed legs apart and waited to dangle the microphone over the actress, who swung open the glass doors, just failing to catch reflections of the film crew. She turned up her wide-lipped smile by fractions of an inch as she strode towards the camera. "Welcome to—"

For a breath Goldman was entranced by how graceful she seemed even at rest, her long pale face smooth as marble scarcely hinting at impatience while her blonde hair glinted in a breeze that left the rest of her tall slim lavender-suited form unmoved, and then he grew aware of the interruption, a voice almost tuneless enough to be merely speaking:

"They come down to the water

To buy themselves a flat.

They've got no room for thin ones here.

Just make way for the fat . . . "

The ballad and the shadow retreated down the alley as Simonette made for them so vigorously one of her pigtails began to unravel. She vanished into a silence that everyone watched until she reappeared. "I can't find anyone," she complained, blinking faster.

"I expect you chased them off," Goldman said, dismissing whatever fool it had been, and turned to his star. "Go again?"

"You're the director."

Simonette picked up her makeup box and was minutely restoring Stephanie Maple's face when Vane; shrugged his free shoulder. "Shot's gone. Too much sun."

"Could you talk us through your flat now, Stephanie, and we'll shoot you coming out same time tomorrow if we aren't putting you to too much trouble?"

The actress inserted her card in the lock to admit them to the lobby. Like the discreetly lit staircase and corridors, it was built of exposed bricks, as though the development was reverting to a past that had never quite existed. No doubt while the warehouses were derelict the walls had been too bare for anyone except the squatters, who would have had bottles and syringes to distract them.

Stephanie Maple led the camera up to her third-floor apartment, where the unplastered walls were adorned with Oriental paintings. Goldman thought those and the austerity with which she'd furnished the huge rooms—dining kitchen, social and recreational area, jacuzzi and amenities room, twin identical bedrooms—ought to appeal to the Japanese developers. Vane; made the most of them while she enthused about them, declaring that they represented what was new and best about the town and vowing she would never abandon her roots despite the international success of her latest film, *Running Mummy,* in which she played an athlete coping with the demands of single motherhood. "And cut," Goldman called at last, close to being mesmerised by the sound of her musical voice in a film of his. "That's it except for the view."

He made his way between two low stark tables to the window even wider than the television. The wind had risen, shattering the track of sunlight on the water. A figure at the river's edge was silhouetted against the ripples, which made it look tattered from head to foot and too thin. It did nothing for the shot, thought Goldman. "We'll leave it till tomorrow," he said.

"Stephanie Maple seems to think I'm the genuine article."

"You'll have to come and talk to my film students."

"I will when I've made enough to impress them."

"You've already done that to me, Jonathan, but I'm only a lecturer."

"I'm not quite Hitchcock yet, Ruth. Once I've got more of a name in advertising, maybe I can make the kind of films I dream about."

"We don't need any hitches, and the rest of you is fine."

The germ of coyness in her voice and in her smile that held back from owning up to itself signified that she wanted to make love before dinner. Goldman followed her into their small bedroom that was cluttered mostly with her clothes, piled on the ironing-board or waiting their turn for space in the solitary wardrobe or the stuffed chest of drawers. She stripped before he could offer to perform the ritual, and then she lay on the plump quilt, her round face framed by a spread of determinedly reddish tresses, her small breasts flattening themselves above sketched ribs, her wide lips and strong broad legs slightly parted. Goldman undressed and went to her with an urgency designed to convince his body as well as Ruth. They weren't overweight, he told himself. All the same, he kept remembering the uninvited ballad that had ruined his first shot of the day—kept almost hearing it and feeling he just had.

They gasped together and lay joined until Goldman's breathing began to lag behind Ruth's. A notion that he still ought to placate her inspired him to suggest dining out or bringing in, but she made it plain he should have known she'd prepared dinner. The vegetables were stubbornly tough, the lamb chops offered a choice of a blackened surface or a pinkish one. Goldman did his best to seem to have no difficulty, and only when the task was more than half complete risked saying "I'll have to be up before dawn again tomorrow."

Ruth pinched the lapels of her housecoat together over her bare breasts and gazed at him across the heavy unclothed second-hand table that occupied a little too much of the room. "What is it this time?"

"More of the same, I'm afraid. Well, not afraid, but the same."

"Another session with your local performer, you mean."

"I think she's a bit more than that, do you? I'm lucky to have her. Don't you think it's good of her to give her services to the community that produced her?"

"I shouldn't imagine there's much of that left." Ruth worried a chop before dropping the bone on her plate. "I thought you were getting all you wanted today," she said.

"There were distractions."

"I'm sure."

They made room for each other while they washed up after dinner. When Ruth caught him glancing at the warehouses across the river, Goldman blurted "It shouldn't matter where you live, just who with." She suffered his hug, and so he ventured to admit "I wouldn't mind going to bed soon."

"I presume you won't object if I stay up and mark some essays."

"We've both got our jobs," said Goldman and sheltered in bed, though it had stored up a chill. Some light seeped in from the living-room, along with the street noise of rowdies who might well have been rehoused from across the water, but he was most aware of how the inside of his throat felt scraped by the beginnings of a cold. He kept checking its ability to swallow until sleep swallowed him. After finding himself alone in bed a few times he began to be regurgitated next to Ruth, which eventually meant he could head off the alarm from rousing her. At least his throat felt no worse, and a hasty shower helped wake him up. He dressed and hurried through a medley of feline smells from the downstairs neighbour's menagerie to ensure Vançc had no excuse for sounding his horn.

In fact the van with PHOENIX PICTURES ON LOCATION on its sides didn't turn up for almost half an hour, by which time Goldman was shivering at the sight of his breath and failing to locate what sounded like someone attempting to carry a tune in their sleep. Simonette and Lezly were sprawled in the back of the van with their equipment between them, and mumbled as Goldman climbed into the front. "It'll be worth beating the dawn for," he felt required to promise.

From the heart of the business district a tunnel-an artery white as the monumental buildings—led under the river to emerge near a square mile of houses the council used to own. Newly made up, every street looked eager to be photographed, while the tenants had been sent across the water to make room for the young and increasingly prosperous employees of a Japanese electronics firm. The far side of the estate was overlooked by the warehouse apartments, where Stephanie Maple stepped out of the lobby as the film crew unloaded the van. Was that a shadow in the alley to her left, a shadow too long and thin even for the hour and very unsteadily outlined? A glance showed Goldman none, but he hurried to reassure himself that wasn't just because the sun had moved. "Whenever you're ready," he called from the alley, and withdrew out of range of the camera.

"Welcome to Riverhaven Apartments," the actress said, "city living for the new millennium, where good jobs and better leisure are just a stroll away from home." She came out of the building a third time to repeat herself in case there had been any problem, and then Vançc ran upstairs to film the last of the dawn from her window. Once the view was captured Goldman said "We're truly grateful to you, Stephanie. I'd love to buy you dinner if you're free, if everyone is."

"It would have to be tonight," the actress said.

Vançc and Simonette proved to be meeting people together, Lezly by herself. After the briefest of silences Stephanie Maple raised her smile. "Shall we say the Japanese along the waterfront?"

Ruth had said more than once she would like to try that restaurant, which was why for the rest of the day Goldman was distracted from editing the film by rehearsing how he should approach her. It might have been too much rehearsal that produced "I don't suppose you'd want to go out for dinner."

"Any night except tonight. I still haven't caught up with my marking."

"Only Stephanie Maple, well, I think she'd like to celebrate successful teamwork."

"Then of course you must go. I'll see to myself, don't worry."

The kiss with which Stephanie Maple greeted him at her door, having remotely admitted him to the apartments, felt like a re-enactment of Ruth's token aloha. At least neither woman ought to catch the cold that was massing like a storm of sneezes in his head. Though the apartment block threatened him with sweating, he could have lived without the enthusiastic compensation of the night air. "We'll stroll it, shall we?" the actress said with what he was surely mistaken to see as a disappointed glance at his Volkswagen.

The short walk along the riverside to the Western Dawn led them past warehouses yet to be renovated. From the depths of one hulk riddled with darkness Goldman thought he heard a mutter that might, given time, have settled on a melody. "Did you . . . "

"What's that, Jonathan?"

"I expect nothing. I mean, I expect it was either me or a tramp."

"No comparison," the actress said with almost too instant a smile.

He tried to open the door of the restaurant for her, but a waiter was ahead of him. Goldman hoped he hadn't offended the man by holding onto the door. The waiter betrayed no emotion as he showed them to the corner of an extensive metal-topped table and, having given them ample time to appreciate the view of the lit city founded on its own bright inversion, brought them menus swarming with ideograms interspersed with translations. "This is kind," Stephanie Maple murmured.

"It's my pleasure," Goldman assured her, largely to suppress his terror at the prices, and was uncontrollably prompted to urge her to order the most expensive items on the menu, then couldn't draw attention to this by ordering more cheaply for himself. As the waiter chopped ingredients in front of them between juggling food and knives Goldman grew aware of having remarked "Lots of tossing, eh?"

"Most people like a bit of spectacle," Stephanie Maple told him.

After that he felt bound to applaud the performance. Having sampled his dwarfish dinner, which seemed reluctant to admit to much taste, he had to say "Good?"

"All I expected."

"Good enough. I'm really pleased we got together." He hoped that was sufficient excuse for him to add "I'd really like to work with you again on something more substantial."

"I prefer younger directors."

"Even younger than me, you mean?"

Her look might have been a rebuke for denigrating himself if it wasn't for the reverse. Once she'd finished a delicate mouthful she said "There could be a chance for you on my next film."

"That would be great," he said, but too much of his attention was entangled in the faint hovering Japanese music or rather in its background. Beneath the tinny plucking and the undercurrent of conversation, most of it Japanese, he heard a discordant voice:

"They chuck your food up in the air
And throw it on the table.
You smile at everything they serve
And swallow if you're able . . . "

Goldman managed to prove to himself that he could before demanding "Can you hear that?"

"I was hearing you."

He had to assume it was a symptom of fever, a thought that seemed to gather most of the heat of the restaurant under his arms. Rather than dab his forehead with his napkin, he excused himself and headed for the toilets identified by a plaque of a samurai warrior. Several Japanese businessmen in suits as dark as the tiles were conversing across the wide room. Goldman stooped to the nearest sink and was splashing cold water on his face when a stupendous sneeze overwhelmed him. A mirror showed him his face dripping not only with water. "Sorry," he choked, snatching a wad of toilet paper out of a cubicle to blow his nose. Once the prolonged routine was completed he went back to the actress, explaining "Just a sneeze and a blow, that was all."

"Not in front of anyone, I hope."

"Why not?" he said, almost remembering.

"It's a terrible insult to blow your nose around Japanese people."

He didn't dare look away from her. "Tell me about this film of years," he came close to pleading.

"It's about a young couple who move into apartments where all the other tenants are criminals. They want to kill the couple for finding out too much but a hit-man's mother tries to protect them. *Hitting It Off*, that's the working title. We may film some of it round here. That's why I thought of you."

"Sounds like a hit. I'm happy I impressed you so much." When she laid her cool hand on his clammy one he asked "Is there someone I should contact?"

"I'll see to that."

Goldman felt it would be ungracious to enquire further. He was relieved to be eventually outside despite the onslaught of night air. "Shall we?" he said.

He meant only to encourage her to move, but she turned from admiring the slow dance of the dim capsized city to give him a look he thought reminiscent of her touch. "We might," she said, and as her card protruded like a coy tongue from the slot beside the lobby entrance "Will you come up?"

"If you'd—Don't say that."

"I didn't mean to confuse you."

"You haven't," he declared without the least sense whether it was true. "Am I all you're hearing?"

"You've got my attention," she said, demonstrating with a wide-eyed gaze that she was unaware of the muffled repetition of a tuneless song in the nearest empty warehouse or inside his equally lightless skull:

"You've got yourself into her life,
You've got into her head.
You'll be inside her body next
And maybe in her bed . . ."

"I won't tonight." Goldman didn't know if he was responding to the song or to the invitation until he added "You don't want my cold."

"Let me know what your backers think of our little film."

"I'm sure they'll fall in love with it even if they don't show it," Goldman said, "show what they feel, I mean," and left her with a kiss that barely made contact. Throughout the drive home his brain stayed clogged with the same inharmonious doggerel. When he admitted himself to the flat he barely heard Ruth's somnolent mumble from the bedroom. "Good evening," it was more likely she asked than said.

"Everything it should have been." Hearing her respond only with measured breaths he took to indicate she was asleep, Goldman retreated to the bathroom, where he could deal with the ballad or the feverish memory of it, he couldn't tell which. "That's a lie," he reiterated until he felt quiet enough to lie beside Ruth.

The morning before the films were to be screened for the developers, Goldman and the crew watched once again and agreed they'd done their best work: the most pointedly edited, the best paced, seductive in their simplicity, the equal of anything of the kind the team had seen . . . "I just want to glance at the footage we didn't use," he cleared his throat to croak.

"Don't you think we made the right choices?" Simonette said with as many blinks as words.

"I'm sure we did." While he was in charge of editing, he always consulted the others. "I think this is the start of our real careers. I only want to check why we didn't use a shot," he said, leading them out of the screening room, where a widescreen television faced two rows of a few old cinema seats, and through the small office into the even smaller editing room.

He watched Stephanie Maple begin "Welcome to—" and fall silent, gazing at him. He ran the shot again and cocked his head so close to the screen he could feel heat rising from it, unless that was fever. "You didn't catch it, then," he said.

"She froze," Lezly retorted, fists on hips.

"No, I mean you didn't catch what stopped her."

"As I remember, you did."

"Only because we were being interrupted. You'll confirm that, Simonette. You went to find whoever it was."

"That's because you looked as if you thought there was somebody," Simonette told him, blinking yet faster.

"One of you must have heard them." When the crew only gazed at him as he coughed and finished coughing, Goldman grabbed the phone. Machines were answering at Stephanie Maple's apartment and on her mobile. He asked both to have her call him and looked up to find the crew watching him. "Would you like some of us to do the presentation?" Vanç said.

"That's still my job," said Goldman, nevertheless adding "Anyway, this will sell itself." He filled his briefcase with copies of the tape and its accompanying glossy brochure and hurried to his car, inside which the March day seemed unreasonably warm. He drove out of the business park beside the tunnel mouth on the renovated side of the river and through the streets of council houses rendered youthful, and left the Volkswagen just out of sight of Teshagihara Enterprises. It wasn't a first impression he cared to make.

The harbourmaster's old building had been turned into offices. A window broad as the reception area contemplated the mouth of the river. While the receptionist, who looked hardly older than school age, hurried to announce him, Goldman kept imagining that the attempts of the air conditioning to relieve the heat were the winds that stirred the waves. He remembered not to bow first to the young executive who came to usher him into the conference room.

It was panelled in pale wood and almost full of a long table and a dozen Japanese businessmen. Though Goldman was wearing his best dark suit, their unobtrusive elegance made him feel overheated because overdressed. "This is Mr Teshagihara," his usher said, having introduced himself as Mr Ichikawa. "I will translate."

Goldman bowed and mumbled an effusive greeting and did less of both to the rest of the men, most of whose names also sounded as if they contained a sneeze, not the only reason why he kept fearing sternutation was about to ambush him. He was almost sure he recognised Mr Teshagihara and several of his minions from the toilet at the

Western Dawn, and couldn't tell whether their lack of expression confirmed it. He had to force himself not to allow a tickling in his throat to cut short his introduction to the film. He was slipping a tape into the projector when his briefcase shrilled.

Ought he to have switched his mobile off, or would it show he was in demand? "Excuse me," he said to Mr Teshagihara with no visible effect, and extracted the phone. "Goldman."

"Jonathan? It's Stephanie. How did your presentation go?"

"I'm in it now."

"Sorry, I thought you might have called to let me know about it. Shall I leave you to wow them?"

"Just very quickly, and don't for a moment think it's a criticism, but can you remind me why you stopped in the middle of your first take?"

"I should think you'd know."

"As I say, remind me."

"I thought you were looking at me to stop. I like to have that kind of rapport with my director."

"But you heard something as well," Goldman insisted with a vigour that made his mouth and throat itch.

"Only your clapper girl running off where you were looking and saying there was nobody."

"That doesn't mean—" All the businessmen were gazing at him, he couldn't tell how patiently. "I'll ring you back when, afterwards," he said and switched the phone off. "That was my star. Let's let her do the talking."

He didn't trust himself to say more. His head was a clammy balloon filled with bewilderment and tickling. He started the tape and tried to admire its image on the wall-sized screen as much as he was sure his clients would. The several promotions were all introduced by Stephanie Maple, some exhibiting her apartment, others the surrounding amenities and growth of opportunity. He would have been happy to let them speak for themselves without the constant muffled accompaniment, a ballad less in any tune at every recurrence:

"You've captured their attention,
So show them what you've got.
Just remember you must never ever

Let them glimpse your snot . . . "

His audience couldn't hear it, he tried to reassure himself. It sounded as though it was skulking rat-like in the walls. He struggled to ignore it and the cold it was threatening to aggravate while Mr Teshagihara discussed matters in Japanese with his subordinates. Eventually he addressed Goldman at length before Mr Ichikawa said "Mr Teshagihara is grateful to you for helping him see clearly."

"I'm glad." When a pause brought nothing further, Goldman asked "How?"

"He sees now the apartments are too large. It will be more efficient to build many smaller ones, Mr Teshagihara says."

"In the warehouses you haven't done yet, you mean. You'll want us to film them when you have, then."

Mr Ichikawa's face remained impassive as he turned to his superior. After an exchange that gave Goldman time to hear the singer's voice grow hoarse with repetition, the executive said "Mr Teshagihara will use your shortest film."

"Punchier, does he think?"

Mr Ichikawa lowered his voice as though confiding a rebuke. "Mr Teshagihara prefers not to see the Chinese rooms."

It became apparent to Goldman that it wasn't enough for Stephanie Maple's apartment to look Oriental-that he wasn't alone in committing a gaffe. "So you'll be using our film to be going on with," he said hastily, "and can you give me any idea when you'll want us to shoot the rest of the development?"

Mr Teshagihara emitted a loud protracted sniff that Goldman told himself couldn't be a signal to his underling to say "Mr Teshagihara will hire another company to do that. Your film will go on local television."

"All over the country, you mean?" Goldman said louder than the meeting appeared to like, but failed to blot out the ballad.

"Your local television."

"But it only reaches a few miles. That wasn't all you asked me for."

Mr Ichikawa communicated some version of this to his superior, who reached stone-faced into a folder for papers that were handed along the table to Goldman. The succession of expressionless faces beneath which they passed made him feel trapped in a masked

Japanese play about commerce. He was leafing in feverish search of a
loophole through the contract that gave Teshagihara Enterprises sole
choice of film and its exhibition when Mr Teshagihara uttered a
prolonged especially liquid sniff and then a sentence. "Mr Teshagihara
will honour what he signed," Mr Ichikawa said.

Presumably he was translating the words rather than the sniff, but it
was the latter that stayed with Goldman. "It's not about honour. It's
about this," he said, jerking two fingers close to his packed nostrils,
and when his voice fell short of obscuring the ballad, joined in. "It's
about don't let them glimpse your snot. Never mind staring at me. It
isn't as if you lot seem to know much about tunes either."

All the consonants of the last word were swept away by a Godzilla
of a sneeze. The contents of his nose sprayed the air and spilled down
his face. For an instant he felt withered by shame, and then he
snatched back the hand that was flinching from finding a handkerchief. "We've got that in common at least," he said and, having wiped
his face on the contract, used it to blow his nose. He crumpled the
pages and shied them at a waste-bin as he backed away from all the
faces he'd provoked into showing emotion. "Don't forget honour," he
said, shutting the door on the sight of them.

Had he placated his tormentor in some way? The only sound that
met him outside the building was a rustle of unseen litter. "This is my
car for anyone who'd like to know," he shouted, and drove home. He
could think of nowhere he wanted to go except bed.

A phone was ringing as he let himself into the house, which no
doubt persisted in smelling of cats. When he realised the phone was
upstairs he dashed to unlock the flat and seize the receiver. "Goldman," he said as clearly as his head allowed.

"Tell us it didn't happen."

"Lezly. You'd rather it didn't, you're saying. You want to make real
films."

"Why would we be saying any crap like that? We want to make
films people see."

"I think we've just done that, haven't we?" Goldman said loud
enough to be heard in the street, where a song seemed to have insinuated itself into a riot of children released from school:

"You've finished making things look good,
And all you made was trouble.
You might as well have given up
And lived among the rubble . . . "

"What do you know about it?" Goldman snarled, and was about to assure Lezly that wasn't aimed at her when she retorted "Everything. The clients faxed us."

"And told us what exactly?" Goldman said, feeling as though he was adding a line to the song.

"They'll pay the contract minimum but they won't let any of the films be shown. Vane; rang to see if he could change their mind and got the feeling you'd offended them somehow."

"I did my best. Forget them. I'd rather work with people more like us. Can you keep some news to yourselves till it breaks?"

"Let's find out."

"It looks as if I'll be directing Stephanic's next feature. You know I'll want you all involved. Forgive me, I ought to have told her you came with the deal."

"We'll need to discuss it."

"We will," Goldman said and pushed himself to his feet by replacing the receiver. The tuneless ballad felt like fog growing solid in his head. Sprinting hotly to the window, he dragged the sash up. Schoolchildren were dodging traffic and scattering litter. The song had trailed off, but for a moment Goldman thought a windblown assortment of papers was a bony figure crawling into an alley. Then he caught sight of Ruth.

She saw him, and her cheerful preoccupied march missed a step while she waved. Goldman was still at the window when she dumped her bag of papers on the creaky sofa. "You're home early," she said.

"Would you rather I weren't here?"

"What on earth makes you ask that?" She took his blazing face in her cool hands. "You're in a strange mood," she said. "Aren't we celebrating?"

"Because I'm directing Stephanic's next film we can if you like, but today's lot don't want what we made for them."

"Oh, Jonathan." He saw her consider enquiring about it and put her questions on hold, instead hugging him and then, with some urgency, rather more than hugging. "We've still got us," she said.

"I don't think you want that much of me just now. I come with a cold, you'll have noticed."

"It's part of you. I expect I'll have caught whatever I'm going to catch."

He didn't feel equal to an argument or, worse, the postponement of one. He led her into the bedroom and, having undressed her as lingeringly as she liked, struggled free of his own humid clothes. The hint of ribs above the wider rest of her left him feeling hot and flabby by comparison, but little else. He knelt between her legs and tried to think of words to murmur while caressing her, but had made little headway along either line when she said "What can you hear?"

"You," he said desperately, dealing her a kiss that felt close to a sneeze. He thought he was safe to mumble another response under cover of it, but Ruth twisted her head aside, crying "What did you say?"

"Nothing."

"You didn't touch who?"

"Nobody," Goldman pleaded, not loud enough to blot out the repetition of the song beneath the window of the next room:

"Just tell her everything you did
Was only for your art.
You didn't take your actress out
And hope she was a tart . . . "

"I didn't and she isn't," he blustered. "Christ, can't you hear that, Ruth?"

"I've heard enough, I think," she said, drawing her legs together and away from him as if they might be needed to support her face, which had grown heavy and slack. "Maybe you were right after all."

"I am. You have to see I am." When she gazed sadly at him he demanded "How?"

"I think I'd rather you weren't here."

"Anything else you want to do to me?" he screamed, lurching into the next room to crane his top half out of the window. A gang of children jeered at him, and one improved on pointing at him by lobbing a plastic bottle in his direction. Its empty clatter failed to distract him from the song that was persisting somewhere up the street. He slammed the window and stumbled into the bedroom. "I wasn't talking about you just now," he tried to assure Ruth.

"Oh, I don't believe you've done that for a while."

"I haven't time for this," he muttered, pulling on his clothes and their clamminess. "I'm going to find—I'm going to—" His inability to explain tethered him to Ruth, though she wasn't looking at him. "All right, goodbye," he blurted and ran downstairs.

The night air might have relieved the heat that made him smell like a tomcat, but he'd hardly set about chasing the unseen singer when he began to feel marinated in sweat. He was sure he knew where his tormentor was bound. Sprinting back to his car, he drove to the tunnel.

All the way through it he kept hearing the singer, though the words were indistinguishable amid the hubbub of the rush hour. Sometimes he thought the voice was in one or other of the vehicles surrounding him, and sometimes on his car radio, though that was switched off. When he emerged from the tunnel the voice fled towards the river, as he knew it would.

He still hadn't glimpsed the singer by the time he reached the warehouses. He parked in front of the derelict building nearest to Stephanie Maple's apartment and was struggling feebly out of his seat belt when a Mercedes drew up outside her block. He didn't know whether to greet her or hide as she was ushered out of the car by a tall wiry muscular man some years younger than her or Goldman. When she caught sight of him he raised a hand and followed it up. "Stephanie," he succeeded in croaking. "Not here for you just now, but looking forward to directing you again."

The man frowned at him as though at an especially unwelcome beggar, and at first the actress only frowned. "Jonathan?" she said. "When would that be?"

"Whenever your next film goes into production. The one about the bad guys living here. The one you want me for."

"As an assistant if I can fix it. I don't know if you'd be directing me."

It was still work, Goldman tried to tell himself, but couldn't help wondering if he might have been hired to direct if he'd accepted whatever had been offered at their last encounter. That seemed as remote and unreal as the future she had just snatched out of reach. He was holding in a shiver that felt like a threat of losing all control when she said "Are you worse, Jonathan? You ought to go home."

"Wherever that is."

She looked as if she hadn't quite heard something, possibly not him. It didn't prevent her from letting herself and her companion into the apartments—if anything, it sped her on her way. Goldman watched the lobby grow deserted and then dark while a song provided a soundtrack:

"It shouldn't matter where you live,

So crawl back in your hole.

It doesn't matter who you are.

You're just another soul . . . "

"Let's see what kind you are," Goldman croaked, and blundered across the parking area that was patterned with bones—with white lines. Under the scrawny floodlights that iced the concrete his car looked abandoned, exhausted of colour. A gathering of shadows fluttered underfoot, eager to drag him down to join them. They helped his legs feel depleted as he staggered to the nearest disused warehouse and peered through a window.

The song was somewhere in the stony dark. It sounded hushed now, almost trapped. "You aren't getting away from me this time," Goldman whispered. The warehouse doors were locked, but he hauled himself up into the glassless aperture and, with an effort that left him sodden and shivering, through.

He lowered himself on his wasted arms and leaned against damp brick while he tried to regather himself. The song had withered into silence, but he could just distinguish a tattered bony shape cowering in the far corner of the vast dark space, and heard the rustling of whatever it used for a bed. When he felt able to manage without the support of the wall he picked his way across the stone floor, avoiding chunks of rubble and drained bottles. Once he almost tripped over a squashed can that stank of lager. Nevertheless he kept his attention on the restless tenant of the dark.

The material in which the figure was attired was dismayingly tattered, he thought, or was that its nest? Surely none of the tremulous fragments could be part of the figure itself. Goldman faltered as he heard the wail of a police car, and as that receded, a last breath of song:

"There was a time when sirens

Didn't give you an alarm . . . "

Something with a mouth or at least a gaping cavity in it wobbled up to greet him, then fell back with a papery sound. At once the figure was indistinguishable from its bed and then not there in any form.

Goldman flattened a hand against the rough chill wall and stooped unsteadily to peer at the items that constituted the bed. They were crumpled pages, thousands of them. He had to wobble lower to lift one to his face. In the glow from the city across the river, he could just make out that he was holding a song sheet. Every page he groped for and let drop was one, but he was unable to read any of the words.

When he tired of letting pages fall back on the mound he followed the last of them down. From so much bending and unbending he felt dizzy and hollow, robbed of substance, scarcely present. He just needed to lie down until he regained himself, he thought. He curled up in the nest, which seemed to have readied a hollow for him, and took a page in each hand as he closed his eyes. He settled into himself and the dark, thinking of Ruth, the Phoenix Pictures team, Stephanie Maple, Mr Teshagihara and his acolytes. When he began to sing, at first it was only to himself.

accident Zone

B LAKE HAD WALKED SOME MILES FROM HIS HOTEL WHEN HE
saw the mirror. He'd exhausted Keswick and its environs within
three days, or the weather had exhausted him; he disliked having to
wait outside his hotel for the hourly bus while rain teemed on his
head, and disliked being blinded by the grey steamed windows as he
rode the bus to the Lakeland coach tour station. Today had been the
first fine day of his holiday in the Lakes. He'd had them make him a
box lunch and had set out from his hotel, away from Keswick. He was
tired of towns.

At noon clouds still overlapped the hills and streamed like smoke
between the trees. The sun glinted dully, then as the afternoon
progressed began to blaze. Blake followed the road for a while, crossing from one meagre verge to the other to protect himself from blind
corners. Eventually, offended by the belches of cars and the glare of
litter, he left the road and climbed a hill. The wet earth smacked its
lips at his feet. He reached the top, where pale rock protruded like
teeth from the grass, and gazed down.

Four hundred feet below, cars scurried like spiders on threads.
Blake took deep breaths and felt victorious. For the first time this year
he could ignore cars. In Keswick they challenged each other in the
narrow streets, snarling; in Liverpool they demanded that he help
design housing projects to accommodate them as well as the tenants.
He stood up and urinated towards them. Then he sat down on the
rocks and ate his lunch.

It was as he threw his head back to catch the dregs of coffee that he saw the mirror. Near the foot of the hill, on the side opposite that he'd climbed, was a hairpin bend. The pin was hardly open. At the hinge of the bend, stuck into a rough green mat of bushes, was a large mirror on a pole. Equidistant from it two cars were parked, at the verge of each approach to the bend.

Blake frowned. He had planned to descend that side of the hill, but the mirror troubled him. It seemed trivial and in bad taste, like a glass-headed pin thrust into a tapestry. Still, he thought, it was absurd enough to be enjoyable. If he responded to it with the shocked laugh it deserved, it wouldn't spoil his landscape. In Liverpool, to the dismay of passers-by, he sometimes laughed at the sight of the white boxes of high-rise flats against blue sky and clouds: Magritte in three dimensions.

We need surrealism more than ever, he thought. For sanity.

The mirror's there to prevent accidents, he responded.

Oh shut up, he thought. This is my landscape today. The drivers can have it tomorrow.

He descended the hill. The ground was beginning to steam; each hundred feet further down he felt as if he'd pulled on another set of clothes. From the top he'd seen a lake, some miles across the fields. He intended to make for it, avoiding the mirror, but the hill seemed patched with sponge, and his zigzag descent across firmer ground brought him slithering to the slope just above the mirror. There he stopped, gasping, for he felt as if he'd stepped from a hot bath and plunged into ice.

It must be an effect of shade, he thought. But he couldn't see how; the sunlight was pouring over him. Perhaps there was a pond near, steeping the area in clamminess. Shivering, he stepped into the road.

The brandished mirror loomed above him. As he crossed the road his head bulged in the mirror and his body dwindled. He recoiled, reminded of humanoid balloons he'd tried to inflate when a child, squeezing air up into the head and blowing again until the head burst. He surveyed both stretches of road, looking for a route to the lake, but both were edged by tangles of bushes beyond which lay muddy fields. He sensed the mirror staring over his head and turned again, angry with himself. God, the quiet ached. Too much so, he thought suddenly, given the nearby cars. Well, there was no point in standing about. He would follow the road away from Keswick. Sooner or later there must be a path toward the lake.

He strode away from the mirror. There was a sign just beyond the parked car; that might help him. Though it seemed odd to park the car with its bonnet between the uprights of the sign. In fact, now Blake came closer, he began to suspect that the car had been dumped. Yes, it had: the front of the car looked like a trampled can. Cursing whoever had abandoned it, Blake came abreast of the car and read the sign. ACCIDENT ZONE, it said. DON'T LET THIS HAPPEN TO YOU.

From the edge of his eye Blake glimpsed movement. He glanced toward the mirror. For a moment he was sure he'd seen an object appear in the mirror and dodge out of sight again. An animal, no doubt, which had brushed the edge of the reflection. From his position by the sign he could see the second car and, prepared now, could make out a wrenched door and a smashed windscreen. The second car was also displayed beneath a sign. Blake stared at the empty rusting cars, the attentive mirror, the emphatic almost suburban silence. Then he began to hurry away down the road.

He had taken only a few paces when heard a car rattling toward him. It swerved around a bend ahead and rushed closer. He retreated onto the verge and the car sped by, deafening him and spouting fumes. Blake stared after it furiously. The students piled inside it ignored the wrecked car. As they reached the mirror Blake was attacked by nausea: hot with rage, he'd suddenly felt as if all his heat had been drained from him. The car skidded across the bend, its reflection squeezed like rubber into a curve, regained control at the last moment and sped on.

Blake took a step toward the mirror. Then he turned and made off down the road. He was still shivering from the gulp of heat that had seemed to be drawn from him. An odd image persisted in his mind; as the car had been caught in the mirror, the glass had trembled like a bubble and small pale globules, or so his memory interpreted them, had appeared around the rim. Distortion caused by the heat and the exhaust of the car, no doubt. But he was sure there must be a flaw in the glass.

He was still shivering as he walked. A wind had started to hiss in the trees bordering the road. The clouds were gathering again, and trickled down the hills. Beyond the trees he encountered a path leading from the road in the direction of the lake; it was composed of brown mud and stones. He would have attempted it, but felt weak. He blamed the chill that had crept into him near the mirror, and an insidious depression that he had taken away with him. Should have known cars wouldn't let me alone, he thought.

He continued walking, but mechanically; the depression had robbed him of motive. Above him chiselled rock caught tatters of cloud. After half an hour's walk the landscape softened; trees swayed, asleep on their roots, and butterflies bloomed on the trunks. He rounded a bend and saw a small white cottage before which stood several white wicker tables and chairs. A pole held up a rotating doubleheaded sign: TEAS.

This time he didn't question its taste. He sat down at a table in the artificial glade. He was still weak, and felt exhausted, and hungry. He glanced about for a waitress and saw a hoarding, which had been screened from him by the trees, on the edge of the glade. Protected by glass, a huge enlargement of a newspaper report gleamed between the trunks. I WAS HOSTILE AND AFRAID, SAYS DRIVER.

A car engine whined like a dentist's drill across the hills. Blake read the hoarding; patches of light surrounded by leaf shadow fluttered and slipped across the words. "In the two year period since the erection of the mirror more fatal accidents have occurred at the bend, five less than in the previous two years. Is there a case for stronger action? Mr. Eric Mayne, 42, of Blubberfosters, survived an accident at the bend. 'I saw a car coming in the other direction,' he told us. 'I slowed down but I still thought we were both going too fast. I was afraid there would be an accident. Then I got angry and turned my headlights on full. I was being very aggressive, I felt it was his turn to slow down. I think the lights blinded him.' Mr. Mayne was lucky; the other driver died. It is up to the drivers not to turn our country into a jungle, and up to us to make sure they do."

Forthright but ungrammatical, Blake thought. He turned his back on the hoarding and gazed across the landscape. Clouds were now pouring down the higher hills. An old lady in an ankle-length kaftan, with white hair like a poodle's fur, emerged from the cottage and took his order for tea and scones. "You're not in a car, are you?" she said. "I saw you looking at my board. Well, I'm glad to see someone's still walking."

Five minutes later she returned with the tea. Shadows were rushing across the landscape. "Yes, I do like the Lakes very much," Blake said.

"Any life would be bearable if it ended here. That was always my scheme of things," she said. "It's the atmosphere I love. In ten years it's made me its own."

"I'm fond of atmospheres," Blake said.

"One thing spoils it. That." She pointed to the hoarding. "Oh, not the report. I put that up myself. I meant the place they're talking about. I wish it weren't so near. The bus to Keswick goes through it, and I dread going."

"I don't think I would dread it, just dislike it," Blake said.

"Ah, but have you been there? Well, tell me your opinion."

"I thought it was grotesque," Blake said. "Entirely out of place. But necessary, perhaps."

"You'll have to take the bus to Keswick to get back to your hotel, unless you intend to walk. You'll probably be soaked if you walk. Now, you remember what I'm going to tell you. Notice what happens when the bus comes near the bend. Everyone will stop talking. They always do, and they couldn't tell you why. They'd probably say they're afraid to distract the driver. But why should they be? Driving's his job, and he knows the road. Why should he crash there, particularly? You tell me that."

"I'm not sure what you're saying," Blake said.

"I'm talking about fear and hostility," she said, gesturing toward the hoarding. "So much of that in a place must leave its mark. It's even there when you're walking, let alone driving. You must have felt it."

"What, fear and hostility?" Blake said. "Not at all."

He stood up and paid. "You're welcome to wait here for the bus," she said. "Look at the sky."

"I'll survive. I think I'll walk until the bus comes," Blake said. "Good for me."

Twenty minutes later he heard the bus behind him. He hesitated, then strode on. The bus swept by, and he hurried up a slope at the edge of the road. From there he could watch the lights of the bus dwindling toward the mirror. Clouds had seeped into the sun, dousing it. He strained his eyes. The lighted windows slipped through the mirror, and as they did so they shuddered. The bus itself negotiated the bend with ease. Blake ran down the slope, frowning. Rage was beginning to sputter inside him. He hurried toward the mirror. He was determined to discover exactly what had spoilt his day.

Near the mirror he left the road. He picked his way in the draining light across the side of the hill. Cars were already casting paths of light before them and rolling them up. He sat on a rock shelving from the hill, and gazed down. The landscape glimmered with the threat of a storm, and the glow coated the wrecked cars. Between them the mirror reared up, an empty eye.

Soon the landscape had lost all its colour. Sky and earth merged. Blake yawned and shivered, for his body heat was dissipating. He'd thought the ground would give out heat at twilight; on the contrary, it seemed to be drinking his own heat. The mirror was only faintly visible now, a thick blob of grey. He drummed his heels on the rock, wishing for the first time in months that he had a cigarette. What the hell he was doing here he didn't know. So much for gestures. No doubt there wouldn't be another bus for almost an hour.

A car crept toward the bend, its headlights awakening almost at the mirror. Blake shook himself alert. The headlights peered out of the mirror, and silhouetted on their reflection a small round shape bobbed up, like a teasing target in a shooting gallery. Blake stood up, squinting, and the headlights swung at him before sweeping away. No, there was nothing except the smouldering impression of the headlights on his eyes. Not so odd, he thought; it had probably been a moth, made to look nearly spherical by the blaze of the lights. The mirror would attract night flyers.

He sat down again. His weakness had returned. Not surprisingly, when it was so cold. If it hadn't been for that bloody woman he would be halfway to Keswick by now. Talking about fear and hostility—well, he wasn't hostile except to the situation he'd allowed to take him over, he wished he could go back and stuff that down her throat. And I'm certainly not afraid, he shouted to himself. Just because he jumped when something appeared in the mirror it didn't mean he was afraid. He would sit for a few minutes to see whether he regained his strength. If not he would walk away.

He watched two cars approaching. Their headlights trickled thinly down the distant roads, then began to widen as they poured closer. As the headlights of one touched the mirror the glass began to shift like a bubble about to burst. No, it wasn't his eyes. The surface of the mirror was perceptibly trembling. It must be a vibration set up by the approach of the car. When the second car drew near and the mirror's shivering increased Blake was sure he was right. The beam was swinging out of the mirror like an uncontrolled searchlight; it roamed across the side of the hill as if searching for him. The second car drew into the verge and allowed the first to pass. Don't blame him, Blake thought. I'd be afraid too.

The second car moved off slowly. As its light returned to the mirror the reflection was surrounded. Blake leaned forward. An iris of small pale shapes had appeared around the light, jostling like bubbles on the rim of a pan coming to the boil.

Blake ran down the hill, fixing his gaze on the mirror. It couldn't be a flaw in the glass, not one that moved around the edge of the mirror and sank back out of sight and reappeared. He ran faster to reach the mirror before the light withdrew, and tripped on a loose rock. He hit the ground with a sucking thud. A prickling touched the back of his neck. The grass before him hissed. It was raining.

Raindrops on a mirror and I almost break my leg, he thought. My God, I'm overwrought. The rain was springing back from the ground. He ran toward the shelter of the bushes behind the mirror. As he passed the mirror he peered up. As far as he could see the glass was beaded by drops, but few of them were around the edge. He shrugged angrily and made for the bushes.

The leaves sizzled about him. After perhaps ten minutes the rain ceased. He emerged, shaking himself like a dog. His hair dripped about his face; his clothes clung to him like seaweed. He stood beneath the mirror and laughed. No, I'm not going to blame you, he thought. This entire absurd business is my own doing.

He heard a car approaching. Perhaps he could thumb a lift. He waited beneath the mirror, leaning forward to avoid its tassels of rain. Points of light flashed from bush to bush as the car neared the bend. No use; it was coming from Keswick. Might have known, Blake thought. Ah well, I'm saved from importuning. He turned to begin walking, then halted. No point in giving the driver more to avoid. The headlights felt their way toward him, and the mirror sprang up at his feet.

It was reflected in a puddle, which had gathered in a dip in the road. For a moment it shone like the moon. Then it shrank. The iris had reappeared; the bubbles crowded and fought for place. Leaning closer, Blake saw that the lowest bubble was nothing of the kind. It contained a vicious grin and glaring eyes.

All his heat rushed out of him. His skin shuddered. He twisted to stare at the mirror. Apart from the probing headlights it was empty. But he had the impression that as he had turned, a darker iris had retreated into the frame of the mirror. He was still staring upward when the car whipped past, lifting a wave from the puddle and drenching him.

Blake shouted in rage, glaring up at the mirror. How many deaths had been focused in the glass? Ten that he'd read of, and there had been more than a dozen small round shapes in the mirror. The puddle might have given them faces, earth for eyes and ripples for grins, he argued with himself. They hadn't been clear. But he was already struggling up the hillside, searching in the sodden grass for the loose rock.

When he found it he slithered down to the mirror. He imagined the faces peering down at him through the dark. You won't take any more with you, he shouted. Shaking with anger and revulsion and renewed cold, he threw the brick.

The mirror was stouter than he anticipated. The rock thudded at his feet. He thought he could hear a dry sound like that of disturbed mice. Oh no you don't, he thought. He hurled the rock again. Three more throws and shattered glass plunged into the earth in front of him.

He smiled grimly and let his shoulders slump. Then he heard two cars converging toward him. My God, what have I done? he shouted. I must be mad. It's the mirror's fault, no, this whole morbid area. Headlights slashed around bends on both sides of him. He threw the rock into the bushes and ran into the road. Perhaps he could stop them. Perhaps one would drive him into Keswick, where he could report someone's act of vandalism on the mirror.

The car coming from Keswick was nearer. He raised his arms and urged it to slow down. He pushed it back with his hands. It slowed for a moment as the driver surveyed him. Then it gathered speed and swerved past him, missing him by inches.

The second car did not.

He heard a metallic squeal and felt a dull agonising thud across the back of his thighs. He was scooped up and slid clawing wildly over metal. His head struck glass. Then the metal whipped from beneath him and he thumped into the mud of the road.

Pain burned through his legs. Above him he heard the chop of car doors, men saying "Oh Christ", "Now for heaven's sake keep calm", and a woman screaming. He turned his head and laid his cheek in bright spotlighted mud. He saw boots walking past his face, squeezing up walls of mud around their footprints. He saw a trailing bootlace drag by, coated with mud like a worm. He heard a voice saying "I think it looks worse than it is, don't worry." Everything, even the pulse of agony in his legs, felt distant as delirium.

Even the mirror at the top of the pole. Even the jagged black hole in it. "I know first aid," someone said. "Give me a few minutes and I think we can move him. We can't leave him here." Even the pale struggling blobs that had appeared at the hole in the mirror, like the contents of a spider's torn cocoon. Someone was tying something around his legs. "We'll have to make a stretcher," a voice said. "Can you hear me? We're leaving you for a minute but we'll still be here. You'll be all right."

No I won't, Blake thought, but he felt detached. He watched the faces stream out of the crack in the mirror, falling through the light like slow leaden bubbles. He watched the string of faces balance on the air and float toward him in disorder, some on their backs, some hanging toward the ground. He closed his eyes. It was worse than delirium. Not until he felt them settle on him like a swarm of insects did he begin to mutter and scream.

"We're coming, just give us a minute, lie still, we're coming," a voice called. But Blake was writhing as his skin crawled, as light soft objects roved over his body, pulling feebly at him, seeking him beneath his skin. They were trying to prise him out. His skin, or his sense of it, was attenuating.

"My God, what's that?" "Moths, I think. Look, there they go. Like bloody scavengers," and he felt himself rolled onto a hard support and lifted. He jolted and sank onto metal. Doors slammed behind him. An engine whirred and he felt the gears engage. He opened his eyes. The mirror and the other car shrank. The displayed wreck swung by, and a chain of pale blobs rose from it and rushed toward the back windows of the car before drifting scattered across the field. Blake moaned. "Hold on. We'll be in Keswick before you know it," the driver said, driving Blake toward a wheelchair in Liverpool, a fear of mirrors, and a crawling of the skin that he would scratch until blood flowed.

The Entertainment

BY THE TIME SHONE FOUND HIMSELF BACK IN WESTINGSEA he was able to distinguish only snatches of the road as the wipers strove to fend off the downpour. The promenade where he'd seen pensioners wheeled out for an early dose of sunshine, and backpackers piling into coaches that would take them inland to the Lakes, was waving isolated trees that looked too young to be out by themselves at a grey sea baring hundred of edges of foam. Through a mixture of static and the hiss on the windscreen a local radio station advised drivers to stay off the roads, and he felt he was being offered a chance. Once he had a room he could phone Ruth. At the end of the promenade he swung the Cavalier around an old stone soldier drenched almost black and coasted alongside the seafront hotels.

There wasn't a welcome in sight. A sign in front of the largest and whitest hotel said NO, apparently having lost the patience to light up its second word. He turned along the first of the narrow streets of boarding houses, in an unidentifiable one of which he'd stayed with his parents most of fifty years ago, but the placards in the windows were just as uninviting. Some of the streets he remembered having been composed of small hotels had fewer buildings now, all of them care homes for the elderly. He had to lower his window to read the signs across the roads, and before he'd finished his right side was soaked. He needed a room for the night—he hadn't the energy to drive back to London. Half an hour would take him to the motorway, near which he was bound to find a hotel. But he had only reached the edge of town, and was braking at a junction, when he saw hands adjusting a notice in the window of a broad three-storey house.

He squinted in the mirror to confirm he wasn't in anyone's way, then inched his window down. The notice had either fallen or been removed, but the parking area at the end of the short drive was unoccupied, and above the high thick streaming wall a signboard that frantic bushes were doing their best to obscure appeared to say most of HOTEL. He veered between the gateposts and came close to touching the right breast of the house.

He couldn't distinguish much through the bay window. At least one layer of net curtains was keeping the room to itself. Beyond heavy purple curtains trapping moisture against the glass, a light was suddenly extinguished. He grabbed his overnight bag from the rear seat and dashed for the open porch.

The rain kept him company as he poked the round brass bellpush next to the tall front door. There was no longer a button, only a socket harbouring a large bedraggled spider that recoiled almost as violently as his finger did. He hadn't laid hold of the rusty knocker above the neutral grimace of the letter-slot when a woman called a warning or a salutation as she hauled the door open. "Here's someone now."

She was in her seventies but wore a dress that failed to cover her mottled toadstools of knees. She stooped as though the weight of her loose throat was bringing her face, which was almost as white as her hair, to meet his. "Are you the entertainment?" she said.

Behind her a hall more than twice his height and darkly papered with a pattern of embossed vines not unlike arteries led to a central staircase that vanished under the next floor up. Beside her a long-legged table was strewn with crumpled brochures for local attractions; above it a pay telephone with no number in the middle of its dial clung to the wall. Shone was trying to decide if this was indeed a hotel when the question caught up with him. "Am I . . . "

"Don't worry, there's a room waiting." She scowled past him and shook her head like a wet dog. "And there'd be dinner and a breakfast for anyone who settles them down."

He assumed this referred to the argument that had started or recommenced in the room where the light he'd seen switched off had been relit. Having lost count of the number of arguments he'd dealt with in the Hackney kindergarten where he worked, he didn't see why this should be any different. "I'll have a stab," he said, and marched into the room.

Despite its size, it was full of just two women—of the breaths of one at least as wide as her bright pink dress, who was struggling to lever herself up from an armchair with a knuckly stick and collapsing red-faced, and of the antics of her companion, a lanky woman in the flapping jacket of a dark blue suit and the skirt of a greyer outfit, who'd bustled away from the light-switch to flutter the pages of a television listings magazine before scurrying fast as the cartoon squirrel on the television to twitch the cord of the velvet curtains, an activity Shone took to have dislodged whatever notice had been in the window. Both women were at least as old as the person who'd admitted him, but he didn't let that daunt him. "What seems to be the problem?" he said, and immediately had to say "I can't hear you if you both talk at once."

"The light's in my eyes," the woman in the chair complained, though of the six bulbs in the chandelier one was dead, another missing. "Unity keeps putting it on when she knows I'm watching."

"Amelia's had her cartoons on all afternoon," Unity said, darting at the television, then drumming her knuckles on top of an armchair instead. "I want to see what's happening in the world."

"Shall we let Unity watch the news now, Amelia? If it isn't something you like watching you won't mind if the light's on."

Amelia glowered before delving into her cleavage for an object that she flung at him. Just in time to field it he identified it as the remote control. Unity ran to snatch it from him, and as a newsreader appeared with a war behind him Shone withdrew. He was lingering over closing the door while he attempted to judge whether the mountainous landscapes on the walls were vague with mist or dust when a man at his back murmured "Come out, quick, and shut it."

He was a little too thin for his suit that was grey as his sparse hair. Though his pinkish eyes looked harassed, and he kept shrugging his shoulders as though to displace a shiver, he succeeded in producing enough of a grateful smile to part his teeth. "By gum, Daph said you'd sort them out, and you have. You can stay," he said.

Among the questions Shone was trying to resolve was why the man seemed familiar, but a gust of rain so fierce it strayed under the front door made the offer irresistible. "Overnight, you mean," he thought it best to check.

"That's the least," the manager presumably only began, and twisted round to find the stooped woman. "Daph will show you up, Mr . . . "

"Shone."

"Who is he?" Daph said as if preparing to announce him.

"Tom Shone," Shone told her.

"Mr Thomson?"

"Tom Shone. First name Tom."

"Mr Tom Thomson."

He might have suspected a joke if it hadn't been for her earnestness, and so he appealed to the manager. "Do you need my signature?"

"Later, don't you fret," the manager assured him, receding along the hall.

"And as for payment . . . "

"Just room and board. That's always the arrangement."

"You mean you want me to . . . "

"Enjoy yourself," the manager called, and disappeared beyond the stairs into somewhere that smelled of an imminent dinner.

Shone felt his overnight bag leave his shoulder. Daph had relieved him of the burden and was striding upstairs, turning in a crouch to see that he followed. "He's forever off somewhere, Mr Snell," she said, and repeated "Mr Snell."

Shone wondered if he was being invited to reply with a joke until she added "Don't worry, we know what it's like to forget your name."

She was saying he, not she, had been confused about it. If she hadn't cantered out of sight his response would have been as sharp as the rebukes he gave his pupils when they were too childish. Above the middle floor the staircase bent towards the front of the house, and he saw how unexpectedly far the place went back. Perhaps nobody was staying in that section, since the corridor was dark and smelled old. He grabbed the banister to speed himself up, only to discover it wasn't much less sticky than a sucked lollipop. By the time he arrived at the top of the house he was furious to find himself panting.

Daph had halted at the far end of a passage lit, if that was the word, by infrequent bulbs in glass flowers sprouting from the walls. Around them shadows fattened the veins of the paper. "This'll be you," Daph said, and pushed open a door.

Beside a small window under a yellowing light bulb the ceiling angled almost to the carpet brown as mud. A narrow bed stood in the angle, opposite a wardrobe and dressing-table and a sink beneath a dingy mirror. At least there was a phone on a shelf by the sink. Daph passed him his bag as he ventured into the room. "You'll be fetched when it's time," she told him.

"Time? Time . . . "

"For dinner and all the fun, silly," she said, with a laugh so shrill his ears wanted to flinch.

She was halfway to the stairs when he thought to call after her "Aren't I supposed to have a key?"

"Mr Snell will have it. Mr Snell," she reminded him, and was gone.

He had to phone Ruth as soon as he was dry and changed. There must be a bathroom somewhere near. He hooked his bag over his shoulder with a finger and stepped into the twilight of the corridor. He'd advanced only a few paces when Daph's head poked over the edge of the floor. "You're never leaving us."

He felt absurdly guilty. "Just after the bathroom."

"It's where you're going," she said, firmly enough to be commanding rather than advising him, and vanished down the hole that was the stairs.

She couldn't have meant the room next to his. When he succeeded in coaxing the sticky plastic knob to turn, using the tips of a finger and thumb, he found a room much like his, except that the window was in the angled roof. Seated on the bed in the dimness on its way to dark was a figure in a toddler's blue overall-a Teddy bear with large black ragged eyes or perhaps none. The bed in the adjacent room was strewn with photographs so blurred that he could distinguish only the grin everyone of them bore. Someone had been knitting in the next room, but had apparently lost concentration, since one arm of the mauve sweater was at least twice the size of the other. A knitting needle pinned each arm to the bed. Now Shone was at the stairs, beyond which the rear of the house was as dark as that section of the floor below. Surely Daph would have told him if he was on the wrong side of the corridor, and the area past the stairs wasn't as abandoned as it looked: he could hear a high-pitched muttering from the dark, a voice gabbling a plea almost too fast for words, praying with such urgency the speaker seemed to have no time to pause for breath. Shone hurried past the banisters that enclosed three sides of the top of the stairs, and pushed open the door immediately beyond them. There was the bath, and inside the plastic curtains that someone had left closed would be a shower. He elbowed the door wide, and the shower curtains shifted to acknowledge him.

Not only they had. As he tugged the frayed cord to kindle the bare bulb, he heard a muffled giggle from the region of the bath. He threw his bag onto the hook on the door and yanked the shower curtains apart. A naked woman so scrawny he could see not just her ribs but the shape of bones inside her buttocks was crouching on all fours in the bath. She peered wide-eyed over one splayed knobbly hand at him, then dropped the hand to reveal a nose half the width of her face and a gleeful mouth devoid of teeth as she sprang past him. She was out of the room before he could avoid seeing her shrunken disused breasts and pendulous grey-bearded stomach. He heard her run into a room at the dark end of the corridor, calling out "For it now" or perhaps "You're it now." He didn't know if the words were intended for him. He was too busy noticing that the door was boltless.

He wedged his shoes against the corner below the hinges and piled his sodden clothes on top, then padded across the sticky linoleum to the bath. It was cold as stone, and sank at least half an inch with a loud creak as he stepped into it under the blind brass eye of the shower. When he twisted the reluctant squeaky taps it felt at first as though the rain had got in, but swiftly grew so hot he backed into the clammy plastic. He had to press himself against the cold tiled wall to reach the taps, and had just reduced the temperature to bearable when he heard the doorknob rattle. "Taken," he shouted. "Someone's in here."

"My turn."

The voice was so close the speaker's mouth must be pressed against the door. When the rattling increased in vigour Shone yelled "I won't be long. Ten minutes."

"My turn."

It wasn't the same voice. Either the speaker had deepened his pitch in an attempt to daunt Shone or there was more than one person at the door. Shone reached for the sliver of soap in the dish protruding from the tiles, but contented himself with pivoting beneath the shower once he saw the soap was coated with grey hair. "Wait out there," he shouted. "I've nearly finished. No, don't wait. Come back in five minutes."

The rattling ceased, and at least one body dealt the door a large soft thump. Shone wrenched the curtains open in time to see his clothes spill across the linoleum. "Stop that," he roared, and heard someone retreat—either a spectacularly crippled person or two people bumping into the walls as they carried on a struggle down the corridor. A door slammed, then slammed again, unless there were two. By then he was out of the bath and grabbing the solitary bath-towel from the shaky rack. A spider with legs like long grey hairs and a wobbling body as big as Shone's thumbnail scuttled out of the towel and hid under the bath.

He hadn't brought a towel with him. He would have been able to borrow one of Ruth's. He held the towel at arm's length by two corners and shook it over the bath. When nothing else emerged, he rubbed his hair and the rest of him as swiftly as he could. He unzipped his case and donned the clothes he would have sported for dining with Ruth. He hadn't brought a change of shoes, and when he tried on those he'd worn, they squelched. He gathered up his soaked clothes and heaped them with the shoes on his bag, and padded quickly to his room.

As he kneed the door open he heard sounds beyond it: a gasp, another, and then voices spilling into the dark. Before he crossed the room, having dumped his soggy clothes and bag in the wardrobe that, like the rest of the furniture, was secured to a wall and the floor, he heard the voices stream into the house. They must belong to a coach party—brakes and doors had been the sources of the gasps. On the basis of his experiences so far, the influx of residents lacked appeal for him, and made him all the more anxious to speak to Ruth. Propping his shoes against the ribs of the tepid radiator, he sat on the underfed pillow and lifted the sticky receiver.

As soon as he obtained a tone he began to dial. He was more than halfway through Ruth's eleven digits when Snell's voice interrupted. "Who do you want?"

"Long distance."

"You can't get out from the rooms, I'm afraid. There's a phone down here in the hall. Everything else as you want it, Mr Thomson? Only I've got people coming in."

Shone heard some of them outside his room. They were silent except for an unsteady shuffling and the hushed sounds of a number of doors. He could only assume they had been told not to disturb him. "There were people playing games up here," he said.

"They'll be getting ready for tonight. They do work themselves up, some of them. Everything else satisfactory?"

"There's nobody hiding in my room, if that's what you mean."

"Nobody but you."

That struck Shone as well past enough, and he was about to make his feelings clear while asking for his key when the manager said "We'll see you down shortly, then." The line died at once, leaving Shone to attempt an incredulous grin at the events so far. He intended to share it with his reflection above the sink, but hadn't realised until now that the mirror was covered with cracks or a cobweb. The lines appeared to pinch his face thin, to discolour his flesh and add wrinkles. When he leaned closer to persuade himself that was merely an illusion, he saw movement in the sink. An object he'd taken to be a long grey hair was snatched into the plughole, and he glimpsed the body it belonged to squeezing itself out of sight down the pipe. He had to remind himself to transfer his wallet and loose coins and keys from his wet clothes to his current pockets before he hastened out of the room.

The carpet in the passage was damp with footprints, more of which he would have avoided if he hadn't been distracted by sounds in the rooms. Where he'd seen the Teddy bear someone was murmuring "Up you come to mummy. Gummy gum." Next door a voice was crooning "There you all are", presumably to the photographs, and Shone was glad to hear no words from the site of the lopsided knitting, only a clicking so rapid it sounded mechanical. Rather than attempt to interpret any of the muffled noises from the rooms off the darker section of the corridor, he padded downstairs so fast he almost missed his footing twice.

Nothing was moving in the hall except rain under the front door. Several conversations were ignoring one another in the television lounge. He picked up the receiver and thrust coins into the box, and his finger faltered over the zero on the dial. Perhaps because he was distracted by the sudden hush, he couldn't remember Ruth's number.

He dragged the hole of the zero around the dial as far as it would go in case that brought him the rest of the number, and as the hole whirred back to its starting point, it did. Ten more turns of the dial won him a ringing padded with static, and he felt as if the entire house was waiting for Ruth to answer. It took six pairs of rings longer than she needed to cross her flat—to make her say "Ruth Lawson."

"It's me, Ruth." When there was silence he tried reviving their joke. "Old Ruthless."

"What now, Tom?"

He'd let himself hope for at least a dutiful laugh, but its absence threw him less than the reaction from within the television lounge: a titter, then several. "I just wanted you to know—"

"You're mumbling again. I can't hear you."

He was only seeking to be inaudible to anyone but her. "I say I wanted you to know I really did get the day wrong," he said louder. "I really thought I was supposed to be coming up today."

"Since when has your memory been that bad?"

"Since, I don't know, today, it seems like. No, fair enough, you'll be thinking of your birthday. I know I forgot that too."

A wave of mirth escaped past the ajar door across the hall. Surely however many residents were in there must be laughing at the television with the sound turned down, he told himself as Ruth retorted "If you can forget that you'll forget anything."

"I'm sorry."

"I'm sorrier."

"I'm sorriest," he risked saying, and immediately wished he hadn't completed their routine, not only since it no longer earned him the least response from her but because of the roars of laughter from the television lounge. "Look, I just wanted to be sure you knew I wasn't trying to catch you out, that's all."

"Tom."

All at once her voice was sympathetic, the way it might have sounded at an aged relative's bedside. "Ruth," he said, and almost as stupidly "What?"

"You might as well have been."

"I might . . . you mean I might . . . "

"I mean you nearly did."

"Oh." After a pause as hollow as he felt he repeated the syllable, this time not with disappointment but with all the surprise he could summon up. He might have uttered yet another version of the sound, despite or even because of the latest outburst of amusement across the hall, if Ruth hadn't spoken. "I'm talking to him now."

"Talking to who?"

Before the words had finished leaving him Shone understood that she hadn't been speaking to him but about him, because he could hear a man's voice in her flat. Its tone was a good deal more than friendly to her, and it was significantly younger than his. "Good luck to you both," he said, less ironically and more maturely than he would have preferred, and snagged the hook with the receiver.

A single coin trickled down the chute and hit the carpet with a plop. Amidst hilarity in the television lounge several women were crying "To who, to who" like a flock of owls. "He's good, isn't he," someone else remarked, and Shone was trying to decide where to take his confusion bordering on panic when a bell began to toll as it advanced out of the dark part of the house.

It was a small but resonant gong wielded by the manager. Shone heard an eager rumble of footsteps in the television lounge, and more of the same overhead. As he hesitated Daph dodged around the manager towards him. "Let's get you sat down before they start their fuss," she said.

"I'll just fetch my shoes from my room."

"You don't want to bump into the old lot up there. They'll be wet, won't they?"

"Who?" Shone demanded, then regained enough sense of himself to answer his own question with a weak laugh. "My shoes, you mean. They're the only ones I've brought with me."

"I'll find you something once you're in your place," she said, opening the door opposite the television lounge, and stooped lower to hurry him. As soon as he trailed after her she bustled the length of the dining-room and patted a small isolated table until he accepted its solitary straight chair. This faced the room and was boxed in by three long tables, each place at which was set like his with a plastic fork and spoon. Beyond the table opposite him velvet curtains shifted impotently as the windows trembled with rain. Signed photographs covered much of the walls—portraits of comedians he couldn't say he recognised, looking jolly or amusingly lugubrious. "We've had them all," Daph said. "They kept us going. It's having fun keeps the old lot alive." Some of this might have been addressed not just to him, because she was on her way out of the room. He barely had time to observe that the plates on the Welsh dresser to his left were painted on the wood, presumably to obviate breakage, before the residents crowded in.

A disagreement over the order of entry ceased at the sight of him. Some of the diners were scarcely able to locate their places for gazing at him rather more intently than he cared to reciprocate. Several of them were so inflated that he was unable to determine their gender except by their clothes, and not even thus in the case of the most generously trousered of them, whose face appeared to be sinking into a nest of flesh. Contrast was provided by a man so emaciated his handless wristwatch kept sliding down to his knuckles. Unity and Amelia sat facing Shone, and then, to his dismay, the last of the eighteen seats was occupied by the woman he'd found in the bath, presently covered from neck to ankles in a black sweater and slacks. When she regarded him with an expression of never having seen him before and delight at doing so now he tried to feel some relief, but he was mostly experiencing how all the diners seemed to be awaiting some action from him. Their attention had started to paralyse him when Daph and Mr Snell reappeared through a door Shone hadn't noticed beside the Welsh dresser.

The manager set about serving the left-hand table with bowls of soup while Daph hurried over, brandishing an especially capacious pair of the white cloth slippers Shone saw all the residents were wearing. "We've only these," she said, dropping them at his feet. "They're dry, that's the main thing. See how they feel."

Shone could almost have inserted both feet into either of them. "I'll feel a bit of a clown, to tell you the truth."

"Never mind, you won't be going anywhere."

Shone poked his feet into the slippers and lifted them to discover whether the footwear had any chance of staying on. At once all the residents burst out laughing. Some of them stamped as a form of applause, and even Snell produced a fleeting grateful smile as he and Daph retreated to the kitchen. Shone let his feet drop, which was apparently worth another round of merriment. It faded as Daph and Snell came out with more soup, a bowl of which the manager brought Shone, lowering it over the guest's shoulder before spreading his fingers on either side of him. "Here's Tommy Thomson for you," he announced, and leaned down to murmur in Shone's ear "That'll be all right, won't it? Sounds better."

At that moment Shone's name was among his lesser concerns. Instead he gestured at the plastic cutlery. "Do you think I could—"

Before he had time to ask for metal utensils with a knife among them, Snell moved away as though the applause and the coos of joy his announcement had drawn were propelling him. "Just be yourself," he mouthed at Shone.

The spoon was the size Shone would have used to stir tea if the doctor hadn't recently forbidden him sugar. As he picked it up there was instant silence. He lowered it into the thin broth, where he failed to find anything solid, and raised it to his lips. The brownish liquid tasted of some unidentifiable meat with a rusty undertaste. He was too old to be finicky about food that had been served to everyone. He swallowed, and when his body raised no protest he set about spooning the broth into himself as fast as he could without spilling it, to finish the task.

He'd barely signalled his intentions when the residents began to cheer and stamp. Some of them imitated his style with the broth while

others demonstrated how much more theatrically they could drink
theirs; those closest to the hall emitted so much noise that he could
have thought part of the slurping came from outside the room. When
he frowned in that direction, the residents chortled as though he'd
made another of the jokes he couldn't avoid making.

He dropped the spoon in the bowl at last, only to have Daph return
it to the table with a briskness not far short of a rebuke. While she and
Snell were in the kitchen everyone else gazed at Shone, who felt
compelled to raise his eyebrows and hold out his hands. One of the
expanded people nudged another, and both of them wobbled glee-
fully, and then all the residents were overcome by laughter that
continued during the arrival of the main course, as if this was a joke
they were eager for him to see. His plate proved to bear three heaps of
mush, white and pale green and a glistening brown. "What is it?" he
dared to ask Daph.

"What we always have," she said as if to a child or to someone
who'd reverted to that state. "It's what we need to keep us going."

The heaps were of potatoes and vegetables and some kind of mince
with an increased flavour of the broth. He did his utmost to eat natu-
rally, despite the round of applause this brought him. Once his
innards began to feel heavy he lined up the utensils on his by no
means clear plate, attracting Daph to stoop vigorously at him. "I've
finished," he said.

"Not yet."

When she stuck out her hands he thought she was going to return
the fork and spoon to either side of his plate. Instead she removed it
and began to clear the next table. While he'd been concentrating on
hiding his reaction to his food the residents had gobbled theirs, he
saw. The plates were borne off to the kitchen, leaving an expectant
silence broken only by a restless shuffling. Wherever he glanced, he
could see nobody's feet moving, and he told himself the sounds had
been Daph's as she emerged from the kitchen with a large cake iced
white as a memorial. "Daph's done it again," the hugest resident
piped.

Shone took that to refer to the portrait in icing of a clown on top
of the cake. He couldn't share the general enthusiasm for it; the

clown looked undernourished and blotchily red-faced, and not at all certain what shape his wide twisted gaping lips should form. Snell brought in a pile of plates on which Daph placed slices of cake, having cut it in half and removed the clown's head from his shoulders in the process, but the distribution of slices caused some debate. "Give Tommy Thomson my eye," a man with bleary bloodshot eyeballs said.

"He can have my nose," offered the woman he'd seen in the bath.

"I'm giving him the hat," Daph said, which met with hoots of approval. The piece of cake she gave him followed the outline almost precisely of the clown's sagging pointed cap. At least it would bring dinner to an end, he thought, and nothing much could be wrong with a cake. He didn't expect it to taste faintly of the flavour of the rest of the meal. Perhaps that was why, provoking a tumult of jollity, he began to cough and then choke on a crumb. Far too eventually Daph brought him a glass of water in which he thought he detected the same taste. "Thanks," he gasped anyway, and as his coughs and the applause subsided, managed to say "Thanks. All over now. If you'll excuse me, I think I'll take myself off to bed."

The noise the residents had made so far was nothing to the uproar with which they greeted this. "We haven't had the entertainment yet," Unity protested, jumping to her feet and looking more than ready to dart the length of the room. "Got to sing for your supper, Tommy Thomson."

"We don't want any songs and we don't want any speeches," Amelia declared. "We always have the show."

"The show," all the diners began to chant, and clapped and stamped in time with it, led by the thumping of Arnelia's stick. "The show. The show."

The manager leaned across Shone's table. His eyes were pinker than ever, and blinking several times a second. "Better put it on for them or you'll get no rest," he muttered. "You won't need to be anything special."

Perhaps it was the way Snell was leaning down to him that let Shone see why he seemed familiar. Could he really have run the hotel where Shone had stayed with his parents nearly fifty years ago? How old would he have to be? Shone had no chance to wonder while the question was "What are you asking me to do?"

"Nothing much. Nothing someone of your age can't cope with. Come on and I'll show you before they start wanting to play their games."

It wasn't clear how much of a threat this was meant to be. Just now Shone was mostly grateful to be ushered away from the stamping and the chant. Retreating upstairs had ceased to tempt him, and fleeing to his car made no sense when he could hardly shuffle across the carpet for trying to keep his feet in the slippers. Instead he shambled after the manager to the doorway of the television lounge. "Go in there," Snell urged, and gave him a wincing smile. "Just stand in it. Here they come."

The room had been more than rearranged. The number of seats had been increased to eighteen by the addition of several folding chairs. All the seats faced the television, in front of which a small portable theatre not unlike the site of a Punch and Judy show had been erected. Above the deserted ledge of a stage rose a tall pointed roof that reminded Shone of the clown's hat. Whatever words had been inscribed across the base of the gable were as faded as the many colours of the frontage. He'd managed to decipher only ENTER HERE when he found himself hobbling towards the theatre, driven by the chanting that had emerged into the hall.

The rear of the theatre was a heavy velvet curtain, black where it wasn't greenish. A slit had been cut in it up to a height of about four feet. As he ducked underneath, the mouldy velvet clung to the nape of his neck. A smell of damp and staleness enclosed him when he straightened up. His elbows knocked against the sides of the box, disturbing the two figures that lay on a shelf under the stage, their empty bodies sprawling, their faces nestling together upside down as though they had dragged themselves close for companionship. He turned the faces upwards and saw that the figures, whose fixed grins and eyes were almost too wide for amusement, were supposed to be a man and a woman, although only a few tufts of grey hair clung to each dusty skull. He was nerving himself to insert his hands in the gloves of the bodies when the residents stamped chanting into the room.

Unity ran to a chair and then, restless with excitement, to another. Amelia dumped herself in the middle of a sofa and inched groaning to one end. Several of the jumbo residents lowered themselves onto folding chairs that looked immediately endangered. At least the seating of the audience put paid to the chant, but everyone's gaze fastened on Shone until he seemed to feel it clinging to the nerves of his face. Beyond the residents Snell mouthed "Just slip them on."

Shone pulled the open ends of the puppets towards him and poked them gingerly wider, dreading the emergence of some denizen from inside one or both. They appeared to be uninhabited, however, and so he thrust his hands in, trying to think which of his kindergarten stories he might adapt for the occasion. The brownish material fitted itself easily over his hands, almost as snug as the skin it resembled, and before he was ready each head as if the performers were being roused from sleep. The spectators were already cheering, a response that seemed to entice the tufted skulls above the stage. Their entrance was welcomed by a clamour in which requests gradually became audible. "Let's see them knock each other about like the young lot do these days."

"Football with the baby."

"Make them go like animals."

"Smash their heads together."

They must be thinking of Punch and Judy, Shone told himself and then a wish succeeded in quelling the rest. "Let's have Old Ruthless."

"Old Ruthless" was the chant as the stamping renewed itself—as his hands sprang onto the stage to wag the puppets at each other. All at once everything he'd been through that day seemed to have concentrated itself in his hands, and perhaps that was the only way he could be rid of it. He nodded the man that was his right hand at the balding female and uttered a petulant croak. "What do you mean, it's not my day?"

He shook the woman and gave her a squeaky voice. "What day do you think it is?"

"It's Wednesday, isn't it? Thursday, rather. Hang on, it's Friday, of course. Saturday, I mean."

"It's Sunday. Can't you hear the bells?"

"I thought they were for us to be married. Hey, what are you hiding there? I didn't know you had a baby yet."

"That's no baby, that's my boyfriend."

Shone twisted the figures to face the audience. The puppets might have been waiting for guffaws or even groans at the echo of an old joke: certainly he was. The residents were staring at him with, at best, bemusement. Since he'd begun the performance the only noise had been the sidling of the puppets along the stage and the voices that caught harshly in his throat. The manager and Daph were gazing at him over the heads of the residents; both of them seemed to have forgotten how to blink or grin. Shone turned the puppets away from the spectators as he would have liked to turn himself. "What's up with us?" he squeaked, wagging the woman's head. "We aren't going down very well."

"Never mind, I still love you. Give us a kiss," he croaked, and made the other puppet totter a couple of steps before it fell on its face. The loud crack of the fall took him off guard, as did the way the impact trapped his fingers in the puppet's head. The figure's ungainly attempts to stand up weren't nearly as simulated as he would have preferred. "It's these clown's shoes. You can't expect anyone to walk in them," he grumbled. "Never mind looking as if I'm an embarrassment."

"You're nothing else, are you? You'll be forgetting your own name next."

"Don't be daft," he croaked, no longer understanding why he continued to perform, unless to fend off the silence that was dragging words and antics out of him. "We both know what my name is."

"Not after that crack you fetched your head. You won't be able to keep anything in there now."

"Well, that's where you couldn't be wronger. My name ... " He meant the puppet's, not his own: that was why he was finding it hard to produce. "It's, you know, you know perfectly well. You know it as well as I do."

"See, it's gone."

"Tell me or I'll thump you till you can't stand up," Shone snarled in a rage that was no longer solely the puppet's, and brought the helplessly grinning heads together with a sound like the snapping of bone. The audience began to cheer at last, but he was scarcely aware of them. The collision had split the faces open, releasing the top joints of his fingers only to trap them in the splintered gaps. The clammy bodies of the puppets clung to him as his hands wrenched at each other. Abruptly something gave, and the female head flew off as the body tore open. His right elbow hit the wall of the theatre, and the structure lurched at him. As he tried to steady it, the head of the puppet rolled under his feet. He tumbled backwards into the mouldy curtains. The theatre reeled with him, and the room tipped up.

He was lying on his back, and his breath was somewhere else. In trying to prevent the front of the theatre from striking him he'd punched himself on the temple with the cracked male head. Through the proscenium he saw the ceiling high above him and heard the appreciation of the audience. More time passed than he thought necessary before several of them approached.

Either the theatre was heavier than he'd realised or his fall had weakened him. Even once he succeeded in peeling Old Ruthless off his hand he was unable to lift the theatre off himself as the puppet lay like a deflated baby on his chest. At last Amelia lowered herself towards him, and he was terrified that she intended to sit on him. Instead she thrust a hand that looked boiled almost into his face to grab the proscenium and haul the theatre off him. As someone else bore it away she seized his lapels and, despite the creaking of her stick, yanked him upright while several hands helped raise him from behind. "Are you fit?" she wheezed.

"I'll be fine," Shone said before he knew. All the chairs had been pushed back against the windows, he saw. "We'll show you one of our games now," Unity said behind him.

"You deserve it after all that," said Amelia, gathering the fragments of the puppets to hug them to her breasts.

"I think I'd like—"

"That's right, you will. We'll show you how we play. Who's got the hood?"

"Me," Unity cried. "Someone do it up for me."

Shone turned to see her flourishing a black cap. As she raised it over her head, he found he was again robbed of breath. When she tugged it down he realised that it was designed to cover the player's eyes, more like a magician's prop than an element of any game. The man with the handless watch dangling from his wrist pulled the cords of the hood tight behind her head and tied them in a bow, then twirled her round several times, each of which drew from her a squeal only just of pleasure. She wobbled around once more as, having released her, he tiptoed to join the other residents against the walls of the room.

She had her back to Shone, who had stayed by the chairs, beyond which the noise of rain had ceased. She darted away from him, her slippered feet patting the carpet, then lurched sideways towards nobody in particular and cocked her head. She was well out of the way of Shone's route to the door, where Daph and the manager looked poised to sneak out. He only had to avoid the blinded woman and he would be straight up to his room, either to barricade himself in or to retrieve his belongings and head for the car. He edged one foot forward into the toe of the slipper, and Unity swung towards him. "Caught you. I know who that is, Mr Tommy Thomson."

"No you don't," Shone protested in a rage at everything that had led to the moment, but Unity swooped at him. She closed her bony hands around his cheeks and held on tight far longer than seemed reasonable before undoing the bow of the hood with her right hand while gripping and stroking his chin with the other. "Now it's your turn to go in the dark."

"I think I've had enough for one day, if you'll excuse—"

This brought a commotion of protests not far short of outrage. "You aren't done yet, a young thing like you." "She's older than you and she didn't make a fuss." "You've been caught, you have to play." "If you don't it won't be fair." The manager had retreated into the doorway and was pushing air at Shone with his outstretched hands as Daph mouthed "It's supposed to be the old lot's time." Her words and the rising chant of "Be fair" infected Shone with guilt, aggravated when Unity uncovered her reproachful eyes and held out the hood. He'd disappointed Ruth, he didn't need to let these old folk down too. "Fair enough, I'll play," he said. "Just don't twist me too hard."

He hadn't finished speaking when Unity planted the hood on his scalp and drew the material over his brows. It felt like the clammy bodies of the puppets. Before he had a chance to shudder it was dragging his eyelids down, and he could see nothing but darkness. The hood moulded itself to his cheekbones as rapid fingers tied the cords behind his head. "Not too—" he gasped at whoever started twirling him across the room.

He felt as if he'd been caught by a vortex of cheering and hooting, but it included murmurs too. "He played with me in the bath." "He wouldn't let us in there." "He made me miss my cartoons." "That's right, and he tried to take the control off us." He was being whirled so fast he no longer knew where he was. "Enough," he cried, and was answered by an instant hush. Several hands shoved him staggering forward, and a door closed stealthily behind him.

At first he thought the room had grown colder and damper. Then, as his giddiness steadied, he understood that he was in a different room, further towards the rear of the house. He felt the patchy lack of carpet through his slippers, though that seemed insufficient reason for the faint scraping of feet he could hear surrounding him to sound so harsh. He thought he heard a whisper or the rattling of some object within a hollow container level with his head. Suddenly, in a panic that flared like white blindness inside the hood, he knew Daph's last remark hadn't been addressed to him, nor had it referred to anyone he'd seen so far. His hands flew to untie the hood—not to see where he was and with whom, but which way to run.

He was so terrified to find the cord immovably knotted that it took him seconds to locate the loose ends of the bow. A tug at them released it. He was forcing his fingertips under the edge of the hood when he heard light dry footsteps scuttle towards him, and an article that he tried to think of as a hand groped at his face. He staggered backwards, blindly fending off whatever was there. His fingers encountered ribs barer than they ought to be, and poked between them to meet the twitching contents of the bony cage. The whole of him convulsed as he snatched off the hood and flung it away.

The room was either too dark or not quite dark enough. It was at least the size of the one he'd left, and contained half a dozen sagging armchairs that glistened with moisture, and more than twice as many figures. Some were sprawled like loose bundles of sticks topped with grimacing masks on the chairs, but nonetheless doing their feeble best to clap their tattered hands. Even those that were swaying around him appeared to have left portions of themselves elsewhere. All of them were attached to strings or threads that glimmered in the murk and led his reluctant gaze to the darkest corner of the room.

A restless mass crouched in it—a body with too many limbs, or a huddle of bodies that had grown inextricably entangled by the process of withering. Some of its movement, though not all, was of shapes that swarmed many-legged out of the midst of it, constructing parts of it or bearing away fragments or extending more threads to the other figures in the room. It took an effort that shrivelled his mind before he was able to distinguish anything else: a thin gap between curtains, a barred window beyond—to his left, the outline of a door to the hall. As the figure nearest to him bowed so close he saw the very little it had in the way of eyes peering through the hair it had stretched coquettishly over its face, Shone bolted for the hall.

The door veered aside as his dizziness swept it away. His slippers snagged a patch of carpet and almost threw him on his face. The doorknob refused to turn in his sweaty grasp, even when he gripped it with both hands. Then it yielded, and as the floor at his back resounded with a mass of uneven yet purposeful shuffling, the door juddered open. He hauled himself around it and fled awkwardly, slippers flapping, out of the dark part of the hall.

Every room was shut. Other than the scratching of nails or of the ends of fingers at the door behind him, there was silence. He dashed along the hall, striving to keep the slippers on, not knowing why, knowing only that he had to reach the front door. He seized the latch and flung the door wide and slammed it as he floundered out of the house.

The rain had ceased except for a dripping of foliage. The gravel glittered like the bottom of a stream. The coach he'd heard arriving—an old private coach spattered with mud—was parked across the rear of his car, so close it practically touched the bumper. He could never manoeuvre out of that trap. He almost knocked on the window of the television lounge, but instead limped over the gravel and into the street, towards the quiet hotels. He had no idea where he was going except away from the house. He'd hobbled just a few paces, his slippers growing more sodden and his feet sorer at each step, when headlamps sped out of the town.

They belonged to a police car. It halted beside him, its hazard lights twitching, and a uniformed policeman was out of the passenger seat before Shone could speak. The man's slightly chubby concerned face was a wholesome pink beneath a streetlamp. "Can you help me?" Shone pleaded. "I—"

"Don't get yourself in a state, old man. We saw where you came from."

"They boxed me in. My car, I mean, look. If you can just tell them to let me out—"

The driver moved to Shone's other side. He might have been trying to outdo his colleague's caring look. "Calm down now. We'll see to everything for you. What have you done to your head?"

"Banged it. Hit it with, you wouldn't believe me, it doesn't matter, I'll be fine. If I can just fetch my stuff—"

"What have you lost? Won't it be in the house?"

"That's right, at the top. My shoes are."

"Feet hurting, are they? No wonder with you wandering around like that on a night like this. Here, get his other arm." The driver had taken Shone's right elbow in a firm grip, and now he and his partner easily lifted Shone and bore him towards the house. "What's your name, sir?" the driver enquired.

"Not Thomson, whatever anyone says. Not Tommy Thomson or Tom either. Or rather, it's Tom all right, but Tom Shone. That doesn't sound like Thomson, does it? Shone as in shine. I used to know someone who said I still shone for her, you still shine for me, she'd say. Been to see her today as a matter of fact." He was aware of talking too much as the policemen kept nodding at him and the house with its two lit windows—the television lounge's and his reared over him. "Anyway, the point is the name's Shone," he said. "Ess aitch, not haitch as some youngsters won't be told it isn't, oh en *ee*. Shone."

"We've got you." The driver reached for the empty bellpush, then pounded on the front door. It swung inwards almost at once, revealing the manager. "Is this gentleman a guest of yours, Mr Snell?" the driver's colleague said.

"Mr Thomson. We thought we'd lost you," Snell declared, and pushed the door wide. All the people from the television lounge were lining the hall like spectators at a parade. "Tommy Thomson," they chanted.

"That's not me," Shone protested, pedalling helplessly in the air until his slippers flew into the hall. "I told you—"

"You did, sir," the driver murmured, and his partner said even lower "Where do you want us to take you?"

"To the top, just to—"

"We know," the driver said conspiratorially. The next moment Shone was sailing to the stairs and up them, with the briefest pause as the policemen retrieved a slipper each. The chant from the hall faded, giving way to a silence that seemed most breathlessly expectant in the darkest sections of the house. He had the police with him, Shone reassured himself. "I can walk now," he said, only to be borne faster to the termination of the stairs. "Where the door's open?" the driver suggested. "Where the light is?"

"That's me. Not me really, anything but, I mean—"

They swung him through the doorway by his elbows and deposited him on the carpet. "It couldn't be anybody else's room," the driver said, dropping the slippers in front of Shone. "See, you're already here."

Shone looked where the policemen were gazing with such sympathy it felt like a weight that was pressing him into the room. A photograph of himself and Ruth, arms around each other's shoulders with a distant mountain behind, had been removed from his drenched suit and propped on the shelf in place of the telephone. "I just brought that," he protested, "you can see how wet it was," and limped across the room to don his shoes. He hadn't reached them when he saw himself in the mirror.

He stood swaying a little, unable to retreat from the sight. He heard the policemen murmur together and withdraw, and their descent of the stairs, and eventually the dual slam of car doors and the departure of the vehicle. His reflection still hadn't allowed him to move. It was no use his telling himself that some of the tangle of wrinkles might be cobwebs, not when his hair was no longer greying but white. "All right, I see it," he yelled—he had no idea at whom. "I'm old. I'm old."

"Soon," said a whisper like an escape of gas in the corridor, along which darkness was approaching as the lamps failed one by one. "You'll be plenty of fun yet," the remains of another voice said somewhere in his room. Before he could bring himself to look for its source, an item at the end of most of an arm fumbled around the door and switched out the light. The dark felt as though his vision was abandoning him, but he knew it was the start of another game. Soon he would know if it was worse than hide and seek—worse than the first sticky unseen touch of the web of the house on his face.

Dead Letters

THE SÉANCE WAS BOB'S IDEA, OF COURSE. WE'D FINISHED dinner and were lighting more candles to stave off the effects of the power cut when he made the suggestion. "What's the point? The apartment's only three years old," Joan said, though in fact she was disturbed by this threat of a séance in our home. But he'd brought his usual bottle of Pernod to the dinner party, inclining it toward us as if he'd forgotten that nobody else touched the stuff, and now he was drunk enough to believe he could carry us unprotesting with him. He almost did. When opposition came, it surprised me as much as it did Bob.

"I'm not joining in," his wife Louise said. "I won't."

I could feel one of his rages building, though usually they didn't need to be provoked. "Is this some more of your stupidity we have to suffer?" he said. "Don't you know what everyone in this room is thinking of you?"

"I'm not sure you do," I told him sharply. I could see Stan and Marge were embarrassed. I'd thought Bob might behave himself when meeting them for the first time.

He peered laboriously at me, his face white and sweating as if from a death battle with the Pernod. "One thing's sure," he said. "If she doesn't know what I think of her, she will for the next fortnight."

I glared at him. He and Louise were bound for France in the morning to visit her relatives; the tickets were poking out of his top pocket. We'd made this dinner date with them weeks ago—as usual, to

relieve Louise's burdens of Bob and of the demands of her work as a nurse—and as if to curtail the party Bob had brought their flight date forward. I imagined her having to travel with Bob's hangover. But at least she looked in control for the moment, sitting in a chair near the apartment door, away from the round dining table. "Sit down, everybody," Bob said. "Before someone else cracks up."

From his briefcase where he kept the Pernod he produced a device that he slid into the middle of the table, his unsteady hand slipping and almost flinging his toy to the floor. I wondered what had happened in the weeks since I'd last seen him, so to lessen his ability to hold his drink; he'd been in this state when they arrived. As a rule he contrived to drink for much of the day at work, with little obvious effect except to make him more unpleasant to Louise. Perhaps alcoholism had overtaken him at last.

The device was a large glass inside which a small electric flashlight sat on top of another glass. Bob switched on the flashlight and pressed in a ring of cork that held the glasses together while Marge, no doubt hoping the party would quieten down, dealt around the table the alphabet Bob had written on cards. I imagined him harping on the seance to Louise as he prepared the apparatus.

"So you're not so cool as you'd like me to think," he said to her, and blew out all the candles.

I sat opposite him. Joan checked the light switch before taking her place next to me, and I knew she hoped the power would interrupt us. Bob had insinuated himself between Stan and Marge, smacking his lips as he drained his bottle. If I hadn't wanted to save them further unpleasantness I'd have opposed the whole thing.

A thick scroll of candle smoke drifted through the flashlight beam. Our brightening hands converged and rested on the glass. I felt as if our apartment had retreated now that the light was concentrated on the table. I could see only dim ovals of faces floating above the splash of light; I couldn't see Louise at all. Silence settled on us like wax, and we waited.

After what seemed a considerable time I began to feel, absurdly perhaps, that it was my duty as host to start things moving. I'd been involved in a few seances and knew the general principles; since Bob was unusually quiet I would have to lead. "Is anybody there?" I said. "Anyone there? Anybody there?"

"Sounds like you've got a bad line," said Stan.

"Shouldn't you say here rather than there?" Marge said.

"I'll try that," I said. "Is anyone here? Anybody here?"

I was still waiting for Stan to play me for a stooge again when Bob's hand began to tremble convulsively on the glass. "You're just playing the fool," Joan said, but I was no more certain than she really was, because from what I could distinguish of Bob's indistinct face I could see he was staring fixedly ahead, though not at me. "What is it? What's the matter?" I said, afraid both that he sensed something and that he was about to reveal the whole situation as an elaborate joke.

Then the glass began to move.

I'd seen it happen at séances before, but never quite like this. The glass was making aimless darting starts in all directions, like an animal that had suddenly found itself caged. It seemed frantic and bewildered, and in a strange way its blind struggling beneath our fingers reminded me of the almost mindless fluttering of hands near to death. "Stop playing the fool," Joan said to Bob, but I was becoming certain that he wasn't, all the more so when he didn't answer.

Then the glass made a rush for the edge of the table, so fast that my fingers would have been left behind if our fingertips hadn't been pressed so closely together that they carried each other along. The light swooped on the letter I and held it for what felt like minutes. It returned to the centre of the table, drawing our luminous orange fingertips with it, then swept back to the I. And again. I. I. I.

"Aye aye, Cap'n," Stan said.

"He doesn't know who he is," Marge whispered.

"Who are you?" I said. "Can you tell us your name?"

The glass inched toward the centre. Then, as if terrified to find itself out in the darkness, it fled back to the I. Thinking of what Marge had said, I had an image of someone awakening in total darkness, woken by us perhaps, trying to remember anything about himself, even his name. I felt unease: Joan's unease, I told myself. "Can you tell us anything about yourself?" I said.

The glass seemed to be struggling again, almost to be forcing itself into the centre. Once there it sat shifting restlessly. The light reached toward letters, then flinched away. At last it began to edge out. I felt isolated with the groping light, cut off even from Joan beside me, as if the light were drawing on me for strength. I didn't know if anyone else felt this, nor whether they also had an oppressive sense of terrible effort. The light began to nudge letters, fumbling before it came to rest on each. MUD, it spelled.

"His name's mud!" Stan said delightedly.

But the glass hadn't finished. R, it added.

"Hello Mudr, hello Fadr," Stan said.

"Murder," Marge said. "He could be trying to say murder."

"If he's dead he should be old enough to spell."

I had an impression of bursting frustration, of a suffocated swelling fury. I felt a little like that myself, because Stan was annoying me. I'd ceased to feel jean's unease; I was engrossed. "Do you mean murder?" I said. "Who's been murdered?"

Again came the frustration, like the leaden shell of a storm. Incongruously, I remembered my own thwarted fury when I was trying to learn to type. The light began to wobble and glide, and the oppression seemed to clench until I had to soothe my forehead as best I could with my free hand. "Oh my head," Marge said.

"Shall we stop?" said Joan.

"Not yet," Marge said, because the light seemed to have gained confidence and was swinging from one letter to another. POISN, it spelled.

"Six out of ten," Stan said. "Could do better."

"Shut up, Stan," Marge said.

"I beg your pardon? You're not taking this nonsense seriously? Because if that's what we're doing, deal me out."

The glass was shuddering now and clutching letters rapidly with its beam. "Please, Stan," Marge said. "Say it's a game, then. If you sit out now you won't be able to discuss it afterwards."

DSLOLY, the glass had been shouting. "Poisoned slowly," Stan translated. "Very clever, Bob. You can stop it now."

"I don't think it is Bob," I said.

"What is it then, a ghost? Don't be absurd. Come on then, ghost. If you're here let's see you."

I heard Marge stop herself saying "Don't!" I felt Joan grow tense, felt the oppression crushed into a last straining effort. Then I heard a click from the apartment door.

Suddenly the darkness felt more crowded. I began to peer into the apartment beyond the light, slowly in an attempt not to betray to Joan what I was doing, but I was blinded by the glass. I caught sight of Stan and knew by the tilt of his head that he'd realised he might be upsetting Louise. "Sorry, Louise," he called and lifted his face ceilingward as he realised that could only make the situation worse.

Then the glass seemed to gather itself and began to dart among the letters. We all knew that it was answering Stan's challenge. We held ourselves still, only our exhausted hands swinging about the table like parts of a machine. When the glass halted at last we'd all separated out the words of the answer. WHEN LIGHT COMS ON, it said.

"I want to stop now," Joan said.

"All right," I said. "I'll light the candles."

But she'd gripped my hand. "I'll do it," Stan said. "I've got some matches." And he'd left the table, and we were listening to the rhythm he was picking out with his shaken matches as he groped into the enormous surrounding darkness, when the lights came on.

We'd all heard the sound of the door but hadn't admitted it, and we all blinked first in that direction. The door was closed. It took a few seconds for us to realise there was no sign of Louise. I think I was the first to look at Bob, sitting grinning opposite me behind his empty bottle of Pernod. My mind must have been thinking faster than consciously, because I knew before I pulled it out that there was only one ticket in his pocket, perhaps folded to look like two by Louise as she laid out his suit. Bob just grinned at me and gazed, until Stan closed his eyes.

aLL For SaLe

ONCE THEY WERE OUTSIDE THE MEDITERRANEAN NIGHTS Barry could hear the girl's every word, starting with "What were you trying to tell me about a plane?"

"Just I, you know, noticed you on it."

"As I said if you heard, I saw you."

"I know. I mean, I did hear, just about." While he gazed at rather than into her dark moonlit eyes that might be glinting with eagerness for him to risk more, he made himself blurt "I hoped I'd see you again."

"Well, now you have." She raised her small face an inch closer to his and formed her pink lips into a prominent smile he couldn't quite take as an invitation to a kiss. Not long after his silence grew intolerable, unrelieved by the hushing of the waves that failed to distract him from the way the huge blurred scarcely muffled rhythm of the disco seemed determined to keep his heartbeat up to speed, she said "So you're called Baz."

"That's only what my friends call me, the guys I was with, I mean. I don't know if you saw them on the plane as well."

"I told you, I saw you."

Her gentle emphasis on the last word encouraged him to admit "I'm Barry really."

"Hello, Barry really," she said and held out a hand. "I'm Janet."

He wiped his hand on his trousers, but they were as clammy from dancing. Her grasp proved to be cool and firm. "So are you staying as long as us?" she said, having let go of him.

"Two weeks. It's our first time abroad."

"There must be worse places to get experience," she said and caught most of a yawn behind her hand as she stretched, pointing her breasts at him through her short thin black dress. "Well, I'm danced out. This girl's for bed."

He could think of plenty of responses, but none he dared utter. He was turning his attention to the jittering of neon on the water when Janet said "You could walk me back if you liked."

As her escort, should he take her hand or at least her arm or even slip his around her slim waist? He didn't feel confident enough along the seafront, where the signs of the clubs turned the faces of the noisy crowds outside into lurid unstable carnival masks. "We're up here," Janet eventually said.

The narrow crooked street also led uphill to his and Paul's and Derek's apartment. Once the pulsating neon and the throbbing competitive rhythms of the discos fell behind, Janet began resting her fingers on his bare arm at each erratically canted bend. He thought of laying a hand over hers, but suspected that would only make her aware of his feverish heat fuelled by alcohol. He became conscious of tasting of it, and was wondering what he could possibly offer her when she clutched at his wrist. "What's that?" she whispered.

He'd thought the trestle table propped against the rough white wall of one of the rudimentary houses that constricted the dim street was heaped with refuse until the heap lifted itself on one arm. Apparently the table served as a bed for an undernourished man wearing not even very many rags. He clawed his long hair aside to display a face rather too close to the skull beneath and thrust out the other hand. "He just wants money," Barry guessed aloud, and in case Janet assumed that was intended as a cue to her, declared "I've got some."

He didn't think he had much. Bony fingers snatched the notes and coins spider-like. At once, too fast for Barry to distinguish how, the man huddled back into resembling waste. "You didn't have to give him all that," Janet murmured as they hurried to the next bend. "You'll be seeing more like him."

Barry feared she thought he'd been trying to impress her with his generosity, which he supposed he might have been. "We like to share what we've got, don't we, us Yorkshire folk."

Before he'd finished speaking he saw that she could think he was making a crude play for her along with emphasising her trace of an accent more than she might like. Her silence gave his thoughts time to grow hot and arid as the night while he trudged beside her up a steep few hundred yards—indeed, overtook her before she said "This is as far as I go."

She was opening her small black spangled handbag outside a door lit by a plastic rectangle that might as well have been a sliver of the moon. "I'm just up the road," he told her.

Did that sound like yet another unintentional suggestion? All she said was "Maybe I'll see you in the market."

"Which one's that?"

She gazed so long into the depths of her bag that he was starting to feel she thought his ignorance unworthy of an answer when she said "What are you going to think of me now."

He had to treat it as a question. "Well, I know we've only—"

"Denise and San have got the keys. I didn't realise I'd drunk that much. Back we go."

She was at the first corner before he'd finished saying "Shall I come with you?"

"No need."

"I will, though."

"Suit yourself," she said and quickened her pace.

He felt virtuous for not abandoning her to pass the man on the table by herself. In fact that stretch was as deserted as the rest of the slippery uneven variously sloping route. The seafront was still crowded, and she had to struggle past a haphazard queue outside the Mediterranean Nights. "I won't be long," she told him.

She was. Once he felt he'd waited longer than enough he tried to follow her, but the swarthy doorman who'd been happy to re-admit her showed no such enthusiasm on Barry's behalf. Even if he'd had the money, Barry told himself, he wouldn't have paid to get back in. He supposed he could have said that Paul and Derek would vouch for him—that was assuming they weren't in an especially humorous mood—but he couldn't be bothered arguing with the doorman. If Janet's friends had persuaded her to have another drink or two, or she'd met someone else, that had to be fine with him.

He did his best to look content as he tramped back along the seafront, and was trudging uphill before he indulged in muttering to himself. He fell silent as he passed Janet's lodgings, the Summer Breeze Apartments, on the way to swaying around several jagged unlit bends that hindered his arrival at his own quarters. Some amusement was to be derived from coaxing the key to find the lock of the street door and from reeling up the concrete stairs, two steps up, one back down. Further drunken fumbling was involved in admitting himself to the apartment, where most of the contents of his and Paul's and Derek's cases had yet to fight for space in the wardrobe and the bathroom. At the end of an interlude in the latter, more protracted than conclusive, he lurched through the room containing his friends' beds to the couch in the kitchen area. Without too many curses he succeeded in unfolding the couch and, having fallen over and onto it, dragging a sheet across himself.

Perhaps all he could hear in the street below the window were club-bers returning to their apartments, but they sounded more like a stealthy crowd that wasn't about to go away. He was thinking, if no more than that, of making for the balcony to look when the slam of the street door sent Paul's and Derek's voices up from the muted hubbub. Soon his friends fell into their room, switching on lights at random. "He's here. He's in bed," Paul announced.

"Thought you'd pulled some babe," Derek protested.

"She didn't have her key," Barry roused himself to attempt to pronounce. "You didn't see her coming back, then."

"You could have brought her up here as long as you let us know," Paul said.

"Put a notice on the door or something," said Derek.

"Next time," Barry told them, not that he thought there was much of a chance. Still, he could dream, or perhaps he could only sleep. He hadn't the energy to ask what was happening outside. The murmur from the street and the blundering of his friends about the apartment receded, bearing his awareness, which he was happy to relinquish.

Snoring wakened him—at first, only his own. The refrain was

taken up by Derek, who was lying on his back, while Paul gave tongue into a pillow. The chorus was by no means equal to the noise from the street. Unable to make sense of it, Barry dragged the floor-length windows apart and groped between them into unwelcome sunlight. Leaning over the rudimentary concrete balustrade, he blinked his vision into focus. The street had disappeared.

Or rather, its surface had. From bend to bend it was hidden by the awnings of market stalls and by the crowd the stalls had drawn. Barry supported himself on his elbows, though the heat of the concrete was only just bearable, until he succeeded in dredging up some thoughts. His mouth was dry and yet oily with reminiscences of alcohol, his skull felt baked too thin, but shouldn't he wander down in case Janet was hoping to encounter him? Mightn't she have waited, not realising he'd given away the contents of his pocket, for him to rejoin her in the Mediterranean Nights? He picked his way to the bathroom and, having made space for it, drank as much water as he could stomach, then showered and dressed. "I'll be in the market," he said, receiving a mumble from one of his friends and an emphatic snore from the other.

In the lobby the owner of the apartments was crammed into a shabby armchair overlooked by a warren of compartments, some lodging keys, behind the reception counter. He wore a flower-bed of a shirt too large even for him, which framed enough chest hair to cover his bald head. He opened his eyes half an inch and used a forearm to wipe his heavily ruled brow as Barry took out his traveller's cheques. "You want pay?" the owner said.

"Please."

"How much you pay?"

"No, we paid in England. My friend Derek had to show you the voucher when we checked in, remember." When the man only scowled at the beads of sweat his tufted forearm had collected, Barry tried to simplify the point. "The paper said we paid."

"Now you pay for things go smash. Nothing smash, money back."

"Derek's in charge of booking and stuff like that. You'll need to speak to him," Barry said, knowing that with a hangover Derek would be even more combative than usual. "He's the man in charge."

"So why I talk to you?"

Barry pointed at the sign beside the pigeonholes: TRAVVLER'S' CHEKS CACHED. "It says you give money."

For a breath that threatened to pop his shirt buttons the man seemed inclined to misunderstand, and then he thrust a ballpoint bandaged with several thicknesses of inky plaster across the counter. "You put name."

Barry signed a cheque for a hundred pounds as quickly as possible—the pen felt unpleasantly clammy—and handed over both, together with his passport. After the merest blink at Barry's signature, the owner ran his gaze up and down him between several glances at the photograph. At last he leaned back, heaving his stomach high with his thighs, to unlock a drawer and count out a handful of large grubby notes. "You pay me nothing," he complained.

Presumably he meant there was no commission. Barry shoved the notes into his shirt pocket—they felt clammier than the pen had—and was holding out the hand when the man dropped the passport in the drawer. "What you want give me?" the owner said, leering at the hand.

"I need my passport."

"I keep now," the owner said and locked the drawer. "You want more pay, you come me."

"I don't think so," Barry told him, but made for the street. Further argument could wait until Paul and Derek were there to join in—all right, and why not, to support him.

As he opened the door he was overwhelmed by heat that competed with the light for fierceness, by the sullen roar of the fire that was the crowd, by the smell of hot wallets, which were all the table nearest the apartments sold. Its immediate neighbour was devoted to leather goods too. The stalls were packed so close together that once he sidled between them he couldn't see the sign above the door—the Summit Apartments, though they were well short of the top of the hill.

Most of the crowd was making its sluggish way upwards, unlike him. Whenever he glanced about for possible souvenirs or presents, and often when he didn't, stall-holders launched themselves and whatever English they had at him. "Good price," they persisted. "Special for you." Beyond the corner was a clump of stalls blue with denim, and past that a stretch of trademarks, each of them almost as wide as the T-shirts and other clothes that bore them. Which stalls were likely to appeal to Janet? That was assuming she was even out of bed. He wasn't sure how either of them would have reacted to the other in sight of the next expanse of tables, which were bristling with phallic statues and orgiastic with couples, not to mention more than couples, carved from stone. He dodged the sellers as the hot crowd pressed around him, and struggled to the lower bend.

Had it brought him back to Janet's lodgings? He was trying to see past stalls heaped with electrical goods when a stall-holder, or surely an assistant, younger than himself stepped in front of him. "What you look?"

"Summer Breeze."

The boy made circles with his hands above the stall as if to conjure Barry's needs into view. "Say other."

Barry's head was so full of heat and light and clamour that he could think of nothing else. "Summer Breeze," he heard himself reiterate.

The boy's thin intense face gave up its frown. "Briefs," he said with a gesture of lowering his own and presumably his shorts as well.

"Breeze." Barry jabbed a finger at the building the stall hid, then waved one limp-wristed hand. "Wind," he said in case that could possibly help.

"Here."

As Barry grew aware that the exchange of gestures had made the nearest members of the crowd openly suspicious, he saw the boy pick up a pocket fan and switch it on. "No, that's not it," he said.

"You try," the boy insisted, thrusting it at him.

"No, it's all ow." Barry meant to wave away the offer, but the whirling blades caught his forefinger. "Watch out, you clumsy bugger," he cried.

The boy turned off the fan, which had developed an angry rattling buzz, and peered at it. "You break. You pay."

"Don't be daft," Barry mumbled, sucking his finger, which tasted like a coin. "Your fault, so forget it."

He'd hardly presented his back to the stall when the boy raised his voice. "Pay now. Pay," he called, and other words that Barry didn't comprehend.

Barry saw a scowl spread like an infection through the crowd, who seemed united in obstructing him. He was willing the commotion to attract Janet and her friends—anyone who would understand him— when the crowd parted downhill. Two policemen were heading for him.

They wore khaki shirts and shorts, and pistols in holsters on their right hips. Their dark moist faces bore identical black moustaches. "What is trouble?" the larger and if possible even less jovial officer said.

"He cut me," Barry blurted, displaying his injured finger, and at once felt guilty. "I'm sure it was an accident, but now he wants me to pay."

"You listen."

It was only when the policeman confined himself to glowering that Barry grasped he was required to observe the interview with the youth, which involved much gesturing besides contributions from nearby vendors and members of the crowd. The conference appeared to be reaching agreement, by no means in his favour, when Barry tried to head it off. "I'll pay something if that'll quiet things down. It oughtn't to be much."

The policeman who'd addressed him brushed a thumb and fore-finger over his moustache, and Barry had a nervous urge to giggle at the notion that the man was checking the hair hadn't come unglued. He stared at Barry as if suspicious of his thoughts before growling "You go other place. No trouble."

"Thanks," Barry said, though his unpopularity was as clear from the policeman's face as from every other he risked observing. To retreat uphill to take refuge with his friends he would have had to struggle through hostility that looked capable of growing yet more solid. He swung around faster than his parched unstable skull appreciated to dodge and sidle and excuse himself down to the next bend, where he saw light through a shop. Once he was out of the back entrance he should be able to find his way to the rear of the Summit Apartments.

He launched himself between two stalls piled with footwear and into the building, only to waver to a halt as darkness pressed itself like coins onto his eyes. Outlines had only started to grow visible as he headed for the daylight, so that he was halfway through the interior before he realised where he was: not in a shop but in somebody's home. Nevertheless the contents of the trestle tables were unquestionably for sale, a jumble of bedclothes, icons, cutlery, a religious tome with dislocated pages, dresses, spanners and other tools, toys including a life-size baby that the dimness rendered indistinguishable from a real one . . . He couldn't judge how many people were crouched in gloomy corners of the single room; of the one face he managed to discern, he saw only eyes and teeth. Their dull hungry gleam prompted him to fumble the topmost note off his wad and plant it between the baby's restless feet as he made for the open at a stumbling run. He barely glimpsed all the denizens of the room flinging themselves at the cash.

He'd emerged into more of the market. Only the space just outside the door was clear. Stall-holders and their few potential customers swivelled their heads on scrawny necks to watch him. They looked as uninviting as the tables, which were strewn with goods like a rummage sale. Here were clothes he and his friends might have packed to slouch in, here were the contents of several bathrooms—shaving kits, deodorants, even unwrapped bars of soap. The stares he was receiving didn't encourage him to dawdle. He set off as fast up the narrow tortuous dusty street as his hung-over legs would bear.

He hoped any rear entrance to the Summit Apartments would be both accessible and open. Though there were alleys between the streets, all were blocked by stalls or vans or refuse. He kept catching sight of the crowd, not including anyone who'd witnessed his difference with the youth. He might have considered dodging through a house to reach his street, but the old people dressed like shadows who were sitting in every open doorway looked worse than inhospitable. At least there weren't many more stalls ahead.

The next offered an assortment of electrical goods: cameras, camcorders and battery chargers, a couple of personal stereos, whose rhythmic whispers reminded him that before he'd gone to university and after he'd left it as well, his parents had often complained the stereos weren't personal enough. Suddenly he yearned to be home and starting work at the computer warehouse, the best job he'd been able to sell himself to, or even not having come away on holiday with his old friends from school. He glanced past the stall into an alley and saw them.

"Paul," he shouted, "Derek," as their heads bobbed downhill, borne by the sluggish crowd. They'd looked preoccupied, perhaps with finding him. He would have used the alley if the bulk of a van hadn't been parked mere inches short of both walls. "I'm here," he yelled, digging the heels of his hands into his chin and his fingertips into the bridge of his nose. "Over here," he pleaded at the top of his voice, and Paul turned towards him.

He would have seen Barry if he'd raised his eyes. Having surveyed the crowd between himself and the alley, he said something to Derek that caused him to glance about before vanishing downhill. The next moment, as Barry sucked in a breath that almost blinded him with the whiteness of the houses, Paul had gone too.

Barry bellowed their names and waved until his finger sprinkled the wall with a Morse phrase in blood. None of this was any use. Members of the crowd scowled along the alley at him while the vendors around him glared at him as if he was somehow giving them away. As he fell silent, the personal stereos renewed their bid for audibility. Wasn't the one at the front of the stall playing his favourite album? He could have taken it for the stereo he'd left in the apartment. He reached for the headphones, but the stall-holder, whose leathery face seemed to have been shrivelled in the course of producing an unkempt greyish beard, tapped his arm with a jagged fingernail. "Buy, you listen," he said.

Barry had no idea what he was being told, and suddenly no wish to linger. He might have enough of a problem at the apartments, since he hadn't brought a key with him. Best to save his energy in case he needed to persuade the owner to admit him to his room, he thought as he toiled past the final stall. It was heaped with suitcases, three of which reminded him of his and Paul's and Derek's. Of course there must be many like them, which was why he'd wrapped the handle of his case in bright green tape. Indeed, a greenish fragment adhered to the handle of the case that resembled his so much.

As he leaned forward to confirm what he could hardly believe, the stall-holder stepped in front of him. He wore a sack-like garment that hid none of the muscles and veins of his arms. His small dark thoroughly hairy face appeared to have been sun-dried almost to the bone, revealing a few haphazard blackened teeth. His eyes weren't much less pale and cracked and blank than the wall behind him. "You want?" he said.

"Where'd you get these?"

"Very cheap. Not much use."

The man was staring so hard at him he could have intended to deny Barry had spoken. Barry was about to repeat himself louder when he heard a faint sound above the awning, and raised his unsteady head to see the owner of the Summit Apartments watching him with a loose lopsided smile from an upper window. "What do you know about it?" Barry shouted.

If the man responded, it wasn't to him. He addressed at least a sentence to the stall-holder, whose gaze remained fixed on Barry while growing even blanker. Barry was about to retreat downhill in search of his friends when he noticed that the vendors he'd encountered in the lesser market had been drawn by the argument or, to judge by their purposeful lack of expression, by whatever the man at the window had said. "All right. Forget it. I will," Barry lied and moved away from them.

At first he only walked. He'd reached the first alley that led to the topmost section of the main market when the owner of the Summit Apartments blocked the far end. Sandalled footsteps clattered after Barry, who almost lost the remains of his balance as he twisted to see the vendors filling the width of the street. An understated trail of blood led through the dust to him. He sprinted then, but so did his pursuers with a clacking of their sandals, and the owner of the apartments managed to arrive at the next alley as he did. Above it there were only houses that scarcely looked entitled to the name, with rubbish piled against their closed doors, their windows either shuttered or boarded up. A few dizzy panting hundred yards took him beyond them to the top of the hill.

Two policemen were smoking on it. Though he saw nothing to hold their attention, they had their backs to him. Beyond the hill there was very little to the landscape, as if it had put all its effort into the tourist area. It was the colour of sun-bleached bone, and scattered with rubble and the occasional building, more like a chunk of rock with holes in. A few trees seemed hardly to have found the energy to raise themselves, let alone grow green. Closer to the hill, several goats waited to be fed or slaughtered. Barry was vaguely aware of all this as he hurried to the policemen. "Can you help," he gasped.

They turned to bristle their moustaches at him. It didn't matter that they were the policemen he'd encountered earlier, he told himself, nor did their sharing a fat amateur cigarette. "All my stuff is in the market," he said. "I know who took it, and not just mine either."

The officer who'd previously spoken to him held up one large weathered palm. Barry kept going, since the gesture was directed at his pursuers. "You come," the man urged him.

Barry had almost reached him when the policemen moved apart, revealing a stout post, a larger version of those to which the goats were tethered. He saw the other officer nod at the small crowd more than Barry had noticed were behind him. As the realization swung him around, his hands were captured, handcuffed against his spine and hauled up so that the chain could be attached to a rusty hook on the post. "What are you doing?" Barry felt incredulous enough to waste time asking before he began to shout, partly in the hope that there were tourists close enough to hear him. "Not me. I haven't done anything. It was him from the Summit. It was them. Don't let them get away."

The stall-holders from the cheapest region of the market were wandering downhill, leaving the owner of the apartments together with three other people as huge and glistening. The only woman looked pained by Barry's protests or at least the noise of them. The policemen deftly emptied his pockets, and while the man who'd spoken to him in the market pocketed his cash, the other folded the traveller's cheques in half and stuffed them in Barry's mouth. Barry could emit no more than a choked gurgle past the taste of cardboard as the Summit man waddled up to squeeze his chest in both hands and tweak his nipples. "You nice," he told Barry as he made way for the others to palpate Barry's shrinking genitals and in the woman's case to emit a motherly sound at his injured finger before sucking it so hard he felt the nail pull away from the quick. All this done, the four began to wave obese wads of money at the policemen and at one another. Barry was struggling both to spit out the gag and to disbelieve what was taking place when he saw three girls appear where the houses gave way to rubble.

The girl in the middle was Janet. Presumably she hadn't been to bed, since she was wearing the same clothes and supporting or being supported by her friends, or both. They looked as if they couldn't quite make out the events on top of the hill. Barry threw himself from side to side and did his utmost to produce a noise that would sound like an appeal for help, but succeeded only in further gagging himself. He saw Janet blink and let go of one of her friends in order to shade her eyes. For an instant she seemed to recognise him. Then she stumbled backwards and grabbed at her companions. The three of them staggered around as one and swayed giggling downhill.

If he could believe anything now, he wanted to think she hadn't really seen him or had failed to understand. He watched the bidding come to an end, and felt as though it concerned someone other than himself or who had ceased to be. The woman plodded to scrutinise him afresh, pinching his face between a fat clammy finger and thumb that drove the gag deeper into his mouth. "Will do," she said, separating her wad into halves that the policemen stuffed into their pockets.

While she lumbered downhill the owner of the apartments handed Barry's passport to the policeman who had never spoken to him, and who clanked open a hulk of a lighter to melt it. The last flaming scrap curled up in the dust as the woman reappeared in a dilapidated truck. The policemen lifted Barry off the post and slung him into the back of the vehicle and slammed the tailgate. The last he saw of them was their ironic dual salute as the truck jolted away. Sweat and insects swarmed over him while the animal smell of his predecessor occupied his nostrils and the traveller's cheques turned to pulp in his mouth as he was driven into the pitiless voracious land.

No Strings

"GOOD NIGHT TILL TOMORROW," PHIL LINFORD SAID, HAVING faded the signature tune of *Linford Till Midnight* up under his voice, "and a special good night to anyone I've been alone with." As he removed his headphones, imitated by the reverse of himself in the dark beyond the inner window, he felt as if he was unburdening himself of all the voices he'd talked to during the previous two hours. They'd been discussing the homeless, whom most of the callers had insisted on describing as beggars or worse, until Linford had declared that he respected anyone who did their best to earn their keep, to feed themselves and their dependants. He hadn't intended to condemn those who only begged, if they were capable of nothing else, but several of his listeners did with increasing viciousness. After all that, the very last caller had hoped aloud that nobody homeless had been listening. Maybe Linford oughtn't to have responded that if they were homeless they wouldn't have anywhere to plug in a radio, but he always tried to end with a joke.

There was no point in leaving listeners depressed: that wasn't the responsibility he was paid for. If he'd given them a chance to have their say and something to carry on chewing over, he'd done what was expected of him. If he weren't doing a good job he wouldn't still be on the air. At least it wasn't television—at least he wasn't making people do no more than sit and gawk. As the second hand of the clock above the console fingered midnight he faded out his tune and gave up the station to the national network.

The news paced him as he walked through the station, killing lights. This year's second war, another famine, a seaboard devastated by a hurricane, a town buried by a volcano—no room for anything local, not even the people who'd been missing for weeks or months. In the deserted newsroom computer terminals presented their blank bulging profiles to him. Beyond the unstaffed reception desk a solitary call was flashing like a warning on the switchboard. Its glow and its insect clicking died as he padded across the plump carpet of the reception area. He was reaching for the electronic latch to let himself into the street when he faltered. Beyond the glass door, on the second of the three concrete steps to the pavement, a man was seated with his back to him.

Had he fallen asleep over the contents of his lap? He wore a black suit a size too large, above which peeked an inch of collar gleaming white as a vicar's beneath the neon streetlights, not an ensemble that benefited from being topped by a dark green baseball cap pulled as low as it would stretch on the bald neck. If he was waiting for anyone it surely couldn't be Linford, who nonetheless felt as if he had attracted the other somehow, perhaps by having left all the lights on while he was alone in the station. The news brought itself to an end with a droll anecdote about a music student who had almost managed to sell a forged manuscript before the buyer had noticed the composer's name was spelled Beathoven, and Linford eased the door open. He was on the way to opening enough of a gap to sidle through, into the stagnant July heat beneath the heavy clouds, when *Early Morning Moods* commenced with a rush of jaunty flourishes on a violin. At once the figure on the steps jerked to his feet as though tugged by invisible strings and joined in.

So he was a busker, and the contents of his lap had been a violin and its bow, but the discovery wasn't the only reason why Linford pulled the door wide. The violinist wasn't merely imitating the baroque solo from the radio; he was copying every nuance and intonation, an exact echo no more than a fraction of a second late. Linford felt as though he'd been selected to judge a talent show. "Hey, that's good," he said. "You ought—"

He had barely started speaking when the violinist dodged away with a movement that, whether intentionally or from inability, was less a dance than a series of head-to-toe wriggles that imparted a gypsy swaying to the violin and bow. Perhaps to blot out the interference Linford's voice represented, he began to play louder, though as sweetly as ever. He halted in the middle of the pedestrianised road, between the radio station and a department store lit up for the night. Linford stayed in the doorway until the broadcast melody gave way to the presenter's voice, then closed the door behind him, feeling it lock. "Well done," he called. "Listen, I wonder—"

He could only assume the musician was unable to hear him for playing. No sooner had the melody ended than it recommenced while the player moved away as though guided by his bunch of faint shadows that gave him the appearance of not quite owning up to the possession of several extra limbs. Linford was growing frustrated with the behaviour of someone he only wanted to help. "Excuse me," he said, loud enough for the plate glass across the street to fling his voice back at him. "If it's an audition you need I can get you one. No strings. No commission."

The repetition of the melody didn't falter, but the violinist halted in front of a window scattered with wire skeletons sporting flimsy clothes. When the player didn't turn to face him, Linford followed. He knew talent when he heard it, and local talent was meant to be the point of local radio, but he also didn't mind feeling like the newsman he'd been until he'd found he was better at chatting between his choices of music too old to be broadcast by anyone except him. Years of that had landed him the late-night phone-in, where he sometimes felt he made less of a difference than he had in him. Now here was his chance to make one, and he wasn't about to object if putting the violinist on the air helped his reputation too, not when his contract was due for renewal. He was almost alongside the violinist—close enough to glimpse a twitching of the pale smooth cheek, apparently in time with a mouthing that accompanied the music—when the other danced, if it could be called a dance, away from him.

Unless he was mute—no, even if he was—Linford was determined to extract some sense from him. He supposed it was possible that the musician wasn't quite right in some way, but then it occurred to him that the man might already be employed and so not in need of being discovered. "Do you play with anyone?" he called at the top of his voice.

That seemed to earn him a response. The violinist gestured ahead with his bow, so tersely that Linford heard no break in the music. If the gesture hadn't demonstrated that the player was going Linford's way, he might have sought clarification of whatever he was meant to have understood. Instead he went after the musician, not running or even trotting, since he would have felt absurd, and so not managing to come within arm's length.

The green glow of a window display—clothed dummies exhibiting price tags or challenging the passer-by to guess their worth, their blank-eyed faces immobile and rudimentary as deathmasks moulded by a trainee—settled on the baseball cap as the player turned along the side street that led to the car park, and the cap appeared to glisten like moss. A quarter of a mile away down the main road, Linford saw a police car crested with lights speed across a junction, the closest that traffic was allowed to approach. Of course the police could drive anywhere they liked, and their cameras were perched on roofs: one of his late-night partners in conversation had declared that these days the cameras were the nearest things to God. While Linford felt no immediate need of them, there was surely nothing wrong with knowing you were watched. Waving a hand in front of his face to ward off a raw smell the side street had enclosed, he strode after the musician.

The street led directly into the car park, a patch of waste ground about two hundred yards square, strewn with minor chunks of rubble, empty bottles, squashed cans. Only the exit barrier and the solitary presence of Linford's Peugeot indicated that the square did any work. Department stores backed onto its near side, and to its right were restaurants whose bins must be responsible for the wafts of a raw smell. To the left a chain fence crowned with barbed wire protected a building site, while the far side was overlooked by three storeys of derelict offices. The musician was prancing straight for these beneath arc-lights that set his intensified shadows scuttling around him.

He reached the building as Linford came abreast of the car. Without omitting so much as a quaver from the rapid eager melody, the violinist lifted one foot in a movement that suggested the climax of a dance and shoved the back door open. The long brownish stick of the bow jerked up as though to beckon Linford. Before he had time to call out, if indeed he felt obliged to, he saw the player vanish into a narrow oblong black as turned earth.

He rested a hand on the tepid roof of the car and told himself he'd done enough. If the musician was using the disused offices as a squat he was unlikely to be alone, and perhaps his thinness was a symptom of addiction. The prospect of encountering a roomful of drug addicts fell short of appealing to Linford. He was fishing out his keys when an abrupt silence filled the car park. The music, rendered hollow by the dark interior, had ceased in the midst of a phrase, but it hadn't entirely obscured a shrill cry from within—a cry, Linford was too sure to be able to ignore it, for help.

Five minutes—less if he surprised himself by proving to be in a condition to run—would take him back to the radio station to call the police. The main street might even feature a phone booth that accepted coins rather than cards. Less than five minutes could be far too long for whoever needed help, and so Linford stalked across the car park, waving his arms at the offices as he raised his face to mouth for help at the featureless slate sky. He was hoping some policeman was observing him and would send reinforcements—he was hoping to hear a police car raise its voice on its way to him. He'd heard nothing but his own dwarfed isolated footsteps by the time he reached the ajar door.

Perhaps someone had planned to repaint it and given up early in the process. Those patches of old paint that weren't flaking were blistered. The largest blister had split open, and he saw an insect writhe into hiding inside the charred bulge as he dealt the door a slow kick to shove it wide. A short hall with two doors on each side led to a staircase that turned its back on itself halfway up. The widening glare from the car park pressed the darkness back towards the stairs, but only to thicken it on them and within the doorways. Since all the doors were open, he ventured as far as the nearest pair and peered quickly to either side of him.

Random shapes of light were stranded near the windows, all of which were broken. The floorboards of both rooms weren't much less rubbly than the car park. In the room to his left two rusty filing cabinets had been pulled fully open, though surely there could have been nothing to remove from them, let alone to put in. To his right a single office desk was leaning on a broken leg and grimacing with both the black rectangles that used to contain drawers. Perhaps it was his tension that rendered these sights unpleasant, or perhaps it was the raw smell. His will to intervene was failing as he began to wonder if he had really heard any sound except music—and then the cry was repeated above him. It could be a woman's voice or a man's grown shrill with terror, but there was no mistaking its words. "Help," it pleaded. "Oh God."

No more than a couple of streets away a nightclub emitted music and loud voices, followed by an outburst of the slamming of car doors. The noises made Linford feel less alone: there must be at least one bouncer outside the nightclub, within earshot of a yell. Perhaps that wasn't as reassuring as he allowed it to seem, but it let him advance to the foot of the stairs and shout into the dimness that was after all not quite dark. "Hello? What's happening up there? What's wrong?"

His first word brought the others out with it. The more of them there were, the less sure he was how advisable they might be. They were met by utter silence except for a creak of the lowest stair, on which he'd tentatively stepped. He hadn't betrayed his presence, he told himself fiercely: whoever was above him had already been aware of him, or there would have been no point to the cry for help. Nevertheless once he seized the splintered banister it was on tiptoe that he ran upstairs. He was turning the bend when an object almost tripped him—the musician's baseball cap.

The banister emitted a groan not far short of vocal as he leaned on it to steady himself. The sound was answered by another cry of "Help", or most of it before the voice was muffled by a hand over the mouth. It came from a room at the far end of the corridor ahead. He was intensely aware of the moment, of scraps of light that clung like pale bats to the ceiling of the corridor, the rat's tails of the flexes that had held sockets for light bulbs, the blackness of the doorways that put him in mind of holes in the ground, the knowledge that this was his last chance to retreat. Instead he ran almost soundlessly up the stairs and past two rooms that a glance into each appeared to show were empty save for rubble and broken glass. Before he came abreast of the further left-hand room he knew it was where he had to go. For a moment he thought someone had hung a sign on the door.

It was a tattered office calendar dangling from a nail. Dates some weeks apart on it—the most recent almost a fortnight ago—were marked with ovals that in daytime might have looked more reddish. He was thinking that the marks couldn't be fingerprints, since they contained no lines, as he took a step into the room.

A shape lay on the area of the floor least visited by daylight, under the window amid shards of glass. A ragged curtain tied at the neck covered all of it except the head, which was so large and bald and swollen it reminded him of the moon. The features appeared to be sinking into it: the unreadably shadowed eyes and gaping whitish lips could have passed for craters, and its nostrils were doing without a nose. Despite its baldness, it was a woman's head, since Linford distinguished the outline of breasts under the curtain indeed, enough bulk for an extra pair. The head wobbled upright to greet him, its scalp springing alight with the glare from the car park, and large hands whose white flesh was loose as oversized gloves groped out from beneath the curtain. He could see no nails on them. The foot he wasn't conscious of holding in mid-air trod on a fragile object he'd failed to notice—a violinist's bow. It snapped and pitched him forward to see more of the room.

Four desk drawers had been brought into it, one to a corner. Each drawer contained a nest of newspapers and office scrap. Around the drawers were strewn crumpled sheets of music, stained dark as though—Linford thought and then tried not to—they had been employed to wipe mouths. Whatever had occurred had apparently involved the scattering about the bare floor of enough spare bows to equip a small string orchestra. By no means anxious to understand any of the contents of the room until he was well clear of it, Linford was backing away when the violin recommenced its dance behind him.

He swung around and at once saw far too much. The violinist was as bald as the figure under the window, but despite the oddly temporary nature of the bland smooth face, particularly around the nose, it was plain that the musician was female too. The long brown stick she was passing back and forth over the instrument had never been a bow—not that one would have made a difference, since the cracked violin was stringless. The perfect imitation of the broadcast melody was streaming out of her wide toothless mouth, the interior of which was at least as white as the rest of her face. Despite her task she managed a smile, though he sensed it wasn't for him but about him. She was blocking the doorway, and the idea of going closer to her—to the smell of rawness, some of which was certainly emerging from her mouth—almost crushed his mind to nothing. He had to entice her away from the doorway, and he was struggling to will himself to retreat into the room—struggling to keep his back to it when a voice cried "Help."

It was the cry he'd come to find: exactly the cry, and it was behind him in the room. He twisted half round and saw the shape under the window begin to cover her mouth, then let her hand fall. She must have decided there was no longer any reason to cut the repetition short. "Oh God," she added, precisely as she had before, and rubbed her curtained stomach.

It wasn't just a trick, it was as much of an imitation as the music had been. He had to make more of an effort than he could remember ever having used to swallow the sound the realisation almost forced out of his mouth. For years he'd earned his living by not letting there be more than a second of silence, but could staying absolutely quiet now save him? He was unable to think what else to do, not that he was anything like sure of being capable of silence. "Help, oh God," the curtained shape repeated, more of a demand now, and rubbed her stomach harder. The player dropped the violin and the other item, and before their clatter faded she came at Linford with a writhing movement that might have been a jubilant dance came just far enough to continue to block his escape.

His lips trembled, his teeth chattered, and he couldn't suppress his words, however idiotic they might be. "My mistake. I only—"

"My mistake. I only." Several voices took up his protest at once, but he could see no mouths uttering it, only an agitation of the lower half of the curtain. Then two small forms crawled out from underneath, immediately followed by two more, all undisguised by any kind of covering. Their plump white bodies seemed all the more wormlike for the incompleteness of the faces on the bald heads—no more than nostrils and greedily dilated mouths. Just the same they wriggled straight to him, grabbing pointed fragments of glass. He saw the violinist press her hands over her ears, and thought that she felt some sympathy for him until he grasped that she was ensuring she didn't have to imitate whatever sound he made. The window was his only chance now: if the creature beneath it was as helpless as she seemed, if he could bear to step over or on her so as to scream from the window for somebody out there to hear—But when he screamed it was from the floor where, having expertly tripped him, the young were swarming up his legs, and he found he had no interest in the words he was screaming, especially when they were repeated in chorus to him.

The Worst Fog of the Year

T HICK FOG HAD BEEN DRAWN OVER THE FIELDS. SINCE THE encircling horizon was invisible, the boundaries of the pale landscape were defined only by a dull silence. The moon was a dab of grey paint on the sky. Ahead, above the surface of the fog, Gaunt saw parallel lines of hedge marking the road that led to the house. With its gables piled askew against the sky the house resembled a waterlogged box soaking out of shape.

Almost before he was ready Gaunt was inside the house and passing along the dark hall, glimpsing a stretched grin on the face which adorned the post at the foot of the banister, a heavy curtain weighted with dust and gradually sagging across a mirror, oak panels displaying framed portraits which appeared to have grown beards of dust. At the end of the hall a fan of electric light lay half closed on the carpet. Gaunt inched past the heavy oak door and its brass meringue of a doorknob, into the room.

Two women sat on couches with rolled arms of thick black leather. Around them the room was piled with silence. The tea in the porcelain cups abandoned on a black table was clouding over like two miniature ponds, and beside the cups and their silver tray an orchid was crushed within a paperweight. Heavy velvet curtains twice Gaunt's height almost curtained a long window. The older woman reached beside her for a poker, which she thrust into the fire beyond the marble proscenium of the fireplace. Her gaze never left her companion's face, and the pistol in her hand never wavered. "What time is it now?" she demanded.

The young woman shook back her black hair from its band and threw out her wrist to consult her watch. "One o'clock."

The gun rose a fraction. "Don't lie to me."

"Twenty to twelve," the young woman said, shivering. "For God's sake, won't you see what you're doing? We can still leave. There's time."

"Almost midnight," the other said happily, and then her voice sharpened. "Don't bring God into it. It's God's will that we're here. Whatever happens will be meant to happen."

"Rubbish," Gaunt snorted.

The woman patted her greying hair into place with her free hand while the girl shrank back into the crook of the couch. "Even if you can't cover your knees, pull your skirt down. Your father won't want to see you looking like that, whatever your boyfriends like."

"You," the girl said wearily, "are mad."

"If you knew that," Gaunt demanded, "why did you let her lure you here?"

The woman raised the gun until the eye of the barrel was level with the right eye of her victim, then she threw the weapon on the hearth. "Go on, and take your atheism with you. God couldn't be so cruel to your father. God will let him come to me."

The young woman made to reach for her, but drew back. "He's dead, mother. He's been dead for months."

"Don't you know I still love him, whoever he married? Do you think I could be frightened of him?" All at once the mother's eyes looked as dangerous as the barrel of the gun. "You're afraid of how he may punish your sins, when you should be weeping for the pain you caused him."

The girl sprang up and kicked the gun, which skidded away beneath the table while the cups chattered like teeth. "That's right, you run," her mother jeered. "He's out there waiting for you. You know you're meant to stay until he comes. Why else do you think tonight is the worst fog of the year?" And behind her the music crept up—for that, of course, was the title of the film.

Outside, over the fields that surrounded the house, patches of fog were wearing thin. A threadbare strip like the ghost of a path, perforated by brittle grass-blades, led towards the house. At the end farthest from the house, blades bent suddenly and sprang up; then others stirred closer to the building. Although the fog hung close to the ground, what troubled the grass was crawling beneath the fog.

For the second time Gaunt wanted to leave. The first had been in London, in a cinema off Tottenham Court Road. Surrounded by snoring men, he'd realised that the young woman was trapped. Her own stupidity and inconsistency had trapped her, or those qualities of the script had, and his feeling compelled to will her to escape had infuriated him. Now, having seen it once, he knew her fate, yet more than ever he was urging the film to let her go. He would have left the cinema, except that he was the entire audience for the press show. At least nobody would know he wasn't watching, and so he closed his eyes. With luck he might nod off, just like one of the Londoners who had nowhere but the cinema to sleep; he'd been lying awake for nights trying to think what to make of his life.

In front of him was dimness not unlike midnight fog, and the sounds of stealthy crawling in the grass. Why was he here? He mightn't even be allowed to review the film. His editor had hinted that his reviews were too analytical for a small-town newspaper and in particular for the cinema manager, a friend of the editor's. If the editor gave way to persuasion then Gaunt would have to, like a minor character required to behave as the script demanded. He heard movement dragging through the grass, and thought he could hear the squeak of soil clenched in a groping fist, though last time he hadn't. He felt as if he was dreaming the film, in which case he had to accept some blame for its absurdity, for that of his own situation, for the absurdity of talking to the film in the dark as though it was as real as himself and as though his feelings could make any difference.

"Pointless," he muttered. "Meaningless, you and me both." He drew a breath to groan as though the film could hear his impatience with it. For a moment he was enclosed in a humming silence; his head swam unpleasantly, and the fog in his eyes seemed to surge at him. Then he heard grass rustling around him.

Had the projectionist turned on the stereophonic sound? He needn't have bothered; it wouldn't improve Gaunt's view of the film. Perhaps the speakers had momentarily gone wrong, because the sound had ceased. Gaunt's eyes lay shut, and his mind lay inert, until behind him he heard the young woman run to draw the curtains.

"He won't come through the window. He'll use the front door as he has every right to," her mother said, and Gaunt opened his eyes. He wasn't in the cinema, he was in the room.

For a moment he thought he was experiencing some new visual gimmick. The room seemed unreal; it seemed somehow to have crammed itself into his eyes. He was nearest the table, and he made himself dip one shaky finger into a cup of tea. The skin of the stagnant brew gave way, and the chill of the liquid shivered up his arm.

He couldn't cry out. The chill had seized his throat, and he couldn't even swallow. His mind was struggling to deny what he was experiencing, but was this really more absurd than his everyday life? As soon as he had the thought, it seized him, and the room opened out around him. "Did he come through the front door for my sister?" the girl cried behind him.

Gaunt lurched aside and stared at her. She was gazing at her mother, who lay in an attitude of regal indifference on the couch. Gaunt shoved one hand almost into the daughter's face, but she didn't flinch. Neither woman could see him. It was he who was unreal.

"No doubt," the mother said.

"And for my brother? Did you lure them both here?"

"They came when they were called," the mother said, and with a hint of bitterness "He let them see him, but he didn't show himself to me."

"But you saw what he did to them. You saw how they were stuffed with earth."

"Don't you say that! Don't you dare suggest he could do that to anyone!"

We're all mad, Gaunt thought wildly. Everything is. He almost touched the girl to convince himself that she was real, but what would that or its opposite prove? He stood in the room, unable to stir, and then he heard a scratching at the front door.

"He's your father!" the woman shouted as her daughter flinched towards Gaunt. "Don't you let him see that you're frightened of him!" She flung herself at the young woman and, grabbing her wrist, dragged her along the hall to the front door. Gaunt felt as if the wake of her violence was carrying him along, past a mirror in which he might or might not be glimpsing himself. There was silence except for the panting of the women; even the front door appeared to be holding itself still. Then something scratched at the foot of the door.

The daughter fought. Gaunt wanted to help her, but the idea felt like a pit into which he would never stop falling. Suddenly several objects like blackened splintered knife-blades were thrust under the door. They were fingernails.

The daughter screamed and, wrenching herself free, fled along the hall. Gaunt thought her flight had released him until he felt himself being rushed after her. As he ended up in the middle of the room, the mother came in and locked the door. "He won't mind if I open the window for him," she said. "It'll be like an assignation."

The daughter caught up the silver tea tray as if it was the only weapon she could bring to mind, sending the cups trundling across the carpet. "After I cleaned up for him," her mother shouted, "and you didn't even wash up!" She captured her daughter's wrists, and the women wrestled for possession of the tea tray. Flashes of light from it blinded Gaunt, who closed his eyes as if that might help him escape. Then they sprang open. At the window, muffled by the curtains, he'd heard a feeble thud of stone on glass.

The woman released her daughter and ran to the curtains. She dragged them open, and the fog bellied forwards to soak up the light from the room. At the bottom of the right-hand pane Gaunt saw a stone rear up slowly, strike the pane and spatter it with mud, fall back to hang suspended for a moment and then thump the glass. Around the stone were five discoloured things like blades.

The blows were growing stronger. From outside the window came a choking cough, and a shower of mud obscured the glass. The mother pulled the upper bolt free of its socket and stooped to the bolt at the foot of the window. Her daughter ran at her, lifting the tray to batter her down. Then the pane gave way, and the stone thudded on the carpet.

Gaunt staggered back, closing his eyes. The gun! He fell to his knees and groped under the table. Nothing. The women screamed, and what sounded like a mound of earth fell through the window into the room.

As Gaunt scrabbled under the table he heard sounds of padding and scraping, like the progress of an injured dog that was causing the floor to quiver. He forced his eyes open, and saw the gun ahead of him, just out of reach. He hitched himself forwards, and the mother bent to pick up the gun as the young woman stumbled to the door. A shadow fell across Gaunt's path. He peered wildly along it and confronted something like a face.

It was crushed and discoloured. It might almost have been a mask shaped of mud and insufficiently baked. Parts of it were moist, other parts were crumbling. The sight of it paralysed him while a frayed hand wavered up from the carpet and reached towards him with its askew nails.

When Gaunt didn't move, the hand faltered to the ragged lips. Deliberately, and with some effort, the mouth produced a handful of glistening mud, and then the hand came swaying towards Gaunt's face. He felt his lips twitching uncontrollably. It was waiting for him to open his mouth.

He couldn't keep it shut now that an outraged scream was building up inside him. The prospect of his fate made not just his mouth but his whole body writhe. The convulsion released him, and he squirmed aside, seizing the wrist, which was mostly bones, and twisting it. Its flimsiness took him unawares. The arm tore loose from the shoulder, and Gaunt went sprawling. Instead of bones and tendons, the arm ended in a bunch of wires and metal rods.

Gaunt staggered to his feet and gave the mutilated dummy a kick to convince himself it had stopped moving. The mother stood frozen, gun in hand, in the act of turning to shoot her daughter in the leg. The daughter was almost at the door, her hand outstretched to grasp the key. How long before the shot revived the action of the scene? Gaunt sprinted to the door and turned the key, then clutched at the young woman's hand.

He didn't know where he meant to lead her, but in any case the knowledge would clearly not have helped. As soon as he tugged at her cold hand, her arm came away at the shoulder.

He felt the walls and floor and his sense of himself begin to give way to the dark. Absurdity was everything. Everything he touched betrayed it. He lurched away from the standing remains of the young woman, towards the husk of her father. Which of them might come lopsidedly for him?

Neither, by the look of it, and the gun would never go off. None of them would ever move again, and there was no point in his moving when there was nowhere for him to go. They were nothing. In destroying them, he'd destroyed nothing. But if he were capable of destroying no more than a symbol of the threat of nothingness then surely he, if nothing else—

He cried out wordlessly, shocked by the pain: the cinema seat had sprung up at last and smacked his arse.

He felt the walls and floor and his sense of himself begin to give way to the dark. Absurdity was everything. Everything he touched betrayed it. He lurched away from the standing remains of the young woman, towards the husk of her father. Which of them might come lopsidedly for him?

Neither, by the look of it, and the gun would never go off. None of them would ever move again, and there was no point in his moving when there was nowhere for him to go. They were nothing. In destroying them, he'd destroyed nothing. But if he were capable of destroying no more than a symbol of the threat of nothingness then surely he, if nothing else—

Before he could finish the thought it went out like a light, and he felt himself come apart in the suddenly total darkness.

The Retrospective

TRENT HAD NO IDEA HOW LONG HE WAS UNABLE TO THINK for rage. The guard kept out of sight while she announced the unscheduled stop, and didn't reappear until the trainload of passengers had crowded onto the narrow platform. As the train dragged itself away into a tunnel simulated by elderly trees and the low March afternoon sky that was plastered with layers of darkness, she poked her head out of the rearmost window to announce that the next train should be due in an hour. The resentful mutters of the crowd only aggravated Trent's frustration. He needed a leisurely evening and, if he could manage it for a change, a night's sleep in preparation for a working breakfast. If he'd known the journey would be broken, he could have reread his paperwork instead of contemplating scenery he couldn't even remember. No doubt the next train would already be laden with commuters—he doubted it would give him space to work. His skull was beginning to feel shrivelled and hollow when it occurred to him that if he caught a later train he would both ensure himself a seat and have time to drop in on his parents. When had he last been home to see them? All at once he felt so guilty that he preferred not to look anyone in the face as he excused his slow way to the ticket office.

It was closed—a board lent it the appearance of a frame divested of a photograph—but flanked by a timetable. Stoneby to London, Stoneby to London . . . There were trains on the hour, like the striking of a clock. He emerged from the short wooden passage into the somewhat less gloomy street, only to falter. Where was the sweet shop whose window used to exhibit dozens of glass-stoppered jars full of colours he could taste? Where was the toyshop fronted by a headlong model train that had never stopped for the travellers paralysed on the platform? What had happened to the bakery displaying tiered white cakes elaborate as Gothic steeples, and the bridal shop next door, where the headless figures in their pale dresses had made him think of Anne Boleyn? Now the street was overrun with the same fast-food eateries and immature clothes shops that surrounded him whenever he left his present apartment, and he couldn't recall how much change he'd seen on his last visit, whenever that had been. He felt suddenly so desperate to be somewhere more like home that he almost didn't wait for twin green men to pipe up and usher him across the road.

The short cut was still there, in a sense. Instead of separating the toyshop from the wedding dresses, it squeezed between a window occupied by a regiment of boots and a hamburger outlet dogged by plastic cartons. Once he was in the alley the clamour of traffic relented, but the narrow passage through featureless discoloured concrete made him feel walled in by the unfamiliar. Then the concrete gave way to russet bricks and released him into a street he knew.

At least, it conformed to his memory until he looked closer. The building opposite, which had begun life as a music hall, had ceased to be a cinema. A pair of letters clung to the whitish border of the rusty iron marquee, two letters N so insecure they were on the way to being Zs. He was striving to remember if the cinema had been shut last time he'd seen it when he noticed that the boards on either side of the lobby contained posters too small for the frames. The neighbouring buildings were boarded up. As he crossed the deserted street, the posters grew legible. MEMORIES OF STONEBY, the amateurish printing said.

The two wide steps beneath the marquee were cracked and chipped and stained. The glass of the ticket booth in the middle of the marble floor was too blackened to see through. Behind the booth the doors into the auditorium stood ajar. Uncertain what the gap was showing him, he ventured to peer in.

At first the dimness yielded up no more than a strip of carpet framed by floorboards just as grubby, and then he thought someone absolutely motionless was watching him from the dark. The watcher was roped off from him—the several indistinct figures were. He assumed they represented elements of local history: there was certainly something familiar about them. That impression, and the blurred faces with their dully glinting eyes, might have transfixed him if he hadn't remembered that he was supposed to be seeing his parents. He left the echo of his footsteps dwindling in the lobby and hurried around the side of the museum.

Where the alley crossed another he turned left along the rear of the building. In the high wall to his right a series of solid wooden gates led to back yards, the third of which belonged to his old house. As a child he'd used the gate as a short cut to the cinema, clutching a coin in his fist, which had smelled of metal whenever he'd raised it to his face in the crowded restless dark. His parents had never bolted the gate until he was home again, but now the only effect of his trying the latch was to rouse a clatter of claws and the snarling of a neighbour's dog that sounded either muzzled or gagged with food, and so he made for the street his old house faced.

The sunless sky was bringing on a twilight murky as an unlit room. He could have taken the street for an aisle between two blocks of dimness so lacking in features they might have been identical. Presumably any children who lived in the terrace were home from school by now, though he couldn't see the flicker of a single television in the windows draped with dusk, while the breadwinners had yet to return. Trent picked his way over the broken upheaved slabs of the pavement, supporting himself on the roof of a lone parked car until it shifted rustily under his hand, to his parents' front gate.

The small plot of a garden was a mass of weeds that had spilled across the short path. He couldn't feel it underfoot as he tramped to the door, which was the colour of the oncoming dark. He was fumbling in his pocket and then with the catches of his briefcase when he realised he would hardly have brought his old keys with him. He rang the doorbell, or at least pressed the askew pallid button that set off a muffled rattle somewhere in the house.

For the duration of more breaths than he could recall taking, there was no response. He was about to revive the noise, though he found it somehow distressing, when he heard footsteps shuffling down the hall. Their slowness made it sound as long as it had seemed in his childhood, so that he had the odd notion that whoever opened the door would tower over him.

It was his mother, and smaller than ever—wrinkled and whitish as a figure composed of dough that had been left to collect dust, a wad of it on top of and behind her head. She wore a tweed coat over a garment he took to be a nightdress, which exposed only her prominent ankles above a pair of unmatched slippers. Her head wavered upwards as the corners of her lips did. Once all these had steadied she murmured "Is it you, Nigel? Are you back again?"

"I thought it was past time I was."

"It's always too long." She shuffled in a tight circle to present her stooped back to him before calling "Guess who it is, Walter."

"Hess looking for a place to hide," Trent's father responded from some depth of the house.

"No, not old red-nosed Rudolph. Someone a bit younger and a bit more English."

"The Queen come to tea."

"He'll never change, will he?" Trent's mother muttered and raised what was left of her voice. "It's the boy. It's Nigel."

"About time. Let's see what he's managed to make of himself."

She made a gesture like a desultory grab at something in the air above her left shoulder, apparently to beckon Trent along the hall. "Be quick with the door, there's a good boy. We don't want the chill roosting in our old bones."

As soon as the door shut behind him he couldn't distinguish whether the stairs that narrowed the hall by half were carpeted only with dimness. He trudged after his mother past a door that seemed barely sketched on the crawling murk and, more immediately than he expected, another. His mother opened a third, beyond which was the kitchen, he recalled rather than saw. It smelled of damp he hoped was mostly tea. By straining his senses he was just able to discern his father seated in some of the dark. "Shall we have the light on?" Trent suggested.

"Can't you see? Thought you were supposed to be the young one round here." After a pause his father said "Come back for bunny, have you?"

Trent couldn't recall ever having owned a rabbit, toy or otherwise, yet the question seemed capable of reviving some aspect of his childhood. He was feeling surrounded by entirely too much darkness when his mother said "Now, Walter, don't be teasing" and clicked the switch.

The naked dusty bulb seemed to draw the contents of the room inwards—the blackened stove and stained metal sink, the venerable shelves and cabinets and cupboards Trent's father had built, the glossy pallid walls. The old man was sunk in an armchair, the least appropriate of an assortment of seats surrounding the round table decorated with crumbs and unwashed plates. His pear-shaped variously reddish face appeared to have been given over to producing fat to merge with the rest of him. He used both shaky inflated hands to close the lapels of his faded dressing-gown over his pendulous chest cobwebbed with grey hairs. "You've got your light," he said, "so take your place."

Lowering himself onto a chair that had once been straight, Trent lost sight of the entrance to the alley—of the impression that it was the only aspect of the yard the window managed to illuminate. "Will I make you some tea?" his mother said.

She wasn't asking him to predict the future, he reassured himself. "So long as you're both having some as well."

"Not much else to do these days."

"It won't be that bad really, will it?" Trent said, forcing a guilty laugh. "Aren't you still seeing . . . "

"What are we seeing?" his father prompted with some force.

"Your friends," Trent said, having discovered that he couldn't recall a single name. "They can't all have moved away."

"Nobody moves any longer."

Trent didn't know whether to take that as a veiled rebuke. "So what have you two been doing with yourselves lately?"

"Late's the word."

"Nigel's here now," Trent's mother said, perhaps relevantly, over the descending hollow drum-roll of the kettle she was filling from the tap.

More time than was reasonable seemed to have passed since he'd entered the house. He was restraining himself from glancing even surreptitiously at his watch when his father quivered an impatient hand at him. "So what are you up to now?"

"He means your work."

"Same as always."

Trent hoped that would suffice until he was able to reclaim his memory from the darkness that had gathered in his skull, but his parents' stares were as blank as his mind. "And what's that?" his mother said.

He felt as though her forgetfulness had seized him. Desperate to be reminded what his briefcase contained, he nevertheless used reaching for it as a chance to glimpse his watch. The next train was due in less than half an hour. As Trent scrabbled at the catches of the briefcase, his father said "New buildings, isn't it? That's what you put up."

"Plan," Trent said, clutching the briefcase on his lap. "I draw them."

"Of course you do," said his mother. "That's what you always wanted."

It was partly so as not to feel minimised that Trent declared "I wouldn't want to be responsible for some of the changes in town."

"Then don't be."

"You won't see much else changing round here," Trent's mother said.

"Didn't anyone object?"

"You have to let the world move on," she said. "Leave it to the young ones."

Trent wasn't sure if he was included in that or only wanted to be. "How long have we had a museum?"

His father's eyes grew so blank Trent could have fancied they weren't in use. "Since I remember."

"No, that's not right," Trent objected as gently as his nerves permitted. "It was a cinema and before that a theatre. You took me to a show there once."

"Did we?" A glint surfaced in his mother's eyes. "We used to like shows, didn't we, Walter? Shows and dancing. Didn't we go on all night sometimes and they wondered where we'd got to?"

Her husband shook his head once slowly, whether to enliven memories or deny their existence Trent couldn't tell. "The show you took me to," he insisted, "I remember someone dancing with a stick. And there was a lady comedian, or maybe not a lady but dressed up."

Perhaps it was the strain of excavating the recollection that made it seem both lurid and encased in darkness—the outsize figure prancing sluggishly about the stage and turning towards him a sly greasy smile as crimson as a wound, the ponderous slap on the boards of feet that sounded unshod, the onslaughts of laughter that followed comments Trent found so incomprehensible he feared they were about him, the shadow that kept swelling on whatever backdrop the performer had, an effect suggesting that the figure was about to grow yet more gigantic. Surely some or preferably most of that was a childhood nightmare rather than a memory. "Was there some tea?" Trent blurted.

At first it seemed his mother's eyes were past seeing through their own blankness. "In the show, do you mean?"

"Here." When that fell short of her he said more urgently "Now."

"Why, you should have reminded me," she protested and stood up. How long had she been seated opposite him? He was so anxious to remember that he didn't immediately grasp what she was doing. "Mother, don't," he nearly screamed, flinging himself off his chair.

"No rush. It isn't anything like ready." She took her hand out of the kettle on the stove—he wasn't sure if he glimpsed steam trailing from her fingers as she replaced the lid. "We haven't got much longer, have we?" she said. "We mustn't keep you from your duties."

"You won't do that again, will you?"

"What's that, son?"

He was dismayed to think she might already have forgotten. "You won't put yourself in danger."

"There's nothing we'd call that round here," his father said.

"You'll look after each other, won't you? I really ought to catch the next train. I'll be back to see you again soon, I promise, and next time it'll be longer."

"It will."

His parents said that not quite in chorus, apparently competing at slowness. "Till next time, then," he said and shook his father's hand before hugging his mother. Both felt disconcertingly cold and unyielding, as if the appearance of each had hardened into a carapace. He gripped the handle of his briefcase while he strove to twist the rusty key in the back door. "I'll go my old way, shall I? It's quicker."

When nobody answered he hauled open the door, which felt unhinged. Cobwebbed weeds sprawled over the doorstep into the kitchen at once. Weedy mounds of earth or rubble had overwhelmed the yard and the path. He picked his way to the gate and with an effort turned his head, but nobody was following to close the gate: his mother was still at her post by the stove, his father was deep in the armchair. He had to use both hands to wrench the bolt out of its socket, and almost forgot to retrieve his briefcase as he stumbled into the alley. The passage was unwelcomingly dark, not least because the light from the house failed to reach it—no, because the kitchen was unlit. He dragged the gate shut and took time to engage the latch before heading for the rear of the museum.

Damp must be stiffening his limbs. He hoped it was in the air, not in his parents' house. Was it affecting his vision as well? When he slogged to the end of the alley the street appeared to be composed of little but darkness, except for the museum. The doors to the old auditorium were further ajar, and as he crossed the road Trent saw figures miming in the dimness. He hadn't time to identify their faces before panting down the alley where brick was ousted by concrete.

Figures sat in the stark restaurants and modelled clothes in windows. Otherwise the street was deserted except for a man who dashed into the station too fast for Trent to see his face. The man let fly a wordless plea and waved his briefcase as he sprinted through the booking hall. Trent had just begun to precipitate himself across the road when he heard the slam of a carriage door. He staggered ahead of his breath onto the platform in time to see the last light of a train vanish into the trees, which looked more like a tunnel than ever.

His skull felt frail with rage again. Once he regained the ability to move he stumped to glower at the timetable next to the boarded-up office. His fiercest glare was unable to change the wait into less than an hour. He marched up and down a few times, but each end of the platform met him with increasing darkness. He had to keep moving to ward off a chill stiffness. He trudged into the street and frowned about him.

The fast-food outlets didn't appeal to him, neither their impersonal refreshments nor the way all the diners faced the street as though to watch him, not that doing so lent them any animation. He couldn't even see anyone eating. Ignoring the raw red childishly sketched men, he lurched across the road into the alley.

He oughtn't to go to his parents. So instant a return might well confuse them, and just now his own mind felt more than sufficiently unfocused. The only light, however tentative, in the next street came from the museum. He crossed the roadway, which was as lightless as the low sky, and climbed the faint steps.

Was the ticket booth lit? A patch of the blackened glass had been rubbed relatively clear from within. He was fumbling for money to plant on the sill under the gap at the foot of the window when he managed to discern that the figure in the booth was made of wax. While it resembled the middle-aged woman who had occupied the booth when the building was a cinema, it ought to look years—no, decades—older. Its left grey-cardiganed arm was raised to indicate the auditorium. He was unable to judge its expression for the gloom inside the booth. Tramping to the doors, he pushed them wide.

That seemed only to darken the auditorium, but he felt the need to keep on the move before his eyes had quite adjusted. The apparently sourceless twilight put him in mind of the glow doled out by the candle that used to stand in an encrusted saucer on the table by his childhood bed. As he advanced under the enormous unseen roof, he thought he was walking on the same carpet that had led into the cinema and indeed the theatre. He was abreast of the first of the figures on either side of the aisle before he recognised them.

He'd forgotten they were sisters, the two women who had run the bakery and the adjacent bridal shop. Had they really been twins? They were playing bridesmaids in identical white ankle-length dresses— whitish, rather, and trimmed with dust. Presumably it was muslin as well as dust that gloved their hands, which were pointing with all their digits along the aisle. The dull glints of their grimy eyes appeared to spy sidelong on him. He'd taken only a few steps when he stumbled to a halt and peered about him.

The next exhibits were disconcerting enough. No doubt the toyshop owner was meant to be introducing his model railway, but he looked as if he was crouching sideways to grab whatever sought refuge in the miniature tunnel. Opposite him the sweet shop man was enticing children to his counter, which was heaped with sweets powdered grey, by performing on a sugar whistle not entirely distinguishable from his glimmering teeth. Trent hadn't time to ascertain what was odd about the children's wide round eyes, because he was growing aware of the extent of the museum.

Surely it must be a trick of the unreliable illumination, but the more he gazed around him, the farther the dimness populated with unmoving figures seemed to stretch. If it actually extended so far ahead and to both sides, it would encompass at least the whole of the street that contained his parents' house. He wavered forward a couple of paces, which only encouraged figures to solidify out of that part of the murk. He swivelled as quickly as he was able and stalked out of the museum.

The echoes of his footsteps pursued him across the lobby like mocking applause. He could hear no other sound, and couldn't tell whether he was being watched from the ticket booth. He found his way down the marble steps and along the front of the museum. In a few seconds he was sidling crabwise along it in order to differentiate the alley from the unlit facade, He wandered farther than he should have, and made his way back more slowly. Before long he was groping with his free hand at the wall as he ranged back and forth, but it was no use. There was no alley, just unbroken brick.

He was floundering in search of a crossroads, from which there surely had to be a route to his old house, when he realised he might as well be blind. He glanced back, praying wordlessly for any relief from the dark. There was only the glow from the museum lobby. It seemed as feeble as the candle flame had grown in the moment before it guttered into smoke, and so remote he thought his stiff limbs might be past carrying him to it. When he retreated towards it, at first he seemed not to be moving at all.

More time passed than he could grasp before he felt sure the light was closer. Later still he managed to distinguish the outstretched fingertips of his free hand. He clung to his briefcase as though it might be snatched from him. He was abreast of the lobby, and preparing to abandon its glow for the alley that led to the station, when he thought he heard a whisper from inside the museum. "Are you looking for us?"

It was either a whisper or so distant that it might as well be one. "We're in here, son," it said, and its companion added "You'll have to come to us."

"Mother?" It was unquestionably her voice, however faint. He almost tripped over the steps as he sent himself into the lobby. For a moment, entangled in the clapping of his footsteps on the marble, he thought he heard a large but muted sound as of the surreptitious arrangement of a crowd. He blundered to the doors and peered into the auditorium.

Under the roof, which might well have been an extension of the low ponderous black sky, the aisle and its guardians were at least as dim as ever. Had things changed, or had he failed to notice details earlier? The bridal sisters were licking their lips, and he wasn't sure if they were dressed as bridesmaids or baked into giant tiered cakes from which they were trying to struggle free. Both of the toyshop owner's hands looked eager to seize the arrested train if it should try to reach the safety of the tunnel, and the bulging eyes of the children crowded around the man with the sugar whistle—were those sweets? Trent might have retreated if his mother's voice hadn't spoken to him. "That's it, son. Don't leave us this time."

"Have a thought for us. Don't start us wondering where you are again. We're past coming to find you."

"Where are you? I can't see."

"Just carry on straight," his parents' voices took it in turns to murmur.

He faltered before lurching between the first exhibits. Beyond them matters could hardly be said to improve. He did his best not to see too much of the milkman holding the reins of a horse while a cow followed the cart, but the man's left eye seemed large enough for the horse, the right for the cow. Opposite him stood a rag and bone

collector whose trade was apparent from the companion that hung
onto his arm, and Trent was almost glad of the flickering dimness.
"How much further?" he cried in a voice that the place shrank almost
to nothing.

"No more than you can walk at your age."

Trent hung onto the impression that his father sounded closer than
before and hugged his briefcase while he made his legs carry him past
a policeman who'd removed his helmet to reveal a bald ridged head as
pointed as a chrysalis, a priest whose smooth face was balanced on a
collar of the same paleness and no thicker than a child's wrist, a
window cleaner with scrawny legs folded like a grasshopper's, a bus
conductor choked by his tie that was caught in his ticket machine
while at the front of the otherwise deserted vehicle the driver displayed
exactly the same would-be comical strangled face and askew swollen
tongue . . . They were nightmares, Trent told himself: some he remembered having suffered as a child, and the rest he was afraid to
remember in case they grew clearer. "I still can't see you," he all but
wailed.

"Down here, son."

Did they mean ahead? He hoped he wasn't being told to use any of
the side aisles, not least because they seemed capable of demonstrating
that the place was even vaster than he feared. The sights they
contained were more elaborate too. Off to the right was a brass band,
not marching but frozen in the act of tiptoeing towards him: though
all the players had lowered their instruments, their mouths were
perfectly round. In the dimness to his left, and scarcely more luminous, was a reddish bonfire surrounded by figures that wore charred
masks, unless those were their faces, and beyond that was a street
party where children sat at trestle tables strewn with food and
grimaced in imitation of the distorted versions of their faces borne by
deflating balloons they held on strings . . . Trent twisted his stiff body
around in case some form of reassurance was to be found behind him,
but the exit to the lobby was so distant he could have mistaken it for
the last of a flame. He half closed his eyes to blot out the sights he had
to pass, only to find that made the shadows of the exhibits and the
darkness into which the shadows trailed loom closer, as if the dimness

was on the point of being finally extinguished. He was suddenly aware that if the building had still been a theatre, the aisle would have brought him to the stage by now. "Where are you?" he called but was afraid to raise his voice. "Can't you speak?"

"Right here."

His eyes sprang so wide they felt fitted into their sockets. His parents weren't just close, they were behind him. He turned with difficulty and saw why he'd strayed past them. His mother was wearing a top hat and tails and had finished twirling a cane that resembled a lengthening of one knobbly finger; his father was bulging out of a shabby flowered dress that failed to conceal several sections of a pinkish bra. They'd dressed up to cure Trent of his nightmare about the theatre performance, he remembered, but they had only brought it into his waking hours. He backed away from it—from their waxen faces greyish with down, their smiles as fixed as their eyes. His legs collided with an object that folded them up, and he tottered sideways to sit helplessly on it. "That's it, son," his mother succeeded in murmuring.

"That's your place," his father said with a last shifting of his lips.

Trent glared downwards and saw he was trapped by a school desk barely large enough to accommodate him. On either side of him sat motionless children as furred with grey as their desks, even their eyes. Between him and his parents a teacher in a gown and mortarboard was standing not quite still and sneering at him. "Mr Bunnie," Trent gasped, remembering how the teacher had always responded to being addressed by his name as though it was an insult. Then, in a moment of clarity that felt like a beacon in the dark, he realised he had some defence. "This isn't me," he tried to say calmly but firmly. "This is."

His fingers were almost too unmanageable to deal with the briefcase. He levered at the rusty metal buttons with his thumbs until at last the catches flew open and the contents spilled across the desk. For a breath, if he had any, Trent couldn't see them in the dimness, and then he made out that they were half a dozen infantile crayon drawings of houses. "I've done more than that," he struggled to protest, "I am more," but his mouth had finished working. He managed only to raise his head, and never knew which was worse: his paralysis, or his parents' doting smiles, or the sneer that the teacher's face seemed to have widened to encompass—the sneer that had always meant that once a child was inside the school gates, his parents could no longer protect him. It might have been an eternity before the failure of the dimness or of Trent's eyes brought the dark.

SLOW

GRADUALLY HE BECAME AWARE OF THE COTTAGE AROUND him, as he emerged from himself again. This time he'd gone back as far as his childhood. A landscape of hills, green beyond green beyond green: he hadn't thought of that for years, he'd decided the memory was more frustrating than useful. He was grateful for it now. It was somewhere to go.

He stretched, taking his time. The clock showed 8:37. He was hungry. No wonder, he thought as he glanced at his wrist: he'd stayed within himself for over two hours, he should have eaten an hour ago. Well, it didn't matter. He'd achieved self-discipline, he needn't overrate routine.

He picked his way between his games to the kitchen, and reached through the trap in the wall for the plate of food. Meat and vegetables—or at least, that was what it looked disgustingly like. For a long time he hadn't been able to touch the food. At last, starving, he'd discovered that it tasted synthetic enough; he could even manage to eat it with his eyes open.

He knelt down and peered through the trap. In twelve hours a larger plate of meat and vegetables would click into place; twelve hours after that, a smaller one again. He could see the plates lined up in their cool colourless store, just beyond his reach. A vague irrational hope—why hope?—made him count them again. But he knew (they) had left him enough food to last almost a year. (They) had gone away.

There was no use denying his feelings. He had been hoping they hadn't really gone; incredibly, he found himself already missing (them).

He shook his head wryly. He would never have believed how much he could adjust to. Returning to the living-room he poked the wall with a finger, and felt the surface yield a little, like rubber. He wouldn't have believed he could grow to bear that, yet now he didn't mind it, so long as he avoided thinking how the appearance of the cottage should have felt. And how soon he'd grown used to the view from the cottage windows, the steely blue shine of the folds of rock, the icy glow they retained for an hour after the white sunsets. Even (they) weren't unpleasant to look at, though sometimes he wondered whether they disguised themselves for him.

Staring out at the empty landscape, he began to wish (they) would appear. Perhaps they hadn't gone far, perhaps they would come back occasionally to look at him. Surely they wouldn't leave him for a whole year without a glimpse of life, with nothing but the bare metallic rock. Not entirely bare, he realised with a disagreeable start. There was something outside the window—the thing (they) had once chased away.

It was almost the colour of the rock. It might have been a shadow, except that there was nothing to cast it. Its head resembled a swollen egg, precariously perched on a long thin neck that bulged toward the midriff. Beneath the belly, if that was what it was, the body tapered; the thing seemed to float on the point of its tail. It was more than a foot taller than he.

It hung in the mouth of a passage through a low table of rock, a metre away. There was no way to tell whether the blank egg was watching. When the thing had first appeared (they) had rushed at it, whirling and blazing; they'd waited until it had retreated into the rock passage. Let it watch, if it was watching. It couldn't reach him.

After a while he tried to assemble the cube, the most difficult of the games (they) had provided. One of these days he would solve it. But whenever he glanced up, his gaze was drawn from the wide retreating levels of rock to the nearby rock table, to the thing hanging balanced on its tail. An hour later he could see that it was coming toward the window.

Let it come. Whatever the windows were made of, they were unbreakable. He'd tried violently enough to break them when first he'd found himself here. He only wished (they) had supplied curtains, so that he could close out the sight of the thing. No, he didn't really need curtains, he wouldn't let it worry him.

The cube defeated him again. It was made of hundreds of slotted metal planes; whenever he fitted them together there were always five or six left over. He'd find the secret. He had plenty of time.

He accepted his defeat. The memory of the green day had calmed him. Somehow the memory seemed to reach back further than itself; it touched something at the centre of him. Tomorrow he might find out what that was, or the next day.

When he'd eaten his evening meal he returned to the livingroom, and frowned. The thing had almost reached the window. How slowly it moved, to have advanced hardly a metre since he'd caught sight of it. Surely it must be vegetarian, surely there couldn't be living prey that was slower than it was. He had no idea what lay beyond the rockscape: there must be vegetation.

He wasn't frowning because of the thing's sluggishness, however. Now the sun had set, the folds of rock were shining like a steely after-image. Something in this light must be playing a trick with the window, for an image of the blank egg on its scrawny neck clung to the glass. Although he moved about the room, changing his angle of vision, the image overlapped its source, blurring the blank head. It was unpleasant to watch; his eyes smarted. Besides, although he knew the thing couldn't reach him, he found its encroaching presence disturbing. It reminded him he was—Perhaps in the morning it would have gone away, baulked.

Around him the cottage began to glow. The furniture, the low beams, the clock-face set at 8:37, glimmered grey; the dim light trembled like almost stagnant water. Perhaps (they) had meant it to imitate electric light, but it was the one thing he found impossible to bear. At least he'd trained himself to sleep once it began. He climbed the luminous stairs. Lying on the bed, eyes closed, he hoped the thing outside was turning away.

When he came downstairs the next morning, it was entering the cottage.

What he'd taken for an image on the glass was nothing of the kind. It looked more solid now than its source outside the window. Nor was it confined to the glass; there was a shadow of the rest of the body, outlined more darkly in the wall beneath the window. In the room, an arm's length in front of the shadow, a faint transparent darkness was forming. It already had the shape of the faceless thing.

Before he could hold on to his control, it broke. He grabbed a handful of planes from the slotted cube and hurled them at the intruder. They passed through the darkness, disturbing it not at all. He threw another handful, then he began to curse (them) for bringing him here. Them. His owners.

For the first time in years all his paranoia flooded over him, all the nightmares and suspicions he'd thought he had disciplined out of himself. Had (they) really rescued him? Or had they snatched him out of space, for a pet?

All the memories he'd dismissed as useless filled him. He had been ferrying supplies between the outer orbits. Suddenly the ferry was whirling helplessly, spinning out beyond the outermost orbit. He'd never known what had happened. Had that been (them) snatching him?

He'd blanked out. Regaining consciousness, he'd recognised he was drifting somewhere beyond the star maps, beyond rescue. His distress beacon was only interorbital. He was going to die. Eventually the knowledge helped him toward peace; there was no point in panicking. He'd used the techniques he had learned to help himself sleep when he'd first gone into space, as a member of a crew: he'd become his breathing, he'd drifted deep into his memories. He had thought of Old Earth, which he'd never seen. Then, as he'd eaten the last of his food and gazed out at space—abruptly: nothing. He had wakened in the cottage.

It was the cottage in the pictures in his book, the book of Old Earth he always kept sealed into his pocket. He'd bought the book in a bazaar; it was centuries old, each page coated with preservative. He'd paid its price, for he had always wanted a glimpse of Old Earth. Now it was as though he'd fallen into the book. It had taken him weeks to soothe his nerves, to regain some sense of inhabiting reality.

And longer to be sure of what he saw through the window: the three glittering veils—crimson, indigo, luminous green, the colours swarming over one another in two-metre curtains of light—that stood fluttering outside the cottage for hours. Eventually he saw them surrounding the food-store; when he looked through the trap, the store had been replenished.

He'd tried to communicate with them, shouting in the close silence of the cottage, gesturing. But the only response he ever got was another, more complicated puzzle or game; the cottage was full of them. (They) never entered the cottage while he was awake, however hard he fought sleep. They simply weren't interested in what he had to say. They'd attempted to provide what they thought was a familiar environment; they gave him food that looked like the food in his book, they pumped something like the ferry's air through a valve in the wall above the staircase; often they watched him for hours. But they didn't think he was so important, they went away somewhere, leaving him at the mercy of the planet's wild life. The faceless egg stood on the stalk of its neck.

He didn't need them to protect him, he thought furiously. He could easily outdistance the thing. It was too slow to trap him, he would outmanoeuvre it all over the cottage, until it became frustrated and went away. He was sure it must be stupid as well as slow; no doubt it wouldn't think to use the empty doorways, it would retard itself further by seeping through the walls.

But it was unnerving. Though he knew he wasn't in danger he found himself unable to look away from the thing. The fascination infuriated him, he felt helplessly resentful; as long as it was in the cottage the thing would distract him from the peace he'd achieved.

He watched the thing enter the cottage. Gradually the outline, hardly more than a misty silhouette, began to round, to fill out. Beyond the window the original shape was suddenly empty air. Now the shape that stained the glass and the wall was fading. The thing in the room swelled darker, opaque now. When the outline in the wall drained completely, he knew the thing was full. It stood next to a low flowered couch. It was in the room with him, little more than a metre away.

For a moment there was nothing between him and terror. The thing stood glistening, dull blue; its bald featureless head almost touched the beams. Close up the thing looked slick and oily. He felt a nervous horror of touching it, of feeling the swollen glistening skin.

Never mind. It couldn't touch him. It was wasting its time, he reassured himself as he saw—with a snigger as much of unease as of mirth—that while entering, it had begun to poise itself to catch him: the head was stooping forward on the neck, and at the top of the egg an orifice was puckering. Within the orifice he could make out rows of fangs, pointing inward. They didn't look like the teeth of a vegetarian. They wouldn't touch him. He could soon be calm.

All he need do was measure the thing's speed. Then he would be able to ignore its impotent menace. He watched the thing creep forward toward him. To reach the window it had moved at a rate of about ten centimetres to the hour. There was no reason to suppose it would move faster now. No reason to suppose so—but it had doubled its speed.

He glared at his chronometer. It never lied, but neither did his eyes in judging distances. The thing had advanced ten centimetres toward him in half an hour. Perhaps the nearness of its prey gave it the impetus. The head had stooped a fraction more, the mouth had opened further, imperceptibly.

He could still stay out of its reach without trying. It couldn't double its speed indefinitely. It couldn't. In half an hour he knew he was right; it had moved only ten centimetres. He snarled at it, at its fatuous empty face, its trailing tail. It didn't frighten him. It just annoyed him. He wished he could block it off so that he needn't look at it.

Block it off. Yes. He might not be able to hide the thing away, but at least he could slow it down further; perhaps then, happily triumphant, he could ignore it. He carried one of the games down from the second bedroom. It was a cubical maze, as high as his waist. He thumped it down in the thing's path. It wouldn't get through that in a hurry.

He forced himself to leave the thing for a while. He gazed out of his bedroom window. The white sunlight bared the landscape, the gleaming metallic corrugations of rock. At the horizon the sky was bright silver. Were there more of the things out there? Oddly, he found himself almost welcoming the notion. At least it made the landscape feel less barren, now the sparkling coloured veils were gone.

He made himself wait for an hour, then went downstairs. The thing had reached the block; a shadow of its tail was seeping into the far face of the cube. Three hours later, when he returned again, two pale silhouettes confronted each other patiently across the cube. Before he went to bed the thing hung half-embedded in the cube, looking exactly like a retarded Jack-in-the-box. He couldn't control his laughter. He wondered whether he might grow fond of the thing. It was beginning to amuse him, in its ugly stupid way.

He lay on the glowing bed. He must be sure to lure the thing into one of the downstairs rooms each evening—never to allow it to reach the hall late in the day, where it could begin coming upstairs while he slept. As the room dimmed slowly, he visualised the layout of the cottage. No, he would never be trapped. He could always keep at least one wall between him and the thing, if he felt he needed to.

He let his breathing carry him down into himself. He remembered the green day, the hills multiplying green to the horizon. For a while, when he'd found himself in the cottage's parody of Old Earth, that memory had seemed flat, false as the cottage's clock—he was sure the clock was empty inside, or solid. The green of his remembered hills had been metallic, not like Old Earth's at all.

But now the green of the metal hills seemed to lead him back further. Perhaps it was inherited memory, perhaps it was only the book: but for a moment the green was the swaying of grass, which he'd never seen. The swaying was peaceful, was sleep.

He awoke refreshed, feeling as if he'd slept for days. The room was dazzling with light. Too dazzling. He twisted round; the white sun stood at the centre of the window. He had overslept.

At once he remembered the thing. He glanced warily toward the doorway, glad (they) had omitted the doors. The landing was empty. He rose hastily, hardly glancing at his clothes beside the bed—he never wore them now, the cottage was too hot. He hurried across the landing. His gasp of shock was the only sound in the cottage.

The thing was waiting for him on the staircase, on the third stair up. The egg had stooped further; if it reached him, it would be on a level with his head—the mouth would, and the mouth had gaped wider now, a fanged ridged hole as wide as his fist.

Did it move faster at night? Had he slept for days? The questions tumbled about in his mind, but his panic was ahead of them. He mustn't be trapped upstairs, there was a nightmare in that somewhere. He mustn't be cut off from food. He climbed over the banisters, hung by his fingertips from the edge of the landing, let himself fall.

Too fast! He hadn't time to bend his knees, the fall jarred his ankles painfully. Panic must be blocking his responses somehow. Well, it was only a four-metre drop, it hadn't killed him. The thing was already backing downstairs toward him. Its averted head wobbled on the thin neck, as if about to turn.

It was moving faster. It was going to overtake him. But he forced himself to time it. The chronometer insisted the thing was still restricted to twenty centimetres an hour. It must be his fear that had lent it the seeming of speed.

He hurried into the kitchen. He felt as if he were trying to run through the marsh of a nightmare. Each step seemed slower than the last. He'd grown unused to panic. He must reach deep into himself for calm, otherwise the situation would overcome him. But first, food. He reached into the trap and took the plate.

Though he knew he should carry the plate across the hall, to manoeuvre further out of reach of the thing, his panic seemed to have exhausted him; he had to make an effort even to cross to the kitchen table. The surface of the table gave like elastic beneath his elbows.

He must time the thing tonight. If it moved faster at night, he could block its path effectively. But if it could somehow make him oversleep—He ate sluggishly, irritably, staring nervously at the blank wall of the kitchen for the thing's outline. He ate, he ate. How much time it took.

He was still eating when the thing glided into the kitchen doorway and stood waiting, head lowered, mouth almost as wide as his head.

His panic burst, flooding him. Then almost at once he felt very calm. So the thing could move faster, but only did so when he wasn't watching. And it must have learned that it could move more quickly through space than through walls. It wasn't as stupid as he'd thought.

But he was still faster. If it could have moved as fast as he, it would have been able to catch him by now. He would always outdistance it. Except that it wasn't pursuing him now; it seemed content to block the doorway.

He laughed out loud. It had trapped him with the food, trapped him in the one place he couldn't have afforded to be blocked from. He could live in here if he had to. There were games and chairs in the kitchen, they would slow the thing down while he slept. Did it expect him to walk over and stuff his head into its mouth? What could it gain by standing there?

Well, let it stand. He felt calm, unnaturally so. He ate slowly—no hurry, the thing was two metres distant. Chew, chew. Chew. His jaws were racing the sun, which had nearly reached the horizon.

When he realised what that meant he felt himself become slowly, slowly cold. He hardly needed to consult his chronometer. Even to raise his wrist toward his face, and turn it to be read, took minutes. At once—although even the thought seemed to drift very slowly into focus—he knew that the thing wouldn't move from the doorway until he was slower than it was.

So that was how it caught its prey. Well, it wouldn't catch him, he would block it. But in the time it took him to rise from his chair the sun sank beneath the horizon. There was no use pretending, he was caught. Time surrounded him thickly, like amber.

Night gathered, and the room began to glow. Beneath his hands the table yielded treacherously, glowing. The walls glimmered grey; the glow shone faintly on the figure waiting in the doorway. The mouth was ready for his head now. The faceless egg was hardly more than a thin stretched frame for the dim fanged tunnel.

He began to writhe frantically within himself, within his stopped body. All he managed was a scream, and even that seemed weak; he tried to make it louder, rawer, but it sank into the silence. Darkness was seeping into the dim glow now. He heard the oppressive silence of the cottage, of the dead clock. He heard his slow harsh breathing, each breath slower than the last. The thing waited near him in the dark, mouth ready.

He heard his breathing. And he knew that the thing hadn't quite trapped him. He couldn't move, but he could still escape.

Perhaps the calm he'd felt before had been false, part of the thing's preying. It didn't matter. He could use that too, to take him to his own peace. He made himself relax, to sink into the green day, the green hills.

The day had gone. There was nothing but the mouth, waiting for him in the darkness. He wouldn't know when it was coming closer, not until it reached him. It might be coming now.

He struggled wildly, feebly within himself, within the dark. At last he gave up, exhausted. That wasn't the way. He couldn't reach for the memory, for escape. It was in him already. He must let it come to him. Listen to his breathing. His slow breathing. Become his breathing, slow. Become all of himself. There was green in the dark, in his mind. There were the hills.

He lay calm, cradled in his breathing. His arrested body stood hunched over the table, but it didn't matter. In a moment the green would begin to sway slowly in the wind, the wind of Old Earth. He knew Old Earth was there at his centre, inherited. He must be aware only of his breathing. The darkness didn't matter. His breathing would take him to his centre. His breathing was slow as the swaying of the leaves.

Worse Than Bones

A S HAMMOND UNPICKED THE STAPLES OF THE PADDED envelope he'd been handed on his way to work, Mrs Middler arrived at her desk. "You'll break your nails if you aren't careful," she informed him, and frowned at the grey stuffing the envelope had begun to shed. "The cleaners won't thank you for that."

"What's someone sent you in a plain brown wrapper, Mr Hammond?" Charl expected to learn, though she wasn't even close to half his age.

"Maybe it's something to make you blush, Charl," Denny said, despite being younger still.

"I know you'd love to see that but you're never going to."

"Let's be polite," Mrs Middler said, Hammond wasn't sure to whom. "So may we see what all the fuss was about?"

Hammond refrained from pointing out that he'd made none of it. He lingered over relinquishing the book once he'd stripped it of its cerements of newspaper. Just enough of the dust jacket remained to show the title, *Tales of the Ghostly,* and the top of a wisp that might have been mist or a bit of a ghost. Mrs Middler's scent, which always led him to expect her to be wearing more makeup, met him as he handed her the book. She lowered her plump smug middle-aged face, presenting him with more of a display of her severely curled blonde hair. "I hope you didn't pay much for this," she said. "Why, it's been scribbled in."

"That's half the charm of old books for me. It makes a book seem lived in if whoever had it before leaves their mark."

Denny poked his thin permanently disappointed face at the book. Three small red spots led like the end of an unfinished sentence from the right-hand corner of his mouth. "Died in, more like," he remarked.

This book belongs to Hettie Close; so, if you've found it, please, return it to—Hammond read that and glimpsed an address down in Cornwall followed by a series of dates, and then Mrs Middler turned the page. "I won't pretend I'm a book person," she said, "but I wouldn't give you tuppence for this one."

Each title on the contents page was accompanied by a handwritten comment. "It's very rare," Hammond felt bound to protest. "The catalogue said it was only a reading copy."

Charl rested a hand on Denny's shoulder. Her hair was nearly the colour of her winter tan, and almost as short as his, both of them seeming eager for baldness. A grimace drew her small face tight. "I wouldn't be seen dead reading that," she declared.

Hammond had never seen her or her colleagues read anything but magazines composed mostly of advertisements. Mrs Middler shut the book and passed it to him, and he tried not to recoil from the sensation of inadvertently touching her hand. He had just grasped that he'd touched only the wrinkled cover when Charl said "Anyway, you can't call it that."

"Why can't I?"

"Not you," she told Hammond with a fragment of a giggle. "You can't just say tales of the ghostly. Tales of the ghostly what?"

Denny emitted a desiccated laugh of agreement and squeezed her arm until she pulled away from him. "It's a perfectly decent title," Hammond was saying meanwhile. "Back then they knew their grammar."

"I believe Charlotte's right," Mrs Middler said and stared past him at the clock beyond the dozens of occupied desks. "Put it away now, Mr Hammond. It's past time to start work."

He was being blamed for an argument of which he'd been simply the victim. He laid the book to rest among the paper-clips and rubber bands in his desk drawer, and didn't look up until his face had stopped burning. He often felt like a schoolboy who'd been given a desk near the teacher's for being unable to spell. More people knew the name of his condition than anyone had when he was at school, which meant that fewer thought he must be able to spell if he could read, but nobody had found a cure that worked for him. That was why he only checked arithmetic he would have been capable of doing, and fetched files so that people younger or much younger than himself could send out yet more correspondence about tax, and replaced files and sorted them into the alphabetical order they seemed unable to retain.

The smell of the files made him hungry for his book long before Mrs Middler sent him to brew tea for the mid-morning break. As soon as he'd dropped the sodden tea bag in his metal bin he resurrected *Tales of the Ghostly* from the drawer. All by itself the contents page made up for the morning so far. Each title allowed him a glimpse of an era when people had the leisure to see ghosts, as did Hettie Close's comments and the painstaking script in which they were expressed. *The Gay Dancers* was judged to be "A-glitter with memories", *The Song in the Church* "Uplifting", *The Plea of a Child* "Good and tearful", *The Mummy's Voice* "Exotic and eerie", *The Phantom Rail-way Signal* "An up-to-date ghost" ... He was savouring the prospect of so many unfamiliar tales—*A Distant Melody* as well, and *The Keeper of the Light,* and *The Padlocked Door*—when Charl, having taken a daintier sip than her coiffure would have led him to predict, blinked at him. "Are you just going to read what they're called, Mr Hammond?"

"Read us a story," Denny presumably joked.

"I liked being read to when I was little," Charl said. "Will you, Mr Hammond?"

He and his parents had read to each other almost as long as he'd had any parents. The thought of reawakening Charl's love of books made him indifferent to Mrs Middler's frown. He was turning to the first tale when he grasped how inadvisable it would be to tell his present audience that a story was called *The Gay Dancers.* He leafed through the warm withered pages to the tale Hettie Close found "Haunting as only true ghosts can be". "This is called *The Path by the Churchyard,*" he announced and, resting his hand on the blank page opposite, read:

"In the twilight of a winter's afternoon of the year 18—, a traveller encountered a countryman on approaching a village in the south-east of our island, where the trees stoop close to the flat land while the winds constantly moan. 'Well met,' says J-to the countryman. 'Pray tell, who is being mourned in yonder churchyard?'

" 'None as I knows of,' responds the countryman.

" 'Then how comes it,' J-enquires, 'that I hear sighs beyond the hedge that bounds it?'

" 'Naught but wind in the trees,' returns the countryman. "Tis thirteen years since yon churchyard was chained and locked.'

"Taking his leave of him, the traveller advanced and saw that it was so . . . "

Hammond became aware that everyone within earshot had hushed to listen to him. He felt as if he'd been discovered at last. He was drawing a breath to do justice to the next sentence when a phone rang, and Denny was the first to laugh. Meanwhile Hammond's flattened hand jerked so nervously he might have thought the page had grown restless beneath it. "They didn't know much about writing in the olden days, did they?" Denny said. "Didn't know what year it was or the poor twat's name."

Charl dealt him a reproachful blink, only to add "Excuse me, Mr Hammond, but I think you mixed up your tenses a bit."

"I never mix up what I read. Come and look if you don't believe me."

Mrs Middler cleared her throat with a sound shriller than the phones. "We've had our break now. Lots of work to be done."

Hammond kept his hot face low for some moments after the book was shut up, then trudged to kneel by Charl, The left-hand drawer of every desk but his contained boxfuls of cards twice the size of a page of his book, each card representing a taxpayer. Hammond carried the first of the boxes to his desk and set about checking the latest column of arithmetic on every card. Charl started at Abel and finished at Bogle, but Hammond had only reached Aycliffe when it was time for lunch.

He went out for as prolonged a walk as he could stand, among buildings much like the squat five-storey concrete office block, except that people lived in them. Plastic cartons dripping red, egged on by lidded cups that sprouted straws for antennae, pursued him through the wasteland relieved only by the twitching remains of young trees. He wished he were on a heath or a hill, where the wind could find something old to enliven. Before long it and its scuttling companions drove him back to the office.

He was about to sit down when his body stiffened, wakening all its aches. The drawer with the book in it, which he'd shut flush with the desk, was open at least an inch. The front cover of *Tales of the Ghostly* was no longer closed but held ajar by a ballpoint pen. "Who's been in my drawer?" he demanded.

Everyone seemed to have agreed to meet him with silence until Charl admitted "I borrowed a paper-clip. I didn't think you'd mind."

"You didn't need to touch my book."

"I didn't," she said, looking hurt. "I was careful not to."

"Well, somebody did. There's a pen in it now."

"Maybe it wants more scribbling in," Denny said.

Hammond confined his response to examining the book for damage. After less of this than he felt entitled to, Mrs Middler said "I'm sure Charlotte would never have interfered with your property, and anyway I don't see anything to make a fuss about. There isn't much that could be done to it that hasn't been."

Hammond shut his lips and the drawer tight, and didn't speak to anyone for hours, even when Mrs Middler told him to make the tea. He was planting Charl's Majorca mug on her Ibiza beer-mat when Charl said "It ought to be called *Tales of Ghostly Things.*"

Mrs Middler clearly thought that deserved more than the grunt he gave it. "Why do you want a book like that?" she apparently needed to know.

He could have said he would rather hold a book than a hand any day. Instead he told her "Most books are ghosts" as he opened his drawer to reassure himself that nothing else had befallen the book. He must have closed the drawer too hard last time; the pen was back under the cover. He transferred the pen to the top of the desk and eased the drawer shut, and would have apologised to Charl if there hadn't been an audience.

When it was time to go home he found that the cleaner had disposed of the padded bag. He slipped the book into a large brown Confidential envelope, challenging Mrs Middler to do more than frown at the use, and buttoned his coat over it. On the dwarfish bus he clung to a metal bar crowded with hands and clutched the package to his bosom with his other arm, much as a woman was holding her child on the seat below him. He couldn't help wondering if the little girl would ever read a book for pleasure. If he'd had both hands free he might have read to her from his book.

The wind rushed him from the bus stop by the park patrolled by litter and stray dogs to his house, a thin red-brick slice of a terrace. A smell of aged paper greeted him as he shut out all but the roar of the wind. He laid his prize on the balding carpet on the stairs while he draped his coat over the post at the foot of the rickety banisters, then shied the crumpled envelope into the splintered wicker wastepaper basket in the front room and sat the book erect in his father's sagging armchair.

Apart from the kitchen and the toilet, which was equally a bathroom, every room was rendered cosier by shelves of books. All his books were second-hand, and he hadn't bought an uninscribed one for years. He took down a few at random to remind himself how inscriptions brought them alive. Here was a volume of Grimm presented as a school prize in 1923, here was an Edwardian Everyday Reciter whose previous owner had indicated all the points at which he should take a breath; an espionage omnibus from a wife to her husband "so you'll remember I've got my eye on you", a dictionary of seashells from a father to his daughter "to answer all those questions you used to ask" . . . Hammond shelved the books and cooked himself two poached eggs on toast to accompany a bowl of cereal, quite enough of a dinner for him these days, especially when more would consume money better spent on books. Having washed up and dried the dinner things with the least tattered of the kitchen towels, he settled himself in the front room.

There must be a draught, and no wonder with the wind flinging its huge soft icy self against the house. *Tales of the Ghostly* had stooped forward on the armchair, propping itself on its open front cover. He glanced at the flyleaf as he retrieved the book. Hettie Close seemed to have needed to reconfirm her ownership every few years; the last date was nine years ago. He scanned the paragraphs he'd read aloud and leafed onward, each page trying to cling to his fingertips like another skin.

As J—walked through the village it began to look familiar, the buildings and the people too, though he had a sense that they were older than they should be. The only innkeeper told him there was no room and gave the impression of being afraid to have J-under his roof. As the night closed in, anyone J—approached fled into their houses and barred their doors against him. Sounds of mourning led him back to the churchyard, where he found a gap in the hedge through which he was able to pass. He followed the sounds to a gravestone, and as the sighs faded into silence, the apparition of the moon through tattered clouds showed him the plot. Carved on the memorial was his own name.

Hammond had thought as much, but the confirmation was a pleasure in itself. It wasn't why he emitted a startled grunt, muffled by the books around him. On the contents page Hettie Close had described the story as "Haunting as only true ghosts can be", yet beneath its final paragraph she had written much less neatly "Falsehood and foolishness". She must have turned against the tale in her old age.

In *The Gay Dancers* a young woman on a visit to friends in a remote part of France was drawn by sounds of revelry to a chateau, where she danced with a mysterious aristocratic youth who promised that their dance and the night would never end. At the height of their waltz she cried out to him to keep her always, and was never seen again. In an epilogue her friends searched for her near a chateau that had been in ruins for a hundred years. Apparently Hettie Close had ceased to find the story "A-glitter with memories"; across the blank half of its last page she'd scrawled "Lies the living want to believe".

Hammond had bought the anthology because the bookseller's catalogue had listed it as extensively annotated by the previous owner, but he was starting to find the annotations disconcerting. He riffled through the book and saw that every tale was followed by a comment, which he might have read if that wouldn't have involved glimpsing the conclusions of the stories. Each final page looked faded, both the print and the progressively effortful scrawl. He'd had enough of Hettie Close's bitter afterthoughts for one night. He turned to the shelves for companionship.

His favourite books proved less congenial than usual, perhaps because he couldn't help wondering how the people who had written in them or been addressed had ended up. Before long the smell of old paper grew oppressive, almost cloying, so that for the first time in his life he was close to wishing he had a television. When a collection of Shelley kept drooping in his hands, he took himself upstairs.

Since all the shelves except those in his room were full, *Tales of the Ghostly* accompanied him. As he lay in the dimness thick as dust he imagined the book had perceptibly added to the smell of old paper. In the depths of the night he was wakened by sounds he put down to a mouse—less than a scratching, just a faint buried restlessness all the more annoying because indefinable. He slapped the bed until the activity ceased or at any rate passed beyond audibility. He had to tell himself it had intensified not the smell but his perception of it before he was able to sleep.

Was his memory as exhausted as he was? In the morning he saw the new book was half out of the shelf, though he seemed to remember pushing it all the way in. He lined it up with its neighbours and got hastily ready for work, having overslept for the first time in his life despite his parents' alarm clock that he'd transferred to his room, never needing it while they were present to waken him.

He was three sweaty panting minutes late for work. Mrs Middler said nothing to him until it was time for tea, and not much then. As he stood her Union Jack mug on the mat depicting a minute map of Britain she relented sufficiently to ask "Did you sort out the business with your book?"

He felt as though she'd noticed something he had overlooked. "What business?"

"Weren't you going to get some money back at least for the condition it was in?"

"I told you yesterday," he said, and was disconcerted to realise he was about to lie. "It was what I expected."

"You'll have to forgive me for being surprised, Mr Hammond. Do you ever write in your books?"

It had never struck him before, but he didn't. "Not yet," he said.

"I hope you never reach that state."

"Pretty soon nobody will read books," Denny told Charl. "Everything worth having will be on the Internet. You'll just need to know how to use it."

"Just because it gives you a big head doesn't mean there's more in there."

Hammond had no wish to become entangled in their flirtation. It wasn't until the afternoon break that he asked Denny "Can you really find anything you want to on your computer?"

"Print it out as well. Go ahead, tell me something to bring you. If it's something Charl shouldn't see, just whisper."

Hammond would have liked to make his distaste clear, but couldn't risk offending Denny. "I'd like to know who lives at an address. I'll give you it tomorrow."

That was one reason why as soon as he reached home he tramped upstairs and took *Tales of the Ghostly* off the shelf. It came so readily it might have been waiting for him. He was sure the smell in the room was stronger. The book wasn't staying where he slept if it smelled that strong. In the kitchen he copied Hettie Close's address onto the message pad for which he never seemed to have any messages, then wrote his name and address on the flyleaf under hers and her trail of dates. He left the book in the front room while he fed himself his eggs and toast and cereal, wondering what second thoughts she might have in store for him. Once upon a time she'd found *The Song in the Church* "Uplifting", but how much had she changed her mind?

In the story a mother returned to churchgoing after the loss of her only child and came to believe that the highest voice in the choir was her daughter's. Having secreted herself in the church overnight, she heard the child alone. Next morning she was found dead, lying on a pew, smiling peacefully. "Smile while you can," Hettie Close had scrawled in ink almost as faded as the print above it. "Smile like the skull you'll be, you fool, before you're worse than bones."

Not only the sentiment dismayed Hammond. His memory must be succumbing to age, because he'd been convinced that each story was followed by far fewer handwritten words. Perhaps this one was the exception; he wasn't yielding to the urge to find out. He took down a shaky tome about ancient Greece, replacing it with *Tales of the Ghostly,* and tried to immerse himself in legends he'd loved to hear and then read as a child.

Tonight he found them too concerned with the underworld, with people who wouldn't stay dead. The idea struck him as both childish and distressing. He nodded over the book and jerked awake convinced he'd heard restlessness somewhere near. He left the book on the couch and climbed the stairs under the bulb that had taken on some of the colour of old paper. He tried to read himself to sleep with Dickens, and then just to sleep, but kept being roused by an impression that there was movement downstairs he couldn't quite hear. Even if only the smell of books was looming over him, in the dark that felt close to solid.

Next morning it was mostly the prospect of speaking to Denny that urged him out of bed and to the office. But Denny was late, and hid his face from Mrs Middler with a heap of files he tried to pretend he'd spent time selecting. Hammond barely waited until her scowl at Denny subsided. "Did you find out what I asked you?" he said low.

"Are you after an old girl, Mr Hammond?" Charl suggested.

"Close," Denny said.

Hammond forgot to keep his voice down. "What are you getting at? What do you mean?"

"The woman who lives there," Denny told him, "she's called Margaret Close."

Charl gave Hammond a secret grin while Mrs Middler's disapproval threatened not to remain mute. Once he was on his knees by Denny, Hammond risked whispering "Did you get a phone number?"

"Obviously," Denny muttered, yanking a folded slip of paper out of a pocket of his jeans along with a bony cigarette he quickly hid.

Nobody was supposed to make personal phone calls from the office, let alone long distance, and nobody as menial as Hammond had a phone at all. The nearest public phone was at least a mile away and unlikely to be intact. He willed Mrs Middler not to stay in the office at lunchtime, and almost sighed aloud when he saw her don her coat. He gave her five minutes away from the building and sat at her desk, ignoring Denny and Charl. As he dialled he feared Margaret Close would be out at work, but the distant bell was stilled before it had finished ringing thrice. "Hello?" a woman's voice said.

He had to take a deliberate breath. "Is that Mrs Close, or is it Ms?"

"I'm the only one there is. It's Ms."

She sounded far too young to have written any of the comments in the book. "Someone else of that name used to live there, didn't they?"

"Were you a friend of my mother's?"

"In, well, I suppose you might say in a kind of a sense, Hammond said, and immediately thought he shouldn't have.

"Are you the man she was always hoping would come back?"

"I never knew her."

"Not you, then. She carried on hoping to the end. Someone she thought she should have spent her life with. Maybe she found him waiting if that's possible. We can't know, can we?"

Hammond felt he wasn't expected to respond, but the next question was sharper. "So what's your interest in her?"

"I've got a book of hers."

"Which book is that? Don't tell me. She's in it, isn't she?"

"You could say that."

"All over it. I know the one. I sold all her books at the market. How much did you pay for it?" the daughter said, and interrupted any answer. "Forget it. I don't want to know."

He had no idea what else to say. After a pause the daughter said "I'm still not getting why you called."

"I suppose I just wondered if you could tell me anything about her or the book. As you say, it seems so full of her."

"That's how she was. You always knew when she was about or even on her way. She'd make sure you did."

"Knew," Hammond ventured to ask, "or know?"

"She's gone. She isn't here, anyway." With some briskness the daughter said "You wanted me to tell you about the book."

"If there's anything to tell."

"She died with it by her bed, if that's what you mean. Presumably realising he hardly could, Ms Close said "She thought the writers back then knew how it was going to be when you were dead, the Victorians with all their spirit stuff, you understand. I tried to make her see once they were just stories, and we had a bad argument even for us."

Hammond had thought of nothing he could say when the daughter admitted "I hope she found what she expected if there's any finding to be done."

"She didn't."

He hardly knew he'd spoken, the thought was so immediate. "I beg your pardon?" Ms Close said, not begging at all.

"Sorry, I shouldn't have—I've got to go," Hammond said and did, not soon enough. Mrs Middler had sailed into view under the clock, carrying a bag of lunch from a salad bar. He retreated to his desk and tried to look as if he'd been there all the time. As she dumped her lunch on her desk, however, her stare provoked him to say "Just borrowing a paper-clip."

Only her stare answered him, and could be avoided by lowering his head. He didn't speak to anyone throughout the afternoon—he was trying to decide whether he wanted to rush home or delay that as long as possible. The end of work was bearing down on him when Mrs Middler tapped on her desk with a pen. "Mr Hammond."

"I'm here."

"Better be over here unless you want everybody knowing what I have to say."

He watched her jab a stubby silver-varnished fingernail at a column of figures, then at another. "You passed these, Mr Hammond, and they're wrong. You'd have had this lady getting a refund she wasn't entitled to and this gentleman paying hundreds of pounds too much back tax. I hope you aren't too old to keep your mind on your job."

He might have kept his peace except for that. "There are more important things than money," he blurted.

"Perhaps you wouldn't think so if you weren't earning any." Apparently in case that wasn't enough of a threat, she added "And don't let me see you sniffing round my desk for stationery again without asking, never mind taking any home."

Another retort found its way to his lips. "I can think of a lot better uses for paper."

Denny had to snort and Charl to giggle under cover of her hand before he realised what he might have seemed to say. He no longer cared. He turned his back on Mrs Middler's incredulous glare and, having retrieved his coat from the hook by the tea urn, marched out of the office.

At least she'd made him eager to go home. In the act of opening the front door he almost called "Hello." He wasn't surprised to find *Tales of the Ghostly* sprawled face down on the front-room carpet as though exhausted by its latest effort—it was more unexpected that the pages on which it lay open had nothing extra written on them. He was examining the book when it seemed to waken in his hand. As he dropped it on the table and tried to rub off his fingertips the sensation of having touched flesh that ought not to have stirred, the front cover fell open. Unlike Hettie Close, he hadn't written a date after his name and address, but one was there now, in a script so large and clumsy as to suggest that the writer was no longer able to see or the writer's hand, if it was one still, to control the scrawl. The date was today's.

He stared until it appeared to writhe, and then he turned the pages with a fingernail. Soon he sucked in a breath and did his best to expel its musty rotten taste. The comment following *The Gay Dancers* had been expanded. After "Lies the living want to believe" words in a larger looser version of the handwriting occupied the rest of the page. "Lies you do, Thomas Hammond."

That was too personal, too aggressive, too close. He tugged the cuffs of his coat over his hands so as to carry the book to the kitchen table, where he used an old redundant knife and fork to turn the pages. The comment at the end of *The Path by the Churchyard* was no longer just "Falsehood and foolishness". The scribble that almost spilled over the margins added "The path leads to me, Tommy boy."

"Good luck to it," Hammond muttered, flicking pages over. Every tale was followed by an extra message now, and even those that didn't include a version of his name seemed aimed at him. The ink on those pages was faded as though drained in order to compose the scrawl. The message at the end of the last story was the most uncontrolled in both handwriting and content. "Don't keep me waiting here in the dark long, old Tom."

He slammed the book shut and stared at its tattered back cover. He didn't know if he was challenging some movement to take place or doing his best to prevent it. When his eyes began to twitch he saw to his dinner while continuing to watch the book. As he ate he grew aware that Hettie Close no longer could. A sense of her hunger sickened him, so that he scraped half his dinner into the bin and abandoned the utensils in the sink.

He'd forgotten to remove his coat, but the house felt too cold for him to do without. He trapped *Tales of the Ghostly* between his cuffs again to transfer the book to his father's armchair, where he could keep an eye on it while he read something else—except that all the favourites he attempted to read, and the inscriptions in them, seemed unreachably remote. Before long he returned to staring at the book propped on the chair.

As the hours passed he began to suspect it of restraining itself until it was unobserved. Once he lurched at it and thumbed through it, but nothing appeared to have changed, except that when he slumped back into his chair he thought the smell of more than aging followed him. Did that herald another transformation? By the time he wondered that, he was as disinclined to stir as the book seemed to be. Only his eyelids could move, and only to droop. He tried to keep them up until he forgot to keep trying.

A secretive movement wakened him. *Tales of the Ghostly* had fallen on its face, and the back cover was wide open. As he wobbled to his feet he saw writing on the rear flyleaf. He was stumbling around his father's chair when the ungainly ill-proportioned scrawl grew clear. "Come to me now, old Hammy, or I'll come to you."

"No you won't," Hammond retorted, "and don't call me Hammy either." Nobody ever had. He seized the book by its rear board and snatched it up, its pages flapping. He was about to thrust it into the space on the shelf when he thought he felt it writhe like some part of a withered body not quite dead. "You won't do that to me again," he yelled, ripping the pages loose from the spine, crumpling them into a wad he pitched into the dusty fireplace. "Let's see you get up to any tricks now," he said, hurling the boards into the fireplace. When there was no response beyond a feeble restlessness of paper that subsided as he watched, he stumped upstairs to bed.

He left the bedroom door ajar in case he heard any mischief downstairs. He almost kept the light on until fury at his own childishness made him tug the cord. He lay listening for indications of stealth in the dark until sleep found him. He dreamed that far too old a woman—so old that she was doing without most of her face had set about crawling up the stairs to him without employing any limbs. As he saw the ragged brownish lump of a head waver above the edge of a stair, then over the next higher, he struggled to waken before he could see it in more detail. He managed to produce a strangled cry, and the object, as misshapen as it was determined, vanished from within his eyelids. When he opened them, however, it was beside him on the pillow.

Even if it was composed of crumpled paper, it had a crooked tongueless grin that gaped wide as he shrank back in the tangle of blankets. He wasn't trying to escape only the mockery of a head. In the twilight before dawn he could just distinguish that the print was fading from the pages while a mist as dark as ink seeped out of them. He hadn't disentangled himself from the bedclothes when the mist rushed into his eyes, filling them with blackness.

He'd hardly begun to cry out with the stinging of his eyes when it ceased. In another moment they cleared, and he tasted ink. On the pillow was nothing but a shapeless wad of paper. Its smell was in his nostrils and then deeper in him. He felt his hands tighten into claws and drag him upright against the headboard. He felt his lips part as the gap in the wad of paper had. "I'm alive," he said, or his mouth did, in a voice delighted to rediscover itself. "I'm alive."

No Story in it

"GRANDAD."

Boswell turned from locking the front door to see Gemima running up the garden path cracked by the late September heat. Her mother April was at the tipsy gate, and April's husband Rod was climbing out of their rusty crimson Nissan. "Oh, dad," April cried, slapping her forehead hard enough to make him wince. "You're off to London. How could we forget it was today, Rod."

Rod pursed thick lips beneath a ginger moustache broader than his otherwise schoolboyish plump face. "We must have had other things on our mind. It looks as if I'm joining you, Jack."

"You'll tell me how," Boswell said as Gemima's small hot five-year-old hand found his grasp.

"We've just learned I'm a cut-back."

"More of a set-back, will it be? I'm sure there's a demand for teachers of your experience."

"I'm afraid you're a bit out of touch with the present."

Boswell saw his daughter willing him not to take the bait. "Can we save the discussion for my return?" he said. "I've a bus and then a train to catch."

"We can run your father to the station, can't we? We want to tell him our proposal." Rod bent the passenger seat forward. "Let's keep the men together," he said.

As Boswell hauled the reluctant belt across himself he glanced up. Usually Gemima reminded him poignantly of her mother at her age—large brown eyes with high startled eyebrows, inquisitive nose, pale prim lips—but in the mirror April's face looked not much less small, just more lined. The car jerked forward, grating its innards, and the radio announced "A renewed threat of war—" before Rod switched it off. Once the car was past the worst of the potholes in the main road Boswell said "So propose."

"We wondered how you were finding life on your own," Rod said. "We thought it mightn't be the ideal situation for someone with your turn of mind."

"Rod. Dad—"

Her husband gave the mirror a look he might have aimed at a child who'd spoken out of turn in class. "Since we've all over-extended ourselves, we think the solution is to pool our resources."

"Which are those?"

"We wondered how the notion of our moving in with you might sound."

"Sounds fun," Gemima cried.

Rod's ability to imagine living with Boswell for any length of time showed how desperate he, if not April, was. "What about your own house?" Boswell said.

"There are plenty of respectable couples eager to rent these days. We'd pay you rent, of course. Surely it makes sense for all of us."

"Can I give you a decision when I'm back from London?" Boswell said, mostly to April's hopeful reflection. "Maybe you won't have to give up your house. Maybe soon I'll be able to offer you financial help."

"Christ," Rod snarled, a sound like a gnashing of teeth.

To start with the noise the car made was hardly harsher. Boswell thought the rear bumper was dragging on the road until tenement blocks jerked up in the mirror as though to seize the vehicle, which ground loudly to a halt. "Out," Rod cried in a tone poised to pounce on nonsense.

"Is this like one of your stories, grandad?" Gemima giggled as she followed Boswell out of the car.

"No," her father said through his teeth and flung the boot open. "This is real."

Boswell responded only by going to look. The suspension had collapsed, thrusting the wheels up through the rusty arches. April took Gemima's hand, Boswell sensed not least to keep her quiet, and murmured "Oh, Rod."

Boswell was staring at the tenements. Those not boarded up were tattooed with graffiti inside and out, and he saw watchers at as many broken as unbroken windows. He thought of the parcel a fan had once given him with instructions not to open it until he was home, the present that had been one of Jean's excuses for divorcing him. "Come with me to the station," he urged, "and you can phone whoever you need to phone."

When the Aireys failed to move immediately he stretched out a hand to them and saw his shadow printed next to theirs on a wall, either half demolished or never completed, in front of the tenements. A small child holding a woman's hand, a man slouching beside them with a fist stuffed in his pocket, a second man gesturing empty-handed at them . . . The shadows seemed to blacken, the sunlight to brighten like inspiration, but that had taken no form when the approach of a taxi distracted him. His shadow roused itself as he dashed into the rubbly road to flag the taxi down. "I'll pay," he told Rod.

"Here's Jack Boswell, everyone," Quentin Sedgwick shouted. "Here's our star author. Come and meet him."

It was going to be worth it, Boswell thought. Publishing had changed since all his books were in print—indeed, since any were. Sedgwick, a tall thin young but balding man with wiry veins exposed by a singlet and shorts, had met him at Waterloo, pausing barely long enough to deliver an intense handshake before treating him to a head-long ten-minute march and a stream of enthusiasm for his work. The journey ended at a house in the midst of a crush of them resting their fronts on the pavement. At least the polished nameplate of Cassandra Press had to be visible to anyone who passed. Beyond it a hall that smelled of curried vegetables was occupied by a doubleparked pair of bicycles and a steep staircase not much wider than their handlebars.

"Amazing, isn't it?" Sedgwick declared. "It's like one of your early things, being able to publish from home. Except in a story of yours the computers would take over and tell us what to write."

"I don't remember writing that," Boswell said with some unsureness.

"No, I just made it up. Not bad, was it?" Sedgwick said, running upstairs. "Here's Jack Boswell, everyone . . . "

A young woman with a small pinched studded face and glistening black hair spiky as an armoured fist emerged from somewhere on the ground floor as Sedgwick threw open doors to reveal two cramped rooms, each featuring a computer terminal, at one of which an even younger woman with blonde hair the length of her filmy flowered blouse was composing an advertisement. "Starts with C, ends with *e,*" Sedgwick said of her, and of the studded woman "Bren, like the gun. Our troubleshooter."

Boswell grinned, feeling someone should. "Just the three of you?"

"Small is sneaky, I keep telling the girls. While the big houses are being dragged down by excess personnel, we move into the market they're too cumbersome to handle. Carole, show him his page."

The publicist saved her work twice before displaying the Cassandra Press catalogue. She scrolled past the colophon, a C with a P hooked on it, and a parade of authors" Ferdy Thorn, ex-marine turned ecological warrior; Germaine Gossett, feminist fantasy writer; Torin Bergman, Scandinavia's leading magic realist . . . "Forgive my ignorance," Boswell said, "but these are all new to me."

"They're the future." Sedgwick cleared his throat and grabbed Boswell's shoulder to lean him towards the computer. "Here's someone we all know."

BOSWELL'S BACK! the page announced in letters so large they left room only for a shout line from, Boswell remembered, the *Observer* twenty years ago— "Britain's best sf writer since Wyndham and Wells"—and a scattering of titles: *The Future Just Began, Tomorrow Was Yesterday, Wave Goodbye To Earth, Terra Spells Terror, Science Lies In Wait* . . . "It'll look better when we have covers to reproduce," Carole said. "I couldn't write much. I don't know your work."

"That's because I've been devouring it all over again, Jack. You thought you might have copies for my fair helpers, didn't you?"

"So I have," Boswell said, struggling to spring the catches of his aged briefcase.

"See what you think when you've read these. Some for you as well, Bren," Sedgwick said, passing out Boswell's last remaining hardcovers of several of his books. "Here's a Hugo winner, and look, this one got the Prix du Fantastique Ecologique. Will you girls excuse us now? I hear the call of lunch."

They were in sight of Waterloo Station again when he seized Boswell's elbow to steer him into the Delphi, a tiny restaurant crammed with deserted tables spread with pink and white checked cloths. "This is what one of our greatest authors looks like, Nikos," Sedgwick announced. "Let's have all we can eat and a litre of your red if that's your style, Jack, to be going on with."

The massive dark-skinned variously hairy proprietor brought them a carafe without a stopper and a brace of glasses Boswell would have expected to hold water. Sedgwick filled them with wine and dealt Boswell's a vigorous clunk. "Here's to us. Here's to your legendary unpublished books."

"Not for much longer."

"What a scoop for Cassandra. I don't know which I like best, *Don't Make Me Mad* or *Only We Are Left*. Listen to this, Nikos. There are going to be so many mentally ill people they have to be given the vote and everyone's made to have one as a lodger. And a father has to seduce his daughter or the human race dies out."

"Very nice."

"Ignore him, Jack. They couldn't be anyone else but you."

"I'm glad you feel that way. You don't think they're a little too dark even for me.

"Not a shade, and certainly not for Cassandra. Wait till you read our other books."

Here Nikos brought meze, an oval plate splattered with varieties of goo. Sedgwick waited until Boswell had transferred a sample of each to his plate and tested them with a piece of lukewarm bread. "Good?"

"Most authentic," Boswell found it in himself to say.

Sedgwick emptied the carafe into their glasses and called for another. Blackened lamb chops arrived too, and prawns dried up by grilling, withered meatballs, slabs of smoked ham that could have been used to sole shoes . . . Boswell was working on a token mouthful of viciously spiced sausage when Sedgwick said "Know how you could delight us even more?"

Boswell swallowed and had to salve his mouth with half a glassful of wine. "Tell me," he said tearfully.

"Have you enough unpublished stories for a collection?"

"I'd have to write another to bring it up to length."

"Wait till I let the girls know. Don't think they aren't excited, they were just too overwhelmed by meeting you to show it. Can you call me as soon as you have an idea for the story or the cover?"

"I think I may have both."

"You're an example to us all. Can I hear?"

"Shadows on a ruined wall. A man and woman and her child, and another man reaching out to them, I'd say in warning. Ruined tenements in the background. Everything overgrown. Even if the story isn't called *We Are Tomorrow,* the book can be."

"Shall I give you a bit of advice? Go further than you ever have before. Imagine something you couldn't believe anyone would pay you to write."

Despite the meal, Boswell felt too elated to imagine that just now. His capacity for observation seemed to have shut down too, and only an increase in the frequency of passers-by outside the window roused it. "What time is it?" he wondered, fumbling his watch upward on his thin wrist.

"Not much past five," Sedgwick said, emptying the carafe yet again. "Still lunchtime."

"Good God, if I miss my train I'll have to pay double."

"Next time we'll see about paying for your travel." Sedgwick gulped the last of the wine as he threw a credit card on the table to be collected later. "I wish you'd said you had to leave this early. I'll have Bren send copies of our books to you," he promised as Boswell panted into Waterloo, and called after him down the steps into the Underground "Don't forget, imagine the worst. That's what we're for."

For three hours the worst surrounded Boswell. **SIX NATIONS CONTINUE REARMING... CLIMATE CHANGES ACCEL-ERATE, SAY SCIENTISTS... SUPERSTITIOUS FANATICISM ON INCREASE... WOMEN'S GROUPS CHALLENGE ANTI-GUN RULING... RALLY AGAINST COMPUTER CHIPS IN CRIMINALS ENDS IN VIOLENCE" THREE DEAD, MANY INJURED...** Far more commuters weren't reading the news than were: many wore headphones that leaked percussion like distant discos in the night, while the sole book to be seen was *Page Turner,* the latest Turner adventure from Midas Paperbacks, bound in either gold or silver depending, Boswell supposed, on the reader's standards. Sometimes drinking helped him create, but just now a bottle of wine from the buffet to stave off a hangover only froze in his mind the image of the present in ruins and overgrown by the future, of the shapes of a family and a figure poised to intervene printed on the remains of a wall by a flare of painful light. He had to move on from thinking of them as the Aireys and himself, or had he? One reason Jean had left him was that she'd found traces of themselves and April in nearly all his work, even where none was intended; she'd become convinced he was wishing the worst for her and her child when he'd only meant a warning, by no means mostly aimed at them. His attempts to invent characters wholly unlike them had never convinced her and hadn't improved his work either. He needn't consider her feelings now, he thought sadly. He had to write whatever felt true—the best story he had in him.

It was remaining stubbornly unformed when the train stammered into the terminus. A minibus strewn with drunks and defiant smokers deposited him at the end of his street. He assumed his house felt empty because of Rod's proposal. Jean had taken much of the furniture they hadn't passed on to April, but Boswell still had seats where he needed to sit and folding canvas chairs for visitors, and nearly all his books. He was in the kitchen, brewing coffee while he tore open the day's belated mail, when the phone rang.

He took the handful of bills and the airmail letter he'd saved for last into his workroom, where he sat on the chair April had loved spinning and picked up the receiver. "Jack Boswell."

"Jack? They're asleep."

Presumably this explained why Rod's voice was low. "Is that an event?" Boswell said.

"It is for April at the moment. She's been out all day looking for work, any work. She didn't want to tell you in case you already had too much on your mind."

"But now you have."

"I was hoping things had gone well for you today."

"I think you can do more than that."

"Believe me, I'm looking as hard as she is."

"No, I mean you can assure her when she wakes that not only do I have a publisher for my two novels and eventually a good chunk of my backlist, but they've asked me to put together a new collection too."

"Do you mind if I ask for her sake how much they're advancing you?"

"No pounds and no shillings or pence."

"You're saying they'll pay you in euros?"

"I'm saying they don't pay an advance to me or any of their authors, but they pay royalties every three months."

"I take it your agent has approved the deal."

"It's a long time since I've had one of those, and now I'll be ten per cent better off. Do remember I've plenty of experience."

"I could say the same. Unfortunately it isn't always enough."

Boswell felt his son-in-law was trying to render him as insignificant as Rod believed science fiction writers ought to be. He tore open the airmail envelope with the little finger of the hand holding the receiver. "What's that?" Rod demanded.

"No panic. I'm not destroying any of my work," Boswell told him, and smoothed out the letter to read it again. "Well, this is timely. The Saskatchewan Conference on Prophetic Literature is giving me the Wendigo Award for a career devoted to envisioning the future."

"Congratulations. Will it help?"

"It certainly should, and so will the story I'm going to write. Maybe even you will be impressed. Tell April not to let things pull her down," Boswell said as he rang off, and "Such as you" only after he had.

Boswell wakened with a hangover and an uneasy sense of some act left unperformed. The image wakened with him: small child holding woman's hand, man beside them, second man gesturing. He groped for the mug of water by the bed, only to find he'd drained it during the night. He stumbled to the bathroom and emptied himself while the cold tap filled the mug. In time he felt equal to yet another breakfast of the kind his doctor had warned him to be content with. Of course, he thought as the sound of chewed bran filled his skull, he should have called Sedgwick last night about the Wendigo Award. How early could he call? Best to wait until he'd worked on the new story. He tried as he washed up the breakfast things and the rest of the plates and utensils in the sink, but his mind seemed as paralysed as the shadows on the wall it kept showing him. Having sat at his desk for a while in front of the wordless screen, he dialled Cassandra Press.

"Hello? Yes?"

"Is that Carole?" Since that earned him no reply, he tried "Bren?"

"It's Carole. Who is this?"

"Jack Boswell. I just wanted you to know—"

"You'll want to speak to Q. Q, it's your sci-fi man."

Sedgwick came on almost immediately, preceded by a creak of bedsprings. "Jack, you're never going to tell me you've written your story already."

"Indeed I'm not. Best to take time to get it right, don't you think? I'm calling to report they've given me the Wendigo Award."

"About time, and never more deserved. Who is it gives those again? Carole, you'll need to scribble this down. Bren, where's something to scribble with?"

"By the phone," Bren said very close, and the springs creaked.

"Reel it off, Jack."

As Boswell heard Sedgwick relay the information he grasped that he was meant to realise how close the Cassandra Press personnel were to one another. "That's capital, Jack," Sedgwick told him. "Bren will be lumping some books to the mail for you, and I think I can say Carole's going to have good news for you."

"Any clue what kind?"

"Wait and see, Jack, and we'll wait and see what your new story's about."

Boswell spent half an hour trying to write an opening line that would trick him into having started the tale, but had to acknowledge that the technique no longer worked for him. He was near to being blocked by fearing he had lost all ability to write, and so he opened the carton of books the local paper had sent him to review. *Sci-Fi On The Net, Create Your Own* Star Wars TM *Character,* 1000 *Best Sci-Fi Videos, Sci-Fi From Lucas To Spielberg, Star Wars* TM: *The Bluffer's Guide* . . . There wasn't a book he would have taken off a shelf, nor any appropriate to the history of science fiction in which he intended to incorporate a selection from his decades of reviews. Just now writing something other than his story might well be a trap. He donned sandals and shorts and unbuttoned his shirt as he ventured out beneath a sun that looked as fierce as the rim of a total eclipse.

All the seats of a dusty bus were occupied by pensioners, some of whom looked as bewildered as the young woman who spent the journey searching the pockets of the combat outfit she wore beneath a stained fur coat and muttering that everyone needed to be ready for the enemy. Boswell had to push his way off the bus past three grim scrawny youths bare from the waist up, who boarded the vehicle as if they planned to hijack it. He was at the end of the road where the wall had inspired him—but he hadn't reached the wall when he saw Rod's car.

It was identifiable solely by the charred number plate. The car itself was a blackened windowless hulk. He would have stalked away to call the Aireys if the vandalism hadn't made writing the new story more urgent than ever, and so he stared at the incomplete wall with a fierceness designed to revive his mind. When he no longer knew if he was staring at the bricks until the story formed or the shadows did, he turned quickly away. The shadows weren't simply cast on the wall, he thought; they were embedded in it, just as the image was embedded in his head.

He had to walk a mile homeward before the same bus showed up. Trudging the last yards to his house left him parched. He drank several glassfuls of water, and opened the drawer of his desk to gaze for reassurance or perhaps inspiration at his secret present from a fan before he dialled the Aireys' number.

"Hello?"

If it was April, something had driven her voice high. "It's only me," Boswell tentatively said.

"Grandad. Are you coming to see us?"

"Soon, I hope."

"Oh." Having done her best to hide her disappointment, she added "Good."

"What have you been doing today?"

"Reading. Dad says I have to get a head start."

"I'm glad to hear it," Boswell said, though she didn't sound as if she wanted him to be. "Is mummy there?"

"Just dad."

After an interval Boswell tried "Rod?"

"It's just me, right enough."

"I'm sure she didn't mean—I don't know if you've seen your car."

"I'm seeing nothing but. We still have to pay to have it scrapped."

"No other developments?"

"Jobs, are you trying to say? Not unless April's so dumbstruck with good fortune she can't phone. I was meaning to call you, though. I wasn't clear last night what plans you had with regard to us."

Rod sounded so reluctant to risk hoping that Boswell said "There's a good chance I'll have a loan in me."

"I won't ask how much." After a pause presumably calculated to entice an answer Rod added "I don't need to tell you how grateful we are. How's your new story developing?"

This unique display of interest in his work only increased the pressure inside Boswell's uninspired skull. "I'm hard at work on it," he said.

"I'll tell April," Rod promised, and left Boswell with that—with hours before the screen and not a word of a tale, just shadows in searing light: child holding woman's hand, man beside, another gesturing . . . He fell asleep at his desk and jerked awake in a panic, afraid to know why his inspiration refused to take shape.

He seemed hardly to have slept in his bed when he was roused by a pounding of the front-door knocker and an incessant shrilling of the doorbell. As he staggered downstairs he imagined a raid, the country having turned overnight into a dictatorship that had set the authorities the task of arresting all subversives, not least those who saw no cause for optimism. The man on the doorstep was uniformed and gloomy about his job, but brandished a clipboard and had a carton at his feet. "Consignment for Boswell," he grumbled.

"Books from my publishers."

"Wouldn't know. Just need your autograph."

Boswell scrawled a signature rendered illegible by decades of autographs, then bore the carton to the kitchen table, where he slit its layers of tape to reveal the first Cassandra Press books he'd seen. All the covers were black as coal in a closed pit except for bony white lettering not quite askew enough for the effect to be unquestionably intentional. **GERMAINE GOSSETT, *Women Are The Wave.* TORIN BERGMAN, *Oracles Arise!* FERDY THORN, *Fight Them Fisheries* . . .** Directly inside each was the title page, and on the back of that the copyright opposite the first page of text. Ecological frugality was fine, but not if it looked unprofessional, even in uncorrected proof copies. Proofreading should take care of the multitude of printer's errors, but what of the prose? Every book, not just Torin Bergman's, read like the work of a single apprentice translator.

He abandoned a paragraph of Ferdy Thorn's blunt chunky style and sprinted to his workroom to answer the phone. "Boswell," he panted.

"Jack. How are you today?"

"I've been worse, Quentin,"

"You'll be a lot better before you know. Did the books land?"

"The review copies, you mean."

"We'd be delighted if you reviewed them. That would be wonderful, wouldn't it, if Jack reviewed the books?" When this received no audible answer he said "Only you mustn't be kind just because they're ours, Jack. We're all in the truth business."

"Let me read them and then we'll see what's best. What I meant, though, these aren't finished books."

"They certainly should be. Sneak a glance at the last pages if you don't mind knowing the end."

"Finished in the sense of the state that'll be on sale in the shops."

"Well, yes. They're trade paperbacks. That's the book of the future."

"I know what trade paperbacks are. These—"

"Don't worry, Jack, they're just our first attempts. Wait till you see the covers Carole's done for you. Nothing grabs the eye like naive art, especially with messages like ours."

"So," Boswell said in some desperation, "have I heard why you called?"

"You don't think we'd interrupt you at work without some real news."

"How real?"

"We've got the figures for the advance orders of your books. All the girls had to do was phone with your name and the new titles till the batteries went flat, and I don't mind telling you you're our top seller."

"What are the figures?" Boswell said, and took a deep breath.

"Nearly three hundred. Congratulations once again."

"Three hundred thousand. It's I who should be congratulating you and your team. I only ever had one book up there before. Shows publishing needs people like yourselves to shake it up." He became aware of speaking fast so that he could tell the Aireys his—no, their— good fortune, but he had to clarify one point before letting euphoria overtake him. "Or is that, don't think for a second I'm complaining if it is, but is that the total for both titles or each?"

"Actually, Jack, can I just slow you down a moment?"

"Sorry. I'm babbling. That's what a happy author sounds like. You understand why."

"I hope I do, but would you mind—I didn't quite catch what you thought I said."

"Three hundred—"

"Can I stop you there? That's the total, or just under. As you say, publishing has changed. I expect a lot of the bigger houses are doing no better with some of their books."

Boswell's innards grew hollow, then his skull. He felt his mouth drag itself into some kind of a grin as he said "Is that three hundred, sorry, nearly three hundred per title?"

"Overall, I'm afraid. We've still a few little independent shops to call, and sometimes they can surprise you."

Boswell doubted he could cope with any more surprises, but heard himself say, unbelievably, hopefully "Did you mention *We Are Tomorrow?*"

"How could we have forgotten it?" Sedgwick's enthusiasm relented at last as he said "I see what you're asking. Yes, the total is for all three of your books. Don't forget we've still the backlist to come, though," he added with renewed vigour.

"Good luck to it." Boswell had no idea how much bitterness was audible in that, nor in "I'd best be getting back to work."

"We all can't wait for the new story, can we?"

Boswell had no more of an answer than he heard from anyone else. Having replaced the receiver as if it had turned to heavy metal, he stared at the uninscribed slab of the computer screen. When he'd had enough of that he trudged to stare into the open rectangular hole of the Cassandra carton. Seized by an inspiration he would have preferred not to experience, he dashed upstairs to drag on yesterday's clothes and marched unshaven out of the house.

Though the library was less than ten minutes' walk away through sunbleached streets whose desert was relieved only by patches of scrub, he'd hardly visited it for the several years he had been too depressed to enter bookshops. The library was almost worse: it lacked not just his books but practically everyone's except for paperbacks with injured spines. Some of the tables in the large white high-windowed room were occupied by newspaper readers. **MIDDLE EAST WAR DEADLINE EXPIRES...ONE IN TWO FAMILIES WILL BE VICTIMS OF VIOLENCE, STUDY SHOWS...FAMINES IMMINENT IN EUROPE... NO MEDICINE FOR FATAL VIRUSES...** Most of the tables held Internet terminals, from one of which a youth whose face was red with more than pimples was being evicted by a librarian for calling up some text that had offended the black woman at the next screen. Boswell paid for an hour at the terminal and began his search.

The only listings of any kind for Torin Bergman were the publication details of the Cassandra Press books, and the same was true of Ferdy Thorn and Germaine Gossett. When the screen told him his time was up and began to flash like lightning to alert the staff, the message and the repeated explosion of light and the headlines around him seemed to merge into a single inspiration he couldn't grasp. Only a hand laid on his shoulder made him jump up and lurch between the reluctantly automatic doors.

The sunlight took up the throbbing of the screen, or his head did. He remembered nothing of his tramp home other than that it tasted like bone. As he fumbled to unlock the front door the light grew audible, or the phone began to shrill. He managed not to snap the key and ran to snatch up the receiver. "What now?"

"It's only me, dad. I didn't mean to bother you."

"You never could," Boswell said, though she just had by sounding close to tears. "How are you, April? How are things?"

"Not too wonderful."

"Things aren't, you mean. I'd never say you weren't."

"Both." Yet more tonelessly she said "I went looking for computer jobs. Didn't want all the time mummy spent showing me how things worked to go to waste. Only I didn't realise how much more there is to them now, and I even forgot what she taught me. So then I thought I'd go on a computer course to catch up."

"I'm sure that's a sound idea."

"It wasn't really. I forgot where I was going. I nearly forgot our number when I had to ring Rod to come and find me when he hasn't even got the car and leave Gemima all on her own."

Boswell was reaching deep into himself for a response when she said "Mummy's dead, isn't she?"

Rage at everything, not least April's state, made his answer harsh. "Shot by the same freedom fighters she'd given the last of her money to in a country I'd never even heard of. She went off telling me one of us had to make a difference to the world."

"Was it years ago?"

"Not long after you were married," Boswell told her, swallowing grief.

"Oh." She seemed to have nothing else to say but "Rod."

Boswell heard him murmuring at length before his voice attacked the phone. "Why is April upset?"

"Don't you know?"

"Forgive me. Were you about to give her some good news?"

"If only."

"You will soon, surely, once your books are selling. You know I'm no admirer of the kind of thing you write, but I'll be happy to hear of your success."

"You don't know what I write, since you've never read any of it." Aloud Boswell said only "You won't."

"I don't think I caught that."

"Yes you did. This publisher prints as many books as there are orders, which turns out to be under three hundred."

"Maybe you should try and write the kind of thing people will pay to read."

Boswell placed the receiver with painfully controlled gentleness on the hook, then lifted it to redial. The distant bell had started to sound more like an alarm to him when it was interrupted. "Quentin Sedgwick."

"And Torin Bergman."

"Jack".

"As one fictioneer to another, are you Ferdy Thorn as well?"

Sedgwick attempted a laugh, but it didn't lighten his tone much. "Germaine Gossett too, if you must know."

"So you're nearly all of Cassandra Press."

"Not any longer."

"How's that?"

"Out," Sedgwick said with gloomy humour. "I am. The girls had all the money, and now they've seen our sales figures they've gone off to set up a gay romance publisher."

"What lets them do that?" Boswell heard himself protest.

"Trust."

Boswell could have made plenty of that, but was able to say merely "So my books . . . "

"Must be somewhere in the future. Don't be more of a pessimist than you have to be, Jack. If I manage to revive Cassandra you know you'll be the first writer I'm in touch with," Sedgwick said, and had the grace to leave close to a minute's silence unbroken before ringing off. Boswell had no sense of how much the receiver weighed as he lowered it—no sense of anything except some rearrangement that was aching to occur inside his head. He had to know why the news about Cassandra Press felt like a completion so imminent the throbbing of light all but blinded him.

It came to him in the night, slowly. He had been unable to develop the new story because he'd understood instinctively there wasn't one. His sense of the future was sounder than ever: he'd foreseen the collapse of Cassandra Press without admitting it to himself. Ever since his last sight of the Aireys the point had been to save them—he simply hadn't understood how. Living together would only have delayed their fate. He'd needed time to interpret his vision of the shadows on the wall.

He was sure the light in the house was swifter and more intense than dawn used to be. He pushed himself away from the desk and worked aches out of his body before making his way to the bathroom. All the actions he performed there felt like stages of a purifying ritual. In the mid-morning sunlight the phone on his desk looked close to bursting into flame. He winced at the heat of it before, having grown cool in his hand, it ventured to mutter "Hello?"

"Good morning."

"Dad? You sound happier. Are you?"

"As never. Is everyone up? Can we meet?"

"What's the occasion?"

"I want to fix an idea I had last time we met. I'll bring a camera if you can all meet me in the same place in let's say half an hour."

"We could except we haven't got a car."

"Take a cab. I'll reimburse you. It'll be worth it, I promise."

He was on his way almost as soon as he rang off. Tenements reared above his solitary march, but couldn't hinder the sun in its climb towards unbearable brightness. He watched his shadow shrink in front of him like a stain on the dusty littered concrete, and heard footsteps attempting stealth not too far behind him. Someone must have seen the camera slung from his neck. A backward glance as he crossed a deserted potholed junction showed him a youth as thin as a puppet, who halted twitching until Boswell turned away, then came after him.

A taxi sped past Boswell as he reached the street he was bound for. The Aireys were in front of the wall, close to the sooty smudge like a lingering shadow that was the only trace of their car. Gemima clung to her mother's hand while Rod stood a little apart, one fist in his hip pocket. They looked posed and uncertain why. Before anything had time to change, Boswell held up his palm to keep them still and confronted the youth who was swaggering towards him while attempting to seem aimless. Boswell lifted the camera strap over his tingling scalp. "Will you take us?" he said.

The youth faltered barely long enough to conceal an incredulous grin. He hung the camera on himself and snapped the carrying case open as Boswell moved into position, hand outstretched towards the Aireys. "Use the flash," Boswell said, suddenly afraid that otherwise there would be no shadows under the sun at the zenith—that the future might let him down after all. He'd hardly spoken when the flash went off, almost blinding its subjects to the spectacle of the youth fleeing with the camera.

Boswell had predicted this, and even that Gemima would step out a pace from beside her mother. "It's all right," he murmured, unbuttoning his jacket, "there's no film in it," and passed the gun across himself into the hand that had been waiting to be filled. Gemima was first, then April, and Rod took just another second. Boswell's peace deepened threefold as peace came to them. Nevertheless he preferred not to look at their faces as he arranged them against the bricks. He had only seen shadows before, after all.

Though the youth had vanished, they were being watched. Perhaps now the world could see the future Boswell had always seen. He clawed chunks out of the wall until wedging his arm into the gap supported him. He heard sirens beginning to howl, and wondered if the war had started. "The end," he said as best he could for the metal in his mouth. The last thing he saw was an explosion of brightness so intense he was sure it was printing their shadows on the bricks for as long as the wall stood. He even thought he smelled how green it would grow to be.

The Word

NOBODY TRIES TO SPEAK TO ME WHILE I'M WAITING FOR the lift, thank Sod. Whenever you want to go upstairs at a science fiction convention the lift is always on the top floor, and by the time it arrives it'll have attracted people like a dog-turd attracts flies. There'll be a woman whose middle is twice as wide as the rest of her, and someone wearing no sleeves or deodorant, and at least one writer gasping to be noticed, and now there's a vacuumhead using a walkie-talkie to send messages to another weekend deputy who's within shouting distance. Here comes a clump wearing convention badges with names made up out of their own little heads, N. Trails and Elfan and Si Fye, and I amuse myself trying to decide which of them I'd least like to hear from. Here's the lift at last, and I shut the doors before some bald woman with dragons tattooed on her scalp can get in as well, but a thin boy in a suit and tie manages to sidle through the gap. He sees my *Retard* T-shirt, then he reads my badge. "Hi there," he says. "I'm—"

"Jess Kray," I tell him, since he seems to think I can't read, "and you sent me the worst story I ever read in my life."

He sucks in his lips as if I've punched him in the mouth. "Which one was that?"

"How many have you written that are that bad?"

"None that I know of."

Everyone's pretending not to watch his face doing its best not to wince. "You sent me the one about Frankenstein and the dead goat and the two nuns," I say for everyone to hear.

"I've written lots since."

"Just don't send any to *Retard.*"

My fanzine isn't called that now, but I'm not telling him. I leave him to ride to the top with our audience while I lock myself in my room. I was going to write about the Sex, Sects and Subtexts in Women's Horror Fiction panel, which showed me why I've never been able to read a book by the half of the participants I'd heard of, but now I've too much of a headache. I lie on the bed for as long as I can stand being by myself, then I look for someone I can bear to dine with.

We're at Contraception in Edinburgh, but it could be anywhere a mob of fans calling themselves fen take over a hotel for the weekend. As I step into the lobby I nearly bump into Hugh, a writer who used to have tons of books in the shops, maybe because nobody was buying them. Soon books will all be games you play on screens, but I'll bet nobody will play with his. "How are you this year, Jeremy?" he booms.

"Dying like everyone else."

He emits a sound as if he's trying not to react to being poked in the ribs, and the rest of his party comes out of the bar. One of them is Jess Kray, who says "Join us, Jeremy, if you're free for dinner."

He's behaving like the most important person there, grinning with teeth that say we're real and a mouth that says you can check if you like and eyes with a message just for me. I'd turn him down to see how that makes him look, except Hugh Zit says "Do by all means" so his party knows he means the opposite, and it's too much fun to refuse.

Hugh Know's idea of where to eat is a place called Godfathers. I sit next to his Pakistani wife and her friend who isn't even a convention member, and ignore them so they stop talking English. I've already heard Hugh Ever say on panels all the garbage he's recycling, about how it's a writer's duty to offer a new view of the world, as if he ever did, and how the most important part of writing is research. He still talks like the fan he used to be, like all the fen I know talk, either lecturing straight in your face or staring over your shoulder as though there's a mirror behind you. Only Kray couldn't look more impressed. Hugh Cares finishes his pizza at last and says "I feel better for that."

I say "You must have felt bloody awful before."

Kray actually laughs at that while grimacing sympathetically at Hugh, and I can't wait to go back to my room and write a piece about the games he's playing. I write until I can't see for my headache, and after I've managed to sleep I write about the rest of the clowns at Contraception, until I've almost filled up the first issue of *Parade of the Maladjusted and Malformed,* which is what conventions are. On the last day I see Kray buying a publisher's editor a drink, which no doubt means he'll sell at least a trilogy. At least that's what I write once I'm home.

Then it's back to wearing a suit at the bank in Fulham and having people line up for me on the far side of a window, which at least keeps them at a distance while I turn them and their lives into numbers on a screen. But there's the smell of the people on my side of the glass, and sometimes the feel of them if I don't move fast enough. Playing the game of never saying what I think just about sees me through the day, and the one after that, and the one after that. I print my fanzine in my room and mail it and wait for the clowns I've written about to threaten to sue me or beat me up. The year isn't over when among the review copies and the rest of the unnecessaries publishers send to fanzines I get a sheet about Jess Kray, the most exciting new young writer of the decade, whose first three novels are going to give a new meaning to fantasy.

Sod knows I thought I was joking. I ask for copies to see how bad they are, and they're worse. They're about an alternate world where everyone becomes their sexual opposite, so a gay boy turns into a barbarian hero and a dyke becomes his lover, and some of the characters remember when they return to the real world and most of them try to remind the rest, except one thinks it's meant to be forgotten, and piles of similar crap. I just skim a few chapters of the first book to get a laugh at the idea of people buying a book called *A Touch of Other* under the impression that it's a different kind of junk. Apparently the books go on to be about some wimp who teaches himself magic in the other world and gets to be leader of this one. It's nine months since I saw Kray talking to the editor, so either he writes even more glibly than he comes on to people or he'd already written them. One cover shows a woman's face turning into a man's, and the second has a white running black, and the third's got a tinfoil mirror where a face should be. That's the one I throw hardest across the room. Later I put them in the pile to sell to Everybody's Fantasy, the skiffy and comics shop near the docks, and then I hear Kray will be there signing books.

How does a writer nobody's heard of put that over on even a shop run by fen? I'm beginning to think it's time someone exposed him. That Saturday I take the books with me, leaving the compliments slips in so he'll see I haven't bought them. Maybe I'll let him see me selling them as soon as he's signed them. But the moment I spot him at the table with his three piles on it he jumps up. "Jeremy, how are you! This is Jeremy Bates, everyone. He was my first critic."

Sod knows who he's trying to impress. The only customers are comics readers, that contradiction in terms, who look as if they're out without their mothers to buy them their funnies. And the proprietor, who I call Kath on account of his kaftan and long hair, doesn't seem to think much of Kray trying to hitch a ride on my reputation, not that he ever seems to think of much except where the next joint's coming from. I give Kray the books with the slips sticking up, but he carries on grinning. "My publishers haven't sent me your review yet, Jeremy."

I should tell him that's because I won't be writing one, but I'm mumbling like a fan, for Sod's sake. "Write something in them for me."

In the first book he writes *For Jeremy who knew me before I was good*, and *To our future* in the second, and *For life* in what I hope's the last. When he hands them back like treasure I stuff them in my armpit and leaf through some tatty fanzines so I can see how many people he attracts.

Zero. Mr Nobody and all his family. A big round hole without a rim. Some boys on mountain bikes point at him through the window until Kath chases them, and once a woman goes to Kray, but only to ask him where the Star Trek section is. Kath's wife brings him a glass of herbal tea, which isn't even steaming and with the bag drowning in it, and it's fun to watch him having to drink that. We all hang around for the second half of the hour, then Kath says in the drone that always sounds as if he's talking in his sleep "Maybe you can sign some stock for us."

I can hear he doesn't mean all the books on the table, but that doesn't stop our author. When Kray's defaced everyone he says "How about that lunch?"

Kath and Mrs Kath glance at each other, and Jess Kidding gives them an instant grin each. "I understand. Don't even think of it. You can buy lunch next time, after I've made you a bundle. Let me buy this one."

They shake their heads, and I see them thinking there'll never be a next time, but Jess Perfect flashes them an even more embracing grin before he turns to me. "If you want to interview me, Jeremy, I'll stand lunch. You can be the one who tells the world."

"About what?"

"That'd be telling."

I want the next *PotMaM* to spill a lot more blood, and besides, nobody's ever bought me lunch. I take him round the corner to Le Marin Qui Rit, which some French chef with too much money built in an old warehouse by the Thames. "This is charming," Kray says when he sees the nets full of crabs hanging from the beams and the waiters in their sailor suits, though I bet he doesn't think so when he sees the prices on the menu. As soon as we've ordered he hurries through the door that says Matelots, maybe to be sick over the prices, and I rip through his books until he comes back with his grin and says "Ask me anything." But I've barely opened my mouth when he says "Aren't you recording?"

"Didn't know I'd need to. Don't worry, I remember everything. My ex could tell you." He digs a pocket tape-recorder out of his trench coat. "Just in case you need to check. I always carry one for my thoughts."

He heard an ex-success say that at Contraception. A sailor brings us a bottle of sheep juice, Mutton Cadet, and I switch on. "What's a name like Kray supposed to mean to the world?"

"It's my father's name," he says, then proves I was right to be suspicious, because it turns out his father was a Jewish Pole who was put in a camp and left the rest of his surname behind when he emigrated with the remains of his family after the war.

"Speaking of prejudice, what's with the black guy calling himself Nigger when he gets to be the hero?"

"A nigger is someone who minds being called one. Either you take hold of words or they take hold of you."

"Which do you think your books do?"

"A bit of both. I'm learning. I want to be an adventurer on behalf of the imagination."

I can hardly wait to write about him, except here's my poached salmon. He waits until I've taken a mouthful and says "What did you like about the books?"

I'm shocked to realise how much of them has stuck in my mind—lines like "AIDS is such a hell you'll go straight to heaven." I want to say "Nothing," but his grin has got to me. "Where you say that being born male is the new original sin."

"Well, that's what one of my characters says."

What does he mean by that? His words keep slipping away from me, and I've no idea where they're going. By the time we finish I'm near to nodding in my pudding, his refusing to be offended by anything I say has taken so much out of me. The best I can come up with as a final question is "Where do you think you're going?"

"To Florida for the summer with my family. That's where the ideas are."

"Here's hoping you get some."

He doesn't switch off the recorder until we've had our coffee, then he gives me the tape. "Thanks for helping," he says, and insists on shaking hands with me. It feels like some kind of Masonic trick, trying to find out if I know a secret—either that or he's working out the best way to shake hands. He pays the bill without letting his face down and says he's heading for the station, which is on my way home, but I don't tell him. I turn my back on him and take the long way through the streets I always like, with no gardens and no gaps between the houses and less sunlight than anywhere else in town. While I'm there I don't need to think, and I feel as if nothing can happen in me or outside me. Only I have to go home to deal with the tape, which is itching in my hip pocket like a tapeworm.

I'm hoping he'll have left some thoughts on it by mistake, but there's just our drivelling. So either he brought the machine to make sure I could record him or more likely wanted to keep a copy of what we said. Even if he didn't trust me, it's a struggle to write about him in the way I want to. It takes me days and some of my worst headaches. I feel as if he's stolen my energy and turned it into a force that only works on his behalf.

When I seem to have written enough for an issue of *PotMaM* I print out the pages. I have to pick my way around them or tread on them whenever I get up in the night to be sick. I send out the issue to my five subscribers and anyone who sent me their fanzine, though not many do after what I write about their dreck. I take copies to Constipation and Convulsion and sell a few to people who haven't been to a convention before and don't like to say no. When I start screaming at the fanzine in the night and kicking the piles over I pay for a table in the dealers' room at Contamination. But on the Saturday night the dealers' room is broken into, and in the morning every single copy's gone.

It isn't one of my better years. My father dies and my mother tells me my ex-wife went to the funeral. The branch of the bank closes down because of the recession, and it looks as if I'll be out of a job, only luckily one of the other clerks gets his back broken in a hit and run. They move me to Chelsea, where half the lunchtime crowd looks like plain-clothes something and all the litter bins are sealed up so nobody can leave bombs in them. At least the police won't let marchers into the district, though you can hear them shouting for employment or life sentences for pornography or Islamic blasphemy laws or a curfew for all males as soon as they reach puberty or all tobacco and alcohol profits to go to drug rehabilitation or church-going to be made compulsory by law . . . Some writers stop their publisher from sending me review copies, so at least I've bothered them. I give up going to conventions for almost a year, until I forget how boring they are, so that staying in my room seems even worse. And at Easter I set out to find myself a ride to Consternation in Manchester.

I wait most of an hour at the start of the motorway and see a car pick up two girls who haven't waited half as long, so I'm in no mood for any crap from the driver who finally pulls over. He asks what I'm doing for Easter and I think he's some kind of religious creep, but when I tell him about Consternation he starts assuring me how he used to enjoy H. G. Wells and Jules Verne, as if I gave a fart. Then he says "What would you call this new johnny who wrote *The Word?* Is he sci-fi or fantasy or what?"

"I don't know about any word."

"I thought he might be one of you chaps. Went to a publisher and told him his ideas for the book and came away with a contract for more than I expect to make in a lifetime."

"How come you know so much about it?"

"Well, I am a bookseller. Those on high want us to know in advance this isn't your average first novel. Let me cudgel the old brains and I'll give you his name."

I'm about to tell him not to bother when he grins. "Don't know how I could forget a name like that, except it puts you in mind of the Kray brothers, if you're not too young to remember their reign of terror. The last thing he sounds like is a criminal. Jess Kray, that's the phenomenon."

I'd say I knew him if I could be sure of convincing this caricature that he isn't worth knowing. I bite my tongue until it feels as if my teeth are meeting, then I realise the driver has noticed the tears that have got away from me, and I could scream. He says no more until he stops to let me out of the car. "You ought to tell your people about this Kray. Sounds as if he has some ideas that bear thinking about."

The last thing I'll do is tell anyone about Kray, particularly when I remember him saying I should. I wait in my hotel room for my headache to let me see, then I go down to the dealers' room. Instead of books a lot of the tables are selling virtual reality viewers or pocket CD-ROM players. I can't find anything by Kray, and some of the dealers watch me as if I'm planning to steal from them, which makes me feel like throwing their tables over. Then the fat one who always wears a sombrero says "Can I do something for you?"

"Not by the look of it." That doesn't make him go away, and all I can think of is to confuse him. "You haven't got *The Word.*"

"No, but Jess sent us each a copy of the cover," he says, and props up a piece of cardboard with letters in the middle of its right-hand side:

JESS KRAY
THE WORD

I can't tell if they're white on a black background or black on white, because as soon as I move an inch they turn into the opposite. I shut my eyes once I've seen it's going to be published by the dump that stopped sending me review copies. "What do you mean, he sent you it? He's just a writer."

"And he designed the cover, and he wants everyone to know what's coming, so he got the publisher to print enough cover proofs for us all in the business."

I'm not asking what Kray said about his book. When Fat in the Hat says "You can't keep your eyes shut forever" I want to shut his, especially when as soon as I open mine he says "Shall we put you down for a copy when it's published?"

"They'll send me one."

"I doubt it," he says, and he'll never know how close he came to losing the bone in his nose, except I have to take my head back to my room.

Maybe he wasn't just getting at me. Once I'm home I ring Kray's new publisher for a review copy. I call myself Jay Battis, the first name that comes into my head, and say I'm the editor of *Psychofant* and no friend of that total cynic Jeremy Bates. But the publicity girl says Kray's book isn't genre fiction, it's literature and they aren't sending it to fanzines.

So why should I care? Except I won't have her treating me as though I'm not good enough for Kray after I gave him more publicity than he deserved when he needed it most. And I remember him thanking me for helping—did he mean with this book? I ask the publicity bitch for his address, but she expects me to believe they don't know it. I could ask her who his agent is, but I've realised how I'd most like to get my free copy of his world-shaking masterpiece.

I don't go to Kath's shop, because I'd be noticed. On the day the book is supposed to come out I go to the biggest bookshop in Chelsea. There's a police car in front, and the police are making them move out of the window a placard that's a big version of the cover of *The Word*—

I hear the police say it has been distracting drivers. I walk to a table with a pile of *The Word* on it and straight out with one in my hand, because the staff are busy with the police. Only I feel as if Kray's forgiving me for liberating his book, and it takes all my strength not to throw it away.

Even when I've locked my apartment door I feel watched. I hide the book under the bed while I fry some spaghetti and open a tin of salmon for dinner. Then I sit at the window and watch the police cars hunting and listen to the shouts and screams until it's dark. When I begin to feel as if the headlights are searching for me I close the curtains, but then I can't think of anything to do except read the book.

Only the first few pages. Just the prospect of more than a thousand of them puts me off. I can't stand books where the dialogue isn't in quotes and paragraphs keep beginning with "And". And I'm getting the impression that the words are slipping into my head before I can grasp them. Reading the book makes me feel I'm hiding in my room, shutting myself off from the world. I stuff *The Word* down the side of the bed where I can't see the cover playing its tricks, and switch on the radio.

Kray's still in my head. I'm hoping that since it's publication day I'll hear someone tearing him to bits. There isn't a programme about books any longer on the radio, just one about what they call the arts. They're reviewing an Eskimo rock band and an exhibition of sculptures made out of used condoms and a production of *Jesus Christ Superstar* where all the performers are women in wheelchairs, and I'm sneering at myself for imagining they would think Kray was worth their time and at the world for being generally idiotic when the presenter says "And now a young writer whose first novel has been described as a new kind of book. Jess Kray, what's the purpose behind *The Word?*"

"Well, I think it's in it rather than behind it if you look. And I'd say it may be the oldest kind of book, the one that's been forgotten."

At first I don't believe it's him, because he has no accent at all. I make my head throb trying to remember what accent he used to have, and when I give up the presenter is saying "Is the narrator meant to be God?"

"I think the narrator has to be different for everyone, like God."

"You seem to want to be mysterious."

"Don't you think mystery has always been the point? That isn't the same as trying to hide. We've all read books where the writer tries to hide behind the writing, though of course it can't be done, because hiding reveals what you thought you were hiding . . . "

"Can you quote an example?"

"I'd rather say that every book you've ever read has been a refuge, and I don't want mine to be."

"Every book? Even the Bible? The Koran?"

"They're attempts to say everything regardless of how much they contradict themselves, and I think they make a fundamental error. Maybe Shakespeare saw the problem, but he couldn't quite solve it. Now it's my turn."

I'm willing the presenter to lose her temper, and she says "So to sum up, you're trying to top Shakespeare and the Bible and the rest of the great books."

"My book is using up a lot of paper. I think that if you can't put more into the world than you take out of it you shouldn't be here at all."

"As you say somewhere in *The Word*. Jess Kray, thank you."

Then she starts talking to a cretic—which is a cretin who thinks they're a critic, such as everyone who attacks my fanzines—about Kray and his book. When the cretic says she thinks the narrator might be Christ because of a scene where he sees the light beyond the mountain through the holes in his hands I start shouting at the radio for quite a time before I turn it off. I crawl into bed and can't stop feeling there's a light beside me to be seen if I open my eyes. I keep them closed all night and wake up with the impression that some of Kray's book is buried deep in my head.

For the first time since I can remember I'm looking forward to a day at the bank. I may even be able to stand the people on my side of the glass without grinding my teeth. But that afternoon Mag, one of the middle-aged girls, waddles in with an evening paper and nearly slaps me in the face with it as though it's my fault. "Will you look at this. Where will it stop. I don't know what the world is coming to."

CALL FOR BAN ON "BLASPHEMOUS" BOOK. I don't want to read any more, yet I grab the paper. It says that on the radio programme I heard Kray said his book was better than the Bible and people should read it instead. A bishop is calling for the police to prosecute, and some mob named Christ Will Rise is telling Christians to destroy *The Word* wherever they find it. So I can't help walking past the shop my copy came from, even though it isn't on my way home. And on the third day half a dozen Earnests with placards saying **CHRIST NOT KRAY** are picketing the shop.

The police apparently don't think they're worth more than cruising past, and I hope they'll get discouraged, because they're giving Kray publicity. But the next day there are eight of them, and twelve the day after, and at the weekend several Kray fans start reading *The Word* to the pickets to show them how they're wrong. And I feel as though I've had no time to breathe before there's hardly a shop in the country without clowns outside it reading *The Word* and the Bible or the Koran at one another. And then Kray starts touring all the shops and talking to the pickets.

I keep switching on the news to check if he's been scoffed into oblivion, but no such luck. All the time in my room I'm aware of his book in there with me. I'd throw it away except someone might end up reading it—I'd tear it up and burn it except then I'd be like the Christ Will Risers. The day everyone at the bank is talking about Kray being in town during my lunch hour I scrape my brains for something else to do, anything rather than be one of the mob. Only suppose this is the one that stops him? That's a spectacle I'd enjoy watching, so off I limp.

There must be at least a hundred people outside the bookshop. Someone's given Kray a chair to stand on, but Sod knows who's arranged for a beam of sunlight to shine on him. He's answering a question, saying "If you heard the repeats of my interview you'll know I didn't say my book was better than the Bible. I'm not sure what better means in that context. I hope my book contains all the great books."

And he grins, and I wait for someone to attack him, but nobody does, not even verbally. I feel my voice forcing its way out of my mouth, and all I can think of is the question vacuumheads ask writers at conventions. "Where did you get your ideas?"

So many people stare at me I think I've asked the question he didn't want asked. I feel as if he's using more eyes than a spider to watch me, more than a whole nest of spiders—more than there are people holding copies of his drivel. Kray himself is only looking in my general direction, trying to make me think he hasn't recognised me or I'm not worth recognising. "They're in my book."

I want to ask why he's pretending not to know me, except I can't be sure it'll sound like an accusation, and the alternative makes me cringe with loathing. But I'm not having any of his glib answers, and I shout "Who are?"

The nearest Kray fan stops filming him with a steadycam video and turns on me. "His ideas, he means. You're supposed to be talking about his ideas."

I won't be told what I'm supposed to be saying, especially not by a never-was who can't comb her hair or keep her lips still, and I wonder if she's trying to stop me asking the question I hadn't realised I was stumbling on. "Who did you meet in Florida?" I shout.

Kray looks straight at me, and it's as if his grin is carving up my head. "Some old people with some old ideas that were about to be lost. They're in my book. Everyone is in any book that matters."

Maybe he sees me sucking in my breath to ask about the three books he wants us to forget he wrote, because he goes on. "As I was about to say, all I'm asking is that we should respect one another. Do me the honour of not criticising *The Word* until you've read it. If anyone feels harmed by it, I want to know."

I might have vanished or never been there at all. When he pauses for a response I feel as if his grin has got stuck in my mouth. The mob murmurs, but nobody seems to want to speak up. Any protest is being swallowed by vagueness. Then two minders appear from the crowd and escort Kray to a limo that's crept up behind me. I want to reach out to him and—I don't know what I want, and one of the minders pushes me out of the way. I see Kray's back, then the limo is speeding away and all the mob are talking to one another, and I have to take the afternoon off because I can't see the money at the bank.

Whenever the ache falters my head fills up with thoughts of Kray and his book. When I sense his book by me in the dark I can't help wishing on it—wishing him and it to a hell as everlasting as my headache feels. It's the first time I've wanted to believe in hell. Not that I'm so far gone I believe wishes work, but I feel better when the radio says his plan's gone wrong. Some Muslim leaders are accusing him of seducing their herd away from Islam.

I keep looking in the papers and listening in the night in case an ayatollah has put a price on his head. Some bookshops in cities that are overrun with Muslims are either hiding their copies of *The Word* or sending them back, and I wish on it that the panic will spread. But the next headline says he'll meet the Muslim leaders in public and discuss *The Word* with them.

A late-night so-called arts programme is to broadcast the discussion live. I don't watch it, because I don't know anyone who would let me watch their television, but when it's on I switch out my light and sit at my window. More and more of the windows out there start to flicker as if the city is riddled with people watching to see what will happen to Kray. I open my window and listen for shouting Muslims and maybe Kray screaming, but I've never heard so much quiet. When it starts letting my head fill up with thoughts I don't want to have, I go to bed and dream of Kray on a cross. But in the morning everyone at the bank is talking about how the Muslims ended up on Kray's side and how one of them from a university is going to translate *The Word* into whatever language Muslims use.

And everyone, even Mag who didn't know what the world was coming to with Kray, is saying how they admire him or how they've fallen in love with him and the way he handled himself, and wish they'd gone to see him when he was in town. When I say I've got *The Word* and can't read it they all look as though they pity me. Three of them ask to borrow it, and I tell them to buy their own because I never paid for mine, which at least means nobody speaks to me much after that. I can still hear them talking about Kray and feel them thinking about him, and in the lunch hour two of them buy *The Word* and the rest, even the manager, want a read. I'm surrounded by Kray, choked by a mass of him. I'm beginning to wonder if anyone in the world besides me knows what he's really like. The bank shuts at last, and when I leave the building two Christ Will Risers are waiting for me.

Both of them wear suits like civil servants and look as though they spend half their lives scrubbing their faces and polishing the crosses at their throats. They both step forward as the sunlight grabs me, and the girl says "You knew him."

"Me, no, who? Knew who?"

Her boyfriend or whatever touches my arm likes a secret sign. "We saw you making him confess who he'd met."

"Let's sit down and talk," says the girl.

Every time they move, their crosses flash until my eyes feel like a whole graveyard of burnt crosses. At least the couple haven't swallowed *The Word,* and talking to them may be better than staying in my room. We find a bench that isn't full of unemployed and clear the McDonald's cartons off it, and the Risers sit on either side of me even though I've sat almost at the end of the bench. "Was he a friend of yours?" the girl says.

"Seems like he wants to be everyone's friend," I say.

"Not God's."

It doesn't matter which of them said that, it could have come from either. "So how much do you know about what happened in Florida?"

"As much as he said when I asked him."

"You must be honest with us. We can't do anything about him if we don't put our faith in the truth."

"Why not?"

That throws them, because they're obviously not used to thinking. Then they say "We need to know everything we can find out about him."

"Who's we?"

"We think you could be one of us. You're of like mind, we can tell."

That's one thing I'll never be with anyone. I nearly jump up and lean on their shining shampooed heads so they won't follow me, but I want to know what they know about Kray that I don't. "Then that must be why I asked him about Florida. All I know is that last time I met him he was going there and he wrote *The Word* when he came back. So what happened?"

They look at each other across me and then swivel their eyes to me. "There are people who came down a mountain almost a hundred years ago. We know he met them or someone connected with them. That has to be the source of his power. Nothing else could have let him win over Islam."

I wouldn't have believed anyone could talk less sense than Kray. "He was like that when he was just a fantasy fan. He's got a genius for charming everyone he meets and promoting himself."

"That must be how he learned the secret that came down the mountain. What else can you tell us?"

I don't mind making them more suspicious of Kray, but I won't have them thinking I tried to help them. "Nothing," I say, and get up.

They both reach inside their jackets for pamphlets. "Please take these. Our address is on the back whenever you want to get in touch."

I could tell them that's never and stuff their pamphlets in their faces, but at least while I've the pamphlets in my fist nobody can take me for a Jess Kray fan. At home I glance at them to see they're as stupid as I knew they would be, full of drone out of the Bible about the Apocalypse and the Antichrist and the Antifreeze and Sod knows what else. I shove them down the side of the bed and try to believe that I've helped the Risers get Kray. And I keep hoping until I see *Time* magazine with him on the cover.

By then half the bank has read *The Word*. I've seen them laughing or crying or going very still when they read it in their breaks, and when they finish it they look as if they have a secret they wish they could tell everyone else. I won't ask, I nearly chew my tongue off. Anyone who asks them about the book gets told "Read it" or "You have to find out for yourself", and I wonder if the book tells you to make as many people read it as you can, like they used to tell you on posters not to give away the end of films. I won't touch my copy of *The Word,* but one day I sneak into a bookshop to read the last page. Obviously it makes no sense, only I feel that if I read the page before it I'll begin to understand, because maybe it can be read backwards as well as forwards. I throw the book on the table and run out of the shop.

At least they've taken *The Word* out of the window to make room for another pound of fat in a jacket, but I keep seeing people reading it in the streets. Whenever I see anything flash in a crowd I'm afraid it's another copy drawing attention to itself. At home I feel it beginning to surround me in the night out there, and I tell myself I've one copy nobody is reading. But I have to take train rides into the country for walks to get away from it—they're the only way I can be certain I'm nowhere near anyone who's read it. And coming back from one of those rides, I see him watching me from the station bookstall.

He looks like a recruiting poster for himself that doesn't need to point a finger. While I'm pretending to flip through the magazine I knock all the copies of *Time* onto the floor of the booking hall, except for the one I shove down the front of my trousers. All the way home I feel my peter wiping itself on his mouth, and in my room I have a good laugh at my stain on his face before I turn to the pages about him.

The headline says **WHAT IS THE WORD?** in the same typeface as the cover of his book. Maybe the article will tell me what I need to put him out of my mind for good. But it says how he bought his parents a place in Florida with part of his advances, and how *The Word* is already being translated into thirteen languages, and I'm starting to puke. Then the hack tries to explain what makes *The Word* such a publishing phenomenon, as she calls it. And by the time I've finished nearly going blind with reading what she wrote I think it's another of Kray's tricks.

It says too much and nothing at all. She doesn't know if the word is the book or the narrator or the words that keep looking as if they've been put in by mistake. Kray told her that if a book wasn't language it was nothing. "So perhaps we should take him at his, you should forgive it, word." He said he just put the words on paper and it's for each reader to decide what they add up to. So she collected a gaggle of cretics and fakes who profess and that old joke "leading writers" and got them to discuss *The Word*.

If I'd been there I'd have mashed all their faces together. It was the funniest book someone had ever read, and the most moving someone else had, and everyone agreed with both of them. One woman thought it was like *The Canterbury Tales,* and then there's a discussion about whether it's told by one character or several or whether all the characters might be the same one in some sort of mental state or it's showing a new kind of relationship between them all. A professor points out that the Bible was written by a crowd of people but when you read it in translation you can't tell, whereas she thinks you can identify to the word where Kray's voices change, "as many voices as there are people who understand the book." That starts them talking about the idea in *The Word* that people in Biblical times lived longer because they were closer in time to the source, as if that explains why some people are living longer now and the rest of what's happening to us, the universe drifting closer to the state it was in before it formed. And there's crap about people sinning more so their sins will reach back to the Crucifixion because otherwise Christ won't come back, or maybe the book says people have to know when to stop before they have the opposite effect and throw everything off balance, only by now I'm having to run my finger under the words and read them out loud, though my voice makes my head worse. There are still columns to go, the experts saying how if you read *The Word* aloud it's poetry and how you'll find passages almost turning into music, and how there are developments of ideas from Sufism and the Upanishads and Buddhism and Baha'i and the Cabbala and Gnosticism, and Greek and Roman and older myths, and I scrape my fingernail over all this until I reach the end, someone saying "I think the core of this book may be the necessary myth for our time." And everyone agrees, and I tear up the magazine and try to sleep.

I can still hear them all jabbering as if Kray is using their voices to make people read his book to discover what they were raving about. I hear them in the morning on my way to the bank, and I wonder how many of them his publisher will quote on the paperback, and that's when I realise I'm dreading the paperback because so many more people will be able to afford it. I'm dreading being surrounded by people with Kray in their heads, because then the world will feel even more like somewhere I've wandered into by mistake. It almost makes me laugh to find I didn't want to be shown that people are as stupid as I've always thought they were.

When posters for the paperback start appearing on bus shelters and hoardings I have to walk about with my eyes half shut. The posters don't use the trick the cover did, but that must mean the publishers think that just the title and his name will sell the book. At the bank I keep being asked if I don't feel well, until I say I'm not getting my Sunday dinner any more since my mother had a heart attack and died in hospital, not that it's anyone's business, but as well as that I can hardly eat for waiting for the paperback.

The day I catch sight of one there's a march of lunatics demanding that the hospitals they've been thrown out of get reopened, and in the middle of all this a woman's sitting on a bench reading *The Word* as though she can't see or hear what's going on around her for the book. And then the man she's waiting for sits down by her and squashes his wet mouth on her cheek, and leans over to see what she's reading, and I see him start to read as if it doesn't matter where you open the book, you'll be drawn in. And when I run to the bank one of the girls asks me if I know when the paperback is coming out, and saying I don't know makes me feel I'm trying to stop something that can't be stopped.

Or am I the only one who can? I spend the day trying to remember where I put the interview with him. Despite whoever stole all the copies of *PotMam* at Contamination, I should still have the tape. I look under my clothes and the plates and the tins and in the tins as well, and under the pages of the magazine I tore up, and under the towels on the floor in the corner, and among the bits of glasses I've smashed in the sink. It isn't anywhere. My mother must have thrown it out one of the days she came to clean my room. I start screaming at her until I lose my voice, by which time I've thrown just about everything movable out of the window. They're demolishing the houses opposite, so some more rubbish in the street won't make any difference, and my fellow rats in the building must be too scared to ask what I'm doing, unless they're too busy reading *The Word*.

By the end of the week, two of the slaves at the bank have the paperback and will lend it to anyone who asks. And I don't know when they start surrounding me with Kray's words. Most of the time—Sod, all the time—I know they're saying things they've heard someone else say, but after a while I notice they've begun speaking in a way that's meant to show they're quoting. Like the girl at the window by mine would start talking about a murder mystery on television and the one next to her would say "The mystery is around you and in you" and they'd laugh as if they were sharing a secret. Or one would ask the time and her partner in the comedy team would say "Time is as soon as you make it." And all sorts of other crap: "Look behind the world" or "You're the shadow of the infinite," which the manager says once as if he's topping everyone else's quotes. And before I know it at least half the slaves don't say "Good morning" any more, they say "What's the word?"

That makes the world feel like a headache. People say it in the street too, and when they come up to my window, until I wonder if I was wrong to blame my mother for losing the tape, if someone else might have got into my room. By the time the next catch-phrase takes root in the dirt in people's heads I can't control myself—when I hear one of the girls respond to another "As Kray would say."

"Is there anything he doesn't have something to say about?"

I think I'm speaking normally enough, but they cover their ears before they shake their heads and look sad for me and chorus "No."

"Sod, listening to you is like listening to him."

"Maybe you should."

"Maybe he will."

"Maybe everyone will."

"Maybe is the future."

"As Kray would say."

"Do you know you're the only one who hasn't read him, Jeremy?"

"Thank Sod if it keeps me different."

"Unless we find ourselves in everybody else . . . "

"As fucking Kray would say."

A woman writing a cheque gasps, and another customer clicks his tongue like a parrot, and I'm sure they're objecting to me daring to utter a bad word about their idol. None of the slaves speaks to me all day, which would be more of a relief if I couldn't feel them thinking Kray's words even when they don't speak them. I assume the manager didn't hear me, since he was in his office telling someone the bank is going to repossess their house. But on Monday morning he calls me in and says "You'll have been aware that there's been talk of further rationalisation."

He was talking before that, only I was trying to see where he's hidden *The Word*. At least he doesn't sound like Kray. "Excuse me, Mr Bates, but are there any difficulties you feel I should know about?"

"With what?"

"I'd like to give you a chance to explain your behaviour. You're aware that the bank expects its staff to be smart and generally presentable."

I hug myself in case that hides whatever he's complaining about and hear my armpits squelch, and me saying "I thought you were supposed to see yourself in me."

"That was never meant to be used as an excuse. Have you really nothing more to say?"

I can't believe I tried to defend myself by quoting Kray. I chew my tongue until it hurts so much I have to stick it out. "I should advise you to seek some advice, Mr Bates," says the manager. "I had hoped to break this to you more gently, but I must say I can see no reason to. Due to the economic climate I've been asked to propose further cuts in staff, and you will appreciate that your attitude has aided my decision."

"Doesn't Kray have anything to say about fixing the economy?"

"I believe he does in world terms, but I fail to see how that helps our immediate situation."

The manager's beginning to look reluctantly sympathetic—he must think I've turned out to be one of them after all, and I won't have him thinking that. "If he tried I'd shove his book back where it came from."

The manager looks as if I've insulted him personally. "I can see no profit in prolonging this conversation. If you wish to work your notice I must ask you to take more care with your appearance and, forgive my bluntness, to treat yourself to a bath."

"How often does he say I've got to have one?" I mean that as a sneer, but suppose it sounds like a serious question? "Not that I give a shit," I say, which isn't nearly enough. "And when I do I can use his book to wipe my arse on. And that goes for your notice as well, because I don't want to see any of you again or anyone else who's got room in their head for that, that . . . " I can't think of a word bad enough for Kray, but it doesn't matter, because by now I'm backing out of the office. "Just so everyone knows I know I'm being fired because of what I say about him," I add, raising my voice so they'll hear me through their hands over their ears. Then I manage to find my way home, and the locks to stick the keys in, and my bed.

There's almost nothing else in my room except me and *The Word*. So I still have a job, to stay here to make sure it's the copy nobody reads. I do that until the bank sends me a cheque for the money they must wish they didn't owe me, and I remember all my money I forgot to take with me when I escaped from the bank.

I'm waiting when they open. At first I think the slaves are pretending not to know me, then I wonder if they're too busy thinking Kray's thoughts. A slave takes my cheque and my withdrawal slip and goes away for longer than I can believe it would take even her to think about it, then I see the manager poke his head out of his office to spy on me while I'm tearing up a glossy brochure about how customers can help the bank to help the Third World. I see him tell the clerk to give me what I want, then he pulls in his head like a tortoise that's been kicked, and it almost blinds me to realise he's afraid of what I am. Only what am I?

The slave stuffs all my money in an envelope and drops it in the trough under the window, the trough that always made me wonder which side the pigs were on. I shove the envelope into my armpit and leave behind years of my life. I'm walking home as fast as I can, through the streets where every shop either has a sale on or is closing down or both, when I see Kray's face.

It's a drawing on the cover of just about the only magazine that is still about books. I have to find out what he's up to, but with the money like a cancer under my arm I can't be sure of liberating the magazine without people noticing. I go into the bookshop and grab it off the rack, and people backing away make me feel stronger. I've only read how *The Word* is shaping up to outsell the Bible worldwide, and how some campus cult is saying there's a different personal message in it for everybody and anyone who can't read it should have it read to them, when a bouncer trying to look like a policeman tells me to buy the rag or leave. I've read all I need to, and I have all I need. The money is to give me time to do what I have to do.

Only I'm not sure what that is. The longer I stay in my room, the more I'm tempted to look in *The Word* for a clue. It's trying to trick me into believing there's no help outside its pages, but I've something else to read. I find the Christ Will Rise pamphlets that *The Word* has done its best to tear up and shove out of my reach, and when I've dragged them and my face out of the dust under the bed I manage to smooth out the address.

It's down where most of the fires in the streets are and the police drive round in armoured cars when they go there at all, and no cameras are keeping watch, and hardly any helicopters. By now it's dark. People are doing things to each other standing up in doorways if they aren't prowling the streets in dozens searching for less than themselves. I'm afraid they may set fire to me, because I see dogs pulling apart something charred that looks as if it used to be someone, but nobody seems to think I'm worth bothering with, which is their loss.

The Risers' sanctuary is in the middle of a block of hundredyearold houses, some of which have roofs. Children are running into one house holding a cat by all its legs, but I can't see anyone else. I feel the front steps tilt and crunch together as I climb to the Risers' door, and I hold onto the knocker to steady myself, though it makes my fingers feel as if they're crumbling. I'm about to slam the knocker against the rusty plate when a fire in a ruin across the street lights up the room inside the window next to me.

It's full of chairs around a table with pamphlets on it. Then the fire jerks higher, and I see they aren't piles of pamphlets, they're two copies of *The Word*. The books start to wobble like two blocks of gelatin across the table towards me, and I nearly wrench the knocker off the door with trying to let go of it. I fall down the steps and don't stop running until I'm locked in my room.

I watch all night in case I've been followed. Even after the last television goes out I can't sleep. And when the dawn brings the wagons to clean up the blood and vomit and empty cartridges I don't want to sleep, because I've remembered that the Risers aren't the only other people who know what Kray was.

I go out when the streets won't be crawling—when the taken care of have gone to work and the beggars are counting their pennies. When I reach Everybody's Fantasy it looks as if the books in the window and the Everything Half Price sign have been there for months. The rainy dirt on the window stops me reading the spines on the shelf where Kray would be. I'm across the road in a burnedout house, waiting for a woman with three Dobermans to pass so I can smash my way into the shop with a brick, when Kath arrives in a car with bits of it scraping the road. He doesn't look interested in why I'm there or in anything else, especially selling books, so I say "You're my last hope."

"Yeah, okay." It takes him a good few seconds to get around to saying "What?"

"You've got some books I want to buy."

"Yeah?" He comes to as much life as he's got and wanders into the shop to pick up books strewn over the floor. "There they are."

I think he's figured out which books I want and why until I realise he means everything in the shop. I'm heading for the shelf when I see *The Word, The Word, The Word, The Word . . .* "Where's *A Touch of Other?*" I nearly scream.

"Don't know it."

"Of course you do. Jess Kray's first novel and the two that go with it. He signed them all when you didn't want him to. You can't have sold them, crap like them."

"Can't I?" Kath scratches his head as if he's digging up thoughts. "No, I remember. He bought the lot. Must have been just about when *The Word* was due."

"You realise what he was up to, don't you?"

"Being kind. Felt guilty about leaving us with all those books after nobody came, so he bought them back when he could afford to. Wish we still had them. I've never even seen them offered for sale."

"That's because he doesn't want anyone to know he wrote them, don't you see? Otherwise even the world might wonder how someone like that could have written the thing he wants everyone to buy."

"You can't have read *The Word* if you say that. It doesn't matter what came before it, only what will happen when everyone's learned from it."

He must have stoned whatever brains he had out of his head. "I felt like you do about him," he's saying now, "but then I got to know him"

"You know him? You know where I can find him?"

"Got to know him in his book."

"But you've got the address where you sent him his books."

"Care of his publishers."

"He didn't even give you his address and you think he's your friend?"

"He was moving. He's got nothing to hide, you have to believe that." Having to give me so many answers so fast seems to have used Kath up, then his face rouses itself. "If you want to get to know him as he is, he's supposed to be at Consummation."

"I've given up on fans. The people I meet every day are bad enough."

Kath's turning over magazines on the counter like a cat trying to cover its turds. "There'll be readings from *The Word* for charity and a panel about it, and he's meant to be there. We'd go, only we've not long had a kid."

"Don't tell me there'll be someone growing up without *The Word.*"

"No, we'd like her to see him one day. I was just telling you we can't afford to go." He shakes two handfuls of fanzines until a flyer drops out of one. "See, there he is."

The flyer is for Consummation, which is two weeks away in Birmingham, and it says the Sunday will be Jess Kray Day. I manage not to crumple much of it up. "Can I have this?"

"I thought you didn't want to know him."

"You've sold me." I shove the flyer into my pocket. "Thanks for giving me what I was looking for," I say, and leave him fading with his books.

I don't believe a whole sigh fie convention can be taken in by Kray. Fen are stupid, Sod knows, but in a different way—thinking they're less stupid than everyone else is. I'll know what to do when I see them and him. The two weeks seem not so much to pass as not to be there

at all. On the Friday morning I have a bath so I won't draw attention
to myself until I want to. For the first time ever I don't hitch to a
convention, I go by train to be in time to spy out the situation. Once
I'm in my seat I stay there, because I've seen one woman reading *The
Word* and I don't want to see how many other passengers are. I stare at
streets of houses with steel shutters over the windows and rivers
covered with chemicals and forests that children keep setting fire to,
but I can feel Kray's words hatching in all the nodding heads around
me.

The convention hotel is five minutes' walk from the station. After
about ten beggars I pretend I'm alone in the street. The hotel is
booked solid as a fan's cranium, and the hotel next to it, and I have to
put up with one where the stairs lurch as if I'm drunk and my room
smells of someone's raincoat and old cigarettes. It won't matter,
because I'll be spending as much time with the fen as I can bear. I go
to the convention hotel while it's daylight and there are police out of
their vehicles. And the first thing the girl at the registration desk with
a ring in her nose and six more in her ears says is "Have you got *The
Word?*"

My face goes hard, but I manage to say "It's at home."

"If you'd like one to have with you, they're free with membership."

It'll be another nobody else can read. I tell her my name's Jay Batt
and pin my badge on when she's written it, and squeeze the book in
my right hand so hard I can almost feel the words mashing together.
"Is he here yet?"

"He won't be."

"But he's why I'm here. I was promised he was coming."

She must think I sound the same kind of disappointed as her. "He
said he would be when we wrote to him, only now he has to be in the
film about him they'll be televising next month. Shall I tell you what
he said? That now we've got *The Word* we don't need him."

I know that's garbage, but I'm not sure why. I bite my tongue so I
won't yell, and when I see her sympathising with the tears in my eyes
I limp off to the bar. It's already full of more people than seats, and I
know most of them—I've written about them in my fanzines. I'm
wondering how I can get close enough to find out what they really

think about *The Word* when they start greeting me like an old friend. Two people have offered to buy me a drink before I realise why they're behaving like this—because I've got *The Word*.

I down the drinks, and more when they're offered, and make sure everyone knows I won't buy a round. I'm trying to infuriate someone as much as their forgiveness infuriates me, because then maybe they'll argue about Kray. But whatever I say about him and his lies they just look more understanding and wait patiently for me to understand. The room gets darker as my eyes fill up with the dirt and smoke in the air, and faces start to melt as if *The Word* has turned them into putty. Then I'm screaming at the committee members and digging my nails into the cover of the book. "Why would anyone be making a film about him? More likely he was afraid he'd meet someone here who knows what he wants us to forget he wrote."

"You mustn't say that. He sent us this, look, all about the film." The chairman takes a glossy brochure out of his briefcase. The sight of Kray grinning on the cover almost blinds me with rage, but I manage to read the name of the production company. "And they're going to do a live discussion with him after the broadcast," the chairman says.

I run after my balance back to my hotel. I can hear machineguns somewhere, and I have to ring the bell three times before the armed night porter lets me in, but they can't stop me now. I haul myself up to my room, snapping a banister in the process, and fall on the bed to let my headache come. Whenever it lessens I think of another bit of the letter I'm going to write. The night and the sounds of gunfire falter at last, and the room fades into some kind of reality. It's like being part of the cover of a book nobody wants to take out of a window, but they won't be able to ignore me much longer.

I write the letter and check out of the hotel, telling the receptionist I've been called away urgently, and fight my way through the pick-pockets to the nearest post office, where I get the address of the television channel. Posting the letter reminds me of going to church when I had to live with my parents, where they used to put things in your mouth in front of the altar. As soon as the letter is out of my hands I don't know if I feel empty or unburdened, and I can't remember exactly what I wrote.

I spend Sunday at home trying to remember. Did I really claim I was the first to spread the word about Kray? Did I really call myself Jude Carrot because I was afraid he'd remember the interview and tell the producer not to let me anywhere near? Won't he just say he's never heard of me? I can't think how that idea makes me feel. I left the other copy of *The Word* in my hotel room as if it was the Bible, and I have to stop myself from throwing the one under the bed out of the window to give them something to fight over besides the trash in the street.

On Monday I know the letter has arrived. Maybe it'll take a few hours to reach the producer of the discussion programme, since I didn't know his name. By Tuesday it must have got to him, and by Wednesday he should have written to me. But Thursday comes, and I watch the postman dodging in and out of his van while his partner rides shotgun, and there's no letter for me.

Twice I hear the phone in the hall start to ring, but it could just be army trucks shaking the house. I start trying to think of a letter I could write under another name, saying I know things about Kray nobody else does, only I can't think of a letter that's different enough. I go to bed to think, then I get up to, and keeping doing those is Thursday and Friday morning. Then I hear the van screech to a halt just long enough for the postman to stick a letter through the door without getting out of his cabin, because presumably they can't afford to pay his partner any more, then it screeches away along the sidewalk. And when I look down the stairs I see the logo of the television company on the envelope.

I'd open it in the hall except I find I'm afraid to read what it says. I remember I'm naked and cover my peter with it while I run upstairs, though everyone in the house is scared to open their door if they hear anyone else. I lock all my locks and hook up the chains and wipe my hands on my behind so the envelope won't slip out of them, then I tear it almost in half and shake the letter flat.

Dear Mr "Carrot"
Jess Kray says

Suddenly my hands feel like gloves someone's just pulled their hands out of, and when I can see again I have to fetch the letter from under the bed. I'm already struggling to think of a different name to sign on the next letter I send, though since now I'll know who the producer is, should I phone them? I poke at my eyes until they focus enough that I can see her name is Tildy Bacon, then I make them see what she wrote.

Dear Mr "Carrot"
Jess Kray says he will look forward to seeing
you and including you in our discussion on the 25th.

There's more about how they'll pay my expenses and where I'm to go, but I fall on the bed, because I've just discovered I don't know what to do after all. It doesn't matter, I'll know what to say when the cameras are on and the country's watching me. Only something's missing from that idea and the absence keeps pecking at my head. It feels like an intruder in my room, one I can't see that won't leave me alone. Maybe I know what I'm trying not to think, but a week goes by before I realise: I can't be certain of exposing Kray unless I read *The Word*.

I spend a day telling myself I have to, and the next day I drag the book out of its hiding place and claw off the dusty cobwebs. I stare at the cover until it feels as if it's stuck behind my eyes, then I scream at myself to make me open it. As soon as I can see the print I start reading, but it feels as if Kray's words and the noises of marching drums and sirens and gunfire are merging into a substance that's filling up my head before I can stop it, and I have to shut the book. There's less than a week before I'm on television, and all I can think of that may work is being as far away from people as I can get when I read the book.

The next day is Sunday, which makes no difference, since there are as many people wandering around the countryside with nothing else to do any day of the week. I tear the covers off a Christ Will Rise pamphlet and wrap them round *The Word* before I head for Kings Cross, and I'm sure some of the people I avoid look at it to see if it's *The Word*. I thump on the steel shutter until the booking clerk sells me a ticket. While I'm waiting for the train I see through the reinforced glass of the bookstall that most of the newspapers are announcing a war that's just begun in Africa. I catch myself wondering if *The Word* has been translated in those countries yet, and then I imagine a world where there are no wars because everyone's too busy reading *The Word* and thinking about it and talking about it, and my fingernails start aching from gripping the book so I won't throw it under a train.

When my train leaves I'm almost alone on it, but I see more people than I expect in the streets. Quite a few seem to be gathering in a demolished church, and I see a whole crowd scattered over a park, being read to from a book—I can't decide whether it's black or white. All their faces are turned to the sun as if they don't know they're being blinded. As the city falls away I'm sure I can feel all those minds clogged with Kray trying to drag mine back and having to let go like old tasteless chewing gum being pulled out of my head. Then there are only fields made up of lines waiting to be written on, and hedges blossoming with litter, and hours later mountains hack their way up through fields and forests as if the world is still crystallising. In the midst of the mountains I get off at a station that's no more than two empty platforms, and climb until I'm deep in a forest and nearly can't breathe for climbing. I sit on a fallen tree, and there's nothing to do except read. And I make myself open *The Word* and read as fast as I can.

I won't look up until I've finished. I can feel his words crowding into my head and breeding there, but I have to understand what he's put into the world before I confront him. The only sound is of me turning pages and ripping each one out as I finish it, but I sense the trees coming to read over my shoulder, and moss oozing down them to be closer to the book, and creatures running along branches until they're above my head. I won't look; I only read faster, so fast that the book is in my head before I know. However much there is of it, I'm stronger—out here it's just me and the book. I wonder suddenly if the pages may be impregnated with some kind of drug, but if they are I've beaten it by throwing away the pages, because you must have to be holding the whole book for the drug to work. I've no idea how long

I've been reading the book aloud, but it doesn't matter if it helps me see what Kray is up to. Though my throat is aching by the time I've finished, I manage a laugh that makes the trees back away. I fall back with my face to the clouds and try to think what the book has told me that he wouldn't want anyone to know.

My body's shaking inside and out, and I feel as if my brain is too. There was something about panic in *The Word*, but if I think of it, will that show me how the book is causing it, or won't I be able to resist swallowing *The Word* as the cure? I'm already remembering, and digging my fingernails into my temples can't crush the thought. Kray says we'll all experience a taste of the panic Christ experienced as we approach the time when the world is changed. I feel the idea cracking open in my brain, and as I fight it I see in a flash what he was trying not to admit by phrasing it that way. He wanted nobody to know that *he* is panicking—that he has something to be afraid of.

I sit up and crouch around myself until I stop shaking, then I go down through the forest. The glade papered with *The Word* seems to have a meaning I no longer need to understand. Some of the pages look as if they're reverting to wood. The night comes down the forest with me, and in a while a train crawls out of it. I go home and lock myself in.

Now it takes me all my time to hold *The Word* still in my head. The only other thing I need to be aware of is when the television company sends me my train ticket, but everything around me seems on the point of making a move. Whenever I hear a car it sounds about to reveal it's a mail-van. At least that helps me ignore my impression that all I can see of the world is poised to betray itself. If this is how having read *The Word* feels . . .

The next day the mail-van screeches past my building, and the day after that. Suppose the letter to me has been stolen, or someone at the television company has stopped it from being sent? I'll pay my own fare and get into the discussion somehow. But the ticket finally arrives, which may mean they'll try and steal it from my room.

I sit with the ticket between my teeth and watch the street and listen for them setting up whatever they may use to smash my door in. Suppose the room itself is the trap? Or am I being made to think that so I'll be driven out of it? I wrap the ticket in some of a Christ Will Rise pamphlet so that the ink won't run when I take it with me to the bathroom, and on the last morning I have a long bath that feels like some kind of ritual. That would be a good time for them to come for me, but they don't, nor on my way to the station, though I'm sure I notice people looking at me as if they know something about me. For the first time since I can remember there are no sounds of violence in the streets, and that makes me feel there are about to be.

On the train I sit where I can watch the whole compartment, and see the other passengers pretending not to watch me. All the way to Hyde Park Corner I expect to be headed off. I'm trudging up the slope to the hotel when a limo pulls up in front of the glass doors and two minders climb out before Kray does. As he unbends he looks like a snake standing on its tail. I pretend to be interested in the window of a religious bookshop in case he tries to work on me before the world is watching. I see copies of *The Word* next to the Bible and the Koran, and Kray's reflection merging with his book as he goes into the hotel. He must have noticed me, so why is he leaving me alone? Because passiveness is the trick he's been playing on me ever since I read *The Word*—doing nothing so I'll be drawn towards him and his words. It's the trick he's been playing on the world.

Knowing that makes me impatient to finish. I wait until I see him arrive in the penthouse suite, then I check in. My room is more than twice the size of the one I left at home. The world is taking notice of me at last. I drink the liquor in the refrigerator while I have another bath, and ignore the ringing of the phone until I think there's only just time to get to the studio before the discussion starts.

A girl's face on the phone screen tells me my taxi's waiting. As soon as we're in it she wants to know everything about me, but I won't let her make me feel I don't know what I am. I shrug at her until she shuts up. There are no other cars on the road, and I wonder if there's a curfew or everyone's at home waiting for Kray and me.

Five minutes later the taxi races into the forecourt of the television studios. The girl with not much breath rushes me past a guard at the door and another one at a desk and down a corridor that looks as if it never ends. I think that's the trick they were keeping in store for me, but then she steers me left into a room, and I'm surrounded by voices and face to face with Kray.

There are about a dozen other people in the room. The remains of a buffet are on a table and scattered around on paper plates. A woman with eyes too big for her face says she's Tildy Bacon and hands me a glass of wine while a girl combs my hair and powders my face, and I feel as if they're acting out some ritual from *The Word*. Kray watches me as he talks and grins at some of his cronies, and once the girl has finished with me he puts a piece of cake on a plate and brings it over. "You must have something, Jeremy. You look as if you've been fasting for the occasion."

So does he. He looks thinner and older, as if he's put almost all of himself into his book, or is he trying to trick me into thinking he'll be easy to deal with? I take the plate and wash a bite of the cake down with some wine, and he gives me the grin. "It's nearly time."

Is he talking about the programme I can see behind him on a monitor next to a fax machine? Someone who might be a professor or a student is saying that nobody he's met has been unchanged by *The Word* and that he thinks it promises every reader the essential experience of their life. Kray's watching my face, but I won't let him see I know how much crap the screen is talking until we're on the air. Then Tildy Bacon says to everyone "Shall we go up? Bring your drinks."

As the girl who ought to learn how to breathe ushers people towards the corridor, Tildy Bacon steps in front of me and looks me in the face. So they've saved stopping me until the last possible moment. I'll wait until everyone else is out of the room, then I'll do whatever needs to be done to make certain she can't follow me and throw me off the air. But she says "We had to ask Jess how to bill you on screen since you weren't here."

If she thinks I'm going to ask what he said I was, she can go on thinking. "I'm sure he knows best," I tell her with a grin that may look like his for all I care, and dodge around her before she can delay me any further, and follow the procession along the corridor.

At first the set-up in the studio looks perfect. The seven of us, including Kray, will sit on couches around a low table with glasses and a jug of water on it while Kray's minders have to stay on the far side of a window. Only I haven't managed to overtake the procession, so how can I get close to him? Then he says "Sit next to me, Jeremy," and pats a leather cushion, and before I have time to wonder what he's up to I've joined him.

Everyone else sitting down sounds like something leathery stirring in its sleep. The programme about Kray is on a monitor in a corner of the studio. A priest says he believes the secret of *The Word* needs to be understood, then the credits are rolling, and a woman who I hadn't even realised was going to run the discussion leans across the table and waits for a red light to signal her. Then she says "So, Jess Kray, what's your secret?"

He grins at her and the world. "If I have one it must be in my book."

A man with holes in his purple face where spots were says "In other words, if you revealed the secret it wouldn't sell."

Is there actually someone here besides me who doesn't believe in *The Word?* Kray grins at him. "No, I'm saying the secret must be different for everyone. It isn't a question of commerce. In some parts of the world I'm giving the book away."

The holey man seems satisfied, but a woman with almost more hair on her upper lip than on her scalp says "To achieve what?"

"Peace?"

Good Sod, Kray really does believe his book can put a stop to wars. Or does he mean he won't be peaceful until the whole world has *The Word* inside them? The woman who was given the signal leans across the table again, reaching for Kray with her perfume and her glittering hands and her hair swaying like oil on water. She means to turn the show into a discussion, which will give him the chance not to be watched all the time by the camera. I'll say anything to bother him, even before I know what. "It's supposed to be . . . "

That heads her off, and everyone looks at me. Then I hear what I'm going to say—that the secret of *The Word* is supposed to be some kind of eternal life. But there is no secret in *The Word,* that's why I'm here. "Jeremy?" Kray says.

I'm wondering if *The Word* has got inside me without my knowing—if it was making me say what I nearly said and that's why he is encouraging me. He wants me to say that for him, and he's talking about peace, which I already knew was his weapon, and suddenly I see what everything has been about. It's as if a light is shining straight into my eyes, and I don't care if it blinds me. "He's supposed to be Christ," I shout.

There's some leathery movement, then someone I don't need to see says "All the characters are clearly aspects of him."

"We're talking about the narrator of *The Word*," the television woman explains to the camera, and joins in. "I took him to be some kind of prophet."

"Christ was a prophet," says a man who I can just about see is wearing a turban.

"Are we saying—" the television woman begins, but she can't protect Kray from me like that. "He knows I didn't mean anyone in his book," I shout. "I mean him."

The words are coming out faster than I can think, but they feel right. "If people don't believe in him they won't believe in his book. And they won't believe in him unless he can save himself."

Ideas are fighting in my head as if *The Word* is trying to come clear. If Christ came back now he'd have to die to make way for a religion that works better than his did, or would it be the opposite of Christ who'd try to stop all the violence and changes in the world? Either way . . . I'm going blind with panic, because I can feel Kray close to me, willing me to . . . He wants me to go on speaking while my words are out of control—because they're his, or because I won't be able to direct them at him? Then I realise how long he's been silent, and I think he wants me to speak to him so he can speak to me. Is the panic I'm suffering his? He's afraid—afraid of me, because I'm . . .

"I think it's time we moved on," the television woman says, but she can't make anything happen now. I turn and look at him.

He's waiting for me. His grin is telling me to speak—to say whatever I have to say, because then he'll answer and all that the world will remember hearing is him. It's been that way ever since the world heard of him. I see that now, but he's let me come too close. As I open my mouth I duck my head towards him.

For a moment it seems I'm going to kiss him. I see his lips parting, and his tongue feeling his teeth, and the blood in his eyes, and the fear there at last. I duck lower and go for his throat. I know how to do it from biting my tongue, and now I don't need to restrain myself or let go. Someone is screaming, it sounds as if the world is, but it can't be Kray, because I've torn out his voice. I lift my head and spit it back into his face.

It doesn't blot out his eyes. They meet mine, and there's forgiveness in them, or something even worse—fulfilment? Then his head falls back, opening his throat so I'm afraid he'll try and talk through it, and he throws his arms wide for the cameras. That's all I see, because there's nothing in my eyes now except light. But it isn't over, because I can still taste his voice like iron in my mouth.

Words are struggling to burst out of my head, and I don't know what they are. Any moment Kray's minders or someone will get hold of me, but if I can just . . . I bang my knees against the table to find it, and hear the glasses clash against the jug. I throw myself forwards and find one, and a hand grabs my arm, but I wrench myself free and shove the glass against my teeth until it breaks. Now the light feels as if it's turning into pain that is turning into the world, but whose pain is it—Kray's or mine? Hands are pulling at me, and I've no more time to think. As I make myself chew and swallow, at least I'm sure I'll never say another word.

afterword

DID THIS BOOK LIVE UP TO ITS TITLE? IN TIME IT WILL, of course. Who knows, perhaps the odd tale may even survive me as a reprint, and until then I won't know if I'll know. Let me chase away some of the shadows. Everything I write, even this, can be seen as the work of a past self—dead, if you like, though I'd prefer to regard all those personalities as having helped to make me whatever I am. Certainly I find the experience of reading my old or even not so old stuff increasingly strange: it's like encountering it for the first time, and from someone else's pen. As I sort through these performances in the order of writing, we'll see what memories they rouse.

"The Previous Tenant" dates from 1968, the year before I met my wife. I'd recently completed *Demons by Daylight,* my first real book, and this story followed. I seem to have felt the need to experiment further (to overcome my sense of having reached an end with *Demons)* rather than consolidate what I'd learned so far. Presumably that's why I denied the characters names. I later saw that the story recalled "The Beckoning Fair One", which I'd read when I was too young to appreciate its subtleties. On the other hand, I've no idea where the central relationship came from except the depths of my head.

Besides meeting Jenny in 1969, I began to review films for the BBC. I'd already been writing about them for years, mainly horror, after my friend Harry Nadler urged me to. He loved the cinema of the fantastic as much as I did, and used reviews of mine in *Alien* and later in *L'Incroyable Cinema,* both of which he co-edited in Manchester. Among much else, he was responsible for my first encounter with

Fritz Lang's *Metropolis*. It was entirely typical of Harry that when he learned I hadn't seen the film, he invited me back to the house where he lived with his mother and proceeded to screen it with an 8mm projector in ten-minute reels on his bedroom wall.

Well, I digress. I may well again in the course of this piece. "After the Queen" (1969) was based on an idea by John Owen of LiG, the Liverpool science fiction group. As Frank Mace he wrote "The Ideal Type" in *Dark Mind, Dark Heart,* and "The Cuckoo Clock" in *London Mystery Magazine.* The latter journal deftly bought all rights by hiding its contract on the back of the cheque. Though I'm sure John is too seasoned to fall for that now, he didn't realise that the tale had been filmed for *Alfred Hitchcock Presents* (adapted by Robert Bloch, no less) until Universal contacted him decades later to inform him it was being remade. It was John who introduced me to Val Lewton's magnificently suggestive horror films, along with the music of Villa-Lobos and Milhaud, and John Collier's splendid novel *Defy the Foul Fiend.* As for "After the Queen", the setting is based on a real cinema, the Woolton, one of the few suburban Liverpool cinemas not to close in the sixties or seventies.

"The Last Hand" (1969) also recalls LiG. For years we had our clubroom at 69A Bold Street, above Helen's Leather Goods, an upstairs business capable of various interpretations. Eventually we were cast out, perhaps because Helen valued privacy on Monday nights, and instead met on Sundays at the house of Norman and Ina Shorrock—one of many reasons for the dedication of this book. They set me appreciating good food and wine: Ina wouldn't leave anyone unfed, and Norman never let a glass stay empty in anyone's hand. I often said that he'd lent me his nose, and Jenny that he had a lovely one. More often than not we played cards: chemin de fer, brag, puddle (Jenny's innovation), knockout whist, ranter go round, many variations of poker . . . Players included Norman Weedall (the late great wine-maker and collector of *Weird Tales),* Eddie Jones (who illustrated my first published story and the cover of *Demons by Daylight* and any amount of science fiction but died in poverty, alas) and, if he was visiting, Phil Rogers (who specified that at his funeral the coffin should be carried off to the strains of the Radetsky March, and so it was). John Roles tended to sit out the games, though he was the only person other than my daughter who could beat me at Nim, which John and I first saw in *Last Year in Marienbad*. A bookseller and creator of the fanzine *Morph,* one issue of which made history by being edible, he was strangled to death at his home in June 1999 by a postcard collector and charity worker, Andrew John Swift. John's bookshop suggested the one in "Cold Print", and he introduced me to the actual setting of "The Cellars". Neither tale is in this book, of course, and so I'd better regain some relevance by mentioning that on trains to science fiction conventions the assembled gamblers of LiG fell to cards. Without this I'm sure "The Last Hand" would never have occurred to me.

"The Worst Fog of the Year" (1970) was suggested by the experience of watching films at press shows, still the best way to avoid the distractions of an audience: the stench of their popcorn, the shrilling of their mobile phones, the mutter of their commentaries or conversation. The story first appeared in the British Fantasy Society's journal *Dark Horizons.* Karl Edward Wagner let me know that he would use it in *Year's Best Horror Stories* if the ending were less jokey, and I made it so. Both endings appear in this book, in case you didn't notice.

For several years Jenny and I spent our summer holidays in Cumbria, generally in the hotel that figures in "Above the World" (not included here). "Accident Zone" (1973) derives from some of our walks. The different views of the landscape the two stories take can be ascribed at least partly to the effects of LSD. When I wrote "Accident Zone" those experiences were a couple of years in the future. My agent Kirby McCauley found the tale "slow and not very attention getting", and I'm inclined to agree with him. Still, enough readers have found something in it to give me an excuse to reprint it here.

I don't generally use friends as characters. In "Dead Letters" (1974) I gave two of the cast the first names of stalwarts of LiG, Stan and Marge Nuttall, but none of their characteristics. I hope they were amused. The story was one of a bunch I wrote in emulation of the notorious but subsequently celebrated EC horror comics of the fifties. The market the stories were meant for had second thoughts about buying prose fiction, and they found a home elsewhere. I also wrote some science fiction, my agent having advised me to try, but my style and imagination tended to stiffen at the challenge. "Slow" (1975) was the last attempt, and relatively sure of itself.

In 1990 I was one of six diners in *The Horror Cafe,* a special extended edition of a BBC television arts programme. Also round the table were Pete Atkins, Clive Barker, John Carpenter, Roger Corman and Lisa Tuttle. As we ate and drank we discussed horror I recall surprising Clive, the elected host, by suggesting that my tales celebrated the unknown—and eventually improvised a round-robin story. At the end of one of his contributions John Carpenter left me to pick up a concept in quantum physics. "Fuck you, John," I was heard to respond, though not in the broadcast version, edited down from three hours to half the length. True to my constitution, I'd taken every opportunity to eat and drink whatever was on offer, an attitude that drew praise from the television reviewer Nancy Banks Smith. When at last the cameras stopped rolling it proved to be Roger Corman's birthday, and much champagne was quaffed. The next day I sat very still for not much less than an eternity outside Euston Station before forcing myself onto a train for Liverpool to sit even stiller. Later that year the *Radio Times* approached me to put the round robin into publishable form to help promote the broadcast, but whoever commissioned the tale felt I hadn't done justice to the material. Is "Facing It" fun in its own right? You'll have judged for yourself.

"The Word" (1993) owes its existence to Douglas E. Winter, the spectacularly talented author of *Run.* Doug conceived an anthology of tales that would span the last century, one long story to a decade. That much I'm sure of, and memory suggests Steve King was originally to evoke the sixties, but wasn't the underlying theme to be a revelation brought down a mountain? I could swear that's why I included it in my piece. For the rest I leave interpretation to the reader, but I'm reminded that I once attracted some hostility with an article on science fiction conventions in *Blazon,* the journal of the Knights of St Fanthony. It was the idea of the editor, Eric Bentcliffe ("Eric the Bent"), who originally asked me to read the early work of John W. Campbell Jr in order to vilify it. I'd earned a reputation for controversy, but if people thought I would produce it on demand, it was time to think again.

"Little Ones" (1996) was written in collaboration with Jenny that is, for once the shared authorship was made plain. My writing from 1969 onwards owes an increasing amount to her and eventually to Tammy and Matt as well. Of course not only the writing does: much of the best of me comes from them. When "Little Ones" appeared in print in an anthology of collaborations between partners it was preceded by our comments, and here they are.

"When Ramsey spoke of a collaboration, my mind went back to when I had a provisional licence previous to passing my driving test, and needed a qualified driver to sit in with me. I'm glad to say that this experience was a much better one than that.

"It brought home to me the sheer professionalism of Ramsey—his ability to return to a story and hone it over an extended period of time as opposed to my short period of concentrated effort followed by a triumphant 'It's done!'

"On the debit side some changes he made to my original I would have argued against if time and the pressure of work had allowed. Maybe next time . . . "

"As so often, Jenny overrates me and underrates herself. I'd say we have collaborated on virtually all the fiction I've written since we met twenty-eight years ago. She's my first editor, the person who reads my initial drafts and makes suggestions and criticisms. Only she could, because she's the only person who can read the handwriting. Mind you, hers is as bad as mine. She had to tell me that Gill's mysterious possession in our story, a plonte quane, was in fact a plaster gnome.

"Jenny's teaching background often figures in my stuff, and even if I wrote some of the details about teaching in the present tale, they're really all hers. I used her story as a first draft and worked at the motivations until I believed in them. Our readers can play at deciding which of us wrote which scenes and which sentences. Jenny and I are so close that I'll bet we fool you. That's love and marriage."

"Twice by Fire" (1997) was commissioned for an anthology of tales about James O'Barr's creation, the Crow. I see now that it's a sufficiently universal concept that I didn't need to set it in America. I can only hope that aspect isn't too unconvincing, though I'm by no means as good at producing an American voice as Pete Crowther or Pete Atkins or, before them, my fellow Wirralian Eric Frank Russell. From the same year, "Never to be Heard" was another commission, based on a painting by Alan M. Clark. His image helped focus my ambition to write a decent story about music. I was indeed in the choir at grammar school and had to mouth rather than sing when we performed Borodin.

"Agatha's Ghost" also dates from 1997. I'm dismayed to have to report that I didn't invent the advice Agatha is offered on the air; I heard a lady much like her being told on a Radio Merseyside phonein to try those solutions—hence the tale. Usually the programme doesn't insult the intelligence. Far worse, to the extent of being horribly fascinating, is *Trisha,* a British television show very much like Jerry Springer with a veneer of concern. Couples and families rant onstage while the audience jeers and the viewer at home is trapped into feeling superior to them all. To quote an actual subtitle from 19 November 2002"

"This family is on self-destruct. What will happen by the end of the show? Don't miss it!" Further drama is always promised "after the break" (during DESPERATE MOTHERS, DYING DAUGHTERS on 2 December 2002, for instance). You see how guiltily obsessed I am. Body language readers and relationship therapists are often trotted out, but the show's most basic appeal involves lie detectors and DNA tests (neither as reliable as Trisha Goddard wants us to think). "Is he the baby's father? Find out after the break!" It's unnerving when reality catches up with my fiction and I can't invent anything worse, but the reality is one reason why I write.

In 1998 I found time to write four short stories, and they're all in here. "Return Journey" was suggested by a trip to Llangollen, where a vintage railway had been dressed up as a wartime ride for the weekend. "The Entertainment" contains echoes of Robert Aickman's "The Hospice" but is its own tale, I hope, not least in its knockabout and its nervousness about growing old. Aickman professed to find some worth in my stuff, or at least implied as much. His correspondence with the late Cherry Wilder betrays the truth.

"No Strings" was written for Michele Slung's anthology about strangers, but she found it insufficiently strange. I'm not complaining: without her invitation the story would never have existed, and it has done well for itself. "Becoming Visible" derives from an incident where I lost my temper with a salesman on the telephone, who did indeed make the mistake of enquiring why I didn't want to buy whatever product he wanted to sell. For some weeks after this he kept making deranged calls to the house, and alas, I couldn't remember the name of the firm he had originally identified. Eventually he went away, leaving me with a story idea. As you see, ideas can be the easy part—indeed, I've more of those in my notebooks than I'm likely to have time to develop.

"No Story in It" (1999) was the second tale I wrote around an image by Alan Clark—the one that haunts the writer in the tale. I had the late John Brunner at the back of my mind, having recently written a memoir of him (which can be found in my non-fiction book *Ramsey Campbell, Probably*). While the unlucky protagonist isn't meant to be him, I fear John would have sympathised with many of his experiences. This was one of several tales of mine to be found wanting on a web site where someone criticises horror fiction from the safety of a pseudonym, a rather asinine genre enterprise. The masked reviewer comments about the story "A difficult read in that I was unable to firmly grasp what might be happening an (sic) any given moment. The dialogue was barely coherent as was the plot at times and the final resolution, quite hollow. I've never been happy or impressed by anything has (sic) Campbell has done, sometimes I wonder why I even bother." Well, quite, not least since the review (dark green typeface on a black background) is barely legible. I suppose I shall just have to live with not being admired by a Guy N. Smith fan that thinks M. R. James wrote "The Jolly Corner".

1999 also produced "Worse than Bones". As far as I'm concerned, inscriptions in second-hand books are a bonus. 2000 saw me complete just one short story, "No End of Fun", a tribute to a J. K. Potter

picture (the mirror, of course, though his image isn't of a mirror).
Then came 2001, which felt like living in science fiction, especially to
someone old enough to have seen the film originally in Cinerama. I
found it a productive year for my short stories; only half of its crop is
included here. "Tatters" came from a reference on Radio 3 to satirical
street ballads, and gave me some scope to joke. "The Retrospective"
felt rather like a tribute to the great Thomas Ligotti, though I'm
certain he would handle the notion quite differently. Because of a
misunderstanding the last three words were omitted from its original
publication and replaced with an ellipsis, an effect I dislike as much as
M. R. James did . . . Here the story is complete. As for "All for Sale", a
street market did indeed spring up overnight around the first hotel
where the family and I stayed in Turkey, and a swarthy hi-fi dealer in
Tottenham Court Road once palpated my tits and declared "You are
nice." Everything can be material, you see.

So I trundle to my latest conclusion. I hope this jumble of observa-
tions has been more rewarding than otherwise. For some of my readers
it will revive memories; it did for me. Among the reasons I find the
film *Hilary and Jackie* so moving (besides our daughter's youthful
career as a cellist) is that the first and final scenes are shot on Freshfield
Beach. Many were the summer picnics LiG and friends enjoyed there
for decades. Jenny and I often still picnic there, and sometimes we
return along the same path we all followed years ago. More than once
I've seemed to see people walking ahead—Norman, Norman, Harry,
Phil, John, Eddie—into that evening glow that feels like perfect stillness, the golden light that transforms everything into peace.

Ramsey Campbell
Wallasey, Merseyside
5 April 2003

acknowledgements

"Return Journey", copyright © 2000 by Ramsey Campbell. From *Taps and Sighs,* edited by Peter Crowther.

"Twice by Fire", copyright © 1998 by Ramsey Campbell. From *The Crow" Shattered Lives and Broken Dreams,* edited by J. O'Barr and Ed Kramer.

"Agatha's Ghost", copyright © 1999 by Ramsey Campbell. From *White of the Moon,* edited by Stephen Jones.

"Little Ones", copyright © 1999 by Jenny and Ramsey Campbell. From *Till Death Do Us Part,* edited by Jill M. Morgan and Martin H. Greenberg.

"The Last Hand", copyright © 1975 by April R. Derleth and Walden W. Derleth. From *Nameless Places,* edited by Gerald W. Page.

"No End of Fun", copyright © 2002 by Ramsey Campbell. From J. K. Potter's Embrace the Mutation, edited by William Schafer and Bill Sheehan.

"Facing It", copyright © 1995 by Ramsey Campbell. From *Peeping Tom* 18, edited by Stuart Hughes.

"Never to be Heard", copyright © 1998 by Ramsey Campbell. From *Imagination Fully Dilated,* edited by Alan M. Clark and Elizabeth Engstrom.

"The Previous Tenant", copyright © 1975 by Ramsey Campbell. From *The Satyr's Head and Other Tales of Terror,* edited by David A. Sutton.

The *Oxford Companion to English Literature* describes Ramsey Campbell as "Britain's most respected living horror writer". He has been given more awards than any other writer in the field, including the Grand Master Award of the World Horror Convention, the Lifetime Achievement Award of the Horror Writers Association and the Living Legend Award of the International Horror Guild. Among his novels are *The Face That Must Die*, *Incarnate*, *Midnight Sun*, *The Count of Eleven*, *Silent Children*, *The Darkest Part of the Woods*, *The Overnight*, *Secret Story*, *The Grin of the Dark*, *Thieving Fear*, *Creatures of the Pool*, *The Seven Days of Cain* and *Ghosts Know*. Forthcoming is *The Last Revelation of Gla'aki*. His collections include *Waking Nightmares*, *Alone with the Horrors*, *Ghosts and Grisly Things*, *Told by the Dead* and *Just Behind You*, and his non-fiction is collected as *Ramsey Campbell, Probably*. His novels *The Nameless* and *Pact of the Fathers* have been filmed in Spain. His regular columns appear in *Prism*, *All Hallows*, *Dead Reckonings* and *Video Watchdog*. He is the President of the British Fantasy Society and of the Society of Fantastic Films.

Ramsey Campbell lives on Merseyside with his wife Jenny. His pleasures include classical music, good food and wine, and whatever's in that pipe.

www.ramseycampbell.com

"Afterword", copyright © 2003 by Ramsey Campbell.

"The Word", copyright © 1997 by Ramsey Campbell From *Revelations*, edited by Douglas E. Winter.

"Afterword", copyright © 2003 by Ramsey Campbell.